PENHALIGON'S PRIDE

1910. Anna Garvey and her daughter are still running the Tin Streamer's Arms in Caernoweth, Cornwall, and it finally seems like she has left her tumultuous history behind in Ireland. Meanwhile Freya Penhaligon has blossomed and is now the object of increasing affection from Hugh, the elder son of the wealthy Batten family. After the dramatic events of the previous months, it feels like everything is finally getting back to normal. But when Anna inadvertently reveals something she shouldn't, she finds herself at the centre of a blackmail plot and it seems like the past she longed to escape is coming back to haunt her.

PENHALIGON'S PRIDE

PENHALIGON'S PRIDE

by

Terri Nixon

Magna Large Print Books
Long Preston, North Yorkshire,
BD23 4ND, England.

British Library Cataloguing in Publication Data.

A catalogue record of this book is
available from the British Library

ISBN   978-0-7505-4655-3

First published in Great Britain in 2017 by Piatkus,
an imprint of Little, Brown Book Group

Published in Large Print 2018 by arrangement with
Little, Brown Book Group Limited

Magna Large Print is an imprint of Library Magna Books Ltd.

Printed and bound in Great Britain by
T.J. (International) Ltd., Cornwall, PL28 8RW

For Michael Green, in thanks and friendship.

Dramatis Personae

Anna Penhaligon: formerly Anna Garvey, she arrived in Caernoweth to take up the inheritance of the local pub. It emerged that she and her daughter had left Ireland in the wake of the death of a local banker's son, killed accidentally by Mairead when he had attacked her on a deserted beach. To protect her daughter, Anna said it was she who'd killed him.

Matthew Penhaligon: a recovering alcoholic. A lifelong fisherman, now forced to take a job as a miner following the death of Roland Fry, his friend and skipper. Matthew and Anna have found peace and happiness together, though they have been unable to officially marry.

Freya Penhaligon: Matthew's daughter. At the age of eight, and worried about her father's safety at sea during a storm, she was washed off the breakwater and almost drowned. Her mother found herself unable to live with Matthew any longer, and took Freya to live in London and attend private school there. Freya returned to Caernoweth after several years to live with her father and grandfather, and works in the struggling family book shop, Penhaligon's Attic. She also works at the Caernoweth hotel with her best friend Juliet Carne.

Mairead Casey: previously known as Mairead Garvey. Anna's daughter, who suffers from mild epilepsy that takes the form of absence seizures. Clever and complicated, with a head for figures, she helped Freya turn the shop around and they soon became close. Freya is the person in whom Mairead confided the truth about the murder in Ireland.

James Fry: a former friend of Matthew's, and the only son of popular fisherman Roland. He left Caernoweth at seventeen to train as an architect, and has returned to try and set up his own business in town. He still blames Matthew for an accident that almost killed his father and lost him half his business. Upon inheriting that business, James sacked Matthew in order to force him into a swap with Penhaligon's Attic. This did not work, and while Matthew works in the mine, James is still the unwilling skipper of the *Pride of Porthstennack*.

David Donithorn: a troubled young man who had been a child working on the *Pride* when the near-fatal accident had happened. But while Matthew was eventually forgiven, and given a second chance, David lost his job and was refused any more work on the boats. Carrying a huge grudge against Matthew, he now works as a miner at Wheal Furzy, and is Matthew's shift captain.

Isabel Webb: Freya's mother, a Spanish stowaway who Matthew met in Plymouth, and who fell for the romantic notion of life with a handsome sailor. Sadly the reality of Matthew's difficult existence did not measure up, and after the accident that almost claimed her daughter's life she and Freya left Caernoweth. Isabel later married a politician and moved to America, allowing Freya to return to live with her father.

Juliet Carne: Freya's friend, and fellow chambermaid at the hotel. She had been having an on-again off-again affair with married David Donithorn, and is now expecting his child. Having also slept with James Fry, who is single, she has told him the child is his. Matthew, Anna and Freya know this is untrue, but James is happy and ready to start building his own family.

Various townspeople, including:

Robert Penhaligon: Matthew's father. He struggled for years with Matthew's alcoholism, and their relationship suffered. Anna's presence in the family home smoothed things over to a degree, and eventually Robert signed the shop over to Matthew. Their relationship is still fragile, but mending.

Joe and **Esther Trevellick:** the elderly couple who work for Anna at the Tin Streamer's Arms.

Ellen Scoble: the first person to approach Anna as a friend. A widow with a young son, she is struggling to make ends meet, and works as a bal maiden at Wheal Furzy.

Doctor Andrew Bartholomew: initially disapproving of Anna, but was so taken by the way she turned the town around and created a sense of community that he suggested he produce a false death certificate for her, to send to the authorities in Ireland.

Susan Gale: his housekeeper. An inquisitive

woman, and grandmother to three unruly young-sters.

Brian Cornish: a friend of James's father, Roland, he took James under his wing when Roland died. He also championed Anna during her difficult first weeks in. Caernoweth. A kindly fisherman, and a regular in the Tinner's Arms.

The Battens: Pencarrack House overlooks the town and is the home of **Charles,** who owns several of the town's properties and businesses; his son **Hugh,** who has formed an attachment to Freya Penhaligon; his two daughters, **Dorothy** and **Lucy,** and Dorothy's illegitimate and adven-turesome ten-year-old son, **Harry.**

Arric: The pub's cat. Found as a kitten by Joe Trevellick by the side of the road, he terrorises the hens and takes every opportunity to show Anna who really owns the Tinner's Arms.

Chapter One

July 1910. Porthstennack harbour

The sun threw the last of the day's light across the calm sea in a defiant golden burst, then, sinking out of sight, finally allowed evening to brush the world with chilly fingers. The sounds that accompanied this new aspect of the diminishing day should have been soothing to the two figures, side by side on the beach; the guttural call of cormorants at their nests in the cliffs, the rush of water over shingle, and the hiss and fizz of the retreating tide. Even, if you listened carefully, the little popping sounds of bubbles settling into the gaps in the pebbles.

But underlying it all, there was that hollow boom, peculiar to the coast, where the sea made contact within the body of the land by way of deep, dark caves, and you could almost feel the ground shaking beneath your feet... A sound like thunder. A terrible weight. A tightness in the chest. A burning in the lungs that could only be eased by opening your mouth, but you mustn't

Freya Penhaligon felt a steadying hand on her arm, and opened her eyes. It took a moment to adjust her vision to the darkening day, and the sound of the air rushing into her mouth and down her throat held a high, helpless note of panic as she looked at the waves, dragging at the shore as they had once dragged at her clothes.

'You're doing well,' Anna said. 'But I'd say that's enough for today, wouldn't you?'

'No. I can go a little bit closer.' But she didn't sound convinced, even to her own ears.

Anna's grip remained firm. 'Not now, sweetheart. This fear has been a long time settling in, you can't expect to banish it in a few days.'

Freya nodded. Knowing she was safe was one thing, but she couldn't deny the uneasiness she felt as she saw the waves come rushing up the beach, as if any attempt to run away would be thwarted by the shingle shifting beneath her boots. The sea still sounded like gnashing teeth when it hit the rocks, angry with the eight-year-old child she'd been for escaping its hungry embrace. It probably always would.

They wound back through Porthstennack the long way, coming off the beach at the far end of Smugglers' Way and walking slowly through the lanes. There were still plenty of people about; the daylight might be fading but there was still enough of it left to finish chores and outdoor jobs, before full darkness forced everyone indoors. Leaving the hamlet and starting up to Caernoweth, to their left lay Priddy Farm, which took up all the land between the school at Priddy Lane and the back end of Porthstennack. They could hear the farmer shouting to the casual workers who were helping with the silage while the days still stretched long and warm, and Freya began to feel the tension melting away under the familiar sounds.

She looked ahead, to the house where she'd

16

lived until the age of eight: Hawthorn Cottage. It lay in its own little yard halfway up the hill, and as they drew level she stared at the lighted window at the front of the house. Did the kitchen still look and smell the same? Did the floorboards still creak by the window in the sitting room? Did the mangle in the outhouse still work, and did they still have to wedge the door open with a rock to let the daylight in? Did Tory, the little girl who lived there now, sit there in the half-dark, dreaming her days away and ignoring her chores, just as Freya had at her age?

'Penny for your thoughts?' Anna said.

Freya shrugged. 'I was only thinking how strange it is, that we're always looking ahead, and wanting to grow up, but still want things to stay the same.'

'Ah, but nothing ever does. Not really. Is that a bad thing though?'

Freya thought for a moment. 'I'm glad enough to have had that time in London, but part of me still wishes I'd never had to leave here.'

Anna put an arm around her. 'Well, we five are going to be making new memories together now. Isn't that worth the odd nostalgic pang?'

'I wish we could all live together though.'

Papá and Anna had gone away for a week, after Anna Casey's "death" had been widely reported and, although the townspeople believed a marriage in Bodmin had necessarily been conducted in secret, only Freya, Grandpa and Mairead knew no such ceremony had taken place; sometimes it was hard to keep the many layers of secrets in order, and now and again Freya found herself

17

hoping for something to happen, to expose every-thing and everyone, so they could begin afresh. Then she'd close her eyes and pray it never would, because that would bring an end to everything.

Anna squeezed Freya's arm. 'One day I hope. But in the meantime, we're still a family, and at least Mairead and I are safe here.'

'As long as you don't get noticed by Constable Couch,' Freya pointed out. 'So don't go robbing any banks.'

Anna laughed. 'You spoil all the fun. Although,' she added, 'a lazier constable I've yet to meet, thank goodness. Sure, doesn't he deserve his name!'

They drew level with the memorial at the bottom of town, and both stopped and stared up at it through the lowering shadows. Malcolm Penworthy's stone eyes gazed up through the rows of houses and shops, as if mesmerised and humbled by the way his little town had grown.

'I'm still more than halfway certain he's why people have accepted us,' Anna mused. 'I know you and Matthew have both said it's more to do with the pub and all, but...' She gestured at the imperious figure looming over them. 'For most people the important thing is still that I'm descended from the war hero who built the town.'

'For some, perhaps,' Freya conceded. 'I sup-pose it's natural though, since we've celebrated him for so long. You've heard of the Penworthy Festival?'

'No. But it sounds fun.'

'It's every fifteenth of August, and nearly the whole town takes the day off work to celebrate.

Shops close too, but they stay open longer the days before and after, to make up for it. Grandpa says the owners of the Tinner's have all been treated like royalty themselves.'

'Well I haven't seen any sign of that so far,' Anna said with a wry smile. 'But we all know why, don't we? I can hardly blame them.'

'At least now everyone knows *why* you had to be so secretive,' Freya said. 'Or they think they do.'

'Hush!' Anna glanced around, but there was no one within hearing. Nevertheless she lowered her voice. 'I still can't believe Mairead told you everything.'

'She had to tell someone, and better me than anyone else.'

'That's true enough. Away home now, and I'll see you tomorrow. Mairead'll be up to the shop before you go to work.' She dropped a quick kiss on Freya's cheek, and the natural, unconscious gesture brought a smile to Freya's face.

At home, and still in the grip of nostalgia, she left off the electric light, and instead lit a candle. Its light was reflected in the mirror of her dressing table and threw a warming glow across the room as she peeled off her dress and chemise, then took down her hair. She'd only recently begun wearing it up, and it still felt like a very new, adult thing, to sit at her dressing table and loosen all the pins, putting them carefully on the table one by one.

She picked up Granny Grace's hairbrush and began to draw it through her tangled hair, wincing as the bristles caught and tugged. The tallow candle threw a yellow colour onto the strands that the brush pulled on, but as they sprang back against her head they turned once more into the rich, dark luxuriant curls so like Mama's. Everyone said she was more her mother's child than her father's, but apart from the colouring she could see none of Mama's exotic Spanish allure in the face that stared back at her now, only her father's short, straight nose, and his particular way of raising one eyebrow.

Hugh Batten, the heir apparent to Pencarrack House, made no secret of his interest in her. Of course he was as far removed from Freya's world as she was from the piskies, and the knockers in the mines. But it didn't matter; Hugh was a nice-looking young man, and she had daydreamed about him often enough, but whenever she let her thoughts roam ahead, to falling in love with someone deeply enough to share her life with him, the face was blank so she knew it could not be Hugh.

She finished brushing her hair and blew out the candle, wrinkling her nose at the pungent, smoky smell. Perhaps some things belonged in the past for a reason – electric light might make you blink and wince at the brightness for a moment, but at least it didn't cling to your clothes and your hair, and make you smell like a dirty outhouse.

She closed her eyes and let herself sink into sleep. As always when she'd tested her fears at the beach, she dreamed of being eaten alive by hungry waves, but when she cried out for help this time, a reaching hand found hers and pulled her onto the shore. She opened her eyes into the darkness of her room, still breathing hard, and struggling, without success, to remember who that hand had belonged to. All she knew was that she could still feel it, and that when she fell back into sleep again she was smiling.

The following morning she was surprised, and momentarily disturbed, by a visit from Doctor Bartholomew. Seeing him approach from the street she glanced worriedly at the ceiling, wondering if Grandpa Robert was ill again, and Papá had sent for the doctor before he'd gone to work. But when Bartholomew came in she saw he was carrying a fairly heavy-looking lidded box, rather than his usual black bag.

'Good morning, Miss Penhaligon.'

'Morning, Doctor Bartholomew.' It was still a source of amazement to many to see how this formerly irascible man had mellowed in the past few months, largely thanks to Anna's steady, calm and firm influence, and her refusal to be cowed by his abrupt manner. Freya had her suspicions that he was drawn to her in other ways too; but the reason for his visit today turned out to have nothing to do with Anna.

He put the box on the counter, and flexed his fingers to ease the stiffness of carrying it up from the bottom of town. 'I've decided to take in a lodger,' he said, 'now that I'm not taking the rents from the Tinner's. So I've been clearing out my attic.' He lifted the lid. 'I'd forgotten all about these old books, but some of them are probably worth a penny or two to the right buyer.'

He unfolded the cloth, and Freya peered into the box. There were about ten or twelve books, of varying sizes, but the one thing they all had in common was a beautiful, well-preserved finish; dark greens with gilt edging, dark reds, and some blues, and the pages were yellowed but didn't appear loose or torn.

'They've been wrapped in goat skins,' Bartholomew said. 'Carried from house to house ever since my father died, but I've had little time for leisure reading I'm afraid, so they've stayed put away. I have the wrappings here if you want them.'

'Are they novels?' Freya was reluctant to pick one of them up in front of him, in case she damaged it in some way.

'I don't believe so. I haven't looked at all of them, but they seem to be local history and that sort of thing. Just up your street, I would think.'

'They're beautiful,' Freya admitted, 'but we don't have the money to buy just at the moment, I'm afraid.'

'Buy?' Bartholomew's eyes widened. 'Good heavens, girl! No, these are a gift. They're doing no good to anyone in my attic, might as well put them in yours!' He smiled at his own little joke. 'Are you interested?'

'Yes!' Freya breathed, before remembering her manners. 'I mean, thank you, yes we'd be thrilled.'

'Well that's that, then. If I find any more I'll pop them along, shall I?'

'That would be wonderful.'

'Splendid. I'll be off, then.' He raised his hat.

'Goodbye, and thank you again. I hope you find a good lodger.'

'I'm sure I shall.' He nodded, and then he was gone.

Freya picked up the first of the books and

opened it gingerly, sensing great age in the heft of it, and her gaze fell on the date inscribed inside: 1723. It was a beautifully illustrated history of an area not too far from Caernoweth, covering half of the south coast of Cornwall.

The next book was older still, and was filled with drawings of a place on Bodmin Moor called Lynher Mill – a burned-out mill graced the frontispiece, its tower stunted and darkened by fire, its roof gone. Freya put the book aside to read later, and pulled out another. They were so well cared for, they must surely be worth a fortune to someone. She was so engrossed she didn't hear the door open, until Mairead's voice cut across the shop.

'It's a good thing I'm not a thief.'

'Hmm?' Freya looked up at last. 'Oh, yes. I was distracted.'

'So I see. What's that?'

Freya told her about Bartholomew's visit. 'I'm dying to look at them properly, but I should go to work; Mrs Bone will take my extra hours away if I'm late even once.'

Mairead grimaced. 'She's a harridan. Go on, I'll catalogue the books.'

'Send the list to Teddy Kempton first,' Freya reminded her. 'He's still collecting them for Mr MacKenzie.'

'I'll send it on this afternoon's post.' Mairead held the door open for Freya, who was checking her hair in her reflection in the window. 'Go on, no one's looking at you, it doesn't matter if you've a hair out of place!'

Such bluntness had long since ceased to cause surprise or hurt feelings. Instead Freya grinned

23

and tweaked Mairead's own hair loose from its coil.

'I'll be back late again, I should think,' she said. 'Tell Grandpa there's a sheep's head in the pot.'

'I will.'

'Have some yourself if you want.'

The look of distaste on Mairead's face was nothing short of priceless. The formerly wealthy Garvey women might have settled into life among the lower classes, but there were some things that would never come naturally. A boiled sheep's head for dinner was one of them.

Chapter Two

Paddle Lane, Porthstennack

The decision was both the easiest and the hardest James Fry had ever had to make, but his pen hovered over the paper, having scratched the words: 'Dear Mr Trubshaw,' and he took a deep breath and lowered it to the table top again. His hand was steady, his mind clear, and yet... He picked up the letter awaiting his reply, and read it once more.

Dear Mr Fry.

I have taken the liberty of writing to you, having found your forwarding details listed with your former employer in Dorset. When we met in Truro a few weeks ago your determination struck me, despite the brief nature of our meeting, and I am contacting you with news of an opportunity for which I feel you might be suited. I set the details below, and urge you to reply to me at this address without delay.

An associate of mine, Mr Gerald Simpson, is in need of a junior partner for his new company, based in Sheffield. I gave him your name and he is most keen to meet. I confess I do not know your circumstances, but you appeared well presented, and this post would suit a man of the trade who has a modest capital sum to invest. As you are no doubt aware, the district of Levenshulme was just last year assimilated into Manchester itself, and is expanding still. Mr Simpson is fast becoming a name in the architecture business, but such business moves faster still, and he will need a reply soonest; he has had a good deal of interest as you might imagine, but thanks to our long-standing acquaintance I have persuaded him to delay making an appointment until I have your response, which I have assured him will be within the week.

Yours faithfully
Charles Trubshaw

James picked up the pen again, and watched the words appear beneath the salutation as if written by someone else:

I thank you most sincerely for your kind thought of introducing me to Mr Simpson. However, since our meeting – on that very day, in fact – I have discovered I am looking forward to impending fatherhood, and so you will understand am unable to sell my property to fund any investment. I must, therefore, regretfully decline your invitation, and hope this letter reaches you in good time.

Before he could change his mind he blotted the ink, and thrust the folded paper into an envelope. Such an opportunity was one he'd dreamed of ever since he'd taken up his apprenticeship with Richard Shaw at Bryanston House. Long years of learning the craft, first as a stone mason and then through studying architecture, had all been leading up to this very moment. He pictured Mr Trubshaw's narrow, bespectacled face as he read this letter, and in his mind's eye he saw that face close down, and knew his bridges would be burned from the moment he put the letter in the post.

But he had a family to consider now. Soon he and Juliet would marry, and their child would have a good, safe home. He looked around at the tiny kitchen and sighed; at least it *would* be safe, once some basic repairs were carried out... His family deserved better. He pulled the stack of paper towards him again.

'Plaster,' he wrote. Then tapped his chin with the pen and closed his eyes briefly, before bending to his paper again.

Paint. Wood. Borrow tools from Brian. November (5 months.) Cradle. Make? (ask Brian) V. Imp – check roof structure.

Gradually the urge to rewrite the letter to Trubshaw faded, and James realised he was actually smiling as he wrote. After a few minutes he laid down his pen and went upstairs, into the bedroom

26

that had been his father's. He hadn't been able to bring himself to move into it, despite its superior size, but perhaps it was time to change all that. He ducked back through the low doorway and stepped across the landing to his own bedroom.

Half the size of Roland's, with a small window and a sloping roof, this room was the warmest during winter, being the one with the chimney breast running up through it. The child would be born in November, and would sleep in with himself and Juliet at first, but during winter the chimney bricks would warm the room, and once the roof was properly fixed it would be perfect.

He knocked at the window ledge, listening with a practised ear as the dull thump changed its note under his knuckles; there was rot in there, which would weaken the frame if left too long. Roland had tried to take care of the place, but there was only so, much you could do with a shattered knee, and James was an architect, and a stone mason; if anyone could put the house to rights it was him.

'Doctor, heal thyself,' he said aloud, with a little smile. He had largely ignored the state of the house since his return, believing he would be long gone to his new premises before extensive – and possibly expensive – repairs were necessary, but things were different now. The letter would go in the post tomorrow, and by the time Trubshaw received it this room would be on the way to becoming the haven for James Fry's own child that it had once been to James himself.

Caernoweth Hotel

The party was lively enough, but to her own surprise Lucy Batten had been fighting boredom from the moment she'd arrived. She'd been excited to get the invitation to what promised to be the party of the year, and relieved that her older sister had pleaded too much work to do; Lucy would have free rein, and not have to put up with sniffy looks every time she laughed too loudly or with the 'wrong' person. With the year at its warmest, the hotel gardens would be full of people, the ballroom would be cooler for their absence, and, best of all, there would be dancing.

But now she was here she was unsettled to find herself becoming unusually impatient and restless although there was no reason tonight should be different... Or perhaps that was exactly it: the same faces laughed over, and into, their wine glasses; the same voices cut through everyone else's, as if what they had to say was so much more important; the same conversations travelled around and around, becoming more embellished and, conversely, more boring as they went. Lucy quickly went from admiration for the Brownsworths' ostentation to being discomfited by their taking over an entire hotel for a whole weekend. It was actually embarrassing, and it wasn't even an important birthday.

It would have been bearable if only her brother had come too, at least Hugh would have pulled her out of this gloom by passing his own jaded but amusing opinions, *sotto voce* of course. But since neither he nor her sister were here Lucy felt pinned beneath the spotlight of expectation; a Batten ambassador, and obliged to act accordingly.

Even the dancing, to which she'd so looked forward, wouldn't be the right kind. Far too sedate, ordered, everyone doing the same thing, with only varying degrees of ability to separate them. Nothing like the kind of dance she performed in her room, to the lonely audience of her own reflection. To listen to dear old Disapproving Dorothy, anyone would suppose Lucy intended to follow in the Paris footsteps of Mata Hari. Or that actress at the Moulin Rouge a few years ago, who'd appeared wearing nothing but a few well-placed shells. Even Lucy had been shocked at that, but the shock had quickly given way to a dark kind of delight, and even envy. The *freedom!* It must have been–

'Lucy! How wonderful.' Clara Brownsworth, twenty-three years old as of today, and acting older than her mother, kissed the air on either side of Lucy's cheeks. 'Amanda's here, and Heather. You must meet Heather's new beau, he's got the most divine accent you've ever heard. American, you know. *So* exciting to meet a real one.'

Lucy gave an inward sigh, but her interest was piqued when she learned that Peter Boden, Heather's latest, was apparently involved in theatre in New York. He was engaging, if a little earnest, pleasantly spoken, and happy to talk, but being so much in demand as a novelty he was whisked away after a few minutes by Clara. His swift departure left Lucy, Heather and Amanda by the French windows overlooking the garden, and Lucy struggled against a yawn. Hugh would

29

have stood behind Amanda and pulled faces over the top of her head in an effort to make Lucy laugh, obliging her then to explain herself. Perhaps he was there in spirit, because the very thought of it brought a twitch to Lucy's lips, which earned a downward turn from Amanda's.

'It's not funny.'

'What isn't?'

'I was just saying how Clara will glue herself to Peter's side all night, and poor Heather here will be lucky to see him again before breakfast.'

'Yes.' It did seem unfair, but despite feeling mildly sorry for Heather, Lucy soon drifted off again. She'd even have welcomed her older sister's company just at the moment; Dorothy could be a bit of a tartar, there could be nothing worse than a reformed gadabout, but at least she made interesting conversation, and would more than likely have given Clara short shrift about monopolising someone else's beau. But Dorothy was at home with little Harry and Father, and Hugh was out with his hunt friends, presumably having a high old time.

She took one last furtive look around, and stepped out into the still-light evening, breathing a deep sigh of relief as the noise fell away behind her. A walk would be just the thing to shake off this creeping sense of impatience and restlessness, so she followed the path around to the front of the hotel, and the generous, spotlessly clean courtyard, and then, rather than turning back as she'd thought she would, she kept walking.

The road through Caernoweth was steep, and her flimsy party shoes were not made for walking, but the change of scenery was too compelling to resist and she started down the hill. She had gone very little distance when she heard voices away to her left and just ahead. Recognising one of them she quickened her pace and, when she drew level with the narrow alleyway between the civic offices and the butcher's next to it, she stopped to listen. Mostly boys, and all of an age, around ten or eleven, whooping and jeering as their marbles smashed into each other and the wall. The voice she had recognised spoke up boldly, claiming the winning throw.

'It was too! Look, Bobby's is all the way out of the circle!'

'You cheated! Yeah, you did, I seen you leanin' forward!'

'I did not cheat!' The voice was heated and verging on pompous, and, despite herself, Lucy couldn't help smiling. Then she straightened her shoulders, assumed a stern look, and stepped into the entrance of the alleyway. As her shadow fell over the assembled boys they all scrambled to their feet. Except one, who just sighed.

Lucy clapped her gloved hands together. 'Master Henry George Batten, there you are!' Using his full name always put him on his guard, and she enjoyed seeing his expression change from defiance to nervousness.

'My name's Harry,' he said. But he rose anyway, and peered around Lucy to the street beyond. 'Is Mother with you?'

'No. Now come along.' The perfect excuse to leave the party – Lucy couldn't have planned it better if she'd tried. *I'm so sorry, Clara, I just popped*

31

out for some air, and found my rascal of a nephew playing with the local children! And I was so enjoying myself... She suppressed a smile, and stopped herself from holding out her hand to Harry. He was a darling, but he wouldn't thank her for making him look like a baby in front of his friends. His *friends?* Good grief, Dorothy would have kittens!

'Quickly now, Harry,' she urged. 'You're needed at Pencarrack, you're the only one who can help your grandfather with a very difficult problem he has.'

Harry cleared his throat, and nodded. 'Of course, Aunt Lucy, I'll come at once.' He brushed the dust off his trousers and nodded to the other boys. 'Good evening, and thank you for the game.' He bent swiftly and swept up the winning marbles, dropping them into his purse to a chorus of protest, then ducked past Lucy out into the street.

'Did you really win that game?' Lucy asked, amused, as she caught up with him.

'Of course!'

She chose not to pursue it; instead she voiced her bigger concern. 'Harry, did you sneak out without your mother knowing?'

'She was busy with Grandfather.'

'Still, it's dishonest, and might have caused a dreadful worry,' Lucy said. 'You mustn't do that.'

'Mother would never let me come out to play by myself. You know she wouldn't.'

'And with good reason. If she knew you were sitting in the dirt and playing marbles with ... with those boys, she'd be right to stop you.'

'I thought you were more fun than that,' Harry said, his voice taking on a sulky tone. 'Uncle

Hugh would understand.'

'Uncle Hugh would do exactly as I have done,' Lucy said archly. 'The point is, fun or not, you're a Batten. You're to behave as such, and that doesn't include–'

'Uncle Hugh talks to the girl in the bookshop a lot.'

'What girl in the bookshop?'

'Miss Penhaligon. He takes me there all the time but he doesn't spend a lot of time looking at the books.'

Lucy bit her lip, not wanting to smile while she was supposed to be playing the stern aunt. 'Is this girl very pretty, then?'

He shrugged. 'Quite, I suppose.'

'And is she nice?'

'Yes. And she's clever, too.'

'Then I'm sure she knows Uncle Hugh is only being polite. He's not playing marbles in an alleyway, in other words.'

Harry sighed again. 'Will you tell Mother?'

'I haven't decided yet.'

Pencarrack appeared above the top of the hill, rising from its grounds just ahead, and Harry's pace slowed. He'd lost his bravado now; the prospect of coming face to face with his irate mother was not a happy one. Not for either of them.

'Go around the back,' Lucy advised. 'Pretend you've been in the garden.'

Harry shot her a grateful look and ran off, with all the enviable energy of a boy about to turn eleven, and left his aunt trailing in his wake. Her shoes were starting to rub and her gloves made her hands sweat, and she felt quite old, suddenly, at twenty-one. By this age some of the best ballerinas were already thinking about how long they had left before they hung up their shoes, and here was she, not even knowing what she wanted to do with her life except it must involve dance and theatre somewhere. She was tempted to return to the party and talk to Peter Boden again, but there would be little hope of prising him loose from his hostess. Besides, she was hot and bothered now, after that brisk walk up through town, and it just wasn't worth the raised eyebrows.

She and Harry needn't have worried about Dorothy missing him; when Lucy went into the library she found her sister and her father poring over figures at the desk, oblivious to the sight of the youngest member of their family directly behind them through the window.

Dorothy looked up. 'I thought you were going to the Brownsworths' party?'

'I did.' Lucy dropped her evening bag on the table, and flopped into a chair. 'Dreadful bore. I shan't be missed.'

'We're busy,' Dorothy pointed out. 'Father's going over the wages budget for the rest of the year.' When Lucy rolled her eyes, she sighed. 'It's a busy time in the real world, Lucy, you'd do well do understand such things if you hope to find a young man one day.' Then her glance wandered to the window and fell on her son. 'Why don't you go out and play with Harry? It'll be his bedtime soon and you know how much he loves to spend time with his Aunt Lucy.' Was there a hint of bitterness in that voice? 'Father and I will be finished soon and I'll read Harry's story.' She lifted a hopeful eyebrow. 'Unless you want to do it?'

'No, that's quite all right, thank you.' Lucy stood and picked up her bag again. 'I'm sure you do it so much better.'

'I doubt that,' Dorothy said, somewhat wryly. 'He always complains I don't do the voices properly.'

'Practice makes perfect. I'll leave you to your work, then. I'm aching to get these awful shoes off.'

Alone in her room Lucy prised the shoes off her feet and gave a sigh of relief as she sat on the edge of her bed. She stretched one leg, and then the other, and then lifted her arms above her head and looked up at them critically. She adjusted the shape she had created, letting her fingers float through the small area of free space she allowed them, and then rose to her feet, drawing one foot up her calf beneath her dress and standing, perfectly poised, on the toes of the other.

Her clothes were getting in the way. Lucy shrugged her way out of the layers until only her underwear remained, and then the corset joined the heap of dress on the floor. The luxury of being able to bend and twist her unrestricted body made her smile, and she began to hum as she danced, imagining herself on a beautifully lit stage, with the Russian greats. Or perhaps she was more like Isadora Duncan? Yes, Isadora, with her Greek style and her barefooted, light movements and precisely positioned limbs.

Lucy danced on until the heat forced her to stop, then she fell across her bed, exhausted, and for once without having danced off her frustration; her family's attitude to anything that had a theatrical flavour was, and always would be, one of infuriatingly casual dismissal. Proper outrage, or at least disapproval, would have at least been fun to defy, but nothing so much as dented the thick, stifling blanket that lay over the Battens, the mines, and the quarry. Dorothy accused Lucy of not being in the 'real world', but if that was reality, this world of dance, music and dreams was where Lucy would stay, even if it meant living in it alone.

The Tin Streamer's Arms

Summer business was slow. At first Anna had been surprised, considering the sun brought more visitors to the town. But she quickly realised that those who did come generally spent their evenings at the hotel, and only ventured into town to take the sea air before scuttling back up the hill for a large dinner in surroundings that smelled more like perfume and less like fish. Apparently even the distant but constant noise of the pumps and stamps at Wheal Furzy was preferable to that.

The workers of town and hamlet were absent for another reason. They were taking advantage of every moment of daylight, working the fields and the seas with a feverish desperation, knowing the darker days would be along all too soon to put an end to warm evenings and late sunsets. Only then would they bring themselves to the comfort and companionship of the Tinner's Arms.

Anna hadn't seen Matthew for several days

either, and each time there was movement anywhere near the door she looked up in the hope of
seeing his dark blond hair, and the smile that still
sent her heart silly. But he was working long hours
at Wheal Furzy, determined to give David Donithorn no excuse to turn him out, and the last thing
he'd want to do when he got home would be to get
changed and go visiting. Especially in a pub.

Knowing all that made missing him no easier
though, and she drummed her fingers on the
polished surface of the bar, as if by doing so she
could rid them of the need to touch his face, to
slide around the back of his neck and into his
thick, soft hair... Tomorrow was Sunday, he had
some repairs to make to the front-facing window
of Penhaligon's Attic after church, but perhaps
later they might walk up to the old fort, the way
they had on his birthday... She felt a faint smile of
anticipation cross her face before Esther Trevellick broke into her thoughts.

'We'm off now, Miz Garvey. Joe's feelin' nashed.'

'Nashed?'

'Not so bright.'

'Oh, he's ill again?'

'Like I said.' Esther hung her apron on the
hook and took down her coat. Even in the warm
summer evening it would have been odd to see
her without several layers of heavy clothing. Anna
wondered how she didn't melt.

'Well, take him home and take care of him. I
hope he feels better soon.'

'He's tired,' Esther said, and some of the curt-
ness in her voice had leaked away, replaced by a
new, quieter tone. 'He needs a good rest now.'

Anna nodded. 'Tell him to take as long as he needs.' She felt the next words forming, and tried to make herself stop before they tumbled out, but she couldn't. 'I'll pay his wage while he's unwell, so don't worry.'

Esther's eyes widened. 'I'll tell him, Miz Garv ... Mrs Penhaligon. Thank you ever s'much. I'll be here bright an' early.'

'Has he seen the doctor?'

'No need to bother the doctor.' Esther gave a rueful little smile. 'We was sayin' last night, it makes us wish we 'ad them witches in our family still.'

'Witches?'

'From back along. People always said Joe's side of the family had witches in. They was healers really, and good ones by all accounts. Twins. But the boy was put to death for bein' a witch. Killed 'is sister, so they do say.'

'Ah, so when you say *back along*, you're not meaning last year then?' Anna had learned that the expression could mean anything from last week to the dawn of time. 'When was this?'

'Couple 'undred years. More, maybe. Could have been useful now, so we needn't trouble Doctor Bartholomew. Nor the savings pot. Joe had brother and sister twins too, but they died from the workhouse.'

'Oh, that's terribly sad.'

'Don't be askin' Joe about it, he feels bad enough. He got out the workhouse when we married and took his parents' place, but he had to leave the young 'uns there. Joe din't want to, but we couldn't do nothin' for 'em.'

This was more than Esther had ever spoken of her and Joe's life, and Anna couldn't help feeling the old woman was delaying her leaving, preferring to remain in the warmth and light of the pub.

'That's a dreadfully sad story,' she said gently. 'Poor Joe.'

''Tis so.' Esther stood silent for a moment, then shrugged. 'Anyway, we'll get off home.'

She went through to the back, and Anna heard the rumble of Joe's voice, raised in surprise as his wife told him the good news about his pay. She wondered at her own impulsiveness, but at the same time she was glad she'd done it; despite everything she had developed a real affection for the Trevellicks. Now there was only the practicality of being a man down that she had to contend with, so perhaps it was a mixed blessing they were quiet after all.

By the time she deducted the rent, and the small wage she paid the Trevellicks, there was barely enough to live on, and her mind turned over all the different ways she might raise the pub's profits. If only she hadn't been so quick to offer free drinks, and a rent-free use of the bar for the Widows' Guild, she might not be feeling such a pinch, but those were the things on which her fragile new life were built. Those and her relationship to the town's founding father. She would just have to work extra hard, and hope Finn didn't become greedy and increase the rent.

Mairead drifted in from the kitchen, and Anna sighed; she had never seen anyone so obviously wishing she was somewhere else. That it was the beach she yearned for came as no great surprise, but the evening was marching on, and the wistful glances at the window did nothing to soften Anna's resolve to keep her indoors, and safe; she still shuddered at the memory of what had happened in January.

Her daughter's horrific experience on the beach by their home in Ireland seemed to have had more of a lasting effect on Anna than on Mairead herself, and she felt sick every time she thought about it, but Mairead would have been more than happy to put down her cloth right now and walk out into the growing dusk. She simply could not imagine it ever happening again, it was past and gone, and now that she had told Freya too, her mind was unburdened of its awful secret. As if that had been the worst part.

The door opened, and Anna looked around, grateful for the distraction as much as the custom. 'Brian, good to see you.'

Brian Cornish nodded, and perched himself on his favourite stool. 'How be diddlin'?'

'I'm ... diddling fine, I think? Will I get you your usual?' She fetched his tankard, but he held up a hand.

'Not yet.' He twisted to look at the door, then turned back and winked at her. 'James'll be in d'rectly. He's still in the mood to drink to his good news. He's gettin' wed, you know.'

Anna blinked. 'Is he now? I'd no idea he was even courting. And who'd be daft enough?'

'Now, come on, you know better'n that.'

Anna relented. 'All right. Who's the lucky girl?'

'The Carne maid.'

'Juliet?'

Brian misinterpreted her doubtful voice. 'She's a good enough girl really, deep down. Bit flighty, but–'

'No, no. It isn't that. I mean, she's friends with Freya, so I'm sure she's lovely. It's just, does James know she's...' She stopped. It really was none of her business, and, until James chose to make it so, none of Brian's either. Her mind was already searching for alternative ways to finish her sentence, but she needn't have worried.

'In the family way?' Brian grinned 'He does. That's why they plan to tie the knot soon.'

Relieved, Anna had to admit to a grudging admiration for James. 'I must say it's good of him to be taking on another man's child.'

'Another man's?' Brian's grin vanished and his voice sharpened, and Anna's heart sank but it was too late. Brian eyed her grimly. 'You'd best tell me. And I think I'll have that ale after all.'

There was no help for it, she'd spoken without thinking, she could only carry on now. 'We, that is *I*, heard her talking to ... to someone else. She told him *he* was the father and I believed her. So did he, I think, but he wasn't going to accept responsibility.'

'That'd be young Donithorn then. I thought they'd stopped knockin' about last year though.' He sighed and shook his head. 'He's more her age at least.'

'But married,' Anna pointed out needlessly, putting his drink in front of him. 'And wanting nothing to do with Juliet. Best let sleeping dogs lie, don't you think?'

41

Brian was clearly wrestling with the new information. 'James deserves to know, though, don't he?'

'James doesn't deserve anything from me,' Anna said curtly. 'Except maybe a poke in the eye.'

'Don't seem fair to let him make a fool of himself. But he's 'appy as Larry at the moment, almost like a different bloke. I don't want to be the one to ruin that.'

Anna winced. 'I'm sorry to have put you in a difficult position. I assumed he'd told you. He must have worked it out though, surely?'

Brian didn't seem to have heard. 'I never had much time for young Fry when he first came back,' he mused. 'Roley was a good friend, and to my mind his boy was far too happy to go his own way. But he's settled nicely now. Works hard enough on that boat even if he ain't a natural. Be a shame to see him put himself into debt for a lie, no one deserves that.'

'No, I suppose not. Will you tell him?'

Brian didn't reply for a while. He took a long drink and then replaced his tankard and stared at it, his hands linked on the bar in front of him. Then he nodded. 'I suppose.'

'Will he be relieved, d'you think, or will it hurt him?'

'I don't know, maid, honest I don't.' Brian sighed again, and finished his drink. 'I think I'll go home after all. I'll see you d'rectly.'

'Yes, see you tomorrow.' Anna removed the tankard for washing, and noted the new slump in Brian's shoulders as he crossed to the door. She wished she could take back her words, but in a way he was right; James was about to give everything up for Juliet, and for a child he believed was his. Perhaps it was better he should find out now, before it was too late.

Chapter Three

The Saturday to Monday birthday celebrations at the Caernoweth Hotel meant long working hours, and even more cleaning than usual. Freya had kept herself entertained throughout her shift by daydreaming she might be spotted by a handsome, mysterious guest of the Brownsworths, who would whisk her out into the night-scented gardens and declare himself to her beneath the branches of the big beech tree by the southern wall. But her duties did not put her in the way of any of the party guests, so there was no hope of an accidental meeting in the corridor, as Juliet and James had done.

Perhaps, though, that was for the best, considering the mess which had resulted from *that* less than fortuitous meeting. Juliet had so far managed to hide her situation from the sharp-eyed Mrs Bone, but it wouldn't be long before she would be forced to ask for lighter duties, and then the secret would be a secret no longer. Freya's conscience had been nagging at her too, since Juliet's confession about the baby's father; James was no friend to the Penhaligons, but he didn't deserve to be tricked.

Outside in the back yard after the long, tiring

shift was over, she waited for Juliet as usual, and watched the comings and goings of people from another world: women in slinky dresses, men in smart jackets and colourful ties, chattering amongst themselves while horses stamped impatiently in unfamiliar stables. The late evening air had a bite to it, and Freya pulled her tartan summer shawl tighter and resisted the urge to just go home on her own. This might be her last chance to steer her friend towards telling the truth.

The sounds of the party drifted from the hotel through open French windows; music and laughter, the occasional voice raised in ire. Now and again a figure would stumble around the yard, looking for a flower bed to be sick into, and on one occasion settled for the water trough. Freya grimaced. Cleaning that would be someone's unhappy task tomorrow, but thankfully not hers.

Juliet emerged at last. 'Thanks for waiting. 'Tid'n a long walk, but it's nice to have company.'

'Long enough on your own,' Freya said. 'And there are a lot of strangers about this weekend.'

'Well it won't matter much longer.' Juliet linked her arm through Freya's as they crossed the yard. 'I'll soon be Mrs James Fry, and me and the baby'll have that nice little cottage on Paddle Lane all to ourselves, while James is out earnin'.'

Freya hesitated in the face of Juliet's contentment. Despite her determination, now didn't seem the time to bring up what she'd meant to say after all. 'Have you thought about what you might call the baby?' she asked instead.

Juliet smoothed her skirts over the bump with her free hand. 'James says if it's a boy he wants to call him Roland, for his pa.'

'That's nice. What if it's a girl?'

'If it's a girl, I'm allowed to choose. I thought … Ellen.'

'After David's sister?' Freya stopped still and stared at her. 'Are you mad?'

'I like the name. And anyway,' she hesitated, looking a little embarrassed, 'it might soften Davey t'wards the babe.'

'But he's...' Freya shook her head, seizing the moment. 'Look, don't you think you ought to tell James the truth?'

'Hush!' Juliet looked around quickly. 'And no, I don't.'

'But it's not fair to—'

'Don't tell me what's not fair!' This time it was Juliet who stopped. She shook off Freya's arm, seemingly less worried now about who was passing them on the darkening street. Frustration had overtaken caution. 'Some people can afford to take over a whole *hotel* for one poxy birthday party, and the likes of me has to tell fibs for the rest of her life just to get by.' She began walking again, quickly, and Freya had to run a few steps to catch her.

'It's not James's fault,' she pointed out reasonably, 'and anyway, neither he nor the Donithorns are the ones having the party.'

'I know that!'

'Then why are you so set on punishing James?'

'Why should you care, after what you've said about him? And anyway, what would you know? You with your family business, your high ideas of takin' up with them at Pencarrack... Oh, don't

45

look like that! I've seen the way you float away whenever someone mentions Hugh Batten!'

'We're not talking about me,' Freya said, hiding her embarrassment beneath the retort. 'And I thought you told me to hush.' Most of those hurrying past them were bal maidens coming down from the Wheal Furzy, mostly unrecognisable in their big straw hats, and scarves that kept out the worst of the dust, but none of them were interested in the gossip of a couple of chambermaids from the hotel. David's wife, who might have been, was not among them as far as Freya could see.

'It don't matter anyway,' Juliet said, subsiding. 'James'll only just be finishin' work. He don't have no reason to come this far up town.'

'I'm sorry. But I'm your friend and–'

'Well act like it then,' Juliet said, but her pleading tone belied her sharp words.

Freya took her arm again, and they moved off down the hill. She was glad she had at least brought the subject up, but another niggling question surfaced. 'Why do you do it?'

'Do what?'

'With men. Why do you cheapen yourself like that?'

Juliet's pace slowed and Freya braced herself for another barrage, and she likely deserved it, but instead her friend was simply thinking. 'It's never *felt* cheap,' she said at last. 'Look, the way people talk, it don't matter one bit. Only thing that matters is that when I get old and die, I in't treated like no sinner. I deserve holy ground just as much as anyone.'

'No one thinks you're a sinner.'

'I've heard people saying I'm a hussy, an' that all I care about is how fast I can make a man want me.' She looked at Freya, and her expression was one of genuine puzzlement. 'But it in't like that. It's the opposite.'

'The opposite? What do you mean?'

'You know how it is when you're talkin' to a man,' Juliet said, frowning as she gathered her words together. 'You get nervous, worried about what'll happen when they want to ... you know. And they all do, don't you go thinkin' otherwise.' She shot Freya a wry look, and Freya hoped she wouldn't mention Hugh again. 'But it spoils things to worry. I want to relax when I like someone, and the best way to do that is to ... to get it out of the way.'

'You say you don't want to be treated like a sinner, but you never even tried to hide it.'

'That's dishonest,' Juliet said simply. 'Lyin's a worse sin than havin' carnal knowledge of someone. It's like Mrs Packem pretending she's the one who makes all them cakes instead of me!' But Freya wasn't fooled by the deliberate attempt to divert the conversation.

'And you think it's better to be honest, and to make no secret of your ... behaviour?'

'Don't you?'

'Not if it'd shame my family.'

Juliet shrugged. 'Tom don't give a damn for our name. And there's no one else left who'd care. Maybe if Ma was alive... Anyway, I do what I do to please *me*. Not the man I'm with.' She looked at Freya anxiously. 'Do *you* understand now?

Because you're about the only other person who might care. Only one who matters, anyway.'

'I think so.' Freya nodded. 'But I'm glad you won't have to do it any more.'

'Me too,' Juliet admitted. When they parted company at Penhaligon's Attic she gave Freya a swift, uncharacteristic hug – startling but deeply touching. 'James is happy too. Don't spoil it.'

'I won't,' Freya said with a smile. 'You'd better get a move on, your brother will be wondering where his supper is.'

'True,' Juliet agreed gloomily. 'Tom would sooner starve than peel a tiddy himself. I'll see you Monday.' She crossed the road, and Freya watched her until she had turned into her lane, then she went in through the back door of Penhaligon's Attic. She switched on the light in the kitchen, and noticed a piece of paper sitting on the otherwise spotless table; a note from Mairead, who had long since gone home.

Dear Freya,

Catalogue updated. List of new books sent to Mr Kempton in Plymouth. Books still in boxes until reply received. I hope we can spend some time together tomorrow after Church. Perhaps the beach?

Mairead.

PS: Do not draw my attention to a sheep's head again, unless it is still attached to the sheep.

Paddle Lane, Porthstennack

The dust was flying, but with the windows open it

48

wasn't unbearable. James straightened the make-shift mask he had put over his nose and mouth, and hefted the hammer again. The old plaster must have been in place since Noah was a lad ... it fell off in dry, raggedly shaped clumps, throwing off-white dust into the air, but now it covered a good part of the floor in the big bedroom and left the stone walls lumpy and bare. There was no wooden slatting beneath it ... that ought to be remedied, but in the meantime it made removing the old plaster a much quicker job.

James stepped back and looked at the room. He and Juliet would be comfortable in here, and it wouldn't take too long either, once he had mixed the lime plaster. He could easily picture the house as it would look in a few short months, and his mouth stretched in a smile behind the mask: two bedrooms furnished and warm instead of one; smells of cooking and of other, more mysterious things connected with women and children; the house would be lived in all day and night, and would feel like a proper home for the first time since his return. As an only child he had been aware of Roland's unspoken hope that their blood would continue, even if the name did not. And now, boy or girl, it would.

James kicked a large chunk of plaster out of the way and stepped closer to the wall; the area around the window would need a more delicate touch. He gave it an experimental tap, but before he could go any further a movement below caught his attention. Brian Cornish, one hand on the gate, looked up at him and waved, but he didn't seem to be enjoying this warm Sunday; his face looked pinched and pale. Perhaps he was ill?

James gestured for him to come in, and dusted his hands against his trousers. He removed the mask as he walked out into the clearer air of the stairway, and wiped the sweat from his face. When he went into the sitting room he found Brian still standing, his hat in his hands.

James frowned. 'Has something happened?'

'No. Yes.' Brian eyed the hammer James still carried, and James put the tool down, his curiosity growing.

'All right, what is it?' A thin, twisting apprehension had begun to worm its way through him. 'Come on, you're as well to just get it off your chest. Is it something to do with Matthew?'

'No. It's Juliet. Or rather, th'babby.'

The apprehension deepened, and James took a deep breath and found the strength to ask, 'Has she lost it?' Brian shook his head. 'What, then? She's run off with a travelling salesman?' It was easier to joke, now he knew the worst had not happened, but Brian didn't share his humour.

'The child's not yours,' he said bluntly. 'It's David Donithorn's.'

James froze into an immovable lump. He said nothing. His mind, however, stumbled on, giving him the memory of his trembling hand on the rounded, solid reality of his family's future beneath Juliet's apron. Or so he'd thought.

He cleared his throat and managed, 'You know that for certain?'

'Certain as can be. Best talk to her yourself.'

'Who told you?'

'Someone heard her talkin' to Donithorn.'

50

Brian shook his head. 'Don't matter who. But I b'lieve 'tis the truth, if that do carry a weight.' He sighed. 'I'm that sorry, lad. I've not wanted to be the one to tell you, but someone had to.'

'Before I make a fool of myself and lose everything, you mean?' James recognised the truth of his bitter words even as he spoke them. He felt light-headed with the suddenness of this collapse of everything. 'When did you find out?'

'Friday. I just couldn't–'

'For God's sake! *Friday?*'

'I know, but... Look, lad, sit down,' Brian said, his voice rough. 'I'll make tea.'

'No.' James still could not move. There was something burning in him, like a line of gunpowder snaking towards old dynamite. Brian ought to leave before the two met. 'Just get out.'

'You're bound to be angry,' Brian said, his voice hardening slightly. 'So I'll do you the courtesy of ignoring that. But 'tidn't me you should be blaming.'

'You should have told me sooner,' James said, low and fierce. The fuse was burning now, and his hands curled into fists. 'Go on.'

Brian went, leaving the front door open, and James followed just for the bleak satisfaction of slamming it shut and knowing the crash would echo along the narrow street. The vibration shook loose some of the broken plaster from the upstairs window, and he heard it hit the floor from the other side of the house.

He went back into the little sitting room, where he'd lately pictured himself with a smiling son or daughter on his knee, and there he stood still,

51

staring at the floor. When he at last opened his mouth, the sound that came out of it took him by surprise; it was not an expression of the betrayed anger he felt building inside him, nor a curse against Juliet, which might have eased the pressure, it was the choking sob of grief. The sound was as unsettling as it was unexpected, and he clamped his lips shut against it. The baby had not died, so why did he feel as if it had?

James sat on the very edge of the settee. The suspicion had been there from the start, but within moments he'd realised he wanted Juliet to be telling the truth, so he'd believed her. His longing for a family had been deep-rooted in him since he'd lost his own mother, and his happiest childhood memories were of those days when he had spent all his free time at Penhaligon's Attic. A real home, filled with noise, affection, frequent scoldings and equally frequent laughter, especially when Matthew's little sister had been alive.

Knowing this of him, Juliet Carne had lied straight to his face. She had pretended a reluctance to force his hand, but she knew he would insist on doing right by her, and she had given him just enough of a glimpse into what life might be like for him. Now it had been snatched away, and the cruelty of the timing was another blow, no less savage: if Brian had only come to him right away, James would still have had the chance to take up Trubshaw's offer.

James rose stiffly and climbed the stairs. He ignored the little bedroom where he'd been sleeping since his return to Porthstennack, and went into the room he'd been preparing for his bride.

He picked up a piece of crumbling plaster and flung it at the wall, where it hit with a muffled thud before sliding down and cracking in two. It wasn't enough. He seized another piece, and this time he threw it at the half-closed window. The noise was scarcely more satisfying; the plaster was soft, and the glass was strong on this side of the house, to withstand the beating of the sea wind. The window simply opened a little further, sending the lump of plaster into the tiny back garden below.

James had a moment to be thankful he had left the hammer downstairs before he realised he was in danger of losing control. He knelt beside the bowl of water he'd put aside for washing his hands, and splashed his face. The shock of the chill on his hot, sweating skin had the desired effect, and he sat back, feeling the water trickling down his neck and through the thin material of his shirt. After a moment concentrating on that simple sensation he grew calmer, and he rose to his feet again and rubbed his wet face with his shirt-sleeve, before closing the window and going downstairs.

Juliet would be at home, cooking Sunday lunch for her brother. He would talk to her, because maybe it wasn't true, maybe Brian had misheard, or misunderstood. One look at her face would tell him all he needed to know, and he could make his decision then. With the unsettling sense that his entire future rocked on the edge of uncertainty he pulled the front door closed behind him, and turned towards Caernoweth and the Carnes' cottage.

Sunday mornings were Anna's favourite time of the week. With most of the town's population at their worship, the streets were quiet, and the scrubby rear garden at the Tinner's was a little haven of quiet solitude. It was in dire need of tidying – especially now Joe Trevellick was so often poorly – and Anna knelt in contentment with her small trowel, digging over the earth in a patch by the gate. She'd never been a keen gardener, but it was nice just to see the pale, gritty, dry earth becoming rich and dark the deeper she dug, and to let her mind wander.

Yesterday news had arrived from Ireland, and while in practical terms it mattered not at all, still it had knocked her gradually mending self-worth. She had waited until this morning to tell Mairead, while they were finishing breakfast, then laid the newspaper cutting back on the table, next to the letter Mairead had just finished reading. 'So, you understand you won't inherit this place after all, that it's going straight to your father?'

Mairead shrugged. 'I was going to transfer ownership of the pub to him anyway. What does the cutting actually say? I only read Da's letter.'

Anna picked up the flimsy piece of paper again, and read aloud: 'The headline says: "Respected General Surgeon Inherits English Property Under Veil of Crime and its Necessary Retribution."'

'It seems needlessly wordy and dramatic,' Mairead observed in dry tones.

'Doesn't it? Anyway, it just goes on to say what your father's letter said. Because of my "conviction for the murder of Liam Cassidy, son of the eminent banker Fergus Cassidy", I've "forfeit all properties and lands, including those listed in my last will and testament." It's all gone to your father. I just wanted to be sure you're of a settled mind about it.'

Mairead had looked above her head, at the whitewashed ceiling, and then around them at the tiny kitchen they had become so quickly used to. 'But we'll still live and work here.'

It wasn't a question, but it was a gladdening thing to hear the satisfied note in her voice, and Anna nodded. 'We will. For as long as he'll let us.'

'What about Matthew? Won't you live with him now you're practically married?'

'We both want to, but there's no room in either house. Besides, this place needs someone living in, to keep it clean and aired. You can't live here alone.' Anna thought of Matthew's previous relationship, and suppressed a little sigh. Two false marriages and no actual wedding ... well it certainly kept the costs down. They could never properly wed now that she was supposedly drowned. She was a non-person. But – she smiled at the thought – she was also a free one.

'Come on,' she said to Mairead. 'As Esther Trevellick would say, *they tables won't wipe their selves.*'

Mairead laughed. 'You're getting altogether too good at the Cornish accent.'

'Give me another six months, you won't be able to tell me from Susan Gale.' Anna folded the newspaper cutting and the letter together, and handed them back to Mairead. There was no mention of her in the letter – bar a line from Finn

55

hoping Mairead was coping well with her mother's untimely death – and in the cutting she was simply referred to as Mrs Finn Casey, now deceased. He had, however, made the suggestion that Mairead take on a manager, and that he'd heard of a Mrs Penhaligon who might suit; Anna couldn't help admiring the smooth, enthusiastic way he had embraced this necessary subterfuge.

This exchange had been going through her mind since breakfast, after which she'd seen Mairead off to the beach and now, as she dug over her little patch of ground in this town that had become her own, she remembered something else. Less than a month ago she had been thinking about the late King Edward passing the throne to George, and in the same way of Robert Penhaligon handing the family business to Matthew: the king is dead, long live the king. Now Mairead, little more than a child, was, officially in charge of her own father's property, and Anna experienced a rush of love and worry that were too closely entwined to separate ... the queen is dead, long live the queen.

'Get on, look at you with your green fingers!'

Anna looked up to find Ellen Scoble at the gate, a small basket on her arm. 'Come on in! No church today?'

'This one's got a bit of a cough.' Ellen pulled her seven-year-old son in front of her and urged him through the gate. 'It's that dusty in chapel, and he'd only get glared at once he started. Go on, Eddie, pick out some of they there stones to help Mrs Penhaligon.'

The boy obediently began to pick out the stones

Anna had turned out of the soil, and to put them in a neat pile by the wall. Ellen gave Anna her hand and pulled her to her feet. 'I'm on my way up to visit Ma, but I saw your Mairead on the beach and thought you might like some company. I made some jam. It's for the Penworthy festival, but I brought an extra jar for you and yours.'

Anna smiled. 'Thank you, that's very kind. Come in and have some tea.' She led the way into the kitchen, and while she cut some bread Ellen took a jar from her basket and removed the paper lid. It was a generous gift, particularly from one who could ill afford it, but Anna had learned better than to try and offer to pay, or even to return the gift straight away.

She watched Ellen with growing curiosity, wondering at her friend's faintly distracted manner. Perhaps she hadn't just called in for company after all. But no other explanation was forthcoming, and Anna didn't like to press; if Ellen wanted to say something, she would say it.

'Freya mentioned the festival,' she said instead, as she poured hot water into the teapot, 'but I don't know much about it. Is it right the whole town takes part?'

Ellen looked glad of the distraction. 'It is. Everywhere shuts for the day, and if it's fine we gather on the moor just below the fort. Nothin' fancy. Games and what-not for the men and the tackers, and stalls and suchlike for those who don't care for games.'

'It sounds fun. What if it's wet?'

'We've been lucky these past years, but now and again Cornwall does its best to drown us all.'

57

She grinned, and the last remnant of tension in her features faded. 'Three years back, we all crushed ourselves into the civic hall. Weren't the best of fun, but at least we all got paid for the day off work.'

'They even close the mine?'

'Not all of it. The tributers wouldn't earn from their pitch, so they keep working. But tut workers, and most of us surface workers, get given the day. The Battens get their due by gettin' us to work at the festival. Makes a nice change though.'

'They must be prepared to lose quite a bit of money for the sake of a memorial day.'

Ellen blinked. 'It's Penworthy!' She shook her head at Anna's ignorance, and chuckled as Anna flicked a breadcrumb at her. 'Anyway, speakin' of the mine, how's Matthew goin' on there?'

'He's getting used to it. Still doesn't like it, but I suppose you'd be hard pressed to find anyone who does.'

'You'd be surprised.' Ellen picked up the teapot and poured. 'Some of them have been doing it for so long they wouldn't know any other way of life. Take them out of the mine and give 'em a job above grass, and they'd not know what to do with themselves.'

'I don't think Matthew will ever be comfortable down there. It doesn't help that he's treated like a child by his shift captain...' Anna belatedly remembered that his shift captain was Ellen's brother, and flushed. 'Sorry.'

But Ellen waved a hand. 'Don't mind me. Davey's got 'is ways, and they're not always the best ways. But I'm not him, and he's not me.' She hesitated, then shrugged. 'It's Ginny I feel sorry for.'

'Ginny? Why, is he cruel to her?' Anna had seen David sullen, and even angry, but she'd not yet seen him violent.

'No, nothin' like that. It's just that she've been tryin' to get a baby started since they wed, and she've heard them stories about him and Juliet Carne. They swear it was over with last year, but I've got my doubts.' She was looking at Anna quite pointedly now, probably because of Freya's friendship with Juliet. Perhaps she expected Anna to stick up for the girl, which she wouldn't, not in a month of Sundays. She'd created her own problems, she had no one but herself to blame.

'Anyway,' Ellen went on, 'Ginny thinks if *she* can't give him children to care for them in their old age, he'll likely leave her and go off with someone who can.'

'I'm sure he won't,' Anna said carefully. She knew perfectly well he wouldn't, but telling Ellen she'd heard as much from his own lips would raise far too many questions.

'That's what I keeps tellin' her!' Ellen said. 'He might've had his head turned by an easy bit of fun, but no matter what people think of him I know he cares for Ginny better'n anything. He just don't ever tell her so.'

'Well, now Juliet's going to marry James, so Ginny needn't worry about her anymore, at least.'

'Thank Heaven.' Ellen put down her cup. 'Now I've talked your ear off I'd better go and see how Eddie's doin'.'

They went back out into the sunshine and

59

talked a little more, watching Ellen's little boy building the pile of stones and then deliberately setting them to wobble, testing the structure. 'He's going to be a builder, I reckon,' Ellen said.

'Not a fisherman?'

'I'd never let him go to sea, not in a million years. Lost my own pa, and two uncles. My Ned's illness wasn't helped by workin' for Roland Fry, neither.'

Anna touched her arm. 'I'm sorry, I hadn't realised.'

'Thing is, just about everyone's lost fathers and sons out there, it's a good thing it don't stop more mothers from thinkin' like me or we'd have no fishing industry left.' She shook her head. 'But know this: I won't set my boy on those waves, not ever. I'd sooner see him down the mine with his uncle David. Come on, Eddie.' As she left, she looked back at Anna, screwing her eyes up against the sun. 'Your man's safer down there than he ever was on the sea, too. Remember that, when the fear takes you.'

Chapter Four

With sweat dripping into his eyes and sticking his shirt to his back, with the blisters on his hands splitting and stinging with each shift of the hammer, and with the knowledge that this was his one day off and he was working through it, Matthew might have expected to be feeling discontented and resentful. Instead he found himself smiling as he tapped yet another nail into the window frame, and gave it an experimental shake; this afternoon he would see Anna... He couldn't argue the necessity of their temporary unsatisfactory living arrangements, but a week without talking to her was at least six days too long.

The ladder wobbled, and he gave a shout, clutching at it before realising how pointless that instinctive action was. Looking down, he was partly amused, partly exasperated, but hugely relieved all the same, to see young Harry Batten looking at him with a grin on his face.

'Good afternoon, Mr Penhaligon,' he said. 'Will you let me help you?'

'You'll be helping me to the ground in a heap if you do that again,' Matthew pointed out. He looked around for a responsible adult. 'On your own?'

'Uncle Hugh is away, and Aunt Lucy thinks I'm in my room.'

'I was thinking more of your mother. She'll tan your hide if she catches you here again.' Matthew descended the ladder and used the rag from his belt to wipe the sweat from his face. 'Come on, I'll walk you back home.'

'Can't I bang some nails in?'

'Sorry, boy.' Matthew put a friendly hand on his shoulder. 'Your family wouldn't thank me for sending you home with a swollen thumb. Come on.' It would actually be nice to stretch his legs in a comfortable walk, and give his bruised hands a chance to let the fresh, healing air at them.

Harry shrugged away. 'I don't want to go home.'

61

Matthew ignored the boy's rare sulkiness. 'Just let me tell Freya where I'm going.' He pushed open the door and called out, 'I'm just going up to Pencarrack to return something! Anna should be here soon. Tell her I won't be long.'

But the voice that responded was his father's. 'Oh, ar? Young master's abroad again, is he? Send'n in 'ere, I'll find somethin' to keep him busy. Got two pairs of boots to clean, as well as the privy. An' they windows upstairs could do with a wash.'

Matthew turned to Harry with an eyebrow raised, and Harry sighed. 'Oh, all *right!*'

'Are you sure? My pa's a fair man to work for. He won't make you miss *too* many meals, and I'm sure he'd have you home by bedtime.'

'I said I'll go.' Harry's face was glum, and Matthew hid a smile, and gestured up the hill. 'Shall we?'

Harry gave him a mutinous look, but after they'd taken only a few steps he'd forgotten his grievance. 'What were you doing up that ladder?'

'Just making a few repairs before the winter sets in.'

'What kind of repairs?'

'The wood gets old, and it warps sometimes. If it's left through the winter it'll just become weak. So we sometimes need to replace bits of the frame before that happens.'

'They look all right to me.' Harry twisted his head to look back and up at the windows of Penhaligon's Attic.

'That's because I take good enough care of them that you have to be close to spot when something needs doing. Why are you so interested?'

'It looked like fun,' Harry said. 'Banging away with a hammer like that.'

'It's certainly the only good excuse to make a noise on a Sunday,' Matthew said. 'I'm sure they'll be making repairs at Pencarrack while the weather's good. Maybe it'd be better if you asked to help your handyman, or at least watch him, instead of wandering around here.'

'Collings doesn't like me to get in his way. He says I'm more trouble than I'm worth.'

Matthew gave him a wry smile. 'I can see his point. But you ought to be more careful, you know.'

'Sorry, I didn't mean to make you nearly fall.'

'I just meant you're very young to be out and about alone.'

Harry immediately pulled himself taller. 'I'm nearly eleven! Besides, Mother won't come with me, she's too busy with Grandfather, talking about boring old mines.'

Dorothy Batten, talking business ... how things had changed. Matthew remembered her from years ago, and a young lady less likely to be interested in figures sheets and profits he couldn't imagine. She'd been in the newspapers every other week in those days, climbing into carriages or onto boats with a variety of men; bluntly telling the gleeful reporters precisely what she thought of them, and why she didn't care what they thought of her; angering and embarrassing her father seemingly just for the fun of it. It had only been a matter of time, in the opinions Matthew had heard around town, before she fell afoul of the laws of nature. And here was the result: ten years old and already searching beyond his own world for excitement, just like his mother.

'Look, lad,' Matthew said. 'You must know that not everyone in town is ... well, not everyone would just let you stay and watch.'

'*You* didn't.'

'Or take time out of their day to walk you back home,' Matthew amended. He would have to think more quickly to get the better of this one.

'I'll be all right,' Harry said, with admirable confidence. 'My friends will look out for me.'

'What, Bobby Gale and those others? How did you get them to stop chasing you anyway?'

'I ran faster than they did.'

'Well then, how did you get them to let you join in their games?'

'I had better marbles. Once I let them win a few, they decided I was decent after all.'

Matthew couldn't help giving a wry chuckle, despite his concerns. 'Don't you have any other friends? From your own ... school?' He had been about to say 'class', but if Harry had not yet grasped how different his wealth made him, Matthew didn't want to be the one to spoil his innocent fun. That would happen all too soon in any case.

'I don't go to school yet,' Harry said, 'I have a tutor. Maddern. But I'm going away next year, to Plymouth.'

'Boarding school?' Matthew gave a little laugh. 'Well then, you're going to have to learn to do as you're told, they won't take any nonsense.'

'It's called St Boniface Catholic School for

Boys,' Harry went on, pronouncing the name carefully. 'Aunt Lucy says I'm too young, but Mother and Grandfather are very keen. And so am I, of course,' he added, but Matthew wasn't wholly convinced. 'I shall stay there in the term times, and come home for holidays. I hope Bobby and the others will still let me play.'

'Well even if they don't, you're sure to make a lot of new friends,' Matthew pointed out. 'And besides, you'll be too old for playing soon. You'll be taking up the pastimes of a gentleman.' If he'd been Matthew's son he would have already gained his sea legs, even if Matthew himself no longer had a boat on which to employ them.

'Uncle Hugh's going to take me hunting,' Harry mused. 'I like riding, but I'm not sure about hunting. Foxes are pretty. What do you think, Mr Penhaligon?'

'I think you've a good heart, lad. But you must do as your uncle tells you.'

'Oh, I shall. But perhaps I won't be as good at hunting as he'd like me to be.'

Matthew glanced down. Was diplomacy at work here already? The innocent look Harry gave him back told him it was, and he felt a tug of affection. This boy would go far.

They chatted as they walked, about the school, Harry's unlikely companionship with the local ruffian, and how his mother would react to that if she knew. It was only when they drew close to Pencarrack House, and Matthew saw the neatly kept gardens stretching away to the huge house, that he remembered he was talking to the grandson of the man who still owned a great deal of

Caernoweth and, by association, most of the people in it. Harry himself might carry no airs or graces with him, but Charles Batten was very much aware, and proud, of his standing.

Harry's voice cut through Matthew's thoughts. 'Look, there's Aunt Lucy! Hie, Aunt Lucy!' Harry waved his arms above his head, and the young woman who'd emerged from the walled garden looked over. Even from this distance Matthew could see her shoulders slump in relief, and she hurried over to them.

She threw Matthew a grateful look, but her attention was on her nephew. 'Henry George Batten, you're for the high jump this time!'

'I only went for a little walk,' Harry protested. 'Mr Penhaligon brought me back.'

Miss Batten turned to Matthew. 'Thank you, Mr Penhaligon. That was kinder than he deserved.' She dropped a hand on Harry's shoulder. 'I do hope he wasn't any trouble.'

'None whatsoever,' Matthew assured her. 'He just wanted to watch me work.'

'Really? What were you doing?'

'Fixing window frames.'

'Ah!' Miss Batten nodded. 'Collings doesn't like to be criticised, and Master Harry does have trouble keeping his ... *suggestions* to himself.'

'Well, it's good to have confidence,' Matthew said. He was already itching to make his way back home; this conversation felt quite laboured, as if he were being humoured and Miss Batten was stretching politeness beyond its natural bounds.

She cleared her throat. 'Penhaligon, you say? With the books?'

'The same, yes, Miss. Penhaligon's Attic.'

'I understand my brother Hugh brings Harry to your shop sometimes.'

'So I gather.'

'He's very taken with your daughter.'

Matthew's eyes narrowed; he didn't like to ask which 'he' Miss Batten was referring to. 'Harry's welcome any time,' he said, rather pointedly. 'A love of books is no bad thing in a lad.'

'Absolutely!' Miss Batten smiled, then glanced over her shoulder, and Matthew followed her gaze. A man was crossing the lawn towards them, leaving the front door standing wide as if he had flung it open in a temper. Charles Batten. Matthew knew him to be only of medium height, and slight of build, but he seemed to fill a space much larger than his physical self, even at this distance.

Miss Batten's voice turned brisk. 'Well, thank you for bringing Harry back, Mr Penhaligon. I'll try and see to it he doesn't wander off again. Harry, go and say good afternoon to your grandfather.' She gave the boy a little push, and he went, throwing a grin over his shoulder that raised a niggle as before – too vague to be labelled a real familiarity, but there was a flicker of something there, for certain.

'I'm just worried about him, Miss,' Matthew said. He wondered why he'd chosen to prolong this after all; he certainly had no wish to exchange either pleasantries or formalities with Charles Batten. But when he thought of Harry wandering alone, maybe up past Furzy Row where dissatisfaction and jealousy were so often fuelled by the cheapest oblivion a man could buy, he went cold.

'A wealthy boy might come to grief, Miss, if his timing's off and his smile's too cheerful.'

'I understand,' Miss Batten said. 'I ... *we*, that is, are very grateful. Harry's mother is very busy just at present, but perhaps it's time I stopped covering up for the little scamp, and let her know exactly what he's doing.'

Matthew nodded. 'That might be wise.'

Harry was halfway to the house and had met his grandfather, but Charles had merely taken the boy's hand and turned him back, continuing his way to the edge of his garden without so much as breaking his stride. A ridiculous tremble fluttered in Matthew's stomach, and he tried to cough it away. Why in the world should he be nervous? He owed Batten nothing. His shop and the tiny piece of land on which it stood were not owned by Pencarrack, as so many – including his old home at Hawthorn Cottage – were. He had no quarrel with the man, and yet there was something about the way Batten was looking at him that made him wish he was anywhere but here ... even back down on the lower levels of Wheal Furzy. But he couldn't leave now, it would be nothing short of rude. He would have to stay and make his polite introductions.

For a frozen moment he couldn't even remember if the man was a peer... How was he to address him? The uncertainty must have shown on his face, because Batten's mouth twisted in dry amusement, as if he recognised the dilemma. When he spoke, his voice was surprisingly soft, his delivery slow and deliberate.

'Good afternoon. I don't believe I know you,

but I gather you've saved Miss Batten the trouble of once again seeking out my grandson.' Even more surprisingly, he held out a hand. 'Charles Batten. *Mister.*'

Matthew guessed from the tone in his voice that this was the source of an old irritation. He shook the hand, belatedly realising he had not first wiped it on his trousers, and hoping the summer heat had not made it too sweaty. 'Matthew Penhaligon. It's a pleasure, sir.'

'Which? Meeting me, or escorting the young master home?' Batten started to smile again, but then his hazel eyes narrowed, and instead of waiting for an answer, he went on, 'Penhaligon, did you say?'

'Yes, sir. From Penhaligon's Attic.'

Miss Batten spoke up. 'Harry spends a good deal of time there, Father. Quite good for him, I thought, a bookshop.'

'Alone?'

'Hugh generally takes him,' Miss Batten said carefully, eyeing her father. 'It's only today that he decided to go by himself.'

'I was quite safe,' Harry piped up, but was ignored by his aunt and grandfather.

Matthew nodded at him. 'And he's very welcome,' he assured Batten. 'Except today I was unable to keep a close eye on him personally, so thought it best to bring him home.'

'Nevertheless,' Batten said, 'I shall ensure he doesn't trouble you again.'

'Really, it's no bother. Freya enjoys–'

'I'll see that Hugh doesn't waste any more of your time.'

69

Matthew looked from Batten to his daughter, who was frowning in surprise. But Batten's voice held a note of finality, and he accepted the brief audience was over, and that he'd just lost Freya a customer.

'Well,' he said, into the faintly awkward silence. 'I do have work to finish. Good day, Mr Batten. Miss Batten.'

'Good day, Mr Penhaligon,' Miss Batten said. 'And thank you again.'

Batten merely nodded to him, and turned to leave, and Matthew did likewise, but stopped as Harry called out, 'Goodbye, Penhaligon!'

He was waving but, despite the friendly smile on his face, the casual way he had dropped the 'Mr' put Matthew firmly in his place. Matthew raised a hand, and allowed himself a wry little smile; it seemed there was no reason to worry about the boy forgetting his station in life after all. He was born to it.

Juliet lived with her brother Tom somewhere along the lane that ran between Kessell's and the civic offices, but as for how long the lane was, how many houses were there, and which one belonged to the Carnes, James had no idea. Similar to his own home in Paddle Lane, there were eighteen houses along this narrow road, built close to-gether, nine on each side of the lane, and with small patches of ground that might, with a little imagination, be labelled gardens. All of them had their doors open; families back from church were taking advantage of the warm weather to get clothing, bedding and rugs dry, and to let a fresh

70

breeze blow through their homes. Children either worked or played, depending on their ages, and in the second-to-last house James found Juliet's brother, digging over a small, scrubby patch ready for planting carrots from a tray at his side.

He hesitated, suddenly unsure whether to blow in like the hurricane he felt like, or to search for an icier calm, but before he could decide Juliet herself came out of the house with a bowl of dirty dish water. She put it beside her brother, ready for him to reuse on the garden, and when she straightened James could clearly see, for the first time, the newly rounded shape of her beneath her thin summer dress. Hot with housework, she wiped her face and turned to go back indoors before she caught sight of James.

A bright smile broke over her face, and James couldn't even tell if he was returning it, so conflicted were his emotions. His determination faltered; if he pretended he didn't know, he could swallow his pride and anger, and have the family after all. Juliet was a decent enough girl. He even *liked* her. And the child would never have to know... James's heart began to thump heavily again, indecision and anger battling inside him.

'What brings you out here, James?' Juliet said, coming over. She reached up to kiss him, and he mechanically returned the gesture. A brief touch of lips to cheek, nothing more; perfectly respectable, as if anyone cared. He was glad of the excuse that they were in public, and unmarried.

'I just wanted to talk.' He kept finding his eyes straying to the swell of her stomach, and what it could mean for him. 'Can you come for a walk?

Just a short one,' he added quickly, seeing the lowering of Thomas's brow.

'She's busy,' Thomas said, sticking his fork into the ground. He knocked aside a stone with his foot, and met James's gaze with a challenging one of his own.

James was embarrassed to find himself searching for a conciliatory tone. 'I won't keep her long.'

'Bugger off!' Juliet glared at her brother. 'I'm not your bloody slave, Tom, I'll be as long as I like. Come on, James.'

Juliet brushed past him at the gate, and led the way further along the lane. James followed, trying to untangle the thoughts which, until now, had been so straightforward. Where the lane met the corner of two fields, Juliet climbed one of the gates and dropped onto the grass on the other side with a heavy thump of her booted feet.

James found himself tightening at the casual way she was flinging herself around. 'Be careful!'

Juliet grinned. 'Don't fuss! Now, what was it you wanted to talk about?' She watched him climb the gate more carefully, a teasing smile on her face, then ran her hand down the buttons of his waistcoat. 'I bet you didn't really want to talk at all, did you?'

'Yes.' He removed her hand gently. 'I did.'

'Freya thinks it's nice you want to call 'im Roland,' Juliet said, the brightness in her voice sounding more forced now. 'I don't mind if you want to choose the name for a girl too, though. What do you think?'

'I think,' James began, then stopped. He recalled the images that had taken over his life lately; of the second bedroom becoming a nursery, and of having a small face turned to him in trust, and even love. Of the way it would feel to be part of a family. 'I think you can choose,' he finished quietly.

As he spoke, he felt the relief loosen his chest. He could still have it. No one need know, and he might still have a child of his own one day.

Juliet's smile trembled a little, and he realised she'd been scared he was going to do exactly what he'd come here to do. 'In that case,' she said, 'I think I'd like to call her Ellen.'

He nodded, barely listening, still battling with the thoughts of forgiveness that sat so at odds with his pride. 'That's pretty.'

'So, what did you want to talk about?' Juliet said again. 'I thought you was going to be busy at the cottage today.'

'I just fancied a breather, while the plaster's drying,' James lied easily. 'And I thought we ought to start talking about things. How it'll be. That sort of thing.'

'It'll be wonderful, is how it'll be!' Juliet laughed, and moved closer to him again. 'You've made me proper happy, James.'

He couldn't stop himself from asking, 'And there's no one else you'd rather be with?'

'No one. It's just you, me, and our little Roland or Ellen, in our sweet cottage down by the sea.' She kissed him, but when he didn't respond she drew back. He met her eyes, and in them he saw only his own reflection. No guile, no guilt. Perhaps that was what made him say the words he said next, he didn't know. Or perhaps it was that he'd suddenly remembered where he'd heard the name Ellen.

'Not even David Donithorn?'

Juliet's laugh was a dismissive, but breathless sound. 'Why on earth would you bring *him* up?'

'Everyone knows you and he have been ... knocking around.'

'That was ages ago. Last year.' She stepped away, and two bright spots of colour flared in her cheeks.

'It was six months ago,' James said quietly.

'All right! Yes, we were together again after that. But I'm five months gone. *Five.* Not six.'

'So you say. You also just said you'd not been with him since last year.'

'Do I look six months to you?'

'How would I know?' he said reasonably. 'I wouldn't have the faintest idea.'

'We've been through this,' Juliet said. 'Here!' She grabbed his hand, and pressed his palm against her stomach. She spoke quickly. 'You might feel it kickin' in a minute. I feel it in the night sometimes, just flutterin' like a little bird.'

'The thing is,' James said, 'I wouldn't mind. That is, even if it's David's baby–'

'It isn't!'

'If it was, though, I'd still give it a home. I'd still care for it.' He pulled his hand away, keeping his voice even. 'But only if I was sure I could trust you from this moment on. Do you still want Donithorn?'

'He's married!'

'That doesn't mean anything.' He sighed. 'Look. Say we got together. Say we married, in front of everyone we know, and claimed the child

74

was mine, even though we both knew it wasn't–'

'James–'

'And then say something happened to Ginny, or they separated for some other reason. Where would that leave me then? David would be free, and you'd be off with him and his baby before I could blink.'

'It's not his! And if that was what I wanted, why would I have asked *you* for the money to let me leave? I'd never see David if I did that, free or not!'

'You'd be back like a shot if he was, we both know that.' James took a deep breath. 'I can only trust you if you tell me the truth now. Is this my child?'

'Yes!'

He closed his eyes briefly, hating her for destroying this fragile chance, just when he thought he had wrestled his doubts away. 'And do you still care for Donithorn?'

'No. I promise you I don't.'

'You promise?' He looked at her, trying to read past the fear on her face and find a genuine, lasting emotion. 'I don't believe you.'

She paled, and swallowed hard. Now, he thought desperately, *tell me now! We can still–*

'I swear on the life of everyone I love,' she said at last, and his heart plummeted. She looked genuinely puzzled at his reaction. 'Why won't you believe me?'

No sense in keeping it secret now. 'I know for a fact you went to Donithorn first, and he turned you away.'

Now her face was more grey than white. 'Who

told you?' she whispered.

His voice came out flat, lifeless. 'You've stopped denying it, then?'

'All right, I lied, but it was *him* I lied to, not you!'

James shook his head. 'You can't stop yourself, can you? Why would you have lied to him? You knew he could neither leave his wife, nor give you any money. But me? I'm single, I have a house and a business... Why didn't you tell me the truth? I'd have still taken you.'

'I did tell the truth.' She reached for his hand again but he stepped away, feeling sick.

'I'm not the soft-hearted idiot you seem to think I am. I have just given up the biggest chance of my working life! You needed a stable home so I turned the job offer down yesterday. This morning I find out you've played me for the biggest fool that ever walked the Earth.'

'Please—'

'The stupid thing is, it would have been worth it.' He gave a tiny laugh that fell between them like a rock. 'I just wanted you to be honest, and then I could have trusted you. But I know you now. You'll be off, the first chance you get. With Donithorn, or with someone else.' His voice dropped, and he sounded oddly calm to his own ears, as if the revelation, so long in coming, had finally quenched all his passion and anger. 'You're nothing but a scheming whore, Juliet Carne. I pity the poor man who falls for your lies.'

Unable to look at her dismayed face, and her tear-filled eyes, he climbed back over the gate and into the lane. He closed his ears to her voice

76

calling him back; she and her unborn bastard were of no consequence to him now. Let her lie to someone else, he wasn't going to become a laughing stock for the sake of a few crocodile tears and a twitching conscience. The child was not his, the woman did not want him. Neither one had any claim on him any longer.

Chapter Five

Freya propped open the shop door and stood there for a moment, enjoying the warm sun on her face. But she couldn't stand idle for long; Sundays were precious but short, and her list of jobs grew each week the fuller her life became.

'Are you sure you're going to be all right alone, Grandpa?'

Robert, hat in one hand, stick in the other, lowered his eyebrows at her. 'I've been able to find my way around town these past sixty-odd years. And the lad'll be back soon enough, so you can send out a search party if I'm not 'ome by teatime.'

'Don't think I won't,' Freya said. 'Just sit and rest if you get tired, don't try to do too much.'

'Women,' Robert muttered. He put on his hat and moved in his new, slow and careful way out into the sunny street. As he passed Freya he squeezed her wrist where it rested atop the long-handled broom she was about to use, and although he didn't look at her she smiled for him.

She watched him for a few minutes as he limped across the road and down towards the lower end of town, and then her attention was caught by Anna, who was coming up the road, carrying a covered basket.

'Where's Mairead?' Freya asked.

'She's helping Esther this afternoon. Joe is still quite poorly. I've said I'll go back early, too, so I won't stay long after tea.'

'That's a shame. Papá is just out at the moment, but he'll be back soon. He said he'd look out for you if you wanted to walk up and meet him.'

'Up where?'

'Pencarrack.'

'Oh, don't tell me; Master Batten's out and about again?' Anna followed Freya into the shop. 'He's a one, that's for sure. I'll go in a minute, but just let me put these things away first.'

'What is it?'

'Only a few eggs, and some jam Ellen gave me.'

'I like Ellen Scoble,' Freya said. 'You'd never think she used to be a Donithorn.'

'That thought occurs to me every time we meet. Although sometimes not until after I've put my foot in it.' Anna disappeared into the kitchen, and presently Freya heard the sound of cupboards opening and closing. Anna was always doing this, dropping off a little something here, a bigger something there … as if she could afford these things any better than they could. But it made the two households feel more part of each other, and so no comment was ever made.

Freya began to poke her broom at the corners of the shop, half-hearted and a little bit resentful;

she'd have loved the chance to walk Harry back to Pencarrack herself. He was a friendly lad, bright and cheerful, and good company when he wasn't shackled by the rarely seen but disapproving frown of his mother. And besides, it was sunny out there, and not a day to be stuck indoors raising dust and–

'Oi!'

Freya looked up, startled. 'Juliet! What's wrong?'

Juliet had paused in the doorway, breathing hard as if she'd been running. Her face was bright red too, but it became quickly apparent that this was less through exertion than through emotion. 'You little *cow!*' Her eyes suddenly brimmed with tears. 'You *told* him!'

'Told who?' Freya rested the broom against the counter, but Juliet shook off her tentative touch.

'Don't! You've ruined everything. I *hate* you!'

'I don't know what you're talking about!' Freya kept her voice low, aware of the open door and the curious glances from beyond it. 'Come in here.' She pulled Juliet into the shop and kicked away the bucket that had propped open the door. 'Who do you think I've told?'

'James!' Juliet took a gulping breath, and when she spoke again she was more in control, but her voice was still edged with fury. 'You had to go and do it, didn't you? All in the name of what's bloody *fair!*'

'I haven't spoken to James!' Freya tried to take Juliet's hand again, but Juliet tugged it free and stepped away behind the counter.

'Don't lie, I'm not stupid! No one else knew except David, and *he* wouldn't tell him!'

79

'Neither did Freya.' The voice in the kitchen doorway cut through accusation and denial, and both girls turned to see Anna, her face pale, her hands twisting into the thin material of a threadbare tea towel. 'It was me.'

'What?' Juliet whispered.

'Anna?' Freya said at last, when it became clear Anna was struggling to find some words that might ease the wire-thin tension. 'What's she talking about? *You* told James?'

'Not as such.' Anna came into the shop, evidently using the time it took to calmly close the kitchen door in order to gather her thoughts. 'I spoke to Brian Cornish, and he must have told him. It wasn't deliberate,' she added, 'I thought he already knew.'

Juliet gave a half-strangled laugh. 'How many more?' She looked at Anna. 'And how did *you* find out?'

'I overheard you and David talking when I was walking by the fort, and I'd sat behind the wall for shelter from the wind. I was half-dozing, but I heard what the two of you said. David knows it's his baby.'

'So you thought you'd make sure James did as well?' Juliet's bitter voice matched her expression. 'Well thanks to you stickin' your nose in where it's never been wanted, James has thrown me over. Me and this one,' she gestured to her belly, 'won't have no nice house to live in now, nor no one to provide for us.'

Freya shook her head. 'Not James's house, no. But Thomas will—'

'Thomas!' Juliet rounded on her. 'The two of

us barely earn enough together, and when I stop workin' things will just get worse, plus the extra mouth to feed!'

'But you'll still have the house?'

'We won't be able to afford the bloody rent, will we? The tannery don't build 'ouses for their men like Wheal Furzy do, and we both know Mrs Packem won't be payin' me to bake for her no more.' Juliet looked around, at the small, cramped shop with its well-stocked bookshelves; at the shelf behind her, filled with knick-knacks, models, and ornaments; at the doors that led to kitchen and hallway. She poked a rigid finger at some of the bits and pieces on the shelf, and gave a derisive snort. 'It's all right for you Penhaligons, and your little mansion here. You've never understood what it's like.'

Freya bristled. 'We only have this place because of Granny Grace. Papá does all the upkeep himself. We're not well off, *you* know that better than anyone!'

'All them years growin' up in London with your rich ma. Tom and me don't *have* no ma. Nor no pa!'

Freya bit back the defensive retort that she'd spent most of her time at boarding school, and anyway her own mother was living in another country. Despite her anger at the name-calling and accusations, she knew Juliet better than anyone else, and understood her fear.

'Anna didn't mean to let it slip,' she said more gently. 'But we'll help wherever we can, won't we, Anna?'

'Of course we will,' Anna said. 'Why don't I go

to Brian and tell him I'd got it wrong?'

'Oh, don't trouble yourself!' Juliet's voice rose again. 'It's too late. James has just come to see me, and he's finished it.'

'Can't you just deny it?' Freya was disturbed to hear herself say. 'I mean, if it's for the sake of your baby?'

Juliet faltered, then shrugged. 'He told me he'd still take me, if I told him the truth and swore I wasn't in love with David.'

'Well there you are, then!' Freya tried on a smile, but Juliet's face did not reflect it.

'I din't say what he wanted me to say.'

'But ... why?' Freya exchanged a glance with Anna, who shook her head in bewilderment.

Juliet looked stricken, as if the truth had only just hit home. 'Because I didn't believe him! I thought he was trying to catch me out.'

'Then go to him and tell him that.'

'It's too *late!*' Juliet repeated. 'He don't trust me, and don't want nothin' to do with me now.' Tears started to her eyes again, and she turned on Anna. 'You've spoiled everything. You don't belong here, and you don't deserve any of *this!*' She turned to the shelf behind her, and seized the first thing that came to hand: Freya's treasured model boat. A moment later it was twisting through the air, and it was only at the ghastly crunching sound it made as it hit the wall that Juliet seemed to realise what she'd done. She stared at Freya, her mouth half-open in wordless, pleading apology.

Freya's shocked gaze moved to the *Lady Penhaligon*. The masts were bent and snapped, a jagged edge ripping through the material of the sails; the glossy wood cracked along the hull, cutting the carefully painted name in two; the bow crumpled and split where it had hit the floor. Ruined. All Papá's hard work and the love that had gone into it... Granny Grace's beautiful sails...

Her eyes were dry, burning, but her heart ached. Juliet had known how much the *Lady Penhaligon* had meant to her. 'Get out,' she said, in a dull, flat voice.

'Freya—'

'Go on.'

'I'll fix it. I'll get Tom to look at it.'

'No.'

'This is your fault,' Juliet flung once more at Anna, but her fire had died, and regret washed over her features as she eased herself out from behind the counter and past a rigid Freya. She pulled open the door, and looked as though she wanted to say more, but eventually just stepped outside and let the door swing shut behind her.

The jangling bell fell into silence, and Freya heard the scrape of wood as Anna picked up the *Lady Penhaligon*. She turned to see it more clearly, and her throat went tight.

'Your da might be able to mend it,' Anna said, but she didn't sound convinced. 'I'm sure he'd be glad to give it a go, at least.'

Freya tore her eyes away from the boat, and looked at Anna instead. 'Why did you have to tell Brian?'

'I just... Look, it really *was* an accident.' Anna put the broken model on the counter. 'He knew

Juliet was in the family way, and I assumed James already knew the truth.'

'Are you sure you didn't do it just to fight back at James?'

Anna looked startled at the accusation. 'Do you think I've nothing better to do? And you know what they say about people in glass houses.' She frowned. 'If only the silly girl had just told him what he wanted to hear.'

'She's not silly,' Freya said tightly. 'She's just desperate.'

Anna took her hand. 'I know, sweetheart. But she'll be all right. The town will look after her, isn't that what we do?'

Freya searched for a smile but couldn't find one. She could only hope Anna was right. She looked once again at the *Lady Penhaligon*. 'Maybe she could move into the Tinner's?'

'We've no spare rooms, or I'd be happy to take her in.'

Freya wasn't at all sure she believed that. 'Mairead could move in here then.' She realised she sounded stubborn, but she didn't care. 'It needn't be forever. I'm sure she won't mind sharing my room, and then Juliet and the baby can have hers at the pub.'

'Why doesn't she come here?'

'My room might just be big enough for Mairead and me, but not for a baby as well. Besides, there's Grandpa to think of. It has to be the Tinner's.'

Anna looked about to protest further, so Freya pressed on, 'I think we owe her, don't you?'

'I don't owe her a home,' Anna pointed out, a little tartly. 'I might have exposed the truth, but I didn't put her in this mess.'

'It was what you said that turned it into a mess, though. It was all settled before you spoke to Brian.'

Anna winced, but they both knew it to be the truth. She hesitated, then nodded. 'All right. If Mairead is happy to come here for a while, then Juliet can stay at the pub. But only until we've found a better arrangement.'

'I'll go after her now.'

'You've work to do,' Anna reminded her. 'Let me go. I'm the mess-maker, after all.'

'Papá is expecting you to meet him,' Freya said. 'There's no need to make him question why you haven't.'

Anna looked from her to the door, clearly torn, and probably hoping Papá would arrive and take the decision out of her hands.

Freya searched for a calmer tone. 'You barely see each other once a week, it's not right.' She took off her apron and draped it over the counter. 'Go and meet him. I'll still have time to finish this later, if you don't mind a late tea.'

'All right.' Anna went to the door and opened it, then looked back. 'Freya?'

'Yes?'

'I really didn't intend to hurt anyone. I'd not do that for the world.'

Freya sighed. 'I know, and I suppose she does too. Or she will, once she's had time to think. We'll look after her, I'll make sure she knows that.'

'Thank you, sweetheart.' Anna straightened her back and cleared her throat. 'All right, I'm away to meet your father. Hurry and find Juliet, tell her I'll talk to Mairead about it later.'

Grandpa Robert was still out enjoying the warmth of the day, so Freya locked the door and stood looking first down the hill, and then up. Would Juliet have gone home? Or would she be walking off her fury and distress along Furzy Row, hoping to see David Donithorn? Perhaps Polworra Quarry, where the pool always calmed her when she was in a snit over anything. She might even have gone to Porthstennack, hoping to change James's mind, to put things back on the trail they had been on before Anna's unthinking comment had sparked this awful situation.

Freya tried to put her sorrow over the smashed boat to the back of her mind – after all, Juliet's troubles were so much worse – but instead of the sounds of a summer-busy community, and of the gulls' cries in their everlasting quest for food, all she could hear was that strange crunching, snapping sound as the *Lady Penhaligon* crashed into the wall. She shivered. It had the feel of an omen.

Despite his assertion that he had work to do, Matthew saw the familiar figure in the distance, and the last half-resentful thought of climbing ladders and fixing window frames flew away. Anna raised a hand to shield her eyes, and there was a visible lift to her shoulders as she saw him and her step quickened. Matthew's eyes were drawn to the graceful movement of her form beneath the cotton dress of light blue as she hurried up the hill towards him. She was hatless, as usual, and her hair was coming loose from its pins, but he had never known it any other way; if she were to

86

suddenly remember her upbringing and dress accordingly, he doubted he would recognise her.

He was still smiling at that thought when they met in the street. Anna's expression melted from an odd sort of tension into the now familiar look of calm, and the urge to capture those gently smiling lips with his grew deeper. But he settled for taking her hand and holding it tightly, crushed between their bodies – a flimsy barrier, but an effective one. He felt her knuckles press into his shirt just above his belt, and then her fingers twisted into the material as if she had no idea she was doing it. 'Are you all right?' he asked quietly. 'You look unhappy.'

'I'm grand.' She released his hand and lifted hers to touch his face. 'Now I am, anyway.'

'Are you sure?'

'Just a silly row. Nothing to fret over.' She slipped her hand into his, and when they turned to walk along Furzy Row and out towards the fort she moved closer to his side, and he contented himself with watching the wisps of dark hair lifting in the breeze, and the stray locks falling against the side of her neck.

He itched to brush the curls aside and replace them with his fingers, to feel the softness of her skin and the movement of life through her body. The thought brought a wave of emotion he could find no name for. *Love* was neither big nor special enough. Anna raised her face to his, a quizzical smile on her lips that died as their eyes met.

Her voice was light, but there was a new solemnity in her expression. 'Penny for them?'

He doubted he could make her understand for

all the pennies in the world, but he tried anyway. 'It's just seeing you, today,' he said, feeling a bit foolish. 'Something's ... changed. Gone even deeper than before. I can't explain it.'

She stopped walking. They had reached the end of the row of run-down miners' cottages, and ahead of them lay the open moor, the quarry, and the fort. They were surrounded on all sides by beauty, industry, history, and by vivid, glorious life, but all Matthew's attention was on the fine lines that fanned the corners of Anna's eyes; the tiny scratch on her forehead, no doubt from the pub's cat; the way her lips had parted, as if to speak before her own words had failed her.

'I can't,' he repeated. 'Is it enough to say I love you?'

'It'll do, for now.' Anna's eyes belied her flippancy as they searched his, and he bent to press his mouth to hers. She gave the tiniest of sighs, and he felt her hands rest on his waist as they kissed, gripping tightly at his belt. When the kiss ended they smiled at one another, in a wordless question and reply, and Matthew knew that he would soon be showing her exactly what her penny had bought.

Walking on, with the warmth of her kiss still on his lips, Matthew laced his fingers into hers. 'You said something about a row,' he ventured. 'Who did you argue with?'

'Just a customer. It doesn't matter. To be honest I'm more distracted by this business of Mairead not inheriting the pub. Did Freya tell you about that?'

'Yes. Some stupid law that punishes Mairead

for what they think you did. It hardly seems fair.'

'The good thing is she's not at all troubled. Being here seems to have pushed it all a long way away, in time as well as in miles. But I have to remember that over in Ireland it's all still very fresh.'

'Will she write to your aunt and uncle?'

'I don't know. I think I'd like to encourage it someday, especially my cousin Keir. Since I married Finn they've had nothing much to do with me, so Mairead never really knew them the way I did, which is the real pity. Keir's the one I was always closest to, but he moved to New Zealand a while ago.'

'It must be hard on you,' Matthew said quietly.

'Ah, sure, you and Freya make up for it.' Anna's voice brightened, and she swung their hands as if the movement could shake off any melancholy thoughts. 'And so does your da, but don't tell him I said that.'

'Oh, don't worry.' Matthew grinned; in his memory echoed his father's voice, just a day or two ago: *that woman's been the best thing for you since the maid come back from London. But don't let on I told you so...*

'So, where do you want to go?' he said aloud. 'Have you seen Polworra Quarry yet?'

'Only from a distance. Seems a noisy, dirty sort of a place for a Sunday walk, though.' She looked at him through lowered lashes. 'Not very ... private?'

He tightened his grip on her hand and lowered his voice. 'They won't be blasting today. We'll have as much privacy as we like.'

'Then lead on, Mr Penhaligon.'

In contrast to the pumps that constantly worked at keeping the shafts at Wheal Furzy dry, even on a Sunday, Polworra was blessedly quiet. To their left, high on the top of the ridge, the ground was a mass of white and grey rubble, wooden huts, and derricks, but ahead lay the tranquil section of the moor that led towards the sea, and the headland overlooked by the ruins of Caernoweth Fort.

Anna stepped away from him and peered closer at the far edge of the quarry, where it gave way to rough moorland. 'What's over there, in front of that hill?'

'That's the pool. Come on, I'll show you.'

The quarry pool lay still; not even the freshening breeze stirred its surface, protected as it was by the steep slopes on three sides. As boys Matthew and James had often come here to throw lumps of stone in, and see who could make the loudest noise... A pang of sorrow for those uncomplicated times caught him unawares, but was banished quickly when Anna slipped her hand into his again.

'It's a gorgeous colour, don't you think?'

'I suppose it is.' Looking at it with fresh eyes Matthew saw how the turquoise and green changed depending on where you were standing, and where the strong afternoon sunlight fell. It was impossible to see more than a foot or so below the surface, and he remembered entertaining James for hours at a time with tales of what might live just out of sight down there. James had listened, wide-eyed and flatteringly terrified, and Matthew's tales had gradually become wilder and wilder... What a pity he'd never thought to write them into that book of his, Freya would have loved them.

'There's a lot of gorse here,' Anna observed. 'Makes it hard to find somewhere to sit.'

Matthew nodded. 'It's where the mine's name comes from. Wheal, for place of work, Furzy, for the gorse. Place is carpeted and it's a bugger to clear. It's better over there though.' He pointed to a spot closer to the pool, and Anna found a patch of clear ground and patted the grass, squinting up at him.

'Are you going to leave me sitting here all by myself?'

He smiled and stretched out beside her, and she moved closer, tucking her head into the hollow below his shoulder. They lay without speaking for a while, Anna's fingers idly playing with the buttons on his shirt. He closed his eyes against the glare of the sun, and wondered if anyone would notice if they didn't return home until after dark. The windows would wait until next week. Drowsily content, it was a moment before he realised Anna had unbuttoned his shirt, but then she slid her fingers inside and he felt her stop in surprise at encountering bare skin.

'No vest,' she murmured.

He remembered what he had been doing immediately before taking Harry Batten home, and winced; he must smell something awful. 'I was working on the windows. It was too hot.'

She rolled over, and he opened his eyes to see her smiling at him. Her loosened hair brushed his face, and then her lips were on his, and her hand slid further up his chest, plucking at the buttons as she went. There was an undeniable thrill at being with a woman so confident, and for a moment he acquiesced; her long fingers spread his shirt open and traced a line from his jaw, down the side of his neck and along his collarbone. His skin jumped at her touch, and he held his breath as she moved her mouth away from his, following the path laid by her fingers.

He grasped her around the waist and lifted her away, so that their positions were reversed. 'My turn,' he breathed, and pressed her back into the ground with a kiss that left them both gasping. Her hands were still on him, exploring the body she already knew so well as if it were brand new to her, and when she stopped tugging at his clothes in order to remove her own every second stretched into a lifetime. When she finally lay exposed to him he spared one brief glance around to make sure they were fully alone, and slipped into her – the low sound that came from his throat was echoed in her own, and he lowered his lips to hers again, capturing the sound between them.

It was necessarily quick, but intense. More so than ever before, and Matthew made sure Anna had wrung every ounce of pleasure he could give her before allowing himself to follow her into mindless, heart-pounding release. He held her close, pressing himself into her as the day gradually returned, intruding into that moment, and felt her quick, shallow breathing on his neck. Each outward breath was a tiny pant of astonished laughter.

'What'll we ever do in the winter?' she managed

at last, when he had withdrawn reluctantly from her.

He had to wait for his own breathing to settle, before lifting himself onto his elbow and looking down at her. 'What do you mean?'

She gave him an impish grin. 'I can't imagine it could ever be so wildly exciting in a boring old bed, even with you.'

Matthew adopted an affronted tone. 'Are you questioning my ability to make you laugh indoors as well as out?'

'That wasn't proper laughter,' Anna pointed out, tugging at his still-flapping shirt.

'No? What was it then?'

'It was...' Anna shook her head, and her smile was broad and happy, showing those beautiful teeth that he could still feel in the skin of his neck. 'I don't know how it's possible, but I believe that was better than anything we've ever done.'

'I told you,' he said, more softly now, 'something's shifted for me. When I saw you walking up the hill I felt this...' He still couldn't articulate well enough, and to try and show her instead he lifted her hand and placed it over his heart. 'That,' he said. 'That's all you, in there.'

She looked as if she wanted to say something light, but instead she swallowed hard, and blinked. 'I wouldn't want to be anywhere else,' she said quietly. She lifted her hand away and touched his cheek, her eyes searching his. 'I only hope you know how much I love you, because I don't think I'm any better than you at saying it.'

They lay in silence, arms locked about one another, as if to let go would result in one of them

93

floating away. Anna's fingers brushed gently across his sun-warmed body for a moment, then fell still, resting on his hip. Presently she went heavy in his arms, and he lay staring at the sky, feeling her slow, peaceful breathing. Every time she shifted slightly in her sleep he pressed his lips to her hair and held her tighter, and as she stilled again he swore silently that soon he would do this every night.

The sun began to slip seawards, and Anna stirred as the air freshened on her bare skin. They dressed, reluctantly, and when she'd laced her boots Anna put out her hand for Matthew to pull her to her feet.

'Freya will be waiting dinner, won't she?'

Matthew nodded. 'Will you stay and eat with us?'

'I can't. Esther's going early, to take care of Joe.' She smoothed her dress and sighed. 'This has been a perfect afternoon. I don't want it to end.'

'Me neither. When can we do it again?'

'Next Sunday? That'd only make us just like most other married couples, after all.'

He smiled and wrapped his arms around her. 'Two false marriages,' he mused. 'But you're more my wife than I ever felt Isabel could be.'

'Don't say what you think I want to hear,' Anna chided gently. 'I know you and she had an exciting life, and for a good while.'

'It felt like it, but I was a father at nineteen. God, Anna, that's Freya's age!'

'And that's where it all started to slide away?'

Matthew shrugged. 'It sounds awful, and it had nothing to do with Freya. But Isabel and I were

94

hardly more than children ourselves.'

'Well, whatever happens, or doesn't, I love calling myself Anna Penhaligon.' She moved back and held him at arm's length. 'I suppose I can bear living apart a while longer, as long as I know that we'll be together some day.'

'We will,' he said. 'But I don't want to wait until the girls leave us. I want us all to be together before that.' It was not right that the only way they could become a family would be to split them apart.

'We'll find the perfect place,' Anna assured him, 'even if it's not Penhaligon's Attic.'

Matthew blinked. How hadn't he thought of this before? 'I think I've found it.'

'Oh?'

'You just said it, the attic! I can convert the roof space, clear it all out. Mairead can move in there.'

'That's a grand idea! Will it cost a lot though?'

'Well it won't be Hampton Court but it'll be cosy. I'll get started next Sunday.'

'Freya will be delighted,' Anna said. 'She's been as keen as anything for Mairead and me to move in.'

'She's always wanted a big family.' Matthew's mind was racing ahead to how it might work, and he itched to take up a pen and begin planning it.

Still discussing the possibilities, and how they might come by what they needed, they left the quarry pool and walked slowly back across the grass to the tail end of Furzy Row once more. Matthew couldn't help throwing a dark look at the house occupied by David and Ginny Donithorn, and Anna saw it and slipped her arm

95

through his.

'Is he that bad to work for?'

'Not for anyone else, apparently.'

She sighed. 'He's sure to come around eventually, isn't he?'

'I wouldn't be too certain. He's got good reason to mistrust me, after all. Better than most.'

'Well he must surely see you're a hard worker, and no threat to anyone's safety, he'd be a fool not to.' She sounded cross on his behalf, and he smiled.

'Let's hope so.' He sought a cheerier subject. 'I met Charles Batten today, when I took Harry home.'

Anna looked surprised. '*Met* him? You mean, for the first time?'

'Never actually spoken to him before,' Matthew said. 'Knew who he was, of course, but the Battens don't spend much of their time around town.'

'The son comes to the shop,' Anna reminded him. 'Hugh.'

'I've never seen him.' His voice tightened. 'Anyway, I've got a feeling those little visits will be coming to an end. The moment I mentioned my name it was as if someone had pressed a switch. Mr Batten made it sound as if it was doing me a favour by keeping Harry away, but that's not what I read on his face.'

'Snobbery?'

'Well, he'd be entitled. But no, I don't think so.' Matthew shrugged and indicated his soiled work clothes. 'He'd have known I wasn't anyone of account, right from the outset.'

Anna nodded. 'I wonder if it's the regularity of

his grandson's visits that bothers him then. And the fact that his son is encouraging it.'

'Maybe. Something Miss Batten said had me wondering. Is it possible her brother has a ... a *liking*, for Freya?'

'Oh, I'd say more than possible,' Anna began, and Matthew frowned. 'But she's far too sensible to encourage him.' She moved her hand along Matthew's arm until her fingers found his, and spoke gently. 'She's nineteen, Matthew, and she's a very attractive young woman.'

'She's just like her mother,' Matthew said, without thinking. Anna's hand twitched in his, and he squeezed it. 'You're going to have to stop worrying, you know.' She looked up at him, and he grinned. 'If you're ever in any doubt, just think about the first time we were together. Down by the fort.'

'What about it?'

He stopped, and affected a hurt look. 'Don't you remember it?'

'Of course!' She nudged him as they walked on. 'How could I forget? But how does it–'

'Just remind yourself of this: I have never, *ever*, knelt on a stone for Isabel.'

Anna laughed. 'The mark of true love is a bruised knee?'

'I would bruise both knees, and even an elbow,' he assured her.

'Then I can ask for nothing more.'

Anna rolled the last empty barrel along the passageway, breathing a sigh of relief that the night's work was over, a sigh that was cut short as the cat slunk out of the storeroom and twisted around her feet, letting her know with a skin-creeping yowl that she had trodden on his tail.

She clicked her tongue. 'Well whose fault is that?' She slid the barrel into its place, and shooed the cat into the yard. 'Go on with you! Mangy thing!'

Arric stayed close to her feet, but the waft of air that brushed Anna's face was welcoming, so she stayed where she was, leaning against the door jamb. The yard was bathed in a bright, bold moonlight that touched everything with silvery fingers, and Anna breathed deeply in the night air, and closed her eyes in quiet enjoyment.

'You owe me.'

Anna jerked as the quiet voice cut through the night. 'Juliet?'

The girl stepped out from behind the hen house. 'I was hopin' to catch you.'

'You're lucky you did, I wasn't intending to come out tonight.' Anna tried to keep her voice calm. 'How long have you been waiting?'

Juliet shrugged. 'How should I know? Long enough.'

'Well, since you're here, Freya came looking for you after you left the shop. She and I were talk-ing, and we thought–'

'Fifty pounds, and I'll go away.'

Anna's words froze in her throat, then she gave a short, disbelieving laugh and Juliet's face twisted.

'It in't funny–'

'Oh, believe me, I know it's not.' Anna's voice turned hard. 'Firstly, why on God's good green Earth would I give you fifty pounds? And

98

secondly, where do you suppose I'd find that sort of money?'

'I told you, you owe me.' Juliet stepped closer. 'I was all set, until you ruined it, so now *you'll* have to give me enough money to get away. Which is only what I asked James for.'

'And instead he proposed?'

Juliet had clearly heard the note of cynical speculation. 'I never forced him to. I give him a chance to be rid of me, and he din't want that, because he's a gent. Then you opened your big fat mouth, so now he won't give me neither money *nor* marriage!'

Anna heard the despair beneath the venom, and guilt tugged at her again. She reached out a hand, but stopped short of touching the girl's arm, and let it fall. 'I know it's hard to believe, but I'm really very sorry. Let me try to make it right. Move in here.'

Juliet stared a moment, and seemed to be struggling with her reply. 'No. I'd still be bringin' up a bastard child. No pa, and no job. I can't work at the 'otel no more, soon as this gets out they won't have me.'

Anna heard herself say, with less conviction, 'Work for me, then. The baby will be well cared for.'

Juliet shook her head. 'I'm not what they say I am, you know. An' I've got *some* pride, no matter what you might think. I've got to go somewhere no one knows me, an' then I can pretend to be a widow.' She gave her own short, humourless laugh. 'You ought to be able to dish out some advice on *that, Mrs Garvey.*'

99

Anna flinched. 'I don't have that sort of money, or I'd give it to you.' Even then, part of her balked at the notion. If she did have it she could think of a hundred things she'd rather do with it.

'Ask your rich "husband".'

'Matthew's not rich! He has the shop, but it's barely–'

'I in't talkin' about him. I meant the doctor, in Ireland. Mairead's pa.'

Anna stared at her, ignoring the insistent butting of Arric's head against her leg, and the shout from indoors that signalled Mairead was retiring for the night. Both seemed to be coming from another land, far away. *Could* she simply write to Finn, and ask him for fifty pounds? Perhaps if she told him it was for some kind of repairs on his pub... She opened her mouth to say she would do her best, but when Juliet spoke again Anna knew she would have to do a good deal more than try.

'If you don't I'll tell everyone Mairead killed that boy, not you.'

For a moment Anna's mind went completely still; all the usual clamour had fallen silent, and there was only the freezing realisation that Mairead's life was once more in danger. Her eyes searched the shadows for Juliet, and found her white-faced but resolute, her chin thrust out, her gaze steady.

'Yeah, I know what really happened, and I've kept quiet. But if you don't get me that money I'm goin' to the police to tell them everythin'. Even Constable Couch'd be proper interested, I reckon.'

At last Anna's voice returned, barely more than

a husky whisper. 'How do you know?'

'Don't matter.'

'Of course it does!' Anna grabbed Juliet by the shoulders, and shook her. 'If *you* know, who else does?'

Juliet jerked herself away from Anna's grasp, looking shaken by the sudden outburst. '*I* only know 'cos I was in James's cottage when they were talkin' about it. The night your Irish husband came for you.'

Ann thought quickly. 'And James wasn't there then?' She shook her head, remembering. 'No, of course not, he was here.'

'He left the house unlocked.' Juliet's voice cracked, and Anna saw all the horrible little realisations clicking into place. 'I *told* Freya that. James said it would be my house soon, so I should come and go as I pleased, so she knew she could get in.' She sniffed, then sounded stronger again as she went on, 'I was in the kitchen when her and your girl arrived, an' I heard everything. Then Freya said she was gunna make tea, so I hid in the pantry.'

'Didn't James want to know why you were there?'

'He never knew. Even Freya thought I was a mouse.' Juliet shrugged. 'Then, while he was out the front seein' them back off to town, I went out through the back door.'

'So you're sure there were only the two of them talking?'

Juliet's eyes narrowed. 'Are you gunna get me that money, or no?'

'How do I know you won't ask for more when

that runs out? Because it will, and quicker than you'd think.'

'I'm no liar. You've got my word. Nuthin' more I can give you. Well?'

'I'll try,' Anna said. She felt sick. 'I'll write to Finn first thing in the morning.'

'See that you do.' Juliet folded her arms. 'I'll be back for it in a week.'

The faint sympathy had turned sour in Anna's mouth, but she kept her tone even, and concerned. 'Will you be all right in the meantime?'

'Why do you care?'

I don't, not any more. 'Because I've done you a disservice, Miss Carne,' she said, with brittle politeness, 'and I want to try and put it right.'

'Put it right next Sunday, then. After the Guild meeting.'

'It might take a little longer to get that kind of money. Doctor Casey isn't at all wealthy despite what you might think.'

'I'm sure you'll persuade him to find it,' Juliet pointed out coldly. 'Just remember what'll happen if he don't.'

'You do realise what'll happen to Mairead if the truth gets out?'

'Yes.'

'And you'd still do it?' Juliet's voice had held a note of regret that gave Anna hope the girl was merely pushing her luck. But the hope did not last.

'I'd feel bad for your girl, but if it's the only thing that'll make her pa pay up, then yes. I'd do it.'

'And we can't make some other arrangement? Surely if you—'

'No. You owe me a life, me and this one.' Juliet put a hand on her belly. 'You just do right by my child, and by yours, an' neither of you has to worry about seeing me again. If you don't, then your girl will pay for what she did.'

She kept her eyes on Anna's long enough to be sure that icy barb had struck home, then turned and walked quickly away down the uneven path. Anna realised she had clenched her fists so tightly her forearms ached. Her heart was pounding, and she wanted to run after Juliet and drag her back, demand to know how anyone with a soul could stand by and watch an innocent, already traumatised girl hauled away to face a murder trial? Anna held her breath, then let it out in a harsh explosion of fury. It was unthinkable. It couldn't happen. It wouldn't. She would do whatever must be done to make sure of it.

Chapter Six

Smeaton Hotel, Plymouth Hoe

The paper rolled in easily enough. It sat waiting for the brilliance promised by the arrival of the Remington typewriter, but yet again it was doomed to be disappointed. Tristan MacKenzie stared at it, not quite gloomy, but with the beginnings of a sense of futility already pressing on him. The typewriter, delivered from New York at vast expense, should have been the answer to everything; who could fail to create magic when this glorious beast was waiting to transfer it from mind, to fingertip, to paper? But although Tristan could type the words, and remarkably quickly too, once he became used to the keys they did not come to life on the page the way he felt them inside.

His research assistant viewed him through a glass-bottomed tankard he was cleaning with a handkerchief. 'Your publishers are happy enough,' he pointed out. 'What do you believe is missing?'

'Life!' Tristan flung his hands into the air. 'Vitality, colour!'

'Well, you have plenty of superb source material.'

Tristan detected an unusually peevish under-current in Teddy's voice, and sighed. 'You do a marvellous job,' he soothed. 'I'm grateful. And I'm glad Turner and Mitchell are pleased with what I send them of course. But I can't seem to bring what's in here,' he thumped his chest, 'out to here!' He hit the space bar on the typewriter with unnecessary force, and Teddy flinched.

'Well, breaking that isn't going to help,' he muttered.

'Perhaps I should send it back. And myself with it.'

'Why?' Teddy looked mystified. 'You're writing about the English Civil War, and Barbary corsairs! What better place to be than in the English west country?'

'That's just it,' Tristan said. 'Perhaps I've chosen the wrong subject. If I wrote about the American war instead, I'd at least have my own first-hand experience to draw on.'

Teddy raised an eyebrow. 'You were in America for two years. And that was a long time ago.'

'A man can learn a lot in two years.'

'Tristan, you were ten years old! At best you might remember how to throw a rope around a tree stump without falling over.'

Tristan looked at him through narrowed eyes. Teddy looked back, unflinching, and finally Tristan grinned. 'All right. But I still think I'm writing myself into a big dark hole with this.' He gestured at his handwritten notes. 'I wasn't entirely joking about going back to America. Dad and the others would be glad of the help, too.'

'Don't do anything hasty,' Teddy cautioned, getting to his feet. 'You haven't given it much of a chance yet.'

'Where are you going?'

'To collect the mail. I shan't be long.'

'But you'll be ready to pack if I need you, won't you?'

'Of course.'

'Good man.'

Tristan flexed his fingers over the keys, taking a moment to appreciate once again the hulking majesty of the Remington, and to ask it to please, *please*, try and draw the passion he was feeling out through his fingers, and infuse the page with it. The Remington glared back at him, flatly refusing to co-operate.

Finally accepting defeat, he pushed himself away from his desk and stood up, placing his hands in the small of his back and easing the stiffness with a crack. He winced at the sound; surely a man in his middle twenties shouldn't be making such a racket after a mere few hours' inactivity? He missed riding more than he'd thought he would, and made a mental note to go back home to Honiton for a while, get some clean country air in his lungs, and take Bill out for a good long thunder across the hills. It was doubtful the horse was getting much more exercise than he was, it'd be good for them both.

As always, the memory of riding out on the moor brought dual pangs of nostalgia and sorrow, and Tristan forced his mind back to his current problem. Outside the window the day had brightened since the last time he'd looked, the clouds lifted and the summer sky once more looked friendly enough to stand beneath without fear of a good wetting. A walk, then. Just half an hour to give his mind a rest, and his body some exercise. The seafront was only a few minutes away and the breeze blowing off it might whip away some of the fog that hampered his thoughts.

From his rooms overlooking Plymouth Hoe it was a short walk to the esplanade itself, and he picked up his hat and coat. In the hallway he passed his landlady, who had never quite overcome the awe in which she held him as an author and a scholar.

'Out for a walk, Mr MacKenzie?'

'Just a short one.'

'Will you be back for dinner?'

'Of course, Mrs Roper. Wouldn't miss it.'

She gave him a gratified smile, and he escaped into the early afternoon sunshine. On the esplanade he looked across at the mighty Citadel that frowned down on the road and wound away towards the Barbican. A pity it hadn't been built until after the Civil War; such a feat of architecture would have been worthy of its own chapter if only it had existed at the right time. And what a tale those walls would have told. Perhaps for his next book?

He shook his head. The time to begin thinking about the next book was when this one had at least found its fire. Harder to dismiss was the thought of how much Caroline would have loved to explore here. He could picture her now, her face eager, her quick mind cataloguing everything and building a history from a few disjointed facts. Between riding out, and researching the same subjects, they had spent almost all their time together and it was little wonder she'd left such a huge hole in his life, and that his writing was suffering.

He set his back to the Citadel and his face towards Smeaton's Tower, the distinctive red and white striped lighthouse that had once warned ships off the Eddystone rocks some miles further along the coast. Against its base now, instead of crashing waves and spraying foam, smartly dressed people sat on blankets, enjoying the balmy weather. Parasols were stuck into the grass to shield fair skin from the early afternoon sun, and children waited until mothers' and nursemaids' backs were turned to push each other over onto the soft grass. Stifling giggles with two hands, rather than saving themselves from the tumble.

Two particularly robust-looking boys of around two years old sat opposite one another and poked each other in turn, prodding stubby fingers into shoulders, bellies and chins, until one of them caught it near the eye, and a very young woman, probably their sister, lifted him, howling, away from his twin. 'Albert Parker! Say sorry to Adie, you little monkey!'

Tristan realised he'd been smiling as he watched, and the smile remained as he moved on down the path. There was something about a busy town and its people that never failed to get under his skin, and everyone was telling him to go to London or to family in New York. His previous three books had been moderately successful, but it was becoming apparent that Plymouth, despite holding his fascination, was just not the right place for him to find the magic his work was lacking.

Remembering the antics of Adie and Albert Parker, he gave a rueful snort. Perhaps staying with either of his two brothers wasn't the best of ideas either, since brotherly love was not a strong MacKenzie attribute, but a loft somewhere in the environs of New York had a certain appeal, at least for a while. A change of direction in his writing, from the history of England to that of the Americas, would be a sticking point with the publishers, but they were likely to capitulate in the end. And if they didn't? Well, then he'd write his dry little Civil War treatment, and his contract would be fulfilled. Time to move on.

He was idly thinking through the people he'd have to inform when he realised someone was shouting his name. He turned to see Teddy Kempton, hurrying past the lighthouse, and brandishing a piece of paper.

'Mrs Roper said you'd come out,' he said, when

he'd drawn close enough to speak again without raising his voice. 'I have the new list.'

'List?'

'From Penhaligon's Attic.' Teddy passed him the paper.

'You came all the way out here to find me because of this?'

'Look at them.' There was something just a little bit suspiciously smug about Teddy's voice, and Tristan favoured him with a look before glancing at the list. His gaze ran down the titles, but none of them nudged his spirits higher and he shook his head. Then he reached the bottom of the page, and his heart gave a little leap.

Set apart from the neatly handwritten titles and their descriptions and prices, like a hastily scribbled and smudged afterthought: '*Several journals by the hand of John Bartholomew and descendants, earliest d'd 1643, latest d'd 1725. Offers welcome.*'

Tristan lowered the paper and raised his face to Teddy's. He knew there must be an expression of blank amazement on it, but the promise of what lay in those journals' pages was tempered with a sense of outrage that they had been dismissed out of hand, and by a shop which supposedly knew the value of this kind of thing. If they could simply tack them onto the end of their list in such a slapdash and uncaring manner, how might they be treating the books themselves? Casting them carelessly in a dark corner? Leaving them exposed to sunlight or even *damp?* And as for mice...

'Wire them,' he said. 'Tell them we'll buy all the journals they have, and not to let them go to

109

anyone else. Anyone! Tell them we'll pay over and above what anyone else offers. Tell them to send them … no, wait.' He looked around, as though inspiration for all he wanted to say lay in the grass, the sea, the lighthouse itself. 'Tell them we'll come down ourselves and collect them.'

'But you have meetings, and academic commitments,' Teddy protested. 'I'll go if you like.'

'No. I want to talk to these people – don't they realise what they have?'

'Well, possibly not,' Teddy said reasonably. 'I mean, dash it all, Tristan, not everyone feels the way you do about this kind of thing!'

'But they're suppliers of quality books!' Tristan insisted. 'If they don't know the value of something like this, they've no business being *in* business! Can you imagine how they're storing these treasures?'

'They're very nice people. I'm sure they–'

'Nice or not, they ought not to be allowed access to books like this. Wire them at once, Teddy. Now!'

'When shall I tell them you'll be down?'

'We'll leave today. How long will it take to get there?'

Teddy considered. 'Well, by the time I've made reservations, and–'

'Tell them we'll be there at opening time tomorrow, and provided the journals are readable, we'll have them.'

'What about the other books on the list?'

'No! I just want those journals. Go, man!'

Teddy hurried off, and Tristan watched him, feeling a twinge of guilt for shouting; Teddy was an exemplary research assistant, and a good friend, and a mere messenger didn't deserve to be shot. But halfway along the path he turned back, and Tristan saw his mouth split in a smile of understanding, and belated, shared excitement ... as well it might. The journals of a man who'd lived through the English Civil War? Provided the man was halfway literate, they would not only give Tristan's new work the injection of lifeblood it needed but they would be invaluable to anyone with a feel for history and its lessons. He returned Teddy's delighted grin, and made a little shooing motion.

The two of them would travel to Caernoweth this afternoon. And to think five minutes ago he had all but packed his belongings and moved to New York! He laughed aloud with relief, and the dark-haired young woman he'd seen before, who was now passing him with a pram, gave him a puzzled but sweet smile. The two squabbling boys were sitting in the pram, and beamed at him. He raised his hat, and his smile widened, and when he turned to go back to his rooms that weight of futility had been replaced by an eagerness and an anticipation he hadn't felt since he'd first begun writing. Cornwall awaited, and with it the discovery of the real day-to-day life of a man who'd lived it over two hundred and fifty years ago.

Late on Monday, with the sun turning the hills orange, Tristan drove his three-year-old Austin into the courtyard of the Caernoweth Hotel, and found a place to park in the surprisingly crowded car park.

'Shop'll be shut now,' Teddy said, checking his pocket watch. 'Why don't we have some dinner and then rest in the lounge?'

'Not on your life!' Tristan flexed his shoulders and swung his arms around, enjoying the movement after the long, cramped drive. 'As soon as we've changed I intend to make the most of this weather, and go out to explore. Don't feel you have to come with me though,' he added, seeing Teddy's face fall. 'I'll leave you to your brandy and cigar, if that's what you want.'

'No, a walk will be ... welcome,' Teddy said, sounding less than convinced. Then he brightened. 'There's a fort just over the hill. We could go there.'

'Sounds perfect. First I want to go and look at this memorial everyone talks about. Chap by the name of Penworthy.'

'Founder of the town, and a thoroughly decent cove by all accounts,' Teddy said. 'He even has his own day in the local calendar, sometime in August, I think. Date he died, anyway.'

'Cheery sort of celebration,' Tristan mused. 'Right. Come on, then.'

The memorial was as he expected; neatly maintained but nothing particularly special. Penworthy was not astride a horse, or brandishing a pike or musket, he simply stood looking up the hill through town like some benevolent father-figure. Presumably he'd been a tall man in a more sentient life although there was nothing here by which to judge his relative height. Tristan read the dates, nodded, then turned towards the pub he'd noticed on their way down: The Tin Streamer's Arms.

'Thirst-quencher?' he said to Teddy, who needed no further urging.

Now the sun had gone down the pub was quite busy, and for a place that looked very basic and a bit grubby from outside it was remarkably clean within. Although the smallish windows were open, the air was blue with pipe smoke, and rich with the yeasty smell of ale and the hoppy scent of beer. Tristan looked around with pleasure; it had been too long since he'd been in a proper ale house.

Behind the bar was a woman who might have been thirty, or twenty, depending on the way the light fell on her. Dark hair, twisted behind her head but coming loose through sweat and hard work, a slender form, but strong-looking hands, and a wide smile that only faltered as she left one customer and was back in place before she reached the next.

The newcomers warranted a few curious glances from the locals, and the universal language of silent speculation between them: the raised eyebrow answered by a shrug. Tristan nodded at whoever caught his eye, and led the way across the small, stone-flagged floor space to the bar. A slenderly built, blond man stood hunched over his drink, and an older man sat on the stool next to him, throwing an occasional concerned look his way but saying nothing. Talk swelled and ebbed, laughter hooted, and now and again a hacking cough would cut someone's conversation short.

Tristan smiled at the woman, who, now he was close to, he put at somewhere in her middle

113

thirties. She smiled back, but it was mechanical and didn't reach her eyes, and her expression was tight, even guarded. 'What can I get for you gentlemen?'

'Two pints of whatever's closest,' he said. 'Thank you.'

Teddy spoke up, sounding pleased. 'I say, nice to see you again!'

The woman looked at him properly, and her smile relaxed into something more natural and friendly. 'Mr Kempton, isn't it? I don't think I introduced myself before. Anna Penhaligon.'

Teddy shook the proffered hand. 'Tristan, this is the lady who found that first book I brought back for you. Mrs Penhaligon, this is Tristan MacKenzie.'

'It's grand to meet you at last, Mr MacKenzie, Mr Kempton spoke well of you. Welcome to my pub.'

'Yours?' Tristan looked around. 'You must be awfully busy, running a pub and a shop.'

'Oh, I don't run the shop. My stepdaughter does that, with my daughter's help. They're the ones who organise the sales lists and so forth.'

'Ah.' So *they* would be the ones who had so carelessly and scruffily listed those precious journals. Well, tomorrow they would be told in no uncertain terms how to go about caring for that which they claimed to hold so dear.

His inner grumbling halted at the crashing open of the pub door, and this time everyone stopped drinking and fell silent. A burly young man stood framed in the doorway, adjusting his eyes to the dimness in the bar room, and then he started towards the bar with long, determined steps.

For a frozen moment, Tristan was oddly certain the young man was coming for him, but instead he grabbed at the shoulder of the blond man, who'd been so deep in his thoughts that he hadn't even looked around.

'Fry! You bastard!'

'What–' The blond man lifted his head at last, and Tristan saw he was extremely drunk, to the point of barely keeping his balance. 'Tom?'

'You've ruined her!'

'Let him alone, Thomas,' the older man said, and slid off his stool. 'He's not fit to fight.'

'He's not fit to bloody draw *breath!*' Tom bellowed. He put his face close to Fry's, and Tristan saw Fry flinch away, blinking and shaking his head like a confused and berated dog.

'Look...' Fry began, and raised his arms to push his assailant away, but let them fall again, limply, to his sides. To Tristan's astonishment he saw a gleam of tears in the bloodshot grey eyes, and Fry tried to speak again. 'She ... she lied, Tom. The kid's–'

'You promised her a home, and you threw her over!'

The next moment he had driven his fist upwards and clipped Fry under the chin. Fry stumbled against the bar, and a few half-hearted shouts went up, but the only person to make a move to protect the drunk man was his elderly companion, who pushed Tom away. Caught off guard, Tom took several stumbling steps back, and as he lunged back towards Fry and his elderly friend, Tristan stepped instinctively into

115

his path.

'Leave it,' he said, trying to sound calm, 'he's obviously unhappy.' He raised his hands and kept a close eye on those large fists of Tom's, not wanting to provoke the same treatment they'd given Fry. He only realised he'd been focusing on the wrong danger when Tom's forehead jerked forward, and smashed into the bridge of Tristan's nose with an ugly crunching sound and a flare of eye-watering agony.

Stunned, Tristan fell back, aware of very little except Teddy's cry of dismay and the choking, metallic taste of blood. His face was sticky with it, his head felt as if it had been filled with burning oil, and he felt sick. Gradually he became aware the space around him was empty, and that he could see again. Not clearly, just vague shapes; a moving mass of people by the door; the crowd assisting someone with their exit, not unkindly, but with determination.

Tristan coughed and spat, trying not to yell out as the movement sent a fresh wave of pain through his head. He felt a firm hand on his back, and one on his arm, and a moment later something blissfully cold and wet was pressed to his face, and he seized it with both hands, trying to get all the cool relief from it he could.

'Bleddy idiot.' The tone was companionable enough, and Tristan cracked open one eye again and saw the elderly man peering at him, concerned. 'What'd you want to go and do that for? Thomas Carne in't known for his sense of right 'n' wrong.'

'Thobas Card, eh?' Tristan managed. He

cleared his throat and spat again. 'Thad's a dame I'll be watchid out for.'

'Don't try and talk.' It was Mrs Penhaligon who spoke this time. She was rinsing out a fresh towel to clean Tristan's bloody spit off the bar.

'Sorry.' He gestured at the mess.

'Don't give it another thought. You saved your man there a pasting.' She looked at Fry who, oblivious to everything, had taken his friend's stool and now rested his head on his folded arms. 'I'm sure he's grateful. How does your nose feel?'

'You said dot to talk,' he pointed out. He was starting to feel a sense of unreality, mingled with an irrepressible urge to laugh. It hurt and he stopped immediately, but the ridiculousness of what he had walked into kept him smiling behind the towel that was warming rapidly against his face. He couldn't tell if that warmth was water or something worse, but even with the blood running down his throat, and stirring his stomach into churning nausea, this evening knocked spots off sitting at his desk back at the Smeaton Hotel, struggling to string an entertaining sentence together.

Anna Penhaligon was looking at him closely, and despite her tense expression he saw both relief and humour in the moss-green eyes, a few shades darker than his own. 'Well, you're a lot hardier than I'd have expected, given your profession.'

'Oh, Tristan's travelled a good deal,' Teddy put in. 'He's not your average sort of scholar at all.'

'So I see.' Mrs Penhaligon gestured for Tristan to lift the towel, and he tried not to notice when she winced. 'Perhaps you'd better come through

117

to the back so we can clean that properly.' She looked around. 'Esther?'

'Here,' came a voice behind Tristan, and a short, stoutish woman bustled past him to take up Mrs Penhaligon's place behind the bar. 'Mr Cornish, you'm best off takin' young Fry home.'

'Not goin' home,' the blond man muttered, the first sign of life since his narrow escape from Thomas Carne's anger. 'S'a bloody mess.'

'Sleep it off on my settee then,' the older man, Mr Cornish, said. He slipped an arm beneath Fry's, and dragged him to his feet. 'Well done, boy,' he said to Tristan, and gave him a brief smile. 'But stay out of Tom Carne's way for a bit, eh?'

In the sitting room of the Tin Streamer's Arms, Tristan perched uncomfortably on the arm of a couch while Mrs Penhaligon dabbed at his face with a cool cloth. Teddy hovered in the background, hissing now and again in sympathy, and it took a great deal of control not to tell him to belt up; he really wasn't helping at all, but he meant well. Eventually the dabbing stopped, and Mrs Penhaligon looked at him critically, her head tilted to the side, presumably waiting to see if any more blood was on its way out. She seemed satisfied.

'Don't move about too much,' she instructed. 'If I were you I'd get some sleep now, and let nature take over. Where are you staying?'

'The hotel at the top of town,' Tristan said, not liking the new, nasal whine in his voice. 'God, I sound like an accordion with a hole in it.'

Mrs Penhaligon was surprised into a laugh, and some of that strained look fell away from her

118

features. Now she looked younger again. 'That's an interesting notion. Do you play?'

'I do,' Teddy offered. 'But I'm afraid I don't have my instrument with me. What a blow!'

Tristan's eyes met Mrs Penhaligon's, and they both looked away quickly.

'A great blow,' Mrs Penhaligon agreed. 'Still, maybe next time?'

'Oh, most assuredly.' Teddy nodded. 'Right, I'd better get the wounded hero back to the hotel.'

'What are your plans during your stay?' Mrs Penhaligon asked, picking up the bowl of bloodied water. Tristan looked away from it, still feeling a little bit queasy.

'Collecting some journals from your shop, and hopefully a walk out to the fort. Then it's back to Plymouth tomorrow afternoon.' He sounded a little better the more he spoke, thank goodness; any rebuke he delivered tomorrow would lose its impact if it sounded as though it came from a broken squeeze box.

'Ah, the fort.' Mrs Penhaligon looked at Teddy. 'New Fort fort, if I remember correctly?'

'You do!' Teddy actually beamed, and Tristan couldn't help smiling too.

'Come on, you little ray of sunshine,' he said, and stood. 'Let's get back up the road.' He held out a hand. 'Thank you, Mrs Penhaligon.'

'Oh, I believe once someone has wiped a gallon of blood from your face you've crossed over to first-name terms.'

Tristan smiled. 'Then thank you, Anna. And I'm Tristan.'

'Have a safe journey back, and I hope the

journals are what you're after.'

'I'm sure they will be.' Although in what state, he hardly dared contemplate. 'Goodbye, Anna, and thank you again.'

'Go through the back if you like,' Anna said. 'Spare yourself the stares from out there.' She nodded towards the bar. 'But watch out for the cat, he's a bit of a so-and-so.'

She showed Tristan and Teddy into the passage, still smiling and chattering, but when Tristan turned back at the gate, to add that he hoped to see her again before he left, she was pressing the back of her hand to her mouth and her face was once again drawn and tight-looking. Two things were immediately obvious: first, that something was troubling her deeply, and second, that she was evidently well-practised and adept at hiding the fact. He couldn't have said why, but it was a disturbing thought.

Chapter Seven

Penhaligon's Attic

At mid-morning on Tuesday, Freya was already thinking glumly ahead to her hotel shift. Yesterday had been difficult enough; Juliet had kept well out of Freya's way, and the two of them had only seen each other from a distance. For the first time, Freya was glad they had been separated for gossiping, and that Juliet's main job now saw her permanently in the laundry with Miss Pawley. Much as she understood the anger that had driven Juliet to throw the *Lady Penhaligon* against the wall, Freya was not yet ready to forgive her for it.

The bell on the shop door signalled the first customer of the day, and she brightened when she saw who it was.

'Teddy!'

'Good morning, Miss Penhaligon.'

'I've told you, it's Freya. I got your wire, the books are ready.' She peered past him at the shadowy figure of his companion, who had remained on the pavement looking in at the window display. 'Is Mr MacKenzie coming in?'

'Tristan! Come in and meet Miss Penhaligon.'

Mr MacKenzie straightened his coat, and came into the shop. At sight of him Freya's mouth dropped open, and she forgot her manners completely.

'Your face!'

He gave her a faint smile, which in no way detracted from the awful sight of two black eyes with swollen lids, and the deep cut across the bridge of a short, straight nose. The upper half of his face was a mass of puffy, purple bruises, and when he spoke his voice was thick and nasal. 'I bet with a slight accident last dight.' He frowned and tried again. 'Last *night.*'

'Chap by the name of Carne,' Teddy supplied cheerfully. 'Tristan here tried to break up the fight. Well, I say *tried,* he actually did manage it.'

'If it was Tom Carne, I'm guessing the man he was fighting was James Fry,' Freya said. 'How is he?'

'Probably suffering from a ghastly hangover,' Teddy said. 'He was too drunk to know what was going on so his friend took him home.'

Freya nodded. 'I do hope you aren't in too much discomfort, Mr MacKenzie.'

'As a batter of fact, I ab!' Mr MacKenzie sighed with disgust at his own inability to speak, and Freya lowered her face to hide a smile. It did look painful but there was no denying he sounded funny.

'It seems to have become worse overnight,' Teddy said, in an apologetic tone, although he couldn't possibly have been at fault. 'We don't think his nose is broken though.'

'Ah. Good.' A difficult silence descended for a moment or two, and eventually Freya said briskly, 'Are you ready to look at those journals?'

MacKenzie's expression darkened further, and he opened his mouth, but before he could do more than draw breath, Teddy spoke up. 'Yes! Let's have a look, shall we?'

'They're here.' Freya bent to lift the heavy box, and as she straightened with it she saw a look flash between the two men. Mr MacKenzie's eyes were unreadable, in fact they were so swollen shut it was a miracle he could see anything at all, but Teddy Kempton's brows were drawn down in what looked like a warning frown.

'Is there something wrong?' Freya asked. 'You look quite cross.'

Teddy cleared his throat. 'Tristan is concerned that you might not have put sufficient importance on these journals.'

'Importance?' Freya looked at Mr MacKenzie,

but again it was Teddy who answered.

'He was a little ... distressed, I think you could say.' He glanced at Mr MacKenzie, and shrugged. 'Well, all right. He was decidedly annoyed by the casual way these journals were listed. He feels ... he's worried that, if you thought so little of their importance, that you might not care for the books themselves.'

Freya's lips tightened. 'That would imply Mr MacKenzie has no faith in our shop. That he thinks we know nothing about books. Is that the case, Mr MacKenzie?'

'The jourdals please?' Mr MacKenzie nodded at the box. 'I don't have all day.'

Freya was about to make a blunt remark until she saw the way his eyes travelled hungrily over the box of books. His hand, lying on the counter between them, slid closer to it and betrayed his eagerness.

'We've taken very good care of them,' she said instead, and when he flicked his gaze towards her she saw a softening in the hard jawline, and he gave a tiny nod.

'I'b sure,' he said. 'Please?'

Freya lifted the lid and pushed the box towards him. She watched carefully as he touched the topmost book and lifted the thick, protective cloth between each volume.

'Mairead catalogued these for us,' she said to Teddy. 'What you have to understand is that she's got a brilliant business mind, and she can see value in the usual kind of books, but it's all based on facts. Like whether or not there are a lot of copies, or the book is damaged. But to her those

123

journals would just be old scrap books.'

Teddy visibly flinched. 'You mean she wouldn't appreciate them for the knowledge? The very *soul* between the pages?' He shook his head. 'That's a dreadful pity.'

'It doesn't mean she would treat them with any less respect and care than she would a Dickens first edition,' Freya pointed out. 'But she wouldn't class them as any more important either.'

'Hence the scribbled afterthought.'

Freya nodded. 'She probably thought you wouldn't be interested, but then realised she ought to inform you anyway.'

'Which is actually more admirable,' Teddy agreed. 'Don't you think so, Tristan?'

But Mr MacKenzie had lifted out all the hard-covered books on the top of the box, and found what he was looking for, and he didn't reply. Freya saw him hold a breath, and found she was doing the same; she let it out, feeling a little silly, but her fascinated attention remained on this historian she had heard so much about. She certainly hadn't expected someone only in his middle twenties; how much could he really know, at such a young age?

He reached into the box and withdrew the first of the journals. Hefting it in his hand, a little smile played at the corners of his mouth and he laid the book on the counter and peeled away the waterproof layer. He pulled at the leather strap and opened the soft cover, and as his slitted eyes rested on the page within, his whole body relaxed. He looked at Teddy, and nodded.

Teddy reached into his jacket and took out his wallet. 'How much, just for the journals?'

Freya looked from one to the other in dawning realisation of what she'd offered them. For a moment she wondered if she ought to pretend interest from another party, but dismissed the idea as both petty, and likely to have entirely the wrong effect. 'How many are there? I only glimpsed them.'

'Six, I think.' MacKenzie peered into the box again. 'Yes. I'll take all six.' The eagerness was now apparent in his voice, and even in what little she could read of his face.

Teddy could clearly see Freya was at a loss. He took out some crumpled, off-white papers. 'Shall we say three pounds for the collection?'

The air left Freya's lungs in a huff of amazement. 'Three *pounds?*'

'I thought you were aware of their value,' MacKenzie said, but he was smiling.

'Well I can only assume they're worth more to you personally than they would be to anyone else,' Freya observed, trying to keep her voice steady.

'Have a care, Miss Penhaligon, you'll talk yourself out of a sale.'

Freya closed her mouth quickly, before she could do just that, and allowed herself a deep breath and a moment to steady her excitedly thumping heart. 'Yes, thank you, Teddy. Three pounds seems ... very fair.'

'Excellent.' Teddy passed the money to her, and she took it in fingers that suddenly felt made of wood.

The guilty thought that she ought to be giving at least some of this to Doctor Bartholomew was quickly quashed; he'd been quite clear that these

125

books were a gift. But as she slipped the notes into the cash register, she thought of Juliet. Perhaps twenty shillings? It wouldn't go far, but added to the promise of a home and a job it would help a little. She remembered the shattered *Lady Penhaligon,* and almost amended the sum downwards until she also remembered the fear and anger that had prompted the outburst.

Mr MacKenzie and Teddy had left the unwanted regular books on the counter, but as Mr MacKenzie lifted the now-closed box a bright splash of blood splattered onto the lid. He gave a grunt of mingled disgust and dismay, and put it back down.

He pressed the back of his hand to his nose. 'Thank God the lid was on.'

'I don't think you're fit to drive all that way today, old man,' Teddy said, a little fretfully, and handed Mr MacKenzie an oversized handkerchief. 'Let's stay one more night. Give the old hooter a chance, eh?' He picked up the box himself.

Mr MacKenzie put the 'kerchief to his nose, and sighed. 'All right,' he muttered. 'I'll have a lie-down, then we'll walk out to the fort this afternoon so it won't be a complete waste of time at least. But just one more night.'

They made polite but hurried farewells and left, and Freya stood looking after them, trying to convince herself it hadn't been some strange and wonderful dream. She opened the cash drawer again, and brushed her finger over the notes. Notes!

But the smile on her face was not wholly due to the money; she couldn't help remembering the

126

boyish excitement, and then the deep reverence, with which Mr MacKenzie had handled the journals, which had clearly gone to the best possible home. She wished she could have seen his face properly; she had the feeling there would have been a warm light in those puffy, watery eyes, and that the teasing note in his voice would have been reflected there too – he'd come to the shop in one frame of mind, and left in quite another, thanks to Teddy Kempton.

Juliet would be baking for Mrs Packem again this morning, so giving her the money would have to wait until work this afternoon. It would surely help mend things between them, and that would have been worth the whole three pounds, if it had been hers to give, but anticipating the look on Papá's face was even more precious; this would make his idea of converting the attic for Mairead an affordable reality. Soon the Penhaligons would all be living together properly, and all for the want of a few scraps of ancient paper, and the words scratched upon them. Mr MacKenzie's fascination for history would have consequences he himself would never have dreamed in a hundred years.

Wheal Furzy

Something had been off, right from the start of the shift. Matthew and David Donithorn had arrived within minutes of one another and were in the boiler house, changing in their customary silence, when young Tommy Trevellick and an older lad came in.

Tommy had greeted his shift captain cheerfully. 'Look, Alan's back! Fit and well, as you can see.'

'Hmm?' Donithorn barely glanced at him. 'Good enough.'

Tommy shrugged. 'Matt, this is my brother. Alan, you'll know Matthew Penhaligon. His wife runs Gran'ma and Gran'pa's pub.' He flushed. 'I mean, she owns the pub where they work.'

Alan nodded at Matthew. 'All right?'

Matthew nodded back. 'You've been off a good while then?'

'Since March.'

'It's his chest,' Tommy said helpfully, and received a casual cuff in return from his brother.

'Belt up. No one's interested.'

Matthew didn't know whether to acknowledge the comment after that, so he just nodded again. 'It'll speed things up a good bit, having a full team.'

'I'll have to go back to trammin',' Tommy said, 'but I'm that glad Alan's back, it don't matter.'

The boy chattered on, and Matthew expected Donithorn to bark his usual complaint that too much talk meant not enough speed, but the remonstration didn't come. Instead Donithorn just led the way out of the changing area and ducked wordlessly through the small, wood-shored mine entrance. The others needed no urging; pay would not be calculated until they reached the level they were working on, and they each seized their daily candle allowance and followed the shift captain.

Matthew had quickly discovered he preferred to

use the ladders at the start of the core, rather than relying on the man-engine; provided he remembered to wrap his hands in leather straps, to protect against splinters when he slid down past the rungs, he often even found it quicker. The hoist was touted as a great step for a medium-sized mine but, aside from the time it took, something in him balked at standing on a flimsy platform, carried up and down the shaft utterly at the mercy of a few rods and brackets. However, at the end of the shift he put those uneasy feelings aside – it still took the best part of half an hour to be raised to grass by that method, but it was faster, and safer, than climbing for an hour or more with tired arms and legs.

On occasion the engine would halt, and the men ordered off while something was checked. At this point they usually took to the ladders themselves, and so when this happened, as it did today, Matthew arrived at the level they were working a few minutes ahead of his workmates. While he waited for Donithorn and the others to arrive he walked ahead, ducking low to avoid the sharp overhead rocks that jutted downward, and examined the rough rock by the light of his candle. It was odd to think, now, that when he had begun working at Wheal Furzy he had struggled to pick out the tin lode at all; now it was as clear to him as if someone had painted it on the rock. It continued strong and wide, and with luck, and a full team, they would get this ore out fast and then set to work to extend the tunnel still further.

Still unable to make a start, he checked the coil of safety fuse. The first time Matthew had seen

Donithorn prepare for blasting he'd been reluctantly impressed by the captain's quick, practised movements; packing the holes with gunpowder, with something that looked a little like a long, narrow spoon; tamping it down; ensuring every bit was pressed in and not stuck to the sides of the rock. He'd then whipped out two lengths of fuse of two feet each, merely by eye, and cut it. Four feet per hole, two minutes' grace in which to move to safety. Matthew had scrambled backwards and begun to run the moment the first fuse had been lit, but Tommy had stopped him. 'Don't run, you'm more likely to fall or smack your head. Just walk fast.'

He'd been right; two minutes underground seemed to stretch into five as the three of them had made their swift way, stooped over, to huddle around the bend in the tunnel. The noise had been deafening, and Matthew's head had rung for a good long while afterwards, but explosions were associated with ore, and ore with money. He soon got used to it.

They were currently drilling the second of three deep holes, but there was an ample supply of fuse. Likewise gunpowder. Next Matthew went to a wooden prop and prised free the stub of candle stuck there. By the time the rest of his team had joined him he had replaced it, and lit the fresh candle from his own, allowing a thin, flickering light to illuminate the rock-strewn floor.

'Proper miner now, look at you,' Tommy said with a grin. Matthew had no idea how he stayed so chirpy, but such enthusiasm tended to be infectious.

He pretended to cuff the boy around the ear. 'Cheeky bugger.' He picked up his hammer, and rolled his shoulder in preparation for work. 'Good to have your brother back. We'll have this out in double-quick time now.'

Alan Trevellick took the hammer Tommy had been using, and Tommy wrapped leather straps around his hands and went back to his old job, filling the wagon with broken ore, and pushing it out to the hoist. Hand tramming in this way, the boy fought for every step, with warped rails to negotiate and lumps of rock blocking the way, but he worked without complaint. Matthew had already learned a great deal from young Tommy Trevellick.

He and Alan alternated blows as Donithorn turned the drill, driving it deep into the rock below the blue-grey vein of tin. Sweat dripped into their eyes and made their grip slippery, and when Matthew rubbed his hand on his trousers to blot it he felt fresh blisters tearing open. Word was that Tobias Able was reckoning on the lode continuing, and was petitioning the Battens for air-driven drills. That day couldn't come soon enough.

Donithorn remained silent for most of the morning. In the muted light of their candles Matthew caught sight of him now and again, but he didn't appear morose. Rather he seemed elsewhere; his mind far away from the dust and darkness in which he had toiled from the age of fifteen. He didn't even make much comment when, his shoulder muscles screaming, Matthew hit the drill awkwardly and his hammer glanced ineffectually off it.

131

Yesterday he would have revelled in the chance to make a snappish comment, but today he merely grunted, 'Steady.' Tommy was passing at the time, and Matthew saw the boy's candle flame tremble with the speed at which he turned his head in astonishment. Perhaps Alan's return had taken some of the pressure of worry from the shift captain's shoulders, and Matthew began to breathe more easily, hopeful his time as whipping boy was over. That had always been the worst of it; the work itself was bearable, if unpleasant; the dark was stifling; the dust was choking, but it was all manageable and if he was just left alone in peace, to do his work and claim his wage, he could concentrate his thoughts on the pleasures that waited above grass: Anna, Freya, Pa, Mairead. Daylight, fresh air and life. Maybe that's what kept Tommy so cheerful.

They broke for crib at around eleven o'clock, and retreated to the area near the tunnel entrance where it was wider, and where there was somewhere to sit that wasn't choked with lumps of broken rock; the planks of wood were narrow, but preferable to the uncomfortable press of rock through thin trousers. Matthew grinned to himself as he remembered his conversation with Anna about kneeling on rocks; if the definition of love was a bruised knee, what did that make the colourful array of purple, yellow and blue that regularly marbled his backside?

Donithorn ate his meal with no outward sign of enjoyment. He didn't even finish it, but soon put the remains of his half-eaten pasty back in his box and got up. 'Blasting after,' he said shortly, and

132

ducked back down the tunnel to where they'd been working. Tommy exchanged a glance with Matthew; normally blasting would happen right at the end of a shift, in order to let the dust settle before they returned to dig out the ore. This would make work very uncomfortable later, for all of them, but particularly for Alan Trevellick.

Alan and Tommy talked about people Matthew did not know well enough to contribute an opinion, so he kept to himself throughout the remainder of the short break, and tried to rediscover that thread of positive thought. It was easier than he'd expected; out here by the shaft it was just as dark as further along the tunnel, but the steady creaking of the man-engine, the constant sound of the pumps taking water away through the adits, and the shouts of men from other levels echoing in the shaft gave him an odd and unexpected sense of community; they were all working for the same thing after all, whether they were tributers, working their own limited lode, or tut workers on a fixed rate of pay. A regular accompaniment to these sounds was the distant booming of detonations, to which they would soon be contributing.

Alan had broken off from talking to cough; a deep, hacking sound, appalling enough in an old man, never mind in a nineteen-year-old. Matthew swallowed hard, wondering if he was imagining the tickle in his own throat, and determined not to cough himself... It sounded as if Alan would never stop. He'd surely returned to work too soon, but during his time working with Tommy Matthew had learned the Trevellicks had no living parents, just aging grandparents Esther and Joe. There had been little or no choice in the matter, Alan's wage was needed.

At thirty-eight, Matthew was probably one of the oldest men working the underground levels, particularly down this far; most had succumbed to injury or illness long before they reached such an advanced age, but then most of the others had been doing it all their lives. He wondered, with a returning bleakness, how long it would be before he too sounded as if he were tearing himself apart inside. The tickle in his throat grew worse, and he cleared it, tasting rock dust. A swig of water helped, but as he pictured the dust swirling down his throat he wished he'd spat instead.

Donithorn came back, and picked up the coil of fuse and the tamping bar. 'Time.' He started back along the tunnel, but Alan spoke up.

'Powder, Cap'n? Or are we not botherin' with that today?' The sarcasm made Tommy visibly flinch, and Donithorn stopped. Matthew couldn't see his face properly, but he gave a little shake of his head, as if coming back from some other place his mind had been inhabiting. 'Yes. And, um ... bring the bar.'

'You've got that,' Alan pointed out.

Donithorn looked down at his hand. 'Right. Swab stick then.' Irritation crept in. 'Just make haste.' Then he was gone into the dark again, and Matthew and the others put their water bottles and lunch tins back in their bags.

'Well he's changed,' Alan observed. 'Time was you couldn't speak to 'un like that without getting a right ear-bashin' back.' He nudged his brother. 'Why din't you tell me he'd turned into a purring kitten? I'd have come back sooner.'

'He's only been like it today,' Tommy said. 'And you wouldn't anyway, you've been too sick.'

'I was joking,' Alan pointed out patiently. 'Come on, boy, grab what's needed, and let's get this bloody stuff out.' As they started along the tunnel he caught at Matthew's shirt. 'You take this. Nature's callin' an' she've got a bleddy loud voice.'

He pushed the swab stick into Matthew's hand and went back out to one of the worked-out tunnels to relieve himself, while Matthew and Tommy rejoined their captain.

When they reached him he had already cut the three fuses, and was neatly recoiling what was left. He dropped the depleted coil of fuse on the floor, and nodded at the cart. 'Tommy, finish getting that loaded, and get it out.'

'Yes, Cap'n.'

'On you go, Pen'aligon, since you've got the stick.'

Matthew cleaned the loose grit and dust out of the three holes, then Alan arrived and began pouring the gunpowder into the scraper. When he and Donithorn started to pack and tamp the shot-holes, Matthew turned to help Tommy push the three-quarters-full cart back out to the main shaft.

'Get in,' he said, when he was sure they were out of Donithorn's hearing.

Tommy looked at him, puzzled. 'What?'

'Get in!' Matthew knocked the side of the cart, and grinned.

Tommy gave a snort of surprised laughter, and climbed into the cart, where he huddled on the lumps of ore, making himself as small as possible. Matthew pushed, enjoying the sound of Tommy's chuckling as they went, and only just remembering in time to duck his own head to avoid an ear-ringing collision with the low, rocky roof. The boy worked so hard it was easy to forget he was still a child, and it was good to be able to give him a rest, even a brief one, though the ground was impossible to navigate without stopping every minute or so to kick rubble out of the way.

Together Matthew and the cart rattled and slid around the last bend, where the tunnel opened up and the ore could be unloaded onto a kibble for its journey to the surface. Tommy climbed out, and Matthew manoeuvred the cart into position. He glanced around as the boy started back along the tunnel.

'Where are you going now? Alan's here, there's no need for either of us to go back.'

'My coat,' Tommy said. 'I tied it around one of the props. It's the only one I got,' he added apologetically, but Matthew was only too well aware of the consequences of losing clothing when you earned so little money.

'I'll fetch it. Stay put.'

Donithorn was removing the candle from his helmet as Matthew returned to the end of the tunnel. 'What're you back for?'

'Tommy's coat.' Matthew stepped past him and saw the coat, tied by the arms around one of the roughly sawn props.

'Get it then, and be quick.' Donithorn touched the candle to the end of the first fuse. 'Fire in the hole!'

136

Alan quickly lit the other two, and flashed a grin at Matthew, who swore and ripped the coat sleeves free. Turning to follow, Matthew's foot slid on loose rubble, and, as he reached out to steady himself on the wall he glanced at the nearest burning fuse and blinked. Something was ... then he froze. It was almost burned through...

'Run!' It came out weak and dismayed, so he snatched a short breath and bellowed, 'RUN!'

Donithorn half-turned to question the sudden panic, but there was no time to explain. Matthew's heart hammered against his ribs, the sweat of terror mingled with that of the natural heat, and made his free hand slip and slide on the rock wall. The hand holding Tommy's coat gave him better purchase, and he leaned hard to his left, pushing against the wall to drive himself forward.

Donithorn, still blankly unmoving, looked past Matthew and, coming to life, gave a low cry of horror. Alan had heeded Matthew's urgency and disappeared around the first bend, but Donithorn was locked in place and his face, in the thin light of the candle, was whiter than ever. 'How...'

'Go!' Matthew ducked low beneath the uneven roof, pushing Donithorn ahead of him. Even as he slipped and slid, and the skin was torn from his hands by sharp rock, he tried to calculate how long they had left. In his mind's eye there was only the sparking burn of the safety fuse, working its lazy but unstoppable way towards the densely packed gunpowder.

When the explosion came, it began as a dull crump from deep within the rock walls. A second later the tunnel was filled with noise and flying

137

rock, and Matthew's head seemed to explode along with it. Something smashed into his back, sending him crashing against the wall to his right – reflexively his hand shot out to break the impact, but the force behind the blow was greater than he'd realised ... his arm gave way, and his right shoulder hit the wall, followed immediately by the side of his head. He felt his helmet fly off.

Second and third explosions followed, double-bursts of shattered rock roaring down the tunnel. Some small pieces were propelled faster and harder than others, and he felt them pepper his back like pellets, shredding shirt and skin. He tried to push himself away from the wall again, but the white heat that travelled up his arm sent the world spinning around him. Pain followed; an agony that choked off the breath in his throat and sent him to his knees on the rock-littered floor.

Donithorn had also fallen, Matthew could hear him swearing and scrabbling in the darkness just ahead of him. Head still ringing from the impact with the wall, he tried to rise but his legs just shifted and slid on the loose rock and he too cursed aloud, blinking against the gritty dust that filled the air and stuck to his eyelashes.

Beside him, Donithorn's voice sounded as if it were coming through a pillow. 'You all right?'

'I will be,' Matthew muttered, not sure that was true. His right arm felt as if it were on fire, and hung limply at his side. Blood was dripping from just below his elbow, and he knew if he reached across he would find the jagged edge of broken bone, and the torn flesh through which it had burst. He swallowed a surge of nausea, the bitter taste on the back of his tongue almost bringing up more, and tried to take a deeper breath without coughing.

The low rumble of falling rock faded, and the pressure in his ears popped, letting the sounds in again; the sense of where he was, and what had happened, returned like a dash of ice-water. He couldn't move, but the longer they stayed here the more dust they would breathe ... damned if he would end up like Alan Trevellick. *Damned* if he would.

'Help me stand.'

To his surprise Donithorn did so without questioning, fumbling around in the dark until he grasped Matthew's left arm, and as he gained his feet Matthew clamped his mouth shut to stifle a shout. His useless arm was growing numb, his shirt was plastered to his back and he was reasonably sure that this time it wasn't sweat that stuck it there. His helmet would be lying somewhere in this pitch-darkness, having probably saved his life. For now.

Donithorn's voice floated out of the dark, urgent now, and speaking Matthew's fears aloud. 'Come on. There's still danger of roof-fall.'

He started away towards the shaft, tripping on the tram line, and in the stifling, choking blackness Matthew followed slowly, shock playing dark and dirty tricks on his racing mind. Donithorn had cut the fuse too short. Half the length. Half the time. He could have killed them all. He remembered the man's warning on his first day: *Let's hope you get well clear before it blows* ... and his breath snagged on the thought. But the suspicion died swiftly; Donithorn's look of shock had been genuine, he would bet all he had on that.

'Cap'n! Are you all right?' Alan's shaky voice drifted through the tunnel towards them. A moment later the bobbing light of his candle appeared at the bend, and Matthew looked past Donithorn and saw the long, pale face beneath it. 'What b'Christ 'appened there?'

Donithorn did not reply, and Matthew kept his thoughts to himself and concentrated on not falling as the tunnel floor dipped away sharply downward. The fingers of his right hand tingled, and he could feel fresh blood dripping into his half-curled palm. His back ached and stung, and each movement rubbed his rough shirt against it and made the breath hiss between his teeth.

Alan coughed, the barking sound bouncing off the walls, and Matthew saw young Tommy at his brother's back. 'Is anyone hurt?'

'No,' Donithorn said. 'Everyone's fine. We'll let the dust die down and then set to.'

'But we—'

'There's tin needs getting out, Tommy,' Donithorn reminded him curtly. 'A man don't complain about a bit of dust. Are you a man?'

'Yes!'

'Then get some water down you, take a breather, and we'll go back in. Get that cart emptied first.'

Matthew straightened as far as the tunnel's roof allowed, but the movement jarred him, and he sank back to a crouch before he could fall.

'Bugger.' Alan had lit a fresh candle, and now he played the light over Matthew. 'You'm gunna need lookin' at.'

140

Donithorn took the candle and squatted for a better look. For a moment he said nothing, then he muttered, 'Looks like you took the brunt of it. No way of tellin' how bad it is until we get you to grass.' He looked at Tommy. 'You take him, lad. Get Doctor Manley to set that arm.'

'Are you paid up?' Tommy asked Matthew. He sounded apologetic, but the mine doctor would ask anyway, even if he hadn't.

It took two attempts for Matthew to find his voice again, and when he did it was thin and shaky. 'I've paid in every week, but I've not been here long.'

'Don't matter. Doctor'll see to you.'

'We'll empty the cart,' Alan said to his brother. 'Go on now, before the poor bloke falls over.' Despite the sympathetic words there was a new hardness in his voice, and as Matthew rose, more carefully than before, he saw the elder Trevellick giving Donithorn a narrow-eyed look. Donithorn met it with a bland one of his own, but Matthew remembered his bewildered dismay, and he knew the questions would start long before the mine captain got wind of the accident.

'Blimey, you fetched it.' Tommy was staring at Matthew's left hand. Matthew followed his gaze, equally surprised to see the boy's coat still clutched in the bloodstained fingers.

He held it out. He wanted to make some comment about how he'd been glad the boy had forgotten it, that if he hadn't then Donithorn and Alan would probably be dead now, but the thought of speaking make him quake inside. Even the vibration of his own voice would be too much.

141

Tommy took the coat and slipped it on, despite the warmth in the tunnel. He picked up his and Matthew's bags, and crisscrossed them over his own shoulders. 'Come on, let's get you out.'

On the hoist, Matthew gripped the grab-rod one-handed, for the first time feeling that the twelve-inch platform was not big enough; he was wavering on his feet, dizzy and sick-feeling, and a shuffle to one side or the other to rebalance might be enough to knock him against the side of the shaft and send him tumbling into the empty blackness below. He rested his head on his forearm, breathed as deeply as he dared, and waited for the platform to stop at the next level, where he stepped off gratefully to await the next. And the next. And the next.

By the time he and Tommy had reached the surface, and Tobias Able had spotted them, Matthew was near fainting. The heavy stickiness at his back had soaked downwards towards his waist, and his shirt no longer rubbed at his flesh; it was stuck too firmly to whatever mess lay beneath it.

In something of a blur he found himself half-carried indoors, where the mine's doctor joined them and then, lying face-down on the table he felt all the tension of his trembling limbs fall away. He heard young Tommy's anxious, questioning voice, was dimly aware of a tugging sensation at his back, and heard the heavy slicing sound of scissors. Then he closed his eyes and searched for a more peaceful darkness. Anna's smile waited there for him, and he moved towards it with deep relief; everything else was distant and unimportant, and would wait for his return. When he was ready.

Chapter Eight

'Go on, I dare you.' Anna squinted at the early afternoon sky, but the good weather looked set to stay, for a while at least. She stepped away from the washing line and gave one more brisk tug to the closest of the sheets hanging over it, pulling it straight. Arric slunk about her feet as usual, but today she was less inclined to shoo him away; she had the odd feeling he was actually missing Joe Trevellick. She stooped to make a fuss of him, her ever-worried mind going over, yet again, the contents of the letter she had sent to Finn.

There was always the possibility someone else might see any correspondence between them and so it was always kept to the barest minimum, and as between a landlord and his employee. As Mrs Penhaligon, she explained the costly and extensive repairs that must be made to the Tinner's Arms before winter, tempering the bad news by claiming it was increased trade that was making such repairs necessary. She had then thought long and hard over the difficult decision, rejecting it several times before continuing:

As for your daughter, I wonder if you could arrange for her to stay with family during these repairs? I understand that her memories would make it too difficult for her to return to her childhood home, but she has mentioned a great aunt and uncle, her mother's family. Perhaps you might make contact with them, and ask if they are willing to extend their hand to her during this difficult time?

Thinking about the words that would tear her and Mairead apart had lit the fire of Anna's anger again, and it burned hot and suffocating. That a girl like Juliet had the power to do this ... if Anna came face-to-face with her right this minute she had no way of knowing what she might do; Freya's friend or not, Juliet Carne had become a greedy, grasping little thief, set on making anyone but herself pay for her own loose morals and thoughtless mistakes.

Anna stooped to pick up her empty washing basket, ready to go back inside; she had done all she could, and all that remained was the waiting. If Finn accepted the news about the repairs she would have the money inside a week, and would be able to pay Juliet for her silence. And Mairead would be safely away from Caernoweth until Anna was sure Juliet had left for good; she did not trust that vile girl, any further than she trusted the Cornish weather.

Her train of thought was broken by the sound of raised voices from inside the passageway, and she straightened just as the door was flung open. A young lad stood there, covered in dust and grime, and with an unmistakeable urgency about him. He was immediately joined by a worried-looking Esther.

'Tommy,' the boy gasped out, by way of introduction.

'My grandson,' Esther added, and Anna went

144

cold; Tommy Trevellick was on the same shift as Matthew at Wheal Furzy. She dropped the washing basket, and folded her arms to stop the sudden shaking of her hands.

'Is it Matthew?' she managed. 'Is he all right?'

'He'm a bit bashed about, Miz Penhaligon, if I'm truthful.' He looked at her earnestly. 'But he in't gone dead.'

Anna didn't share his cautious optimism, and was already loosening the ties of her apron. 'How badly "bashed about"?'

'Arm's broke. It's a bad one so Tobias did send me to fetch you. Doctor Manley was with your 'usband when I left.'

Anna balled her apron in sweating hands as she followed Tommy through the passageway. 'What happened?'

'I don't rightly know,' Tommy confessed. 'Cap'n was blastin', and I was off around by the shaft–'

'*Blasting?*' Anna's heart slithered in her chest. 'Is ... is it just his arm?'

'Mostly. Got some stones in 'is back too, but th'arm's the worst.'

'Show me to him.' Anna threw her apron onto the bar and followed the boy, almost running to keep up.

Never had the road to Wheal Furzy felt so long, and so steep. By the time she arrived, panting and hot-faced, young Tommy had vanished and Anna faltered, uncertain of where to go now she was here. She'd had a vague expectation of a large yard, with an engine-house of course, and some kind of pumping machinery, and a clearly

145

marked office where she would find the mine captain and learn what had happened to Matthew. She'd thought to see a few sheds too, where the finer work was carried out, but nothing like this.

All around her was urgency, industry, and ear-splitting noise; pumps that kept the shafts clear of water, the creaking and squeaking of chains hauling ore to the surface in kibbles, and all topped off with the heavy, water-driven stamps that crushed the already broken-down ore into a finer sand. There *were* some sheds, where goodness only knew what took place, but outside women and children were working at various stations, breaking medium-sized rocks into smaller ones, then smaller still, with different kinds of hammers.

Anna remembered Ellen telling her, the first time they'd met, that she worked at 'spalling', and she had grinned at Anna's blank look, and explained it meant just what these women were doing. Hearing the words had been one thing, and Anna had felt the beginnings of respect even then, but watching the heavy, wrenching work with her own eyes, she was honestly humbled.

The heat, and the dust, as well as the noise, only added to the shock of reality here, so unlike anything she'd encountered in her life at home – some of these children looked barely old enough for school. A woman of around her own age was busily barrowing the ore from one process to the next, her expression blank; no doubt her mind was somewhere altogether more bearable.

As her gaze swept the area, still looking for the office, Anna's attention was caught by the surprising sight of a small group of women at one of the tables, huddled together, and no one appeared to-be castigating them for ceasing work. Recognising Ellen Scoble as one of them, she sighed with relief, and made her way over to ask where she might find Tobias Able.

It became immediately clear why these workers had been left unchastised. In the centre of the huddle was a dark-haired young woman, sobbing hysterically, only held together, it seemed, by her fellow bat maidens, who rubbed her back and her raw, blistered hands. This evidently too-familiar routine was conducted wordlessly due to the noise, but with cautious optimism on the women's faces.

It occurred to Anna that this must be Ginny Donithorn, waiting for news of her husband, and she stopped, unsure whether to go over after all, but Ellen looked up and saw her. Her expression slipped from the comforting smile she was bestowing on her sister-in-law to one of poorly disguised worry for her friend.

She let go of Ginny's hand, and came over, but she still had to shout to be heard over the nearby stamps. 'Have you heard how your man is?'

Anna shook her head, her throat tightening at the concern on Ellen's face. 'Where do I find Captain Able?'

'Come with me. I'll show you.'

'Is David all right?' Anna cast a glance behind them at the group of women, as Ellen drew her away from the worst of the noise.

'So Tommy says. He'll be up to grass d'rectly and Ginny'll be able to see for herself.' She took

Anna's hand. 'I'm that sorry to hear about Matthew. I feel almost like I tempted fate by sayin' how safe he was.'

'Don't. What happened?'

'No one seems to know.' Ellen led the way across the yard, beneath the shadow of the huge, triangular head-gear that rose overhead. Anna looked up at it, partly wary and partly fascinated, and Ellen explained, 'They're sinking a new shaft. That there's for the windin' engine. Here's the captain's office.'

She stopped outside a building, little more than a small hut, and Anna took a deep breath, trepidation once more making her legs shake.

'Thank you.'

Ellen squeezed her hand. 'I've got to get back to Ginny, and to work. But come and see me when you know anything.' She straightened her straw hat, knocked askew by the clumsy hugs with which she had tried to comfort her terrified sister-in-law. 'I hope he's all right, Anna, I do truly.'

'Thank you,' Anna repeated mechanically; she couldn't think of anything now but Matthew. Ellen looked as though she would say more, but the arrival of Tobias Able put paid to any more talk, and she hurried away.

'Mrs Penhaligon.' Tobias shook her hand. 'Try not to worry, he's alive and in one piece. He was lucky, by all accounts. Won't be working for a month or two, though.'

'Longer, if I've any say,' Anna said. Relief allowed an edge of anger to creep into her voice. 'Don't you people have safety measures in place to avoid this kind of thing?'

148

'We don't know what "this kind of thing" is yet,' Tobias said, his attitude cooling considerably. 'And if I might make bold, Missus, *you* might not want him to come back to work right soon, but he'll have a different way of lookin' at it. From what he was sayin' when he came to us in June, he needs the work.'

'Of course.' Anna subsided. 'You're right. I'm sorry. I'm just... Can I see him?'

'Doctor's busy, won't want distracting.'

'Just for a moment?' Now the initial shock had worn off, the first tears pricked at her eyes and thickened her voice.

Tobias relented. 'Hope you've got a strong stomach.'

Anna flinched, but followed him to a shed behind the mine office. Inside was poorly lit, and cluttered with boots, overalls, helmets and jackets; iron rods and wooden ones, hammers, boxes of candles, and one long, grubby-looking table, off which everything had evidently been pushed in a hurry.

Matthew lay face down on the table, stripped to the waist. His back was smeared with blood, and standing over him with a pair of small forceps, and a frown on his face, was a short, neatly dressed man in his late fifties. He turned to see who'd interrupted him, and although he was not a Caernoweth man he realised who Anna must be, and nodded at her, not without sympathy.

Anna took a step closer. 'Will you let me help?'

Matthew's head jerked at the sound of her voice, and the doctor pressed it back down.

'Lie still, lad. This is tricky work.' He looked at

Anna. 'I could use an extra pair of hands to help reset this bone.'

'Of course.' Anna stepped around the table, and for the first time saw the mangled mess that was Matthew's right arm. 'Oh, God...'

'It's all right,' Matthew mumbled into the wooden table. 'It doesn't hurt.'

'That's because you've lost so much blood,' the mine doctor pointed out. 'You're not going to like this next bit.' He lifted the shattered arm, and Matthew jerked again, and this time his hoarse cry tore straight through Anna's heart.

'Have you nothing to give him to dull the pain?'

'He's had morphine. I can't give him any more yet.'

'Freya's on the boat,' Matthew muttered, giving weight to the doctor's words. 'I'll fetch her.'

'It's all right, love. Freya's at work.' Anna spoke softly, but her heart hammered in sudden fear of what he might say next.

Matthew tried to raise his head again, his eyes focused on some other place and time. 'She's frightened...'

'Easy does it, lad,' Doctor Manley said, in a kind voice.

'Tell her I'm sorry...' Matthew's voice tailed out on a sigh and his eyes fluttered closed, and the doctor nodded quickly at Anna.

'Now, before he wakes.'

'What should I do?'

'Hold his upper arm steady. It'll take a lot of strength.' He eyed her slender frame doubtfully. 'I was going to ask Captain Able to do it.'

'No, please, let me. I'm stronger than I look.'

'Right then.' Manley flexed his fingers. 'Whatever happens, even if he wakes and starts screaming, it's vital you don't let go. Are you ready?'

'Yes.' She grasped Matthew's upper arm in one hand, and braced the other against his shoulder blade.

'Hold tight!' the doctor warned again, and began to pull on Matthew's wrist. Slowly he drew the splintered bone back inside while Anna struggled to keep her hold; Manley had exerted an enormous amount of strength, and it was all she could do to stop her hands slipping off Matthew's bloodied skin.

'Almost there...' The doctor was panting now, and Anna looked up to see him blinking sweat from his eyes. 'Come on, you... *There!*' He let out a quick, triumphant breath, and continued to manipulate Matthew's arm until he was satisfied the bone had found its other half, as best it could at least.

Matthew remained thankfully unconscious for the time it took to sew the torn flesh, and set the arm in a splint and a tight bandage. His face was grimy, but he had sweated away the dust and dirt in streaks, and a faint stubble had begun to darken his jaw. Still, Anna couldn't helping thinking he looked absurdly young, lying there. She brushed his hair back from his forehead and bent to kiss him quickly, then busied herself with cleaning the worst of the blood from a nasty-looking gash on the back of his neck. When she thought about how close that flying stone had come to his unprotected head ... she found herself praying under her breath, for the first time she could remember in many years.

Doctor Manley finished all he could do with the arm, and, unable to secure it against Matthew's chest while he lay on his stomach, he turned his attention to the pieces of stone lodged in his patient's back.

'Mostly superficial,' he said, 'except that one, it's gone deep enough to tear the muscle. I'll have to stitch that too, once I've taken out the rock splinter. He's lucky it's not worse.'

He picked up a pair of narrow forceps. 'Must have been quite close to the explosion,' he observed, eyeing Tobias with one eyebrow raised.

Tobias made no reply, but came over to guide Anna away. 'As I said, I don't know what happened yet, but we'll get to the bottom of it.' He frowned at Manley. 'If you'm thinkin' there will be something to hide here, you'd be mistaken. My men matter to me, just so much as they do to their families.'

'Indeed.' Manley's voice was dry, he was clearly not convinced.

Tobias ignored him and took Anna's elbow. 'Come back in an hour, Missus. And bring your man a shirt.' Anna cast a last glance back at Matthew and the doctor, who had resumed his work with the forceps, and forced her feet to move towards the door. Outside Tobias left her to go into one of the bigger sheds, and Anna caught Ellen's attention on her way out of the yard. The women were all working at their stations again, and Ginny Donithorn, although red-eyed and sniffing, was working as fast as the rest; worry would not pay the rent, and bal maidens were paid by the hundredweight and not by the length of time they worked.

Mindful of that fact, Anna just raised a hand and nodded to show all was as well as could be expected. Ellen waved back, though her other arm continued rising and falling, never breaking its rhythm as her spalling hammer sent splinters of stone flying, and Anna found herself wishing she had a similar job to do, on which to work out the fear and the anger. Instead she passed through the gate and onto the road beyond, wondering how she could possibly fill the time.

Her legs, already wearied from hurrying to the mine, felt like lumps of dead wood, barely holding her up, and she sat on the grass by the side of the dusty road, but with all the noise around her she found her thoughts going around in circles. What could they do without Matthew's wage? The thought of giving all that money to Juliet, money that could be spent so much better... Anger flickered again, but it was wasted energy; there was nothing to be done. The sooner that girl was gone, the better.

She gave up trying to plan for an uncertain future long before the allotted hour had passed. Some of that endlessly stretching time had been taken up by a brief conversation with Tristan and Teddy, who'd been on their way to the quarry until she told them how noisy it was, and that they'd be better off waiting until work had finished for the day. The diversion had been welcome, but when she'd then tried to explain about the explosion she'd felt her throat closing up, and excused herself; she couldn't stay out here a moment longer, not while Matthew was so close.

She left the shocked historians still uttering words of concern, and went straight to the office to find Tobias Able, but he was not there. She was instead met by a blacksmith, who had just delivered a pile of reforged drills and was noting them in a ledger.

'Cap'n should be here d'rectly,' he said, and offered Anna his seat before he left, but she was too nervy to relax, and remained standing, looking around her in an attempt to distract herself.

Every surface was covered with inks, ledgers, stubs of candles, boxes of explosive powder, and all manner of other equipment she had no name for. There were coils of something rope-like against one wall, and that one rickety-looking chair behind the cracked desk, with an oilskin hanging over the back of it and one leg braced on a piece of folded card. The smell that hung in the air was an odd, pungent mixture of oil, wax, dust and metal. Anna's eyes kept being drawn back to the coils, and after a moment she realised, with a cold, sliding feeling in her gut, that it must be safety fuse though the word 'safety' was nothing more than a mockery today.

After around ten minutes waiting and winding herself too tight to think straight, she gave in and poked her head out into the yard. Doctor Manley was talking to Tobias Able, and he looked up, saw Anna, and raised his hand. Tobias turned too, but motioned to her to wait a little longer. Anna went back into the office, closed the door with more vigour than necessary, and sat on her hands in the wobbly chair, her feet drumming on the floor.

Patience and nerves were stretched to snapping point before the door opened again, but instead of Captain Able, or the doctor, she saw a familiar face topped with a shock of black hair. David Donithorn.

He nodded to her. 'Mrs Garvey.'

'Penhaligon,' she corrected, her cool tone belying her fears. 'Is Matthew still all right?'

'Seems so.'

She sagged in her seat. 'What happened down there?'

He shook his head, but rather than the quick, angry defence she had expected, he spoke quietly. 'The Cap'n will be in d'rectly. We'll talk it through.'

'Was it Matthew's fault?' Anna could hardly bring herself to ask, but she had to, and Donithorn surprised her again.

'No, t'wasn't nothin' to do with him.'

'But he got caught up in it.'

'He was fetchin' something for young Tommy. That's all I remember. I can't tell you any more, Mrs Garv ... Penhaligon. I'm sorry.'

'Careful there,' Anna said dryly. 'You almost sound as if you mean it.'

'I do mean it.' Donithorn's expression was one of unhappy confusion, and she regretted her words immediately; Matthew was right, the younger man might have held onto that grudge for an unhealthily long time, but it was nevertheless a legitimate one.

Donithorn cleared his throat, and his voice grew stronger. 'Don't misunderstand me, your husband was no hero down there, but he was put

155

at risk and injured through no fault of his own. As shift captain it's my job to get to the bottom of what went wrong.'

He looked about to say more, but Tobias appeared and gestured to Anna to follow him outside. 'He's awake. Did you bring a shirt?'

'Oh. No, I didn't go home after all.'

'Well you can't be walkin' through town with him an' no shirt on. Davey, fetch something for Penhaligon to wear. Bring it into the shed.'

Donithorn went, and as Anna followed Tobias out of the office she watched him cross the yard. His walk had lost the swagger she'd become accustomed to seeing, and his boots kept catching the uneven ground as if he lacked the strength to lift his feet.

But all thought and consideration of David Donithorn vanished as she stepped once more into the dimly lit shed behind the office. The candles had been snuffed, and there was only the natural light coming through the high window, falling on Matthew who sat on a bench with his head bowed. His shoulders were still flecked with blood, and his right arm was bandaged and held tightly against his chest in a snugly fitting sling. His trousers were badly torn from the knees down, and more blood caked them in places, sticking them to his legs.

He lifted his head as the light spilled through the open doorway, and as she hesitated, to allow her vision to adjust, he just stared at her. She realised she would appear only as a vaguely female shape against the glare, and moved into the room so he could see her properly. His taut expression melted

156

into a trembling half-smile of relief, although his voice was little more than a croak.

'Anna. Thank God.'

She pushed away a pair of boots that lay on the bench, so she could sit next to him, and took his good hand in hers. It too was bloodied and torn, but grasped hers with enough strength to ease her worry a little. 'I've come to take you home,' she said.

He nodded, but didn't say anything else, and she didn't want to press him. He swallowed, once, twice, and made a little dry, guttural sound in his throat.

Anna looked around. 'Is there any water?' There were bottles and flasks in abundance, in piles, but the only liquid she could see was a bottle of rum on a shelf and she distracted him quickly. 'Donithorn will be here with something for you to wear in a minute. Then I'll get you home and you can have a cup of tea.'

'Tea.' For the first time, Matthew's eyes flickered in a genuine smile. 'If that doesn't sound like the most perfect thing just now, I don't know what would.'

'There might even be cake, if Freya's been busy again.'

His hand tightened on hers. 'Does she know?'

'Not yet. I didn't think there was any point in telling her until we had to.'

He nodded. 'I suppose you're right. Things will be harder than ever now, and just when things were starting to look up for the business too.'

'She'll be more worried about you than anything else.'

Matthew shrugged, one-shouldered, and winced. 'Still. This is a burden she shouldn't have to bear.'

'What happened down there?' Anna asked. 'No one seems to know. Or want to say.'

Matthew looked beyond her through the open door. 'Not now,' he said quietly.

Anna frowned. 'What do you mean, *not now?*'

'Hush.' He raised her hand to his lips. 'I'm all right. Let's just enjoy that for a while.'

Another figure appeared in the doorway. It was young Tommy Trevellick. 'Matt? Cap'n Donithorn asked me to give you this.' He handed over a rough jacket, torn in more places than not, and smelling unpleasantly ripe. 'All he could find, he says.'

Anna wrinkled her nose, but smiled her thanks and took it. 'Thank you for fetching me today, Tommy.'

'S'all right, Miz Penhaligon.' He looked at them both as if he wanted to say more, then shrugged. 'I've got to go. They're expectin' me in the office.'

Matthew sat straighter. 'Shouldn't I be there too?'

'Not today,' Tobias said from the doorway. 'Come on, Tommy. We'll get your story, and Donithorn's. Penhaligon, we'll speak to you tomorrow and see how it all fits together. Go home now, get some rest. You'll need it.' He waited until Tommy had joined him, and clapped a hand onto the boy's shoulder, guiding him back out into the sunshine.

Feeling Matthew bracing himself to stand, Anna let go of his hand and slipped an arm around his waist, mindful of his back, padded in several places and with fresh blood already show-ing through the bandages. 'Can you walk if I help you?'

He nodded. 'I just went a bit faint when I got out. The mine doctor said there was a lot of bleeding, and I've not really eaten much. Made me a bit...' he whirled a finger around his temple and rolled his eyes.

'Hmm. Not surprising. Hold your arm out.' She slid the sleeve of the smelly, too-big jacket over Matthew's good left arm, and wrapped it across his back to hang from his right shoulder. He looked at her and pulled a face. 'I think some-one died in this.'

'Well,' Anna managed to inject some of her old briskness into her voice, 'let's just be thankful it wasn't you.'

Chapter Nine

Pencarrack House

The bedroom curtains were tightly closed, al-though it was an unnecessary precaution; there was little chance anyone would be walking in the gardens. Dorothy was locked away in the study with Father, as usual, and Harry was, for once, playing in his own rooms while he waited for Hugh to return from his hunting party. Nobody was out there to look up to the window, to wit-ness this scandalising display of abandon.

The music might be trapped inside Lucy Batten's head, but that made it no less real. Wearing only a light cotton chemise, and comfortably barefoot, Lucy closed her eyes and let the music swell, carrying her through an increasingly complex series of movements. She had tied a scarf to each wrist, the lightest she could find, and these floated around her head as she lifted her arms, drifted across her smiling face, and then whipped out to the sides when she leaned and flicked her wrists.

The click of the door brought her out of the moment with a rude jolt, and she stumbled frantically behind her screen before looking out again, breathless, but relieved to see only Harry standing there. Thank goodness she was dressed this time. More so than usual, anyway. 'What have you been told about knocking before barging in?'

Her uncharacteristic sharpness appeared to pass directly over her young nephew's head. 'My window looks the wrong way, and I wanted to watch for Uncle Hugh coming back.' He crossed, uninvited, to the window seat and lifted away one curtain, and while he stared in vain across the gardens Lucy began to dress. She couldn't help resenting the tightness of her finely made clothes, and the restriction of slipping her feet into shoes she had been so excited about when she'd ordered them from London.

When she emerged Harry had let the curtain fall closed again, trapping him between it and the window, and he was no more than a boy-shaped lump shrouded in heavy velvet.

'There he... Oh.' He sighed. 'I thought that was

160

him, but there are two of them and they're not riding.'

Lucy pulled back the curtains and hooked them onto the ties. 'Who is it then?'

'I don't know.' Harry shrugged. 'They're not carrying any luggage, and they're not miners, or delivery men. Look.'

He moved aside, and Lucy peered through the glass to the garden below. Two men were walking along the long pathway, turning this way and that, pointing, evidently discussing what they were seeing. When they drew close enough for Lucy to distinguish features, she frowned.

'One of them seems decent enough, but the other looks a bit of a thug.'

'Thug?'

'Well, perhaps I'm being unfair. He might have had an accident, I suppose. But his face is a dreadful mess.'

'Let me see.' Harry elbowed her aside again, and Lucy gave him a tap on the back of the head.

'Manners, Henry George.'

'Sorry.' But his attention was on the visitors. 'I wonder what they want?'

'There's one very good way to find out. Come away from the window now.' Lucy held out her hand, and led him to the door. As she passed her glass she glanced at it to make sure she wasn't still unbecomingly flushed from dancing, and that her hair was presentable; thug or not, there was something quite appealing about the stature of the taller of the two men, and first impressions were important after all.

By the time she and Harry had arrived in the

161

entrance hall, the visitors had been admitted. The housekeeper had begun to shuffle off in the direction of the library, but Lucy knew her father and sister would not take kindly to an interruption, unless it was of the utmost importance.

'Mrs Andrews, are these gentlemen here to see Father? Or Miss Batten?'

Mrs Andrews stopped and turned back, her relief evident. 'Not as such, Miss Lucy, no.'

'Then don't trouble them, I'm sure I'll be able to help.' Lucy directed this towards the shorter of the two visitors, trying not to stare too hard at the swollen and bruised face of the other one. 'What can we do for you?'

But it was the puffy-faced man who answered. 'Thank you for allowing us into your home. My name is Tristan MacKenzie. I'm an historian.'

He held out his hand, and Lucy shook it. His accent wasn't precisely local, but neither was it noticeably that of another part of England. His voice, however, was polite and low-pitched, and his grip firm. It made her look at him more closely, and she saw he was younger than she'd thought at first; maybe twenty-eight at most, certainly not yet thirty. His eyes were almost shut, and the cut across the bridge of his nose made her wince in sympathy.

'How on earth did you come by that?'

He gave a slightly embarrassed grin. 'There was an altercation in the local pub, and I made a poor choice in choosing sides.'

Lucy was not sure what to make of that, and turned instead to his companion. He was fresh-faced, but rather plain-looking, and shy in a quiet, scholarly kind of way. His shyness might just be because he wasn't used to houses like Pencarrack – neither of the men was dressed poorly, exactly, but they didn't look as if they spent a lot of time with the gentry either. And if they were wont to get involved in bar fights that was probably a good thing. 'How do you do, Mr...?'

'Kempton. Teddy. Edward. Pleased to meet you.'

'Batten. Lucy. Miss. Likewise.' She smiled to show she was teasing rather than mocking, and Teddy relaxed and smiled back.

'And who is the young master?'

'This is Henry Batten. Better known as Harry. My nephew.'

'Pleased to meet you.' On his best behaviour, Harry held out his hand, and both men shook it with due solemnity.

Mr MacKenzie looked around the large hall, paying particular attention to the antique weapons hanging in the alcoves. 'This is a remarkable building, Miss Batten.'

'Isn't it? How can we help?'

'We wouldn't have disturbed you, only we were on our way out to visit the quarry, and bumped into a friend who said we might prefer to visit somewhere quieter. So we came over here, and I couldn't help noticing that little building off the courtyard.'

'What about it?'

'It looks very much older than the rest of the house. I wondered if you had any idea when it was built?'

'You're the historian, Mr MacKenzie,' Lucy said, with a certain impishness. 'Would you like to guess?' Harry tugged at her hand, eager to put his own history lessons to use, but she shushed him.

MacKenzie regarded her for a moment, and accepted the challenge. 'Well, the reason I was drawn to it was because it seems very similar to some buildings I've been studying for my work. I would guess it was built quite early on in the seventeenth century, am I close?'

Lucy smiled. 'Bravo! Father tells me that was the original Pencarrack Cottage. The rest of the estate grew, along with the Batten fortune, from sixteen forty-five onwards when the first of the Caernoweth Battens moved here.'

'I gather the estate name translates as "head of a rocky mass",' Mr Kempton put in. 'It's jolly close to the top of that valley at the back, so that would fit.'

'And what brings you both to Caernoweth?' Lucy asked.

MacKenzie's face underwent a subtle change; it lost its tension, and there was a new enthusiasm in his voice. 'Some journals were donated to the bookshop down the road. Invaluable to my study, so we came to collect them. I'm quite eager to read them in fact so, with thanks for your inform-ation I think we'll—'

'Well, if you like journals,' Lucy broke in quickly, reluctant to lose such interesting com-pany so soon, 'you're very welcome to look at the ones we have in the gallery.'

MacKenzie stopped, mid-turn. 'That would be very kind,' he said, and she noticed a relaxation in the puffiness around his eyes. As if he were willing them to open so he could enjoy reading those stuffy old books, they blinked a little wider and she saw the vivid green of them for the first time. A startling colour, and quite hypnotic. Disturbed to find herself staring, she turned to Mr Kempton.

'Might I call you Edward?'

'I prefer Teddy,' he said. 'It would be awfully decent of you to let us look at whatever you have here.'

'Then follow me.' Lucy led the way back upstairs, and a short distance along the landing she turned right into a long, narrow room. 'We've had to put them under glass to keep them preserved,' she said, then realised the two men had fallen still in the doorway while she had continued walking. She turned back, and smiled to see them staring at the display cabinets with identical expressions of hungry delight. They followed her in as if they were walking into a throne room.

'It's like a museum,' Teddy said, his finger trailing over the glass of the nearest cabinet.

'Father has no real interest in the books in here,' Lucy said, 'but he knows there is a rising interest, and so he has taken great pains to care for them. Mother was keen, but he never comes in here himself.'

'Why ever not?' MacKenzie moved further into the room, peeking behind the curtain of a covered alcove. She couldn't decide whether his boldness was endearing or irritating.

'He's too busy with the mines, and with the clay works.'

'He owns Wheal Furzy?'

'That's one of ours, yes.'

165

MacKenzie frowned and dropped the curtain. 'Dreadful business. I'm not surprised he's busy today.'

'Dreadful?' Lucy felt a tremor of foreboding at MacKenzie's suddenly sombre expression. 'What do you mean?'

'Well, the explosion.'

'What explosion?'

'You didn't know...' MacKenzie looked stunned. 'Surely they'll have told your father?'

'No.' Lucy breathed deeply, hoping the dizzy feeling would pass. 'Was anyone killed?'

'I don't think so. One of your workers was quite badly hurt, though. Matthew Penhaligon. It was his wife who told us about it, she was waiting to bring him home.'

'I must tell Father.' For a split second Lucy couldn't remember where the door was, and she looked around the room in something close to panic before her mind cleared enough to guide her. 'I'll leave you to...' She waved vaguely at the books, and hurried down the stairs. Harry had vanished again, and a good thing too. If he heard his friend Penhaligon was hurt goodness only knows how fast he would run to that god-forsaken hole in the ground to look for him.

She burst into the library without knocking, and blurted the news as Charles Batten's head snapped up and Dorothy's eyes opened wide.

Charles half-stood, keeping his place on his ledger with one finger. 'Anyone dead?'

'I don't think so. Someone was injured, though. You met him on Sunday, Father, it's Mr Penhaligon.'

'But no deaths.' He relaxed a little, though an irritated frown appeared between his eyes. 'Are you sure about this? Because if it's come from Harry you must remind him they're always blasting, it's part of–'

'No. We have visitors. Scholars,' she added quickly, to give weight to their credibility. 'They've heard it from someone who was there. Look, shouldn't you go and see for yourself?' Lucy expected her blunt question to be rewarded at first with anger, but at least then with realisation and swift movement, but instead her father sat back down.

'Tobias Able will be here as soon as he's got to the bottom of it, no doubt.'

'Has work stopped?' Dorothy wanted to know.

Lucy saw her pen hovering over a book of figures, and bit back an angry reply. 'Only for the injured man, I believe,' she said, relying on sarcasm instead. 'But I'd hate to bore you with unimportant details.'

'Don't be petty,' Dorothy said calmly. 'Of course we're glad no one was killed. But rushing down there and demanding their attention is only going to divert it from where it's needed most.'

Her father nodded. 'Dorothy's quite right. We'll be told in good time what we need to know, and in the meantime we'll just be in the way and hold things up. Doctor Manley is on hand, I imagine?'

The wind taken out of her sails, Lucy nodded. 'I expect so.'

'Who are our visitors?'

Lucy blinked. She accepted that her urgency was likely misplaced after all, but surely there was still enough concern to warrant conversation, at least?

'They're a Mr MacKenzie and a Mr Kempton. Historians. I've left them looking at the books in the gallery.'

'How very trusting,' Dorothy said in a dry voice.

'They seem perfectly honest.'

'Do you have any idea how old and valuable some of those books are?'

'Of course I do!' Lucy's voice was tight, and she couldn't resist adding, 'Do *you* have any idea how young and valuable your son is?'

'Lucy–'

'Or even where he is?'

'With Maddern, I assume.'

'He has no lessons today, it's Maddern's day off.'

'Then why isn't he with you?'

'I'm not his mother! Nor his nursemaid.' Lucy turned to go. 'I expect you'll be happiest when he's gone to St Boniface and you won't have to trouble yourself with him any more.'

'Don't be silly.'

'Gosh, silly *and* petty.' Lucy glared at her sister. 'I'm surprised you think I'm fit to look after your son at all.' Before Dorothy could answer, she left and slammed the door shut behind her.

Then she looked at the stairs, and thought about what Dorothy had said. She remembered Tristan MacKenzie's ruffian-type appearance, offset by his charm, and how unexpected had been the appearance of the two men. Strangers, and very inquisitive ones at that. A little qualm crept over her; what if they *had* sent her from the room on purpose, to give them time to steal some of the priceless works that decorated the gallery? Surely they must have known the mine belonged to the Battens, and that she would be alarmed enough to investigate. And come to think of it, why *hadn't* Tobias Able come to fetch them? Had there been an explosion at all?

Lucy groaned. What an idiot she'd been... Heart hammering, she hurried up the stairs, along the short hall, into the gallery, and, at full tilt, into Teddy Kempton. Their heads smacked together with a blinding crack, and Lucy stumbled back with a little cry of mingled pain and shock. She fell backwards and landed heavily, thanking her stars for the padding at the back of her skirt, then became vaguely aware of a firm, gentle hand in the small of her back, helping her to sit upright.

Another hand slipped into her left one, and it was warm and strong. She felt an undeniable tingle as the fingers closed on hers, and the hand at her back stayed in place, its heat and pressure a deeply pleasurable sensation despite the buzzing in her head. She blinked the dizziness away and looked up with gratitude, ready to thank Mr MacKenzie for his help.

Teddy's blue eyes looked back into hers, and she blinked again.

'Oh! It's you.' She shook her head, realising how it sounded. 'I'm sorry, I mean, are you all right?'

'Quite all right,' he said quietly, then smiled. 'Are you?'

Confusion rendered Lucy unable to answer at first, and his smile faded a little. That helped concentrate her mind. 'Yes, thank you.' Her gaze moved to MacKenzie, who looked away but not

169

before she saw the twitch at the corner of his mouth. Teddy's hands stayed where they were for a moment longer, and then the one on her back slid around her waist, while the other pulled her to stand, rather bemused, and with a nasty headache developing. He held her until she nodded her assurance that she wouldn't fall, and then stepped away.

She wasn't altogether surprised at the disappointment she felt, and for a moment entertained the idea of swaying, just a little, to see how quickly he grasped her again. But instead she brushed some imaginary dust off the back of her skirt and drew herself straighter.

'I take it you weren't making off with our family fortune then?' When she saw their looks of astonishment, she shrugged. 'I feel very silly,' she confessed, 'but there's no sense in trying to make up a plausible reason for me careering around the corner like a ... like a...'

'An outraged gazelle?' Teddy ventured.

'Don't worry, Miss Batten,' MacKenzie said with a grin. 'There was a compliment in there somewhere.' He shook his head at Teddy, and raised his eyebrows. He was probably a decent-looking young man beneath all those bruises, Lucy thought, but her gaze was pulled back to Teddy Kempton. He would have a bruise of his own by tomorrow, she could tell by the reddened area by his left eyebrow, and she was half-amused, half-shocked to find herself wanting to touch it, to soothe it.

She turned away before it could show on her face, and demonstrated her trust by leaving the

170

two of them alone again with the books. 'Just come downstairs when you're ready, or if you'd like some tea. I'll be in the garden.'

Harry was, quite predictably, halfway down the path when she saw him, and heading with a very determined stride for the gate.

'HENRY GEORGE!'

The boy stopped, and she could see his shoulders rise and fall in a theatrical sigh. Then he turned and made his moody way back to her. 'I want to go into town,' he complained. 'Bobby Gale said he'd teach me–'

'That is not the way to persuade me,' Lucy cautioned. 'Come on, let's go and see if there are any strawberries left.' She put out her left hand first of all, then switched to her right at the last minute. As they walked across the grass to the walled garden she pressed her left hand against her skirt, glanced up at the gallery window, and smiled. Her headache was fading already.

Tristan watched Teddy pretending great interest in a large book at the far end of the gallery. Beneath the glass at his own hand was the open journal of the very first Batten of Pencarrack, and it was tugging at his attention like an insistent child, but he moved away from it to stand beside his friend.

Teddy didn't look up, but gestured at the book. 'Family bible,' he said. 'Interesting inscriptions.'

'Oh, yes. Very.'

'Great sources of family history, bibles.'

'Indeed.'

171

'Often find family members that don't appear on official trees.'

'No doubt.'

'Bastards and suchlike.'

'Quite.'

'Always worth looking, I find.'

'Teddy?'

'Yes?'

'When you next call on Miss Batten, try not to knock her out, there's a good chap.'

Teddy turned a flushing face on Tristan, but grinned. 'That obvious, was I?'

'A little.'

'Do you suppose she might consider me?'

'It's a strong possibility.' Tristan patted Teddy's shoulder, and crossed the room to squint again through the glass at the Batten journal.

'Are you sure I'm not stepping on any toes?' Teddy persisted.

Tristan looked at him, surprised. 'Mine, you mean? Good grief, no, whatever makes you say that?'

'Well she's a dashed good-looking girl.'

'She is, but even if she were interested in me, which she clearly isn't,' he pointed out with a little smile, 'I have absolutely no interest in forming any kind of attachment while I'm here. Much less with a daughter of the local aristocracy.'

'They're not–'

'All right, gentry, then. Landed or otherwise. My toes are untrodden upon. Which I hope will go for Miss Batten's too, after the two of you have danced.'

'She was the one who crashed into me,' Teddy

reminded him, rubbing his forehead. 'And you're getting ahead of yourself with talk of dancing.'

'Only you can put that right.' Tristan turned his attention to the journal. Open at the very first page, the writing was closely packed and the ink still dark. It was difficult to make out the words, but just the date gave him a *frisson:* 12 October 1645. The journals themselves would take a great deal of study to decipher, but the sight of them revived his eagerness to delve into those he had just bought, which were dated at least two years earlier. Besides, it would be far more rewarding to read the stories of a hardworking member of the general public than what would probably turn out to be little more than a list of the acquisitions and spending of the privileged elite.

'I'm going to start on the Bartholomew books tonight,' he told Teddy. 'And I think I've decided to stay here in town a little longer.'

'We can't afford the hotel for more than one more day,' Teddy said sensibly.

'Then I'll ask around for a room. You needn't stay, if you don't want to.'

'It's not that I don't want to,' Teddy said, and Tristan wondered if he even realised he was staring wistfully at the door through which Lucy Batten had recently vanished. 'But I have work to do in Plymouth. As do you,' he added, in a slightly disapproving tone.

'My work can wait another week.' Tristan found himself wishing the remainder of the day away so that he could start on the Bartholomew books; Teddy's company was always welcome, but those journals deserved every scrap of Tristan's attention. Three pounds just didn't seem enough of a price to pay.

As they left Pencarrack, Teddy craning his neck for a last sight of Miss Batten, Tristan remembered the Penhaligon girl's reaction to the price the books had fetched; her dark eyes had shot so wide he'd half-expected them to fall out. He was reasonably sure he was forgiven for his initial pomposity, which, he was prepared to admit now, mattered to him far more than it should.

Then he remembered her father had been involved in the explosion, and his smile faded.

'How much money do we have left?' They had reached junction where the hotel lay just ahead, and the town sprawled down the hill to their right.

'I shall have to work it out. And deduct payment for the room for another night. Why?'

'I was thinking about the Bartholomew books. Having seen how Charles Batten looks after his, wouldn't you think they'd be worth more than three pounds?'

'We don't know yet,' Teddy said, frowning. 'We'd need to look at them properly.'

'Then that's what we'll do.' Tristan turned sharply into the hotel courtyard, and marched towards the door. 'Come on, we've got a lot of reading to do, and it's going to take several days. It looks rather as if we're staying.'

'Oh dear.' Teddy grinned and followed him into the pleasantly cool lobby. 'What a ghastly thought.'

Chapter Ten

Matthew's eyes opened to darkness. He could hear the continuing low rumble of rock tumbling into the tunnel where he had been standing, and taste gunpowder and thick dust in his throat. The air was heavy and damp, and for a moment he struggled to breathe, fighting a crushing panic, before an involuntary movement sent a spike of pain through his right arm and reality flared, hideously bright. He was out. He was home.

The bitter taste of bile rose in his throat and he swallowed hard, hating the tiny moan that escaped on his breath. Shivering, he stared into the blackness, waiting for his eyes to adjust to the subtle nuances of the shadows in the room. He breathed as slowly as he could, and took stock of what lay beneath the light covering that kept off the night's chill: his feet were bare; his trousers still on, but feeling oddly light about the lower legs.

Beyond that, all he could tell was that the pain was not yet back with its full force; it still felt removed to a distance, where he could study it with a peculiar detachment. His arm was still imprisoned across his chest ... he remembered being sure he had braced it against the wall, and the confusion when it had collapsed beneath him anyway. Now he knew why. His back throbbed, and, lying still, he could pick out six or seven separate places that had felt the snapping sensation of sharp rock, peppering him from behind, but only one where the pain felt deeper, less likely to fade quickly. The doctor had muttered something about muscle damage, and said he'd have the stitches in there for a while.

Matthew braced himself, and shifted one foot. The slide of material over his skin brought painful feeling to life, and he was instantly transported back into the tunnel, stumbling to his knees in the rubble; it was a miracle his legs weren't broken as well.

He suddenly wanted, very badly indeed, to see a friendly face, and after a minute's steady, deep breathing he gritted his teeth and made himself move. It took several attempts to finally lay his feet flat on the floor beside the bed, and to push himself, awkwardly one-handed, to stand on them. His knees shook, and as he stood still, waiting for the strength to return to them, he felt like an old man. The light switch by the door might as well have been in another house for all the inclination he felt to find it, but the last thing he wanted was to stumble over something, so he made his way stiffly across the room and his hand slapped around until it found the switch. He closed his eyes before turning it on, but the brightness still burned for a moment, making him wince and wish for the old days, and the gentler light of the paraffin lamp.

After a minute or so he opened his eyes again, slowly, and blinked a few times. When he could see without squinting he stood before his mirror and saw that whoever had put him to bed – Anna presumably – had sponged as much grime, blood and dirt from his body as they could, and he stood shirtless but at least reasonably clean. In a strange way it made him feel human again.

Anna had promised him tea. It was late, and there was little chance anyone would still be up, but there was an unquestionable appeal to the thought of something to ease the scratchiness in his throat, and loosen his tongue from where it stuck to the roof of his mouth. He took his dressing gown off the back of the door and hung it across his shoulders, and pushed his sore feet into slippers.

Opening the door to the rest of the house was like returning to a world from which he hadn't even realised he felt shut off, and he made his way down the stairs, each step bringing him further back into reality. He rounded the newel post at the foot of the stairs, glad to see a light still shining under the kitchen door, and hobbled towards it.

'Anna?'

'Sent her home.' Robert was sitting at the table, a teapot in front of him, his cup filled with weak-looking tea. No steam came from it. 'She din't want to go, mind.'

Matthew tried not to let his disappointment show. 'What are you doing up, Pa?'

'Worried about you, boy.' Robert's brusque tone belied the surprising words. He touched the teapot with the backs of bent, arthritic fingers. 'Cold. You'll be wanting some fresh, then?'

'I'll make it,' Matthew said, automatically moving towards the range.

'You bleddy won't. Sit, boy.'

Matthew did, partly dismayed and partly touched to see the way his father's hands shook as they lifted the teapot. 'You should go to bed,' he said quietly. 'You'll make yourself ill.'

'I've stayed awake through more nights than you've lived,' Robert said gruffly. 'I'm all right.'

Matthew waited until Robert had refilled the teapot and seated himself back down with a grunt.

'How is Freya?' he asked. 'And what about Anna? Does anyone know what happened yet?'

'No one's said anythin' about what happened. Likely they're still finding out. Anna's gone back down the Tinner's. I had to remind her about the girl needin' her mother, or she'd have stayed all night.'

'And Freya? You didn't answer that.'

'Freya's Freya.'

'What does that mean?'

Robert fixed him with a steady look. 'It means she've had enough worry in her life, and she knows how to live around it.'

Matthew went very still. The air in the kitchen felt chilly now on his bare skin. 'Are you saying I'm to blame for this?'

Robert sighed. 'I'm just sayin' this could be the worst for us all, and we'd better make sure it in't.'

'And how do we do that?' Matthew felt the sting of his father's words. 'If I'm lucky, this,' he gestured to his arm, 'won't get infected, and I'll keep it. If I'm not, who knows what will happen? Either way I'm not going to be back at Wheal Furzy for a good long while.' *If ever.* But he left that unsaid, and from the look on Robert's face it was unnecessary anyway.

'How bad is it?' Robert's voice was softer now, and he half-reached out to touch Matthew's hand before withdrawing again. The father in him had not quite been subdued by the disciplinarian, after all.

'Hurts.' Matthew knew he sounded blunt, but he felt his throat thickening and didn't trust himself to say any more.

'Anna said the bone was ... out through.'

'Yes.'

'Mine doctor did a good job though, she says.'

'Pa, go to bed. Please.'

'Shoulder's looking bad.'

Matthew glanced at it. The bruising had come out while he'd slept, and from the bicep right up as far as he could see was livid with variations of purples and black. 'Hit the wall,' he said. 'Lucky I didn't break that, too.'

'The wall?' Robert was trying, and the feeble joke even raised a half-smile from Matthew.

'Oh, the wall definitely came off worse,' he said dryly, and Robert huffed a soft laugh.

For a long moment they sat in silence, each struggling to hold onto the fragile bond that they had found earlier in the year. Eventually Robert sighed.

'I just worry, boy. For you and for the family.'

Matthew nodded. 'I know. And you know I'll do whatever I can to keep us afloat. But I need you to shore me up, Pa, not tear me down.'

After another silence, during which Matthew gulped his tea with gratitude and relief, Robert sat back in his chair. 'Anna reckons you could get a job in an office.'

'An *office?*' Matthew choked, and replaced his cup hurriedly. 'She said that?'

'She did. She've got a point, mind. You're good with a pen.'

'Pa!'

'I know t'idn't your choice, but it'd be something. If worst comes to worst,' he added, nodding at Matthew's arm. 'Look, I know there's nowhere you'll be happy that isn't all salt and spray, but you've got to think about Freya. About this house.'

'I am, but Anna's dreaming if she thinks I'd get office work. Doesn't she think I'd have tried that before Wheal Furzy, if I thought it likely?'

'Don't dismiss it, boy. Talk to her about it. At least she's thinking forwards, with a sensible head. Better than Freya's idea, anyway.'

'Freya's idea?'

'Remember them stories you used to write? In the old days, when you was...' Robert's hand clenched on the table, and Matthew remembered it crashing into his jaw, the night they'd almost lost Freya. 'She've written to her ma to ask for the book. Reckons you could sell them to a publisher and become rich. First thing she thought of, the daft beggar.'

Matthew wanted to laugh, but instead he felt the hot sting of tears, and the conflict between head and heart left him unable to find any words.

'I told her,' Robert went on, 'no one would want to read them.'

'What did she say to that?' Matthew managed, wishing Freya was there so he might fold her against him, the way he had when she'd been little, and whisper his gratitude to her. No one had understood his stories like Freya, and he had soon stopped sharing them with anyone else.

'She said 'course they would. Said she loved them, so why wouldn't other children?'

'And what did you say?'

'Told her the truth, since she's old enough to know it. She loved them stories because of who wrote them, that's all. They meant you was thinkin' of her, making things for her. Speaking of which...' Robert stood, oblivious to the pain he'd just inflicted on Matthew, who took a deep breath and pushed it away. If Freya was old enough to understand the truth then surely he should be.

'Where are you going?' he asked, glad for a change of subject.

'Just fetchin' something from the shop.'

He returned a minute or two later with a box in his hands. Matthew had a sudden, clear memory of Freya on her eighth birthday, coming back into the kitchen at Hawthorn Cottage carrying the box that had held the birthday gift he'd made for her. That memory was sharpened, and pushed into his heart like a needle a moment later.

Inside the box lay the Cornish lugger he had taken so many months to make. Carving, shaping, smoothing, adding detail ... through dark nights when the drink had him and he'd made so many mistakes he'd had to later rectify, and through the rare, clear-thinking, hopeful hours when he and Isabel had been happy, and their future had a bright outline at last.

Freya's treasured birthday gift now lay broken; the wood split in half in a dozen places; the sails, made by her grandmother, crumpled and torn; the mast snapped in two. The name, painted by Robert with his careful, talented hand, also sheared through the middle, but the broken lettering gleamed in the kitchen light. *Lady Penhaligon.*

Matthew touched a trembling finger to the side of the boat. 'What happened?'

'She wouldn't say.'

'She wouldn't have done this.'

'No, I reckon not.'

'Who, then?'

Robert shrugged, but there was anger in the set of his jaw; he knew how much had gone into the making of this, modelled on Matthew's own boat the *Isabel,* formerly *Julia.* Some said the renaming of the boat for his wife had been the start of all the Penhaligons' difficulties, but Matthew knew better; those problems had their origins in his inability to fulfil Isabel's romantic dreams, and his stubborn unwillingness to admit how bad things were getting. As a couple they had been doomed from the start, and the only good thing to have come out of it was Freya.

He straightened the slender mast, and unwrapped the tangled sail, but Robert lifted the box away from him.

'Go on back up to bed, there's time enough later for fixing things.' He raised his eyes to Matthew's, and added quietly, 'Them that can be.'

Chapter Eleven

The evening was creeping on, and as Tristan climbed the moorland path to the quarry he was amused to find himself actually missing Teddy's grumbling. His friend had reluctantly left early that morning after all, taking Tristan's car, and promising to contact the publishers to enquire after an advance on publication royalties. What they'd read of Bartholomew's journals had given Tristan back the itch to write, and it was tingling in his fingers even now – the books must surely be worth more than he'd paid, for that fact alone.

Enquiries at the pub had revealed it was no travellers' inn, with rooms for hire; there were two bedrooms only, and both occupied. But Teddy had apparently met Freya on her way to work yesterday, and stopped to ask if she knew of a place. She had told them of a room that might be available; Bartholomew's own descendant, the doctor who'd donated the journals, had been pleased to offer Tristan the use of his attic room, at a manageable rent, for the duration of his time in Caernoweth.

And so the journals had returned to the room where they had languished for so long, which couldn't be more perfect, and now they were at last opened, and devoured with hungry fascination. Long years of practice had enabled Tristan to read past the words themselves, with their strange spellings and odd phrasing, to the meaning that lay beneath, and when he looked around out here, on the land where the words had been penned, he could almost hear the lost voice echoing among the gorse and the silent quarry workings.

We have taken the shilling, and march in three days to Sourton Down near Okehampton. My good friend Stephen Penhaligon, and others from Porthstennack, will travel with me, and much as it pains me to leave my sons I would rather be lonely without them, yet see them safe, than bring them with me and deliver them into the hands of the Roundheads.

Daniel, the younger, has cast a shadowed eye on me, I fear he knows I might not return. But Robert sees the adventure that lies ahead as a march to glory— If I do not return, I must beg my sons to forgive me. And should they be called to take up arms in my place I would that they fight for King Charles with the same dedication as their fellow Cornishmen.

John Bartholomew had written in his journal at every opportunity, and the pages were torn, muddied, and hurriedly written – much of it was unreadable, yet seeing those closely packed words, written across the page in every direction to save paper, had given Tristan a deep thrill and a longing to immerse himself in them entirely.

Nevertheless he was glad he'd forced himself to come out after being locked away in Doctor Bartholomew's attic room for most of the day. The fresh air helped clear his stuffy head, which still ached after his run-in with Tom Carne, and the long hours of squinting at the difficult, laboured writings had begun to take their toll on his bruised and puffed eyes. But out here on the high ground, the discomfort ebbed away and was gradually replaced by a settled, contented feeling. There was a great deal of gorse to weave through, but as he drew closer to the quarry pool it began to clear, and he kept walking until he reached the water's edge, looking forward to the breeze off the water to cool his hot face.

The rocks rose to his right and left, and a high, rough wall formed the fourth side, and completed the false illusion of a peaceful, secluded beauty spot. He looked at the pool, imagining it as it would have been before the workings had moved higher up the moor; a quarry of equal size, probably bigger, before it was worked out.

Now the pumping equipment had been removed to the new site, this old one had flooded, and its rugged surrounds gave the impression of a natural lake. But beneath the still surface that reflected the afternoon sunlight with its deceptively beautiful colours, it would be unthinkably deep. Left to rot at the bottom and all along its scarred, steeply-sloping sides would be broken machinery, perhaps even buildings, and almost certainly equipment that had been superseded by new inventions. The lifetimes of so many men, their work and their way of life, hidden forever in the icy depths.

He let his thoughts wander, in familiar contentment, over the past as he climbed the slope, determined to make at least one circuit of the pool before going back to the happy seclusion of the doctor's house. But before he had taken more than a few steps along the ledge, a movement caught his eye, and when he peered into the water from this greater height his breath halted in shock. He closed his eyes, but behind the tightly shut lids he could still see the thin white legs, exposed as the rock snagged the light summer dress, and the limp arms ... the long hair floating on the surface like weed, the cap that had covered it now floating away and bumping gently against the rock wall.

Instinct pushed him to run down the slope, his heart hammering as he readied himself for swimming out and pulling her back in, but he knew it was too late. Standing by the side of the pool he watched the dead girl for a moment, an immense feeling of sadness creeping over him, then drew a heavy sigh and turned back towards town to fetch help.

It was almost dark when he left the constable's house for the second time that day. All that could be done had been done; the girl, who'd turned out to be in the family way, had been pulled from the water, and Tristan closely questioned. He had eventually convinced Constable Couch that he knew nothing about the girl's death, or even the girl herself, and that, despite his fearsome appearance, he was in fact quite respectable. He'd left his name and contact address and stepped out onto the street, unable to shake the notion that, if he and Teddy had followed through with their plan to visit the pool on Tuesday morning, they might have seen the despairing girl, and maybe even helped her.

He turned towards the bottom of town, but had only gone a few paces when he heard his name spoken in a hesitant, questioning tone. He turned to see the young Miss Penhaligon, a tartan shawl loose about her slender shoulders, and looking a good deal friendlier than he deserved after the way he had spoken to her.

'I thought it was you,' she said, drawing closer. 'How is your nose?'

'Improving in feeling, if not in appearance.'

She smiled. 'Well that's something.'

Tristan wasn't altogether surprised to feel something stirring inside him as he looked at her; she was a very pretty girl, after all. But he wasn't prepared for the sudden wash of concern as he saw the shadows beneath her eyes, and the tiny lines between them.

He spoke gently. 'How is your father?'

'He's...' She stopped, then took a deep breath and continued, with determined optimism in her voice. 'He's going to be all right, we think. There doesn't seem to be any sign of infection in the arm.'

'That's very good news,' Tristan said. 'And how are you?'

'I'm well, thank you.' In contrast to her words, she looked at him for a moment as if she wanted to heap every worry she had from her shoulders onto his, and he would have been happy to bear them, if it would have helped. But of course it wouldn't. He nearly told her then, about the chance of an advance from his publisher for re-search materials, but it wasn't certain yet and might only result in disappointment. Better to wait until he knew.

She raised an enquiring eyebrow. 'You were going to say something?'

'Only that I wish I could help,' he added, half truthfully. 'If there's anything you feel I might be able to do, to take the burden from Mr Penhaligon, you must ask.'

'Thank you.'

An awkwardness fell between them, and they both looked around for something to say to escape it.

'I'm walking your way,' Tristan said at last. 'Shall we go together?'

Miss Penhaligon nodded. She looked so small as she walked beside him; too young to bear such responsibilities, but he noted how straight she held herself, and how strong-looking were the hands that pulled the soft shawl closer about her shoulders. He fought the urge to adjust the folds at the back, to allow the shawl to fall straighter and therefore cover her more warmly ... she was nearly home, it would achieve nothing and just embarrass them both.

He noticed her looking keenly into the darkening alleyways as they walked, and the frown between her eyes deepened. 'What are you looking for?'

'Not what, who. A friend.'

'Oh?'

'It seems a bit silly really, seeing as she's a grownup. But she's ... in trouble. If you see what I mean.'

Tristan went cold, but said nothing.

'I wanted to tell her we'd help her,' she went on, 'but I'm certain now that she's run away.'

188

'Help her how?'

'I was going to give her some of the money you paid me for the journals, but she hasn't been to work in two days.'

Tristan couldn't think of a single thing to say. Miss Penhaligon was still casting about as if she would see her friend beneath a covered doorway, or chatting to one of the other townspeople who were hurrying home from work, but he knew she never would, and he had to find a way to tell her so.

'Is she ... a good friend?' he asked, hoping to hear she was not, but he already knew otherwise; Miss Penhaligon had been going to give her money she herself desperately needed, of course they were close.

'To be honest she's my only real friend,' she said. 'Apart from Mairead, and stepsisters don't really count.'

Tristan's heart plummeted further. 'No, of course.' His own voice sounded as if it were coming from someone else, and he put a hand on Miss Penhaligon's arm. She was looking at him now, and didn't complain about the touch ... she must have seen something in his face because she glanced back at the house from which he had emerged.

'That's the constable's house.'

'Yes. Miss Penhaligon, I'm so sorry...'

The sea just kept rolling, uncertain and unpredictable except for the very fact of its presence. James's eyes burned from staring too long into one place, yet he couldn't look away. His father had loved the sea of course, and everyone here depended upon it, it was simply part of life. But how could anyone trust such an ever-changing beast?

Buildings were what they were. They stayed strong if you built them strong, you could walk past the same one every day for a hundred years should you live so long, and see no more change than a weathering of the stone. If you built it well, and cared for it, it would shelter you and keep you safe all your life. But a man could do everything exactly as he should out there on the water, and it would still turn on him in the end; its capricious nature transforming it from sparkling, diamond-strewn beauty to roaring fury in the time it took for a cloud to pass across the sun.

The news had washed over the town in the same way the waves rushed over the shingle here at Porthstennack: with a surge, a noise, a brief moment of supremacy, and then sucked away again, leaving everyone to await the next momentous event. Juliet Carne's short, confused life was over, and her child's with it. Surely he should be feeling something?

He willed his heart towards accepting some kind of grief, or even guilt, but there was nothing but a distant kind of sadness, and a faintly restless sensation that made him shift on the uncomfortable rocks, and break his hot-eyed gaze from the sea.

As he did so he caught sight of two figures standing on the beach near the harbour wall. Unlike the workers, who never stopped moving, these two seemed carved from stone at first, until one of them stepped back and raised her hands to her face. It was only then that he recognised Freya Penhaligon and Mairead Casey. Mairead put her arm around Freya's shoulder, but the way her hand gripped the older girl's arm didn't look like the comforting gesture of a friend, and more as if she was forcing Freya to stay where she was, and not to turn away.

He frowned at the Irish girl's firmness, at a time when Freya's life was falling around her in tatters, but after a moment Freya dropped her hands, and he saw her shoulders come up. Mairead let go, and James relaxed and left them to their business, his thoughts returning instead to everything that had happened.

A visitor in town – apparently the same one who'd stepped into the path of Tom Carne's fury the other night – had found Juliet's body on Wednesday evening, two days ago. As soon as it became obvious that Juliet had been pregnant, and that James had thrown her over, the general acceptance was that the girl had taken her own life. But Constable Couch had been roused from his habitual state of apathy, and begun questioning the town's population. Of course the first person he had come to had been James.

Had Mr Fry known Miss Carne was in the family way?

Yes.

Did Mr Fry know, beyond doubt, that the child was his?

No.

Ah. Does Mr Fry suspect the child was *not* his?

Yes.

How did Mr Fry come to this conclusion?

191

Anna Penhaligon made it known to a mutual friend.
Did Mrs Penhaligon know who fathered the child?
I don't know.
Did Mr Fry visit Miss Carne on Sunday, with the intention of ending their engagement?
No. Yes. Not at first.
What was Miss Carne's reaction? Was she upset?
Yes.
Did Mr Fry consider her to be of a sound mind, after their discussion?
Yes.
Was Mr Fry in a black temper when he left Miss Carne on Sunday?
Yes.
Did Mr Fry see Miss Carne again following their meeting on Sunday?
No.
Does Mr Fry believe Miss Carne might have been unbalanced to the point of ending her own life?
No… Maybe. No.
What does Mr Fry think Miss Carne would have done, given her unfortunate situation?
The Union Workhouse in Truro?
Does Mr Fry feel guilty for putting Miss Carne in that situation?
A little.
Where was Mr Fry when the suspected murder took place?
When was that?
We believe it to have been sometime between Monday night and Tuesday evening.

On Monday evening James had been working on the *Pride of Porthstennack* – a full crew could testify to that – and they'd finished late to catch the last of the sun. The Tinner's Arms had been unusually full that night, James had drunk himself into something approaching a stupor, and had only the vaguest memory of Tom Carne trying to start a fight. Until someone had stepped in, and earned himself a bloodied nose for his trouble. Brian Cornish had brought James back to Porthstennack soon afterwards, where he had fallen asleep on Brian's lumpy settee.

James hadn't even remembered Carne had punched him, until the following morning. He had felt so ill he hadn't managed anything except a spoonful of porridge, thrust on him by Brian's tight-lipped wife, after which he had staggered down to the shore to work. He'd stayed on the beach, unable to face the swell on the sea, but there had been plenty of people around all day who would swear to having seen him. He didn't even care that their testimonies, should they be required, would consist of seeing him quietly puking behind the rocks, and sleeping off a raging headache in the shelter of the breakwater.

But, quite aside from knowing his own innocence, nothing would convince him that Juliet had killed herself. She might have been in a difficult situation, but the people of Caernoweth would have rallied, they wouldn't see her cast out; he knew that from his own past experience, and so would she. If he'd suspected for one minute that his harsh treatment of her would have brought her to such a depth of despair as to take

193

her own life, he'd never have spoken so roughly to her, and he certainly didn't flatter himself that she had done it for the want of his love.

Which left David Donithorn. If she had gone to him in desperation, might he have wanted to silence her? James's skin crept at the thought, but it was the only other explanation. The young man was known to be surly; after the way he'd been turned off the boats he'd loved from early boyhood, it was no surprise. But was he violent? James didn't know him well enough to say, and in any case even the calmest of people sometimes acted, from instinct and self-preservation, in a way they would normally never consider.

'Mr Fry. What's holding your attention so firmly out there?' Mairead's voice pulled him back from the horizon, and he blinked at her. He hadn't even realised they'd walked across to where he was sitting. She followed the direction in which he'd been gazing, but there was nothing out there except whitecaps and seagulls.

'I was just thinking about Juliet.' He turned to Freya, and spoke quietly. 'You have my sympathies, losing a friend is very hard.'

Freya's attention was constantly being pulled towards the water, and her face was pale, as if she expected the next wave to rush up the beach and sweep her away. She swallowed hard, and nodded. 'Thank you, Mr Fry.'

'Please. It's James.'

'James. You must be very upset, too.'

'I'm...' He hesitated, and opted for honesty. 'Sad, more than anything. She was a spirited girl. Hard to believe she would take her own life.' He looked at her searchingly, and she frowned, correctly interpreting his thoughts.

'Is that what you think happened?' she asked.

'No.'

She nodded, looking relieved. 'Have the police spoken to you?'

'They have. I was in a...' He stopped quickly, before he could describe his drunken state; she would recognise that all too well. 'I was in no fit state to be anywhere around people,' he said instead. 'Have they questioned Anna yet?'

'No!' Freya looked shocked. 'Why would they?'

'I had to tell them who it was who told me the child wasn't mine. You did know that, of course?'

'Juliet told me. She accused me of telling you, too.' Freya blinked back tears. 'We fought over it. We never got the chance to make up.'

James bowed his head. 'That must be the hardest thing of all.'

'It is.' She sniffed, and then seemed to remember where she was and took a few quick, instinctive steps away towards the road.

Mairead caught her hand. 'Come back, you're fine. Tide's going out.'

Freya looked at the sea. 'I want to go home. Papá needs me.'

'How is he?' James found the question popping out, with real concern rather than mere politeness.

'He's ... struggling,' Freya said. 'We're helping where we can, but it was a very bad break and the pain keeps him from sleeping.'

'Is there anything I can do?'

Freya looked at him steadily. 'Be his friend.

While you have the chance.'

'I can't,' James said, hearing the helplessness in his own voice. 'We keep trying, but there's always *something*. One of us always breaks whatever flimsy olive branch the other one offers.'

'Then try harder,' Freya said. 'You've been friends since childhood, just like Juliet and me.'

James sighed. 'Your pa doesn't want my friendship, Freya. And I don't blame him. But if I can offer any practical help, please ... come to me. Ask me.'

'Thank you.'

'And tell Anna not to worry about Constable Couch. He's more interested in putting his feet up again than accusing anyone.'

'You're sure he'll want to talk to her, then?'

He nodded. 'And you too, I should think. But as I said, don't worry.'

'Who do you think k-killed her?' Freya stumbled over the word, and James was reminded she was still very young. Mairead held onto her hand, but said nothing. She was even younger than Freya, but there was a strangely mature wisdom about her that James had found quite fascinating in the past, and he saw it again now.

'I would look to David Donithorn,' he said, looking around to ensure they were not being overheard. 'I can't think of anyone else, and can't believe she did it herself.'

'No. She wasn't particularly religious, but I know she'd never do anything that would mean she couldn't be buried in the churchyard with her family.'

'No, this wasn't a suicide.'

196

'Nevertheless that's what we have to tell the constable it was,' Mairead said.

James and Freya stared at her. Freya shook her head. 'What are you talking about?'

'You both know it would be the worst possible thing for my mother to be involved in *any* kind of investigation.'

'God, of course,' James said, 'I hadn't thought. You'll have to come up with a story that takes the attention off her.'

'But what about whoever killed Juliet?' Freya's face was pale. 'He'll get away with it.'

'That can't be helped, if we're to protect Anna.'

'And what about Juliet herself? Don't her wishes mean anything?'

'Juliet's dead,' Mairead said bluntly, and even James flinched. 'But my mother has been given another chance. Freya, you're the one Juliet would have confided in. It *has* to come from you.'

'I have to lie? To condemn my friend to a burial outside the church, in disgrace and with no place waiting in Heaven?'

'Stop it!' Mairead let go of Freya's hand, almost throwing it from her. 'There's no bloody Heaven or Hell! Juliet was a person, and she's gone. She'll be buried for decency's sake, what does it matter which side of a wall she's on?'

'Mairead,' James began, seeing the stricken look on Freya's face.

But Mairead shook her head. 'We'll say words over her if you like. We'll tend her grave. She'll always be part of your childhood and your memories, but she's *dead!* You have the choice now, whether or not to send my mother after her. And if you do, you can be sure you'll be putting her in a grave just as deep, just as cold, and just as unconsecrated.' Breathing hard, Mairead turned her back on Freya and James, and walked a few paces away.

James looked at Freya. 'She didn't mean–'

'Yes. She did. And she's right.' Freya knuckled the tears from her eyes. 'About Anna, at least.'

Mairead turned back to them. Her eyes were as bright as Freya's but it was fear James read in her expression. He wanted to offer her comfort, as she'd offered Freya, but it would be wholly inappropriate. Nevertheless he was disturbed by the strength of his instinct to do so.

'What will you do?' he asked Freya, tearing his own eyes away from the troubled girl.

Freya looked at Mairead, and her voice was barely audible over the crashing tide. 'I'll go and see Constable Couch, and tell him whatever I have to.'

'I'm sorry,' Mairead said. 'That was cruel.' James heard something new in her voice, a kind of realisation. 'I never really understood how words can do that.'

'No one can blame you,' he said. 'You're worried for your ma, we know that.'

'It's all built on sand after all,' Mairead said, sorrow creasing her brow. 'Our life here. All of it. One slip from someone, one wrong word... It was like that when we first left home, but I thought we'd be safe now.'

'You will be.' James tried to make her eyes stay on his, but they slid away and looked out to sea.

'How can you say such a thing, especially now?'

'I'll do what I can,' Freya said. 'I'll go and see the constable.' She turned back to James. 'Don't wait until it's too late,' she repeated.

James nodded, there was no point in telling her again; he and Matthew had set fire to their friendship between them, but if Matthew had laid the kindling, he was the one who had lit the match.

'Try not to worry,' he said to Mairead, instead. 'We'll look after your ma, she's one of ours. You both are.'

She looked at him steadily for a moment, her head tilted slightly; he had the uncomfortable sense that she was measuring his abilities against honest intentions, and finding them wanting. He hoped she was wrong.

The Tinner's Arms

'How are you finding your lodgings, compared to the hotel?'

Tristan looked up from his book and blinked his way back to 1910, but his reluctance faded as he saw Freya Penhaligon, waiting to be invited to sit. She'd had a sad, bemused look about her since the death of her friend, but appeared glad to find company today, and more peaceful in her mind.

He gestured to the chair opposite, and closed the book. 'Doctor Bartholomew is just the kind of host I like, so thank you for telling Teddy about him.'

Freya sat down. 'And what kind of host is it that you like? Attentive? Generous? Keeps a good cellar?'

Tristan grinned. 'The opposite, in fact. Leaves me very much to my own devices. And Mrs Gale makes passable tea, so things couldn't be better, really.'

'And the journals?' Freya gestured to the book on the table. 'I see you're not reading them now. Why not?'

'Good grief!' Tristan stared at her in something close to horror. How could she possibly imagine that bringing such precious things to a smoky, dusty atmosphere would ... then he caught the glint in her eyes. 'Ah, you nearly set me off again.'

'I assure you, at Penhaligon's Attic we do know how to take care of our books,' she said with mock gravity. Then she shifted forward in her seat with curiosity brightening her expression. 'But have you found them of interest? Learned anything new?'

It was impossible not to respond with the same enthusiasm, and he too sat forward, which brought his face quite close to hers. She no longer flinched when she looked at him, which was encouraging, but in the glass this morning he had seen, with rising frustration, that his eyes still looked slitted, and his nose still swollen. Freya was clearly becoming accustomed to his puffy appearance, and he wished it didn't matter to him in any case. But it did. And it had since their first meeting, if he was being honest with himself. Her somewhat fiery annoyance had been a small part of it, another contributing factor had been her poorly concealed delight at her windfall, and he told himself that her natural, unadorned beauty was completely by-the-by ... but that was where honesty failed him.

'I've learned a great deal,' he said, trying not to stare too deeply into her eyes. So dark, soft as velvet, and those lashes... He moved back a little. 'I wanted to talk to you about the journals, as it happens.'

'Oh?'

'Yes, it's recently come to my attention that they might be worth a great deal more than we'd thought at first, so I would like to make a further offer.'

Freya didn't move for a moment, but a light flush came to her smooth cheeks. 'And what made you decide that?'

'Talking to Miss Batten, at Pencarrack. Her family keep all their journals under glass, and – under normal circumstances I'm sure – under close scrutiny. Locked even, for safe-keeping.'

Freya's eyes narrowed. 'You're not saying this because you feel sorry for my family?'

'I don't have the funds to be doling out charity,' Tristan pointed out truthfully. 'If I tell you the books are worth more than we first offered, you can be sure I'm merely trying to pay you what's fair. And I'll take another look at the rest of those books, too.'

There was another silence, while Freya assessed the truth of his words. Around them conversation rose and fell, chairs scraped, glasses thumped onto tables, and there was the odd sound of drinks being poured at the bar. Tristan looked over to see Anna watching him with a speculative frown, and he hurriedly shifted his gaze back to Freya.

'Well?'

Freya's solemn face broke into a smile, and Tristan was mildly alarmed to feel his insides leap at the sight of it. That spelled trouble, and honesty be damned: she was more than pretty. She was probably the most beautiful girl he had ever met. She shook her head, but it was not in refusal, more in bewilderment. 'Then thank you, Mr MacKenzie, I'll hear your offer.'

'Hear it?' He couldn't help an appreciative grin at her sudden move from eager young girl to shrewd businesswoman. 'Do you have others to consider, then?'

'Of course! Hundreds.' Freya assumed a haughty look. 'Only this morning I had two rare book merchants down from London, fighting it out, right in the middle of our shop. Grandpa had to separate them by throwing a jug of water over them. They did cause a fuss.'

Tristan's loud laugh brought another look from Anna, but this time he was relieved to see her own mouth turn up at the corners before she turned away to serve someone. 'You have quite an imagination!'

Freya smiled. 'I must get that from Papá. He used to write fanciful stories when I was little.'

'Ah. And how is Mr Penhaligon?'

'He's improving a little, thank you. Tomorrow he has to go to the mine to talk to the captain about what happened. He's been unable to until now.'

'And do you know yet what caused the explosion?'

'No. He's still confused about it all. He hopes

he'll understand more once he's spoken to them.'

'Sensible, I suppose. My sympathies. It must be very hard for you all.'

'Thank you.'

'On another subject, I thought we'd moved on to first name terms?'

'Not in business,' she told him with a little smile. 'For business purposes you are Mr Mac-Kenzie, world-famous author, and valued customer of Penhaligon's Attic.'

'World-famous!' Tristan snorted. 'But glad to be considered valued, in whatever capacity.'

Their eyes locked, just for a heartbeat, and Tristan looked away hurriedly. 'Now, about those books. Teddy has gone through our finances, and contacted my publisher on my behalf to tell them what a difference it will make to my work. He believes we can afford to offer you another two pounds, on top of what we paid. Does that suit?'

To his alarm, instead of the wide, happy smile he had anticipated, Freya's eyes suddenly filled with tears and he realised she'd been holding her emotions tightly in check until now. She wiped her face with her sleeve, and sniffed.

'I'm sorry,' she said. 'It's just so generous, and–'

'Let's go outside,' Tristan said, rising to his feet. 'Some fresh air, and the privacy to do as much crying as you like. I shan't mind.' His voice had gone a little hoarse, and he wondered how close he was to putting an arm around her, pulling her to him, and letting her weep against his shoulder.

The scrape of his chair on the stone floor drew Anna's attention, and, seeing Freya's tears, she shot a suspicious look at Tristan.

203

'If you've no objection, I'm going to accompany Freya on a little walk,' he said.

'I'm just a bit tired,' Freya said. 'I'm all right.'

Anna looked at the window. 'It's getting dark,' she pointed out. 'Don't go beyond the memorial, or the hotel.'

'We'll stay where it's well lit,' Tristan assured her. He put a hand on Freya's back to guide her through the door ahead of him, and the warmth of her beneath the thin cotton of her work dress almost made him snatch it away again. He'd felt this only once before, and had never dreamed he would again ... but Caroline was gone.

Outside in the lowering dusk, the street thrummed with activity. People were making the most of the day's fast-fading light, hurrying between houses and work places, and the lamplighter was already beginning at the Penworthy memorial. He would work his way up through town, and by the time he reached the top of the hill those lights would be very much needed.

'Shall we?' Tristan nodded down the hill, and Freya nodded. Her tears had dried, and she gave him a faint smile.

'I'm sorry,' she said. 'It just all hit me at once, but we'll be all right, I'm sure. Especially with your generous help.'

Tristan didn't know what to say; he'd never been in the kind of dire financial straits most of these people lived with; the MacKenzies were by no means rich, but they'd always been in work, at least.

'What did you mean when you said Teddy had written to your publisher?' Freya asked.

'Turner and Mitchell have been very generous in their advance payments,' Tristan said. 'Teddy will have laid it on pretty thickly – though with just cause – that these books will make all the difference to my work. So the arrangement is that they will advance me a little extra money, in anticipation of sales, to secure the kind of research I need. They'll wire funds in a day or so.'

'And how long are you planning on staying in Caernoweth?'

'Another week, perhaps. I'm just reaching some intriguing observations in Bartholomew's journals.' He hesitated, then plunged on. 'Perhaps you might be interested in seeing them?'

'I'd like that,' Freya said quietly. She looked at him, and her smile was suddenly shy.

Tristan pictured his restraint like a man stepping off a safe but boring path into a crevasse, scrabbling at the sides but losing the handholds that would keep him on solid ground. He seized one more, stepping away from Freya to look more closely at the plaque on the memorial.

'I'm starting to read some things about this so-called hero that don't quite match up to local opinion.' He looked back at her, expecting to see curiosity of some kind, polite interest at worst, but not that suddenly wary look.

'What sort of things?'

He shrugged. 'I'd need to read further before I say anything, but I'd be very happy to tell you all about it when I have, and I might even find I've grasped the wrong end of the stick.'

'Do you do that a lot?'

He laughed. 'At the very real risk of harming

my reputation, you'd be surprised. Would you like to know what I turn up?'

Freya nodded, though she still looked uncertain. 'I ought to be going home now,' she said, and Tristan flattered himself that she sounded reluctant. 'I only went to the pub to return one of Anna's cooking pots, and Papá and Grandpa will be waiting for their supper.'

'Will you let me walk you up the hill?'

Freya nodded. 'Thank you.' Her voice was soft, and Tristan held out his arm, feeling his insides tighten with the anticipation of her touch. Freya slipped her hand around it, resting her fingertips lightly on his wrist.

'Shall I bring the journals to the shop tomorrow morning?' he asked, wishing for the first time that this ridiculously steep hill was twice as long.

'Perfect. I'll expect you,' Freya said. Was that a suddenly increased pressure from her hand? It was taking all his self-control not to bring his arm closer to his side.

All too soon they arrived at Penhaligon's Attic. This time when Freya looked at him, Tristan saw something of his own feelings reflected in her little frown of regret. She slid her hand out from under his arm, but she did so very slowly. His heartbeat quickened, and from a great distance he heard himself say, 'I've never met anyone like you before.'

Freya didn't answer and, as he looked at her anxiously for some clue as to her reaction, he saw her lips close on a smile, and her luxuriant eyelashes sweep down as she lowered her face.

'I mean to say,' he stumbled on, abandoning all

the handholds afforded him now, 'everything I've seen of you only convinces me more.'

She raised her eyes to his again. 'Convinces you of what?'

'That you're quite, quite extraordinary.'

Freya looked at him, open-mouthed, then laughed. 'I shall take that as a compliment, although for the life of me I don't know why!'

'Please do.' Tristan smiled back, feeling faintly foolish, but glad to have at least lessened the pressure in his chest, no matter how clumsily. 'Well, I'd better go back to my books, but I look forward to showing you my findings tomorrow. Shall we say around ten o'clock?'

'Can you come at nine?' Freya's flush was picked up by the newly lit gas light above them. 'I mean, I don't want to rush through things, and I have extra hours at the hotel. If that's not too early for you,' she added.

He nodded. 'Nine it is.' Best not to tell her he would be happy to camp out on the doorstep until first light, but the thought made him smile as he said goodbye and turned back down the hill. An impulse made him turn back, to see that Freya had not yet gone inside but stood with one hand on the door handle, her eyes following him. He raised a hand, and she raised hers in return, and Tristan returned to his room at Doctor Bartholomew's house with a light step, and a lighter heart.

Tomorrow he would make a better job of what he wanted to tell her.

Chapter Twelve

Wheal Furzy

'Sit, lad.' Tobias gestured to the single chair in his office, and Matthew accepted without demur. He felt more than a little light-headed after the walk, and his entire right side throbbed, making him feel queasy and unsteady. Tobias gave him a moment to gather himself, and then opened a large notebook that lay on the table between them. The facing pages were covered in messy writing in three blocks of blue, black and green, and a space remained at the end of the second page.

Tobias uncorked a bottle of red ink. 'Right. I've talked to the others. Davey's account's in blue, Tommy's black, Alan's green, what there is of it. Just your piece missin' now. So tell me what you remember.'

Matthew had done little else but think about what he would say when the question was laid at his feet. He could vividly remember the horror of seeing one short fuse, sparks coming off it, burning away to nothing before his eyes. Just thinking about it made him swallow hard and close his eyes.

He also remembered Donithorn's face. And if he'd had the slightest suspicion that the younger man could have done this deliberately, he would have said so, but Donithorn had told him and Tommy to make themselves scarce; he had no way of knowing that Tommy's financial problems would have persuaded either of them to return for the boy's coat.

Whatever had happened, and whatever had been on Donithorn's mind, he was no danger to anyone now and nothing would be gained by having him sacked. Besides, Matthew owed the man a livelihood, and now was his chance to put that right.

'Last thing I remember is fetching Tommy's coat,' he said. His eyes met Tobias's, and did not flinch away. No one could dispute a man's memory, after all. 'After that I woke up on the table here, and my arm was already fixed as it is now. I'm told the doctor gave me something for the pain that addled my head a bit. I don't know what I might have said but it likely meant nothing.'

'I see.' Tobias scribbled quickly, the ink sprawling across the page like freshly spilled blood. 'Who cut the fuses for the blast?'

'I don't know. I was out by the shaft finishing crib.'

'So t'wadn't you, then?'

'No.'

'Were it Davey?'

'I don't know,' Matthew repeated patiently. 'I wasn't there.'

Tobias stopped writing, and stared at the page without speaking. He shifted his attention to the scrawl of blue. 'Now then.' He looked at Matthew. 'Did you take the ladders that day?'

'I did, yes.'

'And the others went on the hoist?' Matthew nodded, and Tobias went on, 'Someone reported a loose rod, so the hoist was stopped and the rest of the shift took to the ladders too. That right?'

'So I gather.'

'Now then. Young Davey did say he picked up the fuses *you* cut, when you got there ahead of everyone.'

Matthew felt as if he'd been punched. 'I didn't cut them.' *The black-hearted bastard...*

'And him sayin' that,' Tobias went on, 'does it maybe shake your memory about a bit? I mean, if he's passin' the blame on to you–'

'No,' Matthew said, with a hard edge to his voice. 'I told you, I wasn't there.' He grasped the edge of the desk and pulled himself to his feet. He wasn't ready to walk anywhere yet, but he had to get out of this office before he lost his temper, and his job along with it. Assuming he still had one.

Before he could announce his intention to leave, however, the door opened and Donithorn came in. He looked from Matthew to Tobias and back again. 'Pen'aligon. You doin' all right?'

'Tell him,' Matthew said, through gritted teeth, ignoring the question. 'Go on, tell him you were lying.'

Donithorn's eyes widened. 'Lying?'

'I didn't cut the bloody fuses!' Matthew sat down again, too heavily, and his back flared with pain where the deep muscle damage was trying to heal. He closed his eyes to stop the room from tilting.

'I never said you did,' Donithorn said, puzzled. 'I said I didn't remember.'

'What?' Matthew opened his eyes again and looked at Tobias, who flushed. He shook his head, anger pulsing in his temples. 'I had you down for decent.'

Tobias met his furious stare without flinching. 'I had to make sure you was tellin' the truth.'

'So you thought you'd trick me? And if you'd spoken to me first, you think *he* would have stuck to the truth?' he gestured at Donithorn.

'I would have,' Donithorn said. He seemed a different man from the one Matthew had known; he looked lost, and it was hardly any wonder, with his livelihood on the verge of being destroyed. Matthew was struck by the twelve-year-old guilt for the last time he had ruined the man's life.

Donithorn took a deep breath, but Matthew spoke up quickly. 'You can't be blamed for not remembering anything, Donithorn, it was a hell of a time. If the fuse was faulty, none of us is to blame.'

'Faulty?' Tobias frowned. 'First I've heard of it. Alan Trevellick said he thought it was short.'

Matthew met his gaze squarely. 'Alan wasn't there when it was cut either, he was answering a call of nature. Did anyone recover the coil from the level?'

'No, it was buried,' Donithorn said. He was eyeing Matthew thoughtfully, and a faint colour had returned to his cheeks. He cleared his throat. 'I recall it did smell a bit off, now you mention it.'

'For Christ's sake!' Tobias ground out. 'You came here to tell the truth!' Then he shook his head, scowling. 'Ah, get on with you both. You were the only ones hurt, and if you're goin' to cover for one another why the hell should I waste any more time? Davey, get back and finish your shift. Penhaligon?' His voice changed again, now tinged with weary acceptance. 'Go home, lad. Rest up. So far as I'm concerned your job'll be here waitin' when you're fit, but don't forget, they'll be slow-goin' while you mend, so if Davey here wants to take on that's his choice. I can't answer for him.'

He looked at the two younger men, and then, still shaking his head, he left the office and slammed the door behind him, shutting out the worst of the noise from beyond. There was a silence between Matthew and Donithorn, and eventually Donithorn spoke.

'That was a good thing you did.'

'I'm sorry I accused you of lying.'

'Not your fault, t'was Toby.'

Another pause fell, then Matthew rose again, more steadily this time. 'Look, I don't know what it was that had you away with the fairies down there, but I've got my suspicions, and if anyone comes to me and asks, I'll have to tell them.'

Donithorn frowned. 'Suspicions?'

'Juliet.'

'What? I didn't find out she was dead 'til Wednesday.'

'That's my point. No one knew about it, except whoever it was who killed her.' He shrugged. 'You were distracted that whole shift.'

Donithorn went white. 'You're one of the few who knows the truth, d'you think I'd kill my own *child?'* He choked on the word, and Matthew frowned; he hadn't considered that part of it.

'All right, but then why–'

'Besides, I've got witnesses'll tell you, *Constable Penhaligon*, that I was workin' double shift on Monday night.'

'Double shift?'

'When we finished work on the two thirty-six level, and you went scuttlin' off to your nice cosy supper at home, Ginny brought me my supper here, in a box. Then I went to the new shaft and put in another eight hours. Maybe that's why, Tuesday, I *was away with the bloody fairies!* You should try it, see how you cope on no sleep and two and a half shifts.'

Matthew studied him for a moment, then nodded. 'I'm glad,' he said truthfully.

'Juliet killed herself. I don't like to think of it, and I don't doubt I had something to do with it. But I didn't kill her. I swear on my own life, and on...' Donithorn cast about for something convincing to say. 'And on the lode we work,' he finished, and Matthew bit back an unexpected smile.

'The lode, eh? Well, that's convinced me.'

'Wait,' Donithorn said. 'Before you go.'

'What?'

Donithorn took a deep breath, and met Matthew's gaze. 'What happened down there. It *was* my fault, we both know that. But I won't make that mistake again.'

'I know you won't. I saw your face before the blast. Otherwise I wouldn't have covered for you.'

'I take the blame for what happened to you, and

I'm that sorry for it.' Donithorn gestured at Matthew's strapped arm, just a bump beneath his shirt. 'And for you keepin' quiet about the fuse, I'm grateful. But ... this don't make us friends.'

'No. But does it at least make us even?'

Donithorn hesitated, then nodded. 'I reckon.'

'Then that's good enough.' Matthew pulled open the door, and flinched at the brightness of the sun that spilled into the room. 'If you need to take on, do it. If not, I'll be back when I can lift a hammer again.'

'Go careful,' Donithorn said, and despite the younger man's assertion that they would never be friends, his words were a curtain, closing gently on a part of Matthew's past that had haunted him for more than a decade. The past was gradually healing, the present was difficult but manageable... Heaven only knew what the future had in store, but at least he had one.

On Saturday morning Freya dressed with a great deal of care. Later she would visit the place where Juliet had been laid to rest in a quick, business-like burial, without a service and outside the consecrated ground of the churchyard, thanks to the need to protect Anna. What most people didn't know, and wouldn't have spared a thought for, was that today was Juliet's twentieth birthday. There was nothing Freya could do about where her friend was buried, but she could at least make sure she wasn't alone today.

It was exactly nine o'clock, and she had just twisted a small bunch of wild flowers together and tied it with a narrow ribbon, when the door

214

opened and Tristan came in.

'Good morning,' he said, returning her hesitant smile. 'I hope I find you well?'

Freya put the posy aside. 'Good morning. You keep good time.' For a moment she couldn't place what was different, then, as he came closer she realised she could see his eyes properly; the swelling had gone down overnight, and the only remnant of his foolish intervention on Monday was the healing cut across the bridge of his nose.

'You're looking well yourself,' she said. 'Quite different.' *And you have the most astonishing eyes I have ever seen...* She lowered her gaze, embarrassed in case he had read the unspoken words in her face, and gestured at the books he carried. 'I see you've only brought two with you.'

'The first and the second.' He put them on the counter. 'To show you the difference, and what I've found.'

'About Penworthy.'

He nodded. 'It's ... interesting.'

'Will *I* find it interesting, or disturbing?'

'I suppose that depends on how determined you are to hold on to false stories concerning your town's past.' He read her frown correctly, and went on, 'Look, there's no doubt he was a hero, he saved the life of the man who wrote these.' He gestured to the carefully wrapped journals. 'Probably a number of people besides. And he did provide housing for his tenants at extremely low rents, and helped the town to flourish. But after that, accounts have clearly been muddled along the way.'

'Then I'd suggest we keep whatever it is you've

215

found between us, at least for the time being.'

'Agreed.' Tristan looked relieved that she hadn't shut him out. She was finding it hard now to look at him without staring ... it had been so much easier when she couldn't see his eyes. They were the most vivid and arresting green, and fringed by thick dark lashes that only enhanced their colour by comparison. His entire face was changed; the reduction of the swelling revealed a beauty of bone structure that suddenly invited her touch, and she pressed the tips of her fingers together, amused and a little shocked.

'How did you get the swelling to go down at last?' she asked, busying herself with straightening a pile of lists that stood on the counter ready to post.

'Tea,' Tristan said, and she turned in surprise to see him grinning. 'Doctor Bartholomew has it delivered from London in little pouches, and Mrs Gale chilled two of them, then told me to lie down and put them on my eyes. I couldn't imagine it would work, but then nothing else had, so there was nothing to lose but an hour's reading.' He shrugged. 'I woke this morning to find they had done the trick. She says she's used it often on her grandchildren when they get into scrapes.'

'And is the pain lessened too?'

'Very much so. I just have to be careful not to sneeze without bracing myself first.'

Freya laughed. 'Then it's a good thing you'll soon be heading back to Plymouth, since the barometer tells me we're expecting rain soon.'

'Yes, a good thing.' But Tristan sounded less than convinced, and Freya's insides gave the

216

same little twist they had last night, when she'd put her hand around his arm to walk home. She took a deep breath, ready to shatter all this polite pretence between them, but he spoke first.

'Freya, I said last night that I found you extraordinary. What I should have said was that I like you, very much.'

'Well thank goodness for that.' Freya smiled at the look on his face. 'I was getting a bit bored by all the dithering.'

'Dithering? We only met a few days ago!'

'True enough. But the day you came in here to buy these, with your face all messy and dripping blood everywhere, not to mention giving me what-for about the way I run my father's business–'

'I'm sorry about that. I realised soon enough I'd got that wrong.'

'You didn't say so,' Freya pointed out. 'Anyway, I saw something. Enthusiasm. I understood it, and I liked it.'

He grinned. 'So you weren't drawn to my noble, handsome features then?'

'It was hard to know which drew me the most,' Freya said thoughtfully, 'the way you growled at me, or the fact you looked like a street wrestler. But in the end I ignored both, and...' She broke off, suddenly shy.

'And?' he prompted gently. 'Life is short, Freya. Tell me.' He reached out and took her hand, and she wrapped her fingers around his. It felt completely natural.

'And, I trusted my instincts about you.'

'Good,' he whispered, and lifted her hand to his lips.

Freya almost tugged it away, aware of her rough, work-reddened skin, but the press of his lips left a feeling of warmth that spread right through her. Instead she took an unconscious step closer, only realising what she'd done as he lifted his head again, and his face was close enough for her to feel the faint stirring of his breath on her skin as he let out a sigh and stepped back.

'The journals,' he said, but with clear reluctance for the first time since he'd first seen them. He seemed to gradually become aware that he still held her hand, but instead of letting go he gave it a gentle squeeze, and then cupped it in both of his. 'Perhaps later I could walk you to work?'

'That would be ... oh.' She subsided. 'I nearly forgot. I'm not going straight to work, I have something to do first. Another time, perhaps?'

'I could walk you to wherever you're going, then?'

Freya recovered some of her composure, and smiled. 'You are quite insistent, aren't you?'

'I feel we've wasted enough time with our "dithering", don't you?' he countered. 'Let me walk with you. Please?'

But as much as she wanted it, she shook her head. 'I couldn't ask you to. It's not something ... nice.'

'Visiting your friend?' he said softly.

She blinked. 'How did you guess?'

'These.' He picked up the twist of wild flowers and put it in her hand. 'Go now, you'll only feel the need to rush if you're on your way to work.' He wrapped her fingers around the stems, and dropped a kiss on her temple. 'I'll mind the shop.

Take your time.'

'It's her birthday today,' Freya said quietly. 'She was a wild one, but she had the best heart. People didn't know it, but she did.'

'She had your friendship, that's all the recommendation she needed.' He drew her closer. Her arms remained at her sides, one hand still clutching the flowers, and it was at this moment the shop door opened and Papá's voice sliced across the room.

'What the hell...? Let her go, man!'

Freya stiffened and went to move away, but Tristan's hands tightened, holding her against him.

'She's upset, sir. Give her a moment, please.'

'Papá, this is Tristan MacKenzie,' Freya said. To her mingled relief and disappointment, Tristan at last released his hold. 'He's the one who bought the Bartholomew journals.'

Papá's gaze dropped to the flowers she held. 'Juliet's birthday,' he said. 'Of course.'

'You remembered?'

Papá gave her a little smile. 'Don't *you* remember? The day she turned seven was the same day I renamed my boat after your ma. You misheard me when I was explaining that the *Julia* was now the *Isabel,* and you spent the next three days trying to convince Juliet that I'd given her a new name for her birthday.'

Freya found an unexpected smile breaking through her tears. 'I'd forgotten. Juliet wasn't at all pleased.'

'No,' Papá said. 'But your mama was.' He gestured at Tristan. 'So this is how you treat our customers is it? No wonder the shop's doing better.'

Freya could tell Tristan was about to react with indignation on her behalf, and she spoke up first, knowing her father's humour somewhat better. 'You know full well it's not! It's true he was only comforting me just now. But he and I are getting to know one another.'

'Quite well, it seems.'

'Papá!'

He relented. 'A scholar, eh? Much preferable to the landed gentry.' He held out his left hand to shake Tristan's, missing Freya's startled look at the reference to Hugh. 'If you're going to be paying visits to my daughter in future, Mr MacKenzie, we ought to at least get to know one another.'

'Tristan's going to mind the shop,' Freya said, preparing to leave. 'Mairead will be here before noon, Tristan. You won't be inconvenienced any longer than that.'

'No inconvenience at all.'

'And I'm here, don't forget,' Papá put in. 'I might not be able to do much, but I can open a cash drawer if it's needed.'

'You're supposed to be resting,' Freya told him sternly. 'You won't mend if you're constantly doing things. How did it go at the mine?'

'It seems the fuse was faulty.' He was clearly disinclined to say anything more, but he looked easier in himself, and Freya took that to be a good sign.

She said her goodbyes and left the men together in the shop, and walked slowly up the hill, past the chapel, and out into the rough ground beyond the cemetery wall. No headstone marked the spot where Juliet lay, but she was surprised to see someone had erected a roughly made cross, and painted Juliet's name and dates on it. Likely that was Tom since the two of them had no one else to care. She knelt beside it, and placed the flowers she'd brought alongside those that had been left by Juliet's brother.

'Happy birthday,' she whispered, then sank back onto her heels, and set her mind free to play with all the memories, good and bad, of a lifetime of friendship.

She didn't see Tristan again until the evening and, with the shop quiet, and the day drawing to a close, they sat quietly together in the kitchen at Penhaligon's Attic. Grandpa was at Brian Cornish's; Brian would bring him back in John Rodda's pony trap later. Papá had also considerately made himself scarce, and gone to the Tinner's, where he would sit in the back room and read.

Freya watched Tristan's face as he carefully unwrapped the books, enjoying his look of reverence and pleasure.

'The first of these was written by John Bartholomew himself, in his own hand,' he said. 'Look.' He pushed it across, and she looked at it with growing fascination. It was dated 1643, and the first entry had been made in April of that year.

Freya squinted at the writing: close-packed, and with sentences written sideways on the paper as well as in the normal way. Every part of the paper had been utilised, but it made it very hard to read.

Tristan took it back and found a sentence to read aloud. 'The spelling and the language is quite different to what we're used to,' he said, 'but roughly it says: "We have taken the shilling, and march to Sourton Down..." Actually, the "we" he refers to might be an ancestor of yours, he's named as Stephen Penhaligon.'

'Yes, that's likely,' Freya said, 'our ancestors were Royalists. Several were killed over Bude way, we think.'

Tristan nodded. 'Stratton Hill. The very battle-field from which John Bartholomew was brought back, along with another man named Trevannion, by Malcolm Penworthy. He'd been blinded, and Penworthy risked life and limb, when he was wounded himself, to drag him back to safety. After that, his son took over the writing of the journals, but John continued to dictate them. You can see the difference in the writing, look.'

He opened the other book, and turned it to show her. The writing was lacking in practice, more scrawled, uncertain, and blotched many times with puddles of ink. But as the book progressed it became neater, although still very different from his father's.

'Well then, what is it you've found against Penworthy?' Freya asked. 'It still sounds as though he was quite heroic.'

'I'm still working my way through,' Tristan confessed. 'But it seems that after the war, Penworthy developed an unhealthy liking for a young local girl. A Sarah Trevellick.'

'Trevellick? One of Esther and Joe's ancestors,

it must be.' Then she frowned. 'An unhealthy liking?'

'It didn't seem to start out as such. Penworthy was troubled by his wound for several years, and she was a gifted healer.' Tristan turned the pages of the second book with extreme care, searching for the right part. 'It says here that John had been granted a cottage on Penworthy's land. I think it might have been that which later became the top of town, just near the hotel. Anyway, it was close to Penworthy's home. Close enough so that...' He broke off. 'I'm not sure I should go on with this.'

'I think you ought to.'

Tristan looked at her a moment, his eyes searching hers, and she nodded at him to continue. He sighed. 'Well, he would go to Bartholomew's cottage, claiming he didn't want to distress his wife by letting her witness his pain, and have the girl visit him there. Bartholomew might have been blind, but he was neither deaf nor insensible, and while the girl tended Penworthy's wound he heard Penworthy make several ... indecent suggestions. All rebuffed, of course.'

'Then why did she continue to go back?' Freya asked, dry-mouthed.

'She didn't, at first. Her twin brother Sebastian tried to go in her place, but, as it says here: "the Master was filled with ire that Sebastian did visit rather than the girl. He swore never to pay one penny 'til she did return." So she went back. Her brother used to wait beside the gate for her to finish, then walk her home.'

'And Penworthy continued to ... to bother her?'

'I don't know,' he confessed. 'I haven't had the

chance to read further yet. But it's likely he would have continued with his attentions. Or worse.'

'But if Bartholomew's son was having all this dictated to him, why didn't *he* do anything to stop it?'

'You have to remember the attitudes of the time,' Tristan said. 'You and I know the man's behaviour was unacceptable, but the girl was unharmed, and at fourteen she was of marriageable age. Besides, there was the cottage ... Penworthy would have a great hold over Bartholomew, even amounting to life or death.'

'Will you tell me what else you find out?'

'Of course.'

'And...' Freya glanced at the door, although she knew they were alone, 'you mustn't let anyone else know about this.'

'But it's history!' Tristan looked honestly puzzled. 'Surely even though this man's held as some kind of shining example, it couldn't hurt to let people know he was human after all? It can't do anyone any harm now.'

'It might! Anna is directly descended from him. She's certain the town has only accepted her because of her lineage, so if people find out the truth it would throw a very ugly light on things. It sounds silly, but Anna would be the one to suffer by it.'

'Oh, come on now, that's just–'

'There are people here who still don't trust her.'

'*Trust* her?' Tristan looked blank. 'Is there something I ought to know?'

'She's an outsider, that's all.' Freya could hardly

believe how close she had come to blurting out something she shouldn't have. But he ought to know as much as the rest of Caernoweth did, at least; someone else would be happy enough to tell him and much better if it came from her.

'Anna and Mairead came here under ... difficult circumstances.'

'Freya.' He put his hands on her shoulders, firmly enough to prevent her turning away, even if she'd wanted to. 'Before you decide whether to tell me anything, listen to what I'm going to say to you.' He took a quick breath, then pushed on. 'I have only once before felt what I'm feeling for you, which is how I know it for what it is. I'll tell you about Caroline one day, but just for now I'm going to tell you she's gone.'

Freya's heart contracted at the look in his eyes. 'I'm–'

'I loved her with my entire, sorry soul. It hurt like the devil, and I never thought I would be lucky enough to feel that pain again.' He kissed her brow. 'It doesn't matter that we don't know each other yet, nor that you have secrets you need to keep to yourself. I can never be a part of your past, but I very much hope you'll let me be in your future.'

He leaned in close and their lips brushed, barely a touch at all, and his fingers caressed her jaw, holding her at that same, tantalising distance.

Freya wanted to keep her eyes open, to watch how the little line between his thick, straight eyebrows deepened with the effort of restraint, but she could no longer choose how her body reacted. The kiss became firmer, deeper, and as his hands dropped from her face to her shoulders again, her eyes closed, shutting out everything that didn't matter.

A marching band might have played outside the window; the door might have opened to admit a cavalry charge; Papá might have struck up a one-man-band with saucepans on the table ... Freya would have noticed none of it. It wasn't until Tristan at last broke away that she came back to her senses.

'Well...' she managed, but no more words followed for a while, and they both remained silent, side by side at the table, absorbing the remnants of such an intense moment.

'Can I assume you have some of those same feelings then?' Tristan said at last, though his smile told her he was confident of her reply.

'Well, I don't *dis*like you,' she said slowly, considering him with her head slightly tilted. 'You're a little bit more handsome than you were, which helps.'

'Ah, but you tolerated my company before, when I had the look of a lump of dough about me,' he reminded her. 'Which proves it's not my appearance that draws you.'

'And how can I know it's not *my* appearance that draws *you?*'

'My darling, it's entirely your appearance. I care absolutely nothing for good humour, gentleness, common sense, kindness, generosity, or selflessness.' After each word he kissed a different part of her face, finishing with the tip of her nose and making her laugh. She found her thoughts going to Juliet, and her reasons for giving in to the wishes of the men who'd bedded her: *'I want to relax when I like someone, and the best way to do that is to ... to get it out of the way.'* If Freya had met Tristan a week ago she'd have been able to tell Juliet it was laughter that created that bond, not the giving of her body. But she'd discovered it for herself too late to help her friend.

She looked at Tristan, who was watching her with a new light in his eyes, but wearing a more solemn expression, waiting for her to begin her story. He moved his chair still closer, and eventually she started to tell him about Anna and Mairead, but it took all her concentration to keep the story as the rest of the town knew it: that Anna was the one Liam Cassidy had attacked; Anna who'd wielded the rock and struck the killing blow; and that, as far as everyone outside the town, and still a good many in it, knew, Anna Casey was dead and buried. Anna Penhaligon was someone else entirely.

He remained silent when she'd finished, and Freya watched him anxiously, wondering if she'd done the right thing after all. She'd discovered he had a very strong sense of right and wrong but could only hope it would lead him to accept what was morally right, over what the law dictated.

Aware her hands were becoming sweaty, she removed the one that lay on Tristan's arm, and the movement brought him back into the moment. 'You have my word I won't pass any of this on.'

She slumped in relief. 'Not even to Teddy?'

'Especially not to Teddy.'

'Why especially?'

Tristan gave her a little grin. 'He seems to have formed a bit of an attachment to Miss Lucy Batten. And, dare I say it, she seems to return it. I would imagine the very last people you'd want anything getting out to would be the Battens.'

'You'd imagine right,' Freya said. 'In which case no. Definitely not Teddy.'

The sound of hooves outside drove them apart and Freya rose. 'That'll be Grandpa.' She brushed down her skirt and went to make sure the front door was unlocked, and when she came back in Tristan had closed both journals, and was wrapping them back up.

'Your grandpa has a pony?'

'Not anymore. He lost it back along, while I was living in London. He gave the trap to John Rodda, so in return Mr Rodda lets him use his pony now and again.'

Tristan raised an eyebrow. 'I could tell from your accent that you didn't do all your growing up here, but London! Very impressive.'

'Not really. Mama and I moved there for a while after her and Papá separated.'

'I'm sorry to hear about that. It must have been difficult.'

'I missed Papá. Mama did too, I know that, but she could never settle here, she always wanted more. That hasn't changed, I don't think. Sometimes I think she'll never be really happy.'

Tristan piled the books carefully on the table. 'And you? Do you take after her, or your father?'

'Actually I think I'm more like Granny Grace, Papá's mother. She was determined to make a success of Penhaligon's Attic, and put everything

228

she had into it.'

'Well that certainly sounds like you,' Tristan said with a smile. 'It's common enough for strong characteristics to get passed down through several generations. Good as well as bad. I know I said I'm not looking to rake over your past, but I'd like to hear more about your family sometime.'

'You will.' She moved closer again, eager to make him talk a little longer. 'It's your turn. Tell me a little about *your* family.'

'My family.' Tristan shook his head. 'If you're looking for a tale of woe, you've found it. In brief, my father's in America with one of my two brothers, and my stepmother, my sister Sophie and my half-sister are all back in Honiton. Making lace, of all vitally important things.'

'So your parents are apart too.'

'Not through Dad's choice. Catherine, my stepmother, came back to England when she fell pregnant with my half-sister. Janet's six now, and Sophie's thirteen, but Catherine still refuses to rejoin Dad. She says it's too dangerous. She's probably right.'

'What's he doing in America?'

'Running a paper mill. Probably into the ground.' He glanced past her at the door that led out to the hall. It was still closed, and he reached for Freya's hand, pulled her close with a jolt that fell just short of roughness, and fastened his mouth on hers. She responded by tangling her hands in his hair and leaning against him. He stilled, just for a moment, then his hold on her tightened.

The slam of the front door was their signal to

break apart again. Tristan released her so slowly she was sure Grandpa would walk in while they were still indecently close to one another.

But by the time the kitchen door opened, Tristan was safely on the other side of the kitchen, his books in his hand, and a polite smile in place. He spoke for a few minutes with Grandpa, and then Freya walked with him out into the porch. The farewell kiss he dropped on her forehead was chaste and sweet, but she only had to look at his face to know that whatever happened between them would be more than simply 'getting it out of the way'.

Chapter Thirteen

In the late afternoon of the first Wednesday in August, Matthew sat in the shop that had been his mother's joy and her pride, and that his daughter loved and worked so hard for, and tried to absorb some of that pleasure. He ought to be grateful, after all; he was alive; he was mending; he had a job waiting for him when he was well enough... He could hear Anna in the kitchen even now, muttering over one of Grace Penhaligon's recipes, and that made him smile; she'd seemed tense lately, and he didn't like to think it was he who'd put the shadows beneath her eyes, but his conscience was pricked every time he saw them. Quite apart from the pain of knitting bones, and fading bruises, reaching the end of each day sober and of positive mind was proving a struggle he dared not tell anyone about.

He put down the book he'd been reading, and levered himself off the chair. Now he'd become used to keeping his arm still, and curbed the instinct to use it, he was finding it easier to move around. The dressings on his back needed changing less often, and the same with his legs, but there was a deep ache that had settled in at his collarbone and spread through his right side. Likewise his upper back, just below the shoulder, gave him frequent, eye-watering pain, and although he'd been told to expect it, it still struck him breathless now and again.

To counter the inactivity he experimented with a few twists of his upper body, and although he stifled his groan when he pushed it too far, Anna had heard and was at the kitchen door a second later, her face dusted with flour and looking cross.

'What are you trying to do now?'

'Move,' he grumbled.

She sighed and came over to him. 'Love, be patient. No sense trying to run before you can walk.'

'Walk?' He put his good left arm around her and drew her to him. 'That sounds like a good idea. I can manage that, at least. Come with me.'

'Your da is upstairs sleeping.' She held him tightly around the waist. 'I love that we're spending more time together, but I understand how hard it is for you.' She drew back, and as her eyes searched his he realised that keeping his daily battle with temptation from her was pointless –

of course she knew, even if she didn't utter the words.

He rested his forehead against hers. 'Don't worry about me,' he said quietly. 'I'll do everything right this time.'

'I know you will,' she whispered, holding him close again. 'I trust you completely.'

He gently stroked the back of her head, and she sighed with contentment. 'Go on then,' she said at length, and with obvious reluctance. 'Get some fresh air while it's still dry out.'

'I'll go down to the beach and see if Brian's about.' He let her go and unhooked his waistcoat from the back of his chair. 'Will you come to meet me, when Pa wakes?'

'I will.' Anna smiled. 'I like how things go when I meet you from your walks.'

Matthew chuckled. 'You might have to wait a little longer for that sort of thing.' He started to button his waistcoat one-handed, and glanced at the greying skies through the window. 'Rain tonight. Have you got anything you want help with, before it starts?'

Anna shook her head. 'Mairead's keeping an eye on the laundry at the pub, and it's all safely gathered in here. Go on then, if you don't want a wetting on your way home.' She helped him with the last button, and handed him his hat. 'I'll see you soon.'

Matthew gradually loosened up as he walked, and made up his mind to do more of it as he fought his way back to full recovery. He was passing Hawthorn Cottage, with no more than a mildly curious glance at the place he'd once been so glad to have found for his new young family, when someone called his name. John Gilbert's widow, Nancy, was hurrying across the yard to the gate.

'I'm that glad I caught you,' she said, shielding her eyes from what remained of the thin sunshine, and looking up at Matthew. She had a high colour in her cheeks, and was breathing quite hard, and one hand rested at her breastbone. 'I in't used to runnin' that fast, except when Matty's climbin' the wall.'

Matthew smiled politely, keen to resume his walk, but it looked as if Mrs Gilbert needed help with something. 'What can I do for you? I only have the one arm though, as you see.'

'Of course, I'd heard. How are you?' she asked, her voice dropping into a soft, concerned tone.

'Mending, thank you.'

'I'm glad to hear it.' Mrs Gilbert's eyes, an unusually light blue, even for one with such light-coloured hair, held Matthew's until he felt obliged to feign a cough, just to break the contact.

'How can I help, Mrs Gilbert?'

'You can start by callin' me Nancy,' she said, and smiled. 'Then after you've mastered that, perhaps you could come in and look at the hatch to the attic?'

'Well I can look, but your landlord should make any repairs. The house is still owned by the Battens, I take it?'

'Yes, but t'idn't so much repairs.' Nancy un-latched the gate to allow Matthew into the yard. 'It's only that you lived here for so long, an' I'm

233

sure there's a knack to gettin' the hatch to shut tighter. Before the winter sets in, you know? It do rattle in the wind, and the little ones sleep right under it.'

Matthew was more than a little unnerved by the way Nancy was looking at him. He thought back to the way he and Isabel had managed when they'd lived here. 'It doesn't shut properly at first. So when it feels like you've slid the bolt all the way, you'll probably notice it just needs an extra push until it's properly in.'

Nancy's sudden wicked grin made him groan inwardly at his choice of words. She was even more forward than he'd thought.

'Can you show me?' She held out her hands, their long, slender fingers red with detergent and hard work, but not at all strong-looking. 'If there's a knack it'd help to see it.'

Matthew looked up the hill, in the vain hope of seeing Anna, but Pa hadn't been asleep long, he'd be another hour at least before he could take over minding the shop.

'I won't keep you,' Nancy went on.

Matthew sighed. 'That's all right,' he said. 'We're in for a summer storm before long, so best to get it sorted now. Lead the way.'

'As if you don't know it!' Nancy gestured for him to go ahead, and he heard her latch the gate shut behind him. He chided himself for the way his heartbeat quickened at the sound. What was he expecting her to do?

In the cottage, however, the smile fell away. From the outside, it was just a building, much like the others that dotted the hillside between

Porthstennack and Caernoweth, not exactly the same, but still, just a house. Inside, he was struck by memory after memory as he passed through the small living room: Isabel, sitting curled up by the fire late at night, her dark hair gleaming, her eyes soft on his, inviting him with an outstretched hand. Isabel again, those same beautiful eyes filled with tears when she thought he wasn't looking, rubbing lard into her knuckles to heal the broken skin. Freya, wobbly in her first steps, crowing with triumph when she reached the settee, and with her tiny face screwed tight in fury when she was denied extra playtime.

'Are you all right?'

He turned. Nancy was standing closer than he'd realised, so lost had he been in the past.

He swallowed. 'Yes. Come on, I'll show you how to fix the hatch.'

'I don't want to put you to any trouble.' She followed him through to the hall, and up the stairs. The room he had once shared with Isabel was now where Nancy's four children slept, being the bigger of the two bedrooms, and the entrance to the attic was in the centre of the ceiling. Matthew determinedly kept his eyes away from where his and Isabel's bed had been.

Nancy stood at his side, her arm brushing his. Looking down, he noticed her breathing had not slowed after her run to catch him on the road, her chest still rose and fell rapidly, and when she turned her face onto him, he realised his suspicions had been right after all. The flush on her pale cheeks, and the sparkle in her eyes, were both unmistakeable; Matthew was not a vain man, but he had seen this look before.

'Nancy ... Mrs Gilbert, I–'

'Let me bring you somethin' to drink,' she said quickly, then hurried on as she saw his face. 'Tea, I mean.'

'The bolt goes all the way across there, see?' he said, ignoring her offer. He knew he sounded curt, but it was best she understand right away. 'If you give it one last push...' he reached up with his left arm, glad of the excuse to move away from the pressure of her against him, 'it'll go another inch, and that'll stop the rattle when the wind gets in under the eaves.'

'Thank you,' she said in a small voice. She sounded so different from the bold, confident woman who'd called out to him on the road that he questioned again what he'd read in her face. He was hardly a great romantic catch, after all, and certainly not a good financial one.

She followed him at a distance out to the gate again. 'I'm sorry if I made you uncomfortable, an' if it hurt to come back in there,' she said, gesturing at the cottage.

Safely on the other side of the gate, Matthew was able to smile, and dismiss her concerns. But she didn't smile back. Her face, clear-eyed and almost heart-breakingly pretty, was devoid of expression as she looked at him. He patted the top of the gate, unable to think of anything to say, except, 'Well, I hope your children sleep sound now.'

'And I hope you recover soon,' Nancy said. Her eyes travelled over him, resting a moment on the open collar of his shirt, where the bruise on his collarbone showed an ugly brownish-yellow.

'My wife's helping me,' he said, gently but pointedly. 'I couldn't have managed without her and Freya.'

Her tone altered abruptly. 'Ah yes. The lovely Anna. You might want to ask Tom Carne what he thinks of your perfect wife an' her big mouth.'

Matthew's eyes narrowed. 'What do you mean by that?'

'Only that if it weren't for her, Juliet and James would still be gettin' wed. Not that it matters now, the girl's dead. Still, makes you wonder. Why'd she put a damper on that, unless she has an eye for James for herself?' Still expressionless, Nancy put a hand on top of his where it lay on the gate. 'You deserve better'n that, Matthew. An' now you know where to find it.'

She turned away and went back indoors, leaving Matthew blinking at the unnerving changes in her manner. Now, at least, there was no question that he had allowed his ego to convince him of something that wasn't there; he didn't know where Nancy Gilbert's children were today, but if he followed her into that house now she'd have the shirt off him before he could close the door.

Shaking his head, he left his old house and started down the hill again. He didn't believe for one moment that Anna had deliberately scuppered poor Juliet's marriage plans, not for any reason, but he couldn't help wondering if Nancy was one of the few who knew – or thought they did – what had happened in Ireland. For Anna's sake, he hoped not.

Porthstennack harbour

James looked at the lowering clouds, and then out to sea. Ern Bolitho would know to turn back if things got rough out there, but summer storms could be unpredictable. He felt a moment's guilt that, yet again, he had passed that responsibility on to his temporary skipper, especially when it was clear the man was doing it more out of lingering respect for his former boss than for his present one; Roland's legacy was apparent in every polite nod James received, every acquiescence to his instructions, every gentle correction of an order that went against one Roland would have given. James Fry had come to realise he was tolerated at best, unlike Matthew, who had been viewed as Roland's equal from the moment he had taken over.

James frowned. He'd hoped the sting of that would have faded by now, particularly in the light of what had happened at Wheal Furzy last week. When he'd heard about the explosion he'd gone icy-cold right through, and he knew then that he still missed his old friend, despite the nagging jealousy. The relief of discovering Matthew was alive, and not likely to lose his arm after all, was the one thing he and his crew members had shared aloud, and in complete harmony.

A low growl in his stomach made him put aside the lobster pot he'd been reweaving, and look towards home. A couple of pasties sat in his pantry, made by Brian's wife and handed to him without a word yesterday as she'd passed on her

238

way to the salting house. She was an odd one, and James didn't even know her name; Brian only ever referred to her as 'th'wife', and she never spoke to anyone but her husband unless she absolutely had to. But she was a very good cook, and the more James thought about those pasties, the louder the grumbling in his belly grew. At length he called over the boy who was watching over Mrs Gale's laundry, spread out on the shingle to catch the last of the dry weather.

'Hie, Bobby!' The boy looked up from where he was moodily stabbing at the stones with the toe of his boot. 'A penny if you'll watch these pots while I fetch my dinner?'

Bobby Gale brightened, and with good reason – after all it would involve no more effort to watch a few lobster pots than he was already expending watching his grandmother's sheets.

'I'll pay you when I get back. Provided the pirates haven't got the better of you.'

Bobby grinned. 'They pirates know better, Mister Fry.'

'Either that, or they know their boss.' James winked, and patted Bobby's shoulder as he passed to go back home. The boy's laugh gave him a sudden, sharp, and completely unexpected pang for what he might have had, and his own smile faded as he walked homeward.

Halfway along Paddle Lane he was met by the unusual, and puzzling, sight of Esther Trevellick sitting on her own front step. She didn't look up as he approached, so he scuffed his feet on the road a little, in order not to startle her before he spoke.

'Mrs Trevellick? Esther? Are you all right?'

'Oh, Mr Fry.' She rose, holding on to the door jamb, and James moved forward quickly and took her arm.

'What is it?'

'Joe've passed on, Mr Fry.' Her voice wavered, and she scowled, as if cross with herself for the display of emotion. 'I found 'im just ten minutes since.' She sniffed, and tried on a smile. 'I'll miss the silly old bugger.'

James put his hand over hers. 'I'm so very sorry, Esther. Really. What can I do to help? Does he have family somewhere else that I can contact for you?'

'Bless you, but no.' Esther visibly pulled herself together, standing straighter, and taking a deep breath so she could speak more strongly. 'He 'ad a brother and sister but they went missin' from the workhouse back in 'sixty-four. Never did see 'em again. There in't no one else, except our Alan and Tommy, and they'll be below grass a good few hours yet.'

'Then let me fetch the doctor for you.'

For a moment Esther looked puzzled, then she nodded. 'Yes. I s'pect he'll need to do somethin' official, won't he?' She blinked, and a tear appeared on her lined cheek. 'An' I s'pect I ought to let Miz Garvey know. Mrs Penhaligon, I mean.'

'Let me do that while I fetch Doctor Bartholomew.' James helped the woman into her home. Despite her roundness she suddenly seemed small, and old. Even as children, and trying their luck in the couple's garden, he and Matthew had known that if one of the Trevellicks was around, the other was not far away; Esther would be lost for a good long while.

The house was small, and dark inside, as were most of the cottages along Paddle Lane, including his own. There was a smell of damp already permeating the air, and that was before the rain – it signalled a deeper problem than a mild leak, and while half his mind considered offering to get it fixed, the other half was on Joe. Perhaps he was simply sleeping, after all? There was always that hope.

He followed Esther up the narrow passageway to the stairs, noting the differences with his own house, here in the same row. His stairway rose from the centre of the narrow hallway, whereas these stairs ran parallel to the back wall of the cottage, with the bedroom door directly at the top. He could feel the damp from the sea air in the walls as he went up, trailing his hand over the painted plaster, and made a mental note to check the corresponding wall in his own house.

'He'm in there,' Esther said, pointing to the bedroom door, but she didn't follow James in. The open window was to his immediate right as he opened the door, and its curtain billowed inwards and into his face. For a second he welcomed the distraction, then he brushed the curtain aside.

Joe was not sleeping. He lay with his twisted, sweat-soaked nightshirt dragged halfway up his skinny white thighs, and his gaze fastened on the bumpy ceiling. The blankets were tangled around his knees, as if he'd tried to free himself from their constraints, and his mouth was slack and half-open. It did not look as if it had been an easy death – if such a thing existed – slipping away in sleep, unaware that the time had finally come... Joe Trevellick had not gone without protest. But he had been elderly, and ill, and it was not for him that James's heart ached.

He went back out to the kitchen, where Esther had begun making tea but had stopped, in the middle of spooning the leaves into the pot, and stared into the distance. 'I'll make it,' he said quietly. 'Sit down.'

While he waited for the water to heat he watched her closely. She sat with her chin propped on one roughened hand, her eyes fixed on the dresser in front of her, but clearly not seeing it. James guessed she was locked into another time, one where Joe would wake up and ask her if she'd darned his socks yet, and where he could still smile, and talk to her, and touch her in passing.

Everyone knew the Trevellicks, that they had been lucky enough to inherit Joe's parents' cottage, and that they had run the Tinner's Arms for twenty years – if badly. But it was only just sinking in that they'd once been young, newly wed and hopeful; they would have worried, and then grieved, for Joe's brother and sister; then later for the deaths of their own son and his wife, the parents of Alan and Tommy. Real people, with real emotions, not just 'The Trevellicks from Porthstennack'.

When he had given Esther her tea he set off up to Caernoweth, belatedly remembering he had promised Bobby Gale he wouldn't be long, but his own hunger had subsided and he didn't think he'd be able to eat for a while after all.

He called in at the doctor's house, and passed on the news through Mrs Gale, whose pleasant but stern face had crumpled. 'God bless Joe,' she said quietly. 'Doctor'll be down to Esther d'rectly. Thank you, Mr Fry.'

James left her in the doorway and continued up the hill. The Tinner's Arms was still closed; the evening had not yet brought workers to their leisure time. James went through the still-broken back gate, and pulled open the door at the bottom of the passageway. The pub's cat lay in a patch of sunlight thrown down by the skylight midway along the passage, and gave him a sleepily suspicious gaze as he stepped over it. Looking back he watched it yawn widely, shake its head, and settle back down. He envied it.

He knocked at the door leading to the house, and when there was no response he pushed it open and found himself in a cluttered but clean kitchen; the smell of carbolic soap tickled his nose, and he saw a tin bath on the table, in which soaked several bar mats from the pub. There was a door at the other side of the room, and it stood open to show the staircase.

He went over to it and stood at the bottom of the stairs. 'Anna? Are you here? It's James Fry.'

Movement at the top of the house turned out not to be Anna, but her daughter, who appeared from one of the rooms holding a piece of paper.

'Mother's at the shop,' she said. She sounded a little shaken, and came downstairs, still clutching what he now saw was a letter. 'Mrs Trevellick's caring for Joe until Alan gets back from work.

What can I do for you?'

'Actually it's Esther I came about,' James said. He told her what had happened, and she nodded slowly.

'I suppose we all knew it was going to happen,' she said. 'Thank you, I'll run and tell Mother, so she knows not to delay coming home later. I suppose we'll have to interview for a pot man now.'

James wasn't quite sure what to say to that. Of course she was right, they had expected it, and sooner rather than later, but he was taken aback by her calm appraisal of the practicalities. However, she seemed to sense that something more was required from her.

'Of course I'm dreadfully sorry for Esther,' she said. 'She must be at a loss. Can you take something back to her from us?'

'That'd be kind,' James said. He wasn't sure he'd ever understand this young woman, still considered 'simple' by most, 'backward' by the kindlier people, and 'childlike' by those who had taken her to their hearts – he was quickly learning that she was none of those things.

'What's in the letter?' He pointed to the crumpled paper in her hand.

She looked down, as if surprised to see she still held it. 'It's from Mother's family. My family too, I suppose. It came this morning, with a letter from my father.'

'And how is your father?'

'He's well. He sent money for Mother to arrange the repairs.'

'Repairs?' James's trained eye instinctively roved over every building he saw, assessing the state of

244

it, and the Tin Streamer's Arms had always appeared to be in good condition. On the surface, at least. 'What's wrong with it?'

'I don't know. But something in my room I think, as I'm to go and stay with Great Aunt Oonagh and Uncle Colm while it's being fixed.'

'I see. And...' He watched her expression, curious to see whether he was learning to read it yet. 'You're not happy about that? You're worried?'

'What if I say the wrong thing? They think...' Her voice dropped to a whisper and she looked instinctively over her shoulder. 'They think she's dead!'

'Surely they won't expect you to talk about what happened?'

Mairead shook her head. 'Mother tells me not. She says they'll just want to know about my life here, and that I can tell them all about that, and it'll be true. Except the part about her.'

'So it was her idea to send you?' Mairead nodded, and James smiled. 'Well then, that's all right, isn't it? You can talk about her too, just refer to her as Mrs Penhaligon, your friend's mother, and someone who works for your father.'

'But what if I say "Mother" by accident?' Mairead looked anywhere but at him, her gaze fluttering around the kitchen like a trapped fly, landing on nothing.

'Sorry? Did you say "martha"? That'd be Martha Penhaligon then, would it?'

Mairead stilled. Her panicked expression dropped away and she smiled, and James was appalled to find his heart leaping at the sight of it crossing her face, like that bright strip of sunlight

245

in the passage.

'Yes, that's right,' she said slowly, deliberately. 'Martha Penhaligon works as the publican in the Tinner's Arms.' She reached for James's hand, and he had to fight not to snatch it away as her fingers closed over his in gratitude. 'Thank you, James.'

'Does it make you feel better?'

'It does.'

'And will you have a nice time in Ireland, do you think?'

'I'm looking forward to meeting the cousins Mother talks about so much, except one of them lives in New Zealand now. He's a farmer, so Mother says.'

'You've never met?'

'Not that I remember. If I ever did then I was tiny at the time.' Mairead crossed to the larder, where she opened a tin and found a half a fruit cake wrapped in wax paper. James's appetite woke up again as the smell wafted to him, rich and sweet. 'That looks delicious. I'd love some, thank you.'

'Fingers off it!' Mairead shut the lid firmly. 'It's for Esther.'

James grinned, surprised at the lack of embarrassment he felt, despite her sharp tone. 'You'll have to trust I don't eat it on the way back, then.'

Mairead eyed him narrowly. 'I'll be checking with Esther.'

'I'm certain you will. Why have you never met your cousins before?'

'They thought Mother was wrong to marry a medical student, and she thought they were wrong not to see his potential. So she married him anyway.' She handed him the tin. 'There you are. I've counted the currants.'

'Even the burned ones?'

'Especially the burned ones.'

James affected a look of hurt betrayal, and was rewarded by one of the girl's rare, bright smiles. 'I'm sure Esther will be glad of it,' he said. 'And now I've got lobster pots to put back together, so I'd better be off.'

'And here I thought you were an architect,' Mairead said. 'Architects don't sit around fixing lobster pots.'

'This one does,' James said on a sigh. 'It's not my choice of job, but it's all I have.'

'And you're happy with it?'

He shrugged. 'Fishing's a fine profession. We all benefit from it.'

'That's not what I asked. Are you happy?'

'No.'

'Well then I'd say you're not trying hard enough.'

James felt a flicker of annoyance at her offhand tone; she had no idea how hard he'd tried, but one thing and then another had slapped him back down. The offer from Charles Trubshaw had been the last straw. 'I've been looking for premises in town,' he said. 'If I find one, I'll sell the trawler and start my own business, just as I planned.'

'Why in town?'

'I beg your pardon?'

'Well,' Mairead shrugged, 'you came back because your father lived here, and you stayed because he left you his boat. Which you don't want.

Juliet's gone too, God love her. So what's keeping you in Cornwall now? Sell your boat. Rent your house out.' She moved ahead to show him out into the passageway. 'It's a big world out there, James. Don't get tangled up in lobster pots and fishing nets.'

She closed the door quietly behind him, leaving him standing in the dappled sunlight that played across the earthen floor, staring at the place where she'd been. She was right. He'd been so wrapped up in making enough money from the business to start up here in town, and then in thoughts of building a life here with Juliet and the baby, that he'd forgotten the reason he'd taken the apprenticeship to begin with. He wanted to build. To renovate. To create.

And he'd better start with his own house, if he expected anyone else to live in it.

Chapter Fourteen

Freya put her rain-sodden hat on Mairead's dressing table, and noticed one of the drawers was still open. She closed it, not liking to see it empty; it felt too final. 'Have you got everything?' She tugged at the shoulders of Mairead's coat, feeling more the anxious mother than the stepsister. 'You look very smart.'

'Doesn't she?' Anna said, coming into the bedroom. 'Hurry now, Matthew has the trap ready at the front.'

'Will he be all right travelling in that thing?' Freya asked, frowning.

'He insisted. I told him not to come, but he's concerned about the road flooding. Don't worry though,' she added. 'I'll be the one driving, and we can stop and rest as we like.' She shooed them towards the door. 'Go on now, the two of you, I'll be down in just a minute.'

Mairead at last climbed into the back of the trap, with Freya's help, then looked around. 'I thought Mother said she'd be down?'

Freya sighed. 'After all the times she nagged at us,' she grumbled, and went back through the pub, to the house. 'Anna! Come on!'

There was a sliding thump from above Freya's head somewhere, and then the click of a door latch.

'Sorry!' Anna hurried down the stairs. 'Now, your da and I'll more than likely be back before opening time, so you needn't stay here.'

'Leave me the spare key anyway, just in case.'

'No need. Besides, you've got work to go to, anyway.'

'I'm not working today. I can even come here tonight and help out in Mairead's place if you like.'

'Still–'

'It's no trouble.'

Anna's lips tightened, then she took the key from her pocket and held onto it for a moment before passing it over. 'Just don't go getting into trouble at the hotel. And where's your hat?'

Freya put her hand to her head, but the pony was already shifting in her traces, impatient to be

249

off, so she pulled her shawl over her head and followed Anna out to the road. The rain wasn't so heavy now, but it was still coming down steadily, and the air was heavy and warm.

'I don't like the look of this,' Papá said, looking skywards. 'The Bodmin road can be nasty when it gets washed out.' He didn't look well today, his eyes were dark and half-hooded, and Freya wished she could tell him to stay home. She watched until the trap turned the corner at the top of town then, shivering in a sudden gust of wind, she hurried back into the Tinner's Arms.

Upstairs she pushed open Mairead's bedroom door, and saw her hat on the dressing table, sitting in a little puddle. She wiped the wood dry with her sleeve, but as she turned to go she noticed that the drawer she'd closed earlier sat crookedly in its runners; this room would stand unused for at least a month, and if the wood warped in the warm, damp weather it would never be a useful drawer again. Anna wouldn't thank her for that. Glad she'd seen it before it was too late, she worked it open, and lifted the displaced side back into position, but as she pushed it closed again she caught sight of something sliding towards her. An envelope, tied with string. The drawer had definitely been empty before...

She remembered the hurried slamming sound, and Anna's reluctance to leave her the key, and she looked at the envelope, her curiosity growing. She shouldn't pry, but such secretive behaviour niggled and prodded; it was too much like when Anna and Mairead had first arrived. She picked up the envelope, scolding herself aloud even as

250

she pulled at the knot to loosen the string, and for a moment thought she was looking at the plain backs of a handful of letters written on crumpled white paper. Then she remembered the papers given to her by Teddy Kempton, and her heart skipped a beat; these were pound notes! She turned them over, and was so stunned to see there must be at least ten of them that for a moment she didn't register the word standing out in bold type that said, not 'One Pound', but 'Five Pounds'. It must have come from Mairead's father to fix the pub, but surely it wasn't in so much disrepair? And why was the money hidden up here?

Unless ... Freya sat on Mairead's stripped bed, not liking the direction her thoughts were going in. *Unless Anna planned to leave Caernoweth, and Papá, and run away again.*

What if Juliet's death, and the ensuing short investigation, had alerted her to the fragility of her life here? Maybe Mairead wasn't going to Ireland at all! Anna might be planning to come back and get the money, then, when Papá was otherwise engaged, to meet her daughter somewhere. Plymouth perhaps. Hadn't Anna just told her she was determined to travel alone, but he had insisted on going with her? This was enough to get them passage to America, where they could start yet another new life, but in far more safety than they had here.

Freya thrust the money back into the envelope, tied the string with shaking fingers, and worked the drawer back off its runner again so it once more sat crookedly and not-quite closed. She

251

pushed the envelope out of sight, and wiped her sweating hands on her coat. Anna loved Papá, but that might not be enough, and if fear had driven her from her home once before it could do so again, only this time the man she left behind was one who'd given her his heart and soul. It would destroy him.

Freya left the room exactly as she found it, including putting her hat back on the dressing table, and went home, thinking furiously all the way. She just hoped she would have the chance to find out the truth from Anna, before it was too late.

Papá and Anna arrived home in good time for Anna to open the Tinner's as usual. Freya watched from the attic window as Papá dropped Anna at the pub then carried on to Porthstennack to return John's pony and trap. She left a note on the kitchen table, advising him to go to bed as soon as he returned, told Grandpa to enforce it, and then hurried down the road to the pub.

Anna's greeting was so warm, light-hearted and comfortable that Freya found herself questioning her earlier darker thoughts; perhaps the money *was* for repairs. After all, Freya had no real knowledge of how expensive building works could be ... she might be worrying for nothing. If James Fry came in tonight she would be able to ask, without raising Anna's suspicion that she had been snooping.

'You forgot your hat again,' Anna said, and handed it to her. 'You left it in Mairead's room.'

'Thank you. How was she when she left?'

'She was still a little nervous, but much better. I think I was worse than she was.' Anna smiled. 'She started to call me Martha halfway to Bodmin, and says it's her way of remembering not to refer to me as "Mother". Clever idea, I thought. Right, let's get that door unlocked.'

Freya's concerns gradually faded as work took over her concentration. She was unfamiliar with the pump, and after one disastrous attempt at drawing beer from it she spent most of her time doing what Mairead did: picking up glasses and clearing spills. Papá called in on his way back home from Porthstennack, and he and Anna chatted quietly in the passage for a few minutes. Freya watched them carefully but nothing seemed amiss; Anna didn't seem nervy or eager for him to leave, in fact the short trip out of town together looked to have brought them even closer, and Anna's eyes were shining when she closed the door behind him, and turned back to Freya.

'I've a confession to make.'

Freya's heart thumped. 'Have you?'

'I always thought I'd do anything to see my family again. I was convinced I'd be horribly envious of Mairead seeing them without me, while knowing they only have terrible thoughts of me, and that I'd wish I was going too.' She smiled. 'But if it meant leaving you and your da behind I'd have to think very hard about how badly I wanted it. Does that make me an awful person, would you say?'

Freya relaxed. 'Not at all. You love him, don't you?'

Anna looked taken aback by the question. 'I love

253

the both of you. Very much. And I even love your cantankerous grandpa.' She squeezed Freya's arm and went to fetch the clean bar towels.

It was only August, but the poor weather had darkened the evenings prematurely, and by nine o'clock people were seeking companionship outside their normal workmates. The small bar was busy, and Anna and Freya were kept occupied for most of the time. Tristan came in at around nine o'clock, his gaze went straight to Freya, who met it head-on, and for a moment everything and everyone around them disappeared. Then a chair scraped somewhere in the room, and noise and life flooded back. He smiled, and Freya's heart responded with a now-familiar leap.

He chose the table next to the bar, his book open on the table in front of him as usual, and Freya took a short break to sit with him while he told her how much more he'd read of the Bartholomew journals, and what he'd learned. There was still a faint tension between them when it came to whether or not he revealed Penworthy's true nature, but tonight they avoided the topic.

'Remember he was writing about marching to the battle at Sourton Down?' he said. 'Well, it was a disaster.' He showed her the notes he'd made earlier. 'Look, there was a massive storm, and the Royalists had to retreat.'

'That makes sense, if they're fighting with pikes and things,' Freya said. 'That'd bring the lightning down on them faster than anything.'

'But,' Tristan said, 'they were so keen to get away, they left King Charles's portmanteau behind, to fall into Roundhead hands.'

'His what?'

'All his battle plans! Right there for the enemy to find. Which is why there was another set-to, at Stratton Hill. The one where John Bartholomew was blinded, and your ancestor Stephen was killed. Which means all this,' he waved at his notebooks, 'happened because of the blasted *weather!*'

Freya knew she ought to find it as funny as he clearly did, but her smile was a response to his amusement, which was hard to resist, rather than the tale itself; thoughts of any storm would never sit easily with her.

'Mr MacKenzie, I owe you a debt. Or at the very least, a drink.'

They looked up to see James Fry holding out his hand to Tristan, who shook it, frowning slightly. Then his expression cleared.

'You're the one Tom Carne was after that night.'

'James Fry.' He nodded at Freya. 'Nice to see you, Miss.'

'You too.' Freya smiled back. 'Oh! Anna, what needs doing to fix up the pub? I was thinking earlier that maybe James could help?'

Anna's hand stilled on the pump handle, and she looked from Freya to James and back again. 'James isn't a builder, sweetheart. He's an architect.'

'I'd be happy to have a look,' James offered. His eagerness was evident, and Freya understood it only too well – bad feeling had a way of eating away at your insides, and he seemed as frustrated as her father by this ongoing feud.

'It's nothing,' Anna said, shooting Freya a warning look. 'Just a little leak. I think it just needs some fresh plaster or something.' She continued to draw the beer, her attention on the glass in her hand, and Freya subsided. Perhaps Anna thought Papá would be cross if James was the one helping, when he was unable. She didn't think he would, but it was hardly her place to say so.

But James pressed on. 'A bit of plaster won't take long, especially since the room is empty. Look, I'm making some for my own house anyway, and it'll save you paying someone. It's Sunday tomorrow, I could do it then.'

'It's quite all right,' Anna insisted. 'Finn has sent five pounds to cover everything.'

'Ah, well. That's only right, after all,' James said, but Freya only half-heard the rest of the conversation. *Five* pounds? Anna had ten times that amount hidden away upstairs.

She realised she'd fallen still, and that Tristan was looking at her oddly, so she smiled and turned to James, making sure her voice matched her bright expression. 'Perhaps you could go upstairs now, Mr Fry, and see what you think?'

'Freya!' Anna sounded shocked and annoyed. 'James is our customer!'

'Oh, I don't mind in the least.' James rose and came around the bar. 'Stairs are through the kitchen, aren't they?'

'How do you know that?'

'I called in the other day, to tell you about Joe, but spoke to Mairead instead. She'd been upstairs.'

Freya noted the panic-stricken look on Anna's

face, and hesitated; ought she to give her the chance to tell the truth, before anyone else became involved?

'Forgive me, Anna. You're right.' She turned to James. 'I'm sorry, I shouldn't have asked.'

Anna gave him his drink. 'Your offer *is* very much appreciated,' she said, visibly relaxing as James sat back down. 'And if I have need of your expertise I'll certainly come to you.'

Anna wouldn't look at Freya for the rest of the evening, which couldn't pass fast enough, but eventually Freya locked and bolted the door behind the last customer. She turned to Anna, who was clearing glasses from the tables, and although her mouth opened to frame a calm, well-considered question about the money, instead she blurted, 'Are you leaving?'

'Leaving? Leaving town, you mean?' Anna looked genuinely stunned. 'What's put that in your head?'

'Are you?'

'No!'

Freya sat at one of the empty tables. 'Do you promise?'

'Sweetheart...' Anna put the glasses down and sat opposite her. 'Why on Earth would you think such a thing?'

Freya felt tears start to her eyes, partly of relief, and partly of mortification. 'I'm so sorry ... the drawer was crooked, I just wanted to fix it before the weather turned and the wood warped, and I know I shouldn't have opened the envelope, but I thought...' She became aware she was babbling, and fell silent. But Anna didn't look angry. She looked pale, and a little bit ill. 'I'm sorry,' Freya said again. 'But why did you say there was only five pounds? And why did he send so much?'

Anna did not answer for moment, and her gaze remained fixed on the smeared table-top. Eventually she looked up again. 'I've kept this from you because you've been coping so well, I couldn't bear to hurt you with the truth. But I think you ought to know now.' She linked her hands on the table, and thought for a moment, then sighed. 'The money was to pay Juliet.'

Freya stared, then gave a little laugh of relief. 'But why keep that secret? It's so kind of you to–'

'It wasn't kind at all. It was to pay for her silence.'

'Her silence? What do you mean?'

'She demanded it of me,' Anna said. 'She was in James's kitchen the night Mairead told you what happened to Liam Cassidy.' Anna carried on talking, quite calmly, but when she came to the part where Juliet had threatened Mairead her voice lowered. 'I couldn't let her tell anyone, so I lied to Finn about the pub needing extensive repairs, and he sent the money.'

Freya tried to picture Juliet demanding payment, threatening Mairead, but she couldn't. Anna had offered her a home, a job. Why wasn't that enough? Then she relived the moment when the *Lady Penhaligon* had hit the wall, and heard again the venom in her friend's voice. Her eyes prickled. 'What will you do with the money now Juliet's gone?'

'I don't know. I know I ought to send it back, but, Freya, think what your da could do with even half that much! We could fix up the attic, and we could all live together at last. Besides, Finn took enough of my money in the past – he used up all my savings, as well as the money settled on me by Uncle Colm when we married. He's even got this place, which should have been his daughter's ... I can't help feeling he owes us.'

'Well it's lucky for you Juliet died, then.' Freya couldn't keep the bitterness from her voice, and she didn't try very hard.

'Sweetheart, I'm sorry. That's not what I meant, you know that.'

'Why haven't you told Papá? You said there were no more secrets between you.'

'Because of how it looks.' Anna rose and went to the window, peering out as if she expected the street to be filled with people listening. 'I know you're furious, and upset, but think about it for a moment. Juliet was *blackmailing* me! Then out of the blue she commits suicide, and I find myself with all this money... Put that together with what people think I did back in Ireland, and it'd be a very generous, or foolish, person who doesn't believe I pushed her into that pool myself!'

She turned back, her mouth set in a straight line, and Freya blinked as the full import of her words hit home. She was right; it would take very little for suspicions to take hold again, and to spread – particularly to the ear of Constable Couch – only this time it would be impossible to deflect them with Anna's illustrious ancestry, and her generosity. Who would believe her? The chilly suspicion even began to creep through Freya, and, appalled, she pushed it aside.

'Surely you can trust Papá,' she said instead. '*He* would help you, you know he would.'

Anna shook her head. 'I can't let anyone else become involved, much less Matthew. I was all set to tell him until Juliet killed herself, but now ... well, it'd ruin him.'

'What do you mean?'

'If people thought she'd been murdered after all, and that I was involved, he'd lose everyone's trust all over again. I can't let that happen. You know why.' Her gaze flicked to the shelf behind the bar, and Freya's followed it.

She shivered, then turned her attention back to Anna. 'But he wouldn't let anyone else become involved. He'd keep your secret. You know that, surely?' She peered more closely. 'But that's not the whole reason, is it? You think *he* won't believe you!'

'And what if he doesn't?' Anna blurted. She seemed to become aware that her hands were twisting together, and forced them to stop. 'What if he loses all the faith he has in me?'

'Are you worried for him, or for you?'

'Both of us! I'd hate, more than anything, to think he thought me capable of such a thing. You're right, I'd have to go, to protect Mairead and myself, and now I have the money to do it. But what worries me more than leaving you all is that Matthew will feel let down and alone, and what if he turns to the drink again?'

'He's a good person–'

'The best of people! You'll get no argument from me. But God love him, Freya, that one weakness ... it's part of his make-up, and he can't change it. Look what happened when I betrayed him before, and was all set to move back with Finn. I won't be the one who pushes him to it again. He needs time to get past the accident, to become steady again in his mind. When he's strong again we can tell him everything. Just not yet. Please?'

Freya didn't say anything, and eventually Anna spoke again, more quietly. 'My first thought, when Juliet said what she did, was to get Mairead away from here.' She gave a short, humourless laugh. 'I never thought I'd feel she was safer back in Ireland than she is here. But how could I be sure Juliet wouldn't stay in town after all, and keep asking for more?'

'She wouldn't have. She wasn't bad, just desperate.'

'Oh, these people you think you know so well, Freya! Your da wouldn't doubt me, and Juliet wouldn't push her luck a bit further... People will do awful things. You have to learn that, my girl, before you're led a merry dance by the people you think you can trust.'

Was that a warning? Freya stared, appalled at the bitterness on Anna's face. 'What?'

'Juliet knows ... I mean, she *knew*, I would do absolutely anything to protect my daughter.'

Freya's anger returned. 'And now you don't have to, so were you just going to keep the money anyway?'

'It only came a few days ago, at the same time as the invitation from Aunt Oonagh. I don't know *what* I was going to do.' Anna lowered her voice and went on, in calmer tones. 'I'm sorry.

Look, I didn't even know for sure that the money was coming, and when it did it was already too late. Juliet was gone.'

Freya's head was spinning, but that icy thought was back, washing at the edges of her mind like the incoming tide, and just as unstoppable: Malcolm Penworthy, a man with a knack for outward displays of generosity, and for winning people's trust. A violent man. And then Tristan's words: *'It's common for strong characteristics to get passed down through several generations. Good as well as bad...'*

She stood, hoping her thoughts were not reflected in her face. 'I'm going home,' she said quietly. 'Will you still come for dinner tomorrow?'

'Wait!' Anna came over and touched her arm. 'Of course I will, and I'm sorry for shouting. But please – this *has* to stay between us. For your father's well-being as much as Mairead's.'

Freya searched her eyes, hoping to find the answer to the poisonous question that she could no longer ignore, but there were no answers there.

'I won't tell anyone,' she said quietly, and she meant it. But not for Anna's sake.

Chapter Fifteen

Tristan watched Freya closely as she closed the door behind her father and grandfather. She'd been wearing her usual cheerful smile as she saw them off on their daily walk to Porthstennack, and it was still in place when she turned back to Tristan to offer him tea, but today it looked pasted on, and held there by determination rather than genuine pleasure.

'Is it helping them both?' he asked, nodding at the closed door.

'I think so. Papá stiffens up so easily, and Grandpa needs the fresh air before it gets too cold out.' She came back to the counter, where Tristan had laid open the journal he'd been reading. 'Anyway, it helps me to get them out from under my feet for an hour or so.'

Tristan took a deep breath; better to get this over with. 'Look,' he began, 'I know it isn't what you want for Anna, and it's not what I promised, but when it comes time to write the history of the town I'm going to have to tell the truth about Penworthy.' He held up a hand before she could say anything, and hurried on, '"I'm sorry, and I'm nowhere near finished with this investigation, but I'm an historian, not a writer of fiction.'

She didn't answer, and he had the feeling she was battling with her conscience as he had done with his. He adopted a gentler tone. 'Look, I still hope to find out that what Bartholomew's saying is nothing more than the bitterness of a proud man, reliant on his squire for everything.'

'I hope so too.' Freya's eyes held his, and the soft shine had gone; they were flat, dull, opaque. Completely lacking any of the fight for which he'd prepared himself. It was unsettling.

'What's wrong?' He took her hand, and it lay in his like a small, sleeping creature; she made no attempt to return the pressure of his fingers. 'It's

263

more than Penworthy, isn't it? Please, tell me.'

'I can't.' She withdrew her hand and stepped away. 'At least, not yet.'

'Is it something to do with Juliet?'

She paled. 'Why do you ask that?'

'Because I know what it's like to lose someone you care about,' he said softly. 'It hits you hardest over the unexpected things.'

'Yes, it does.' Freya gave him a sad smile, and it was like a thread from her soul to his, tugging at him.

He touched her face, but made no closer contact. 'I want you to be happy, Lady Penhaligon.'

'Lady?' Freya threw a look over her shoulder, at a box that lay on the shelf behind the counter. 'Why did you call me that?'

'Well ... your name. The meaning of Freya, as Teddy pointed out to me, is Lady.'

'Papá called me Lady Penhaligon, on my eighth birthday. It's why I named his gift that.' She took down the box, and showed him its contents; a beautiful, hand-crafted boat with broken sails and an ugly split along the side. 'I didn't know that's what my name meant, I never asked. Mama chose it.'

'Freya was a Norse goddess,' he said, running his finger over the smooth, polished wood of the broken boat. 'I thought your mother was Spanish? It seems odd she would choose a Scandinavian name for you.'

'She called Papá her Viking,' Freya said, 'because he has fair hair, and lives for the sea.'

'Did he make this?'

'Yes. Just before I left for London.'

264

'What happened to it?'

Freya shook her head. 'We'll talk later, when we have more time. You might as well tell me what you've found.' She gestured to the journal, and brought a tall stool closer, so she could sit while he deciphered the difficult handwriting.

He had read scarcely more than two sentences aloud before the door opened, the jangling bell cutting through his words. He didn't even realise he was frowning as he looked up, until the new arrival laughed.

'Well there's a jolly greeting, I must say! And here I've brought your beloved motor back!'

'Teddy!' Freya smiled properly at last, and Tristan felt a pang that he had not been the one to inspire it. 'So nice to see you again.'

Teddy's face clouded a little as he took her hand. 'Tristan told me about your sad loss,' he said quietly. 'I'm so sorry, dearest girl. So terribly sorry.'

Freya nodded her thanks, and Tristan's fingers itched to stroke her smooth cheek, to bring some colour back to it. Perhaps she was thinking twice about becoming entangled with him, especially now that she knew he would publish his findings no matter what.

'I've brought one or two bits of paperwork too, and a letter that looks personal.' Teddy handed a small pile to Tristan, who noted that the letter was from his stepmother. Immediately he felt the worm of anxiety uncurl in his stomach, and he tore the letter open quickly. He scanned the contents, and the worry faded a little, but he still felt uneasy.

'What is it?' Freya asked.

'My father's having trouble with the union at the mill in America. Catherine – my stepmother – tells me he's being a stubborn fool about it and she wants me to intercede.'

'What will you do?'

Tristan shook his head. 'Write to him, I suppose. I only have half the story here.' He put the letter back in the envelope, then looked at Teddy. 'I'm sure Freya and myself won't be the only ones pleased to see you.' Teddy flushed, but Tristan remembered something else and abandoned his teasing for the moment.

'Have you brought anything else, by chance?'

'No, but I'm having all our post forwarded to the hotel.' Then he brightened as he caught Tristan's meaning, and turned to Freya. 'I don't have anything just yet, but Turner and Mitchell are wiring the funds within the next day or two, to enable us to pay you the full worth of the Bartholomew journals.'

'Does this mean you'll have to stay in town for a few days?' Tristan asked innocently. 'It seems you could have waited, you know, and come later.'

'I thought you might need to see those papers,' Teddy said, shooting him a look. Tristan smiled, and turned his attention to Freya, who was looking pleased at the news, but with a faint shadow darkening her expression. He wanted to talk to her properly but there was that barrier she had thrown up between them, and he didn't know how to break it down without driving her away.

Luckily Teddy hadn't noticed any tension, and his lively chatter formed an easy connection between the three of them. Tristan told him an edited version of what he'd found in the books, and Teddy's enthusiasm kept conversation flowing easily, until Freya glanced at the clock.

'Can I leave the two of you here to mind the shop? I'm due back at work today and Mrs Bone will be watching for any lateness, more so than usual.'

'Of course,' Tristan said.

'Papá shouldn't be too long, he's probably got caught up talking to his old crew mates.'

Tristan followed her into the hall. 'I'll meet you from work,' he said. 'I was wrong, I do want us to talk. Properly.' He gave her as gentle a smile as he could. 'Not about what's troubling you, if you're not ready. About the rest of it. That storm, your father. Why you and your mother left.' He caught her hand, and this time she returned his grip. 'Freya, I am completely besotted with you, yet I don't know much about you at all. I want to put that right.'

Freya nodded. 'It's a long story, and not a very nice one. And it might change things. How you think about Papá, for one. But I want to tell you.'

'And whatever else it is that's got your thoughts all wrapped up, I hope it's something you can mend.'

Freya kissed him, a soft brush of her lips on his cheek. 'So do I.'

Tristan went back into the shop, where Teddy was looking at him with ill-concealed excitement, and he gave an inward groan – he'd been so keen to talk to Freya that he'd left the Bartholomew books right in front of Teddy's ever-curious eyes.

Teddy put down the one he'd picked up. 'Have you read ahead of where you were making these notes?'

'No, I'm making them as I go. Why?'

'Because I've just gone on a few pages. And what I've just found out about our revered Malcolm Penworthy throws an entirely different light on him.'

'I know,' Tristan said patiently, pointing at his own scribblings. 'Haven't you looked at those?'

'Oh, I don't mean a little bit of wrongly directed and unrequited lust, or even the fighting and the cruelty.'

Tristan sighed, and tried to keep the irritation from his voice. 'Don't talk in riddles, you know I've no patience for guessing games.'

Teddy took a deep breath, and put his hand flat on the open book. 'Penworthy was worse than a lustful botherer of young women. He was a cold-hearted, cold-blooded murderer.'

Pencarrack House

'Where are you off to?'

Lucy stopped, her hand outstretched to open the front door. She turned to see Hugh coming down the stairs, looking as bored as she felt. 'I'm going for a walk. Would you like to come?'

He glanced at his pocket watch, and Lucy knew full well he was checking to see whether it was worth it, or whether Miss Penhaligon would have gone to work already. Then he shrugged. 'Why not? Where's Harry?'

'I'm not his mother,' Lucy pointed out yet again.

'No, but his mother depends on you to keep an eye on him. You know, since you have nothing better to do, and she's working.'

Lucy narrowed her eyes at him. 'Since when have you been Dorothy's champion?'

'I'm not,' he replied with a grin, clearly enjoying her predictable response. 'But you don't, do you? Have anything better to do, I mean?'

'Nor do you,' Lucy retorted.

'Ah, but I'm a gentleman.'

'That's a matter of opinion.'

'Oh, don't be a mizz, Luce. Come on, let's find Harry and take him with us, you know he likes to get out and about.'

'He's with Maddern, if you must know.'

As if on cue, their nephew appeared at the top of the stairs. 'Are you going into town?'

'You have lessons,' Lucy reminded him.

'I've finished. Maddern says I can leave.'

'Come on then,' Lucy sighed. 'But fetch your coat.'

As they passed the Caernoweth Hotel, Lucy glanced automatically at the cars in the court-yard, and her heart gave a little flicker, quickly followed by recognition of what had caused it: Tristan MacKenzie's rather battered Austin was back, which could only mean Teddy Kempton had brought it.

'What's that smile for?'

'Nothing.' But it widened anyway. 'I was thinking about that author who's in town. Wouldn't it be useful for him to have proper access to the

269

Batten journals, whenever he likes, I mean? Do you suppose Father would object if I invited him? And his ... assistant, of course.'

'This is the one you told me about, that called in on the day of the explosion?'

'Yes. He bought some books from that shop in town, apparently, of the same kind as ours.'

Hugh's mouth pursed. 'What's he like?'

Lucy smiled slyly. 'Charming. Very charismatic. Awfully clever, of course.'

'Really.'

'Oh, yes. And I'm sure he's terribly good-looking too, under all that bruising. But it gives him a real ... masculine air.'

'I see, taken your fancy, has he?'

'No,' Lucy said, with perfect honesty. 'I can just appreciate a handsome man when I see one. And I imagine Miss Penhaligon can, too.'

Hugh looked at her sharply, but if she'd expected to see a humorous reaction to her teasing she was disappointed. 'Beats me why he felt the need to hang around,' he said. 'I'm sure he can read just as well in his own home as here.'

'Never mind that. Do you think I should invite him?'

'Definitely. And wear your prettiest dress.' Hugh walked ahead, leaving Lucy staring after him. Perhaps his liking for Miss Penhaligon went deeper than she'd thought – he clearly wanted her to entice Tristan away from the girl. Her curiosity was aroused, too; she'd never seen Freya Penhaligon, but Hugh was notoriously difficult to please when it came to women. What in the world could a working-class shopkeeper and hotel maid have, to

270

interest him so?

She hurried to catch up, and when they drew level with Penhaligon's Attic she glanced in at the window. 'Hugh, look. There's Mr MacKenzie now. Gosh, his bruises have gone down and he's really quite a dish underneath it all. Perhaps you'd like to ask him why he chooses to remain in town?'

With an impish grin at her brother, brought on by the sudden thumping of her heart and lightness of spirit, she pushed open the door. Harry gave an ungentlemanly whoop, and ducked under her arm to vanish into the tightly packed shelves at the back of the shop. Hugh made no secret of his disappointment on learning that Freya had already left for work, and remained standing by the door as if ready to make an escape.

After an awkward greeting, during which a flatteringly overwhelmed Teddy was clearly vacillating between shaking her hand and kissing it, and eventually just squeezed it, Lucy offered the use of Pencarrack for their research. 'Mrs Andrews will be told of course, you only need to ask for the key. What do you think?'

The question was directed at Tristan, but Lucy's eyes went to Teddy to gauge his response. He was smiling, but it wasn't the flushing, embarrassed reaction of before, it was a slow, slightly tilted smile, more of a quirk of the mouth, and his eyes were warm on hers. She cleared her throat and looked at Tristan, who was also smiling.

'That would be very kind,' he said. 'Thank you.'

Lucy peered at the open book on the counter. 'Have you found anything useful in there?'

Teddy beamed. 'I'll say–'

'No,' Tristan said. 'That is, nothing I'm sure of, yet.'

'But–'

'We need to read on, and very carefully,' Tristan said firmly. 'John Bartholomew wasn't writing these at this point, remember. It's his son. There are certain things about the area we ought to cross-check if we can.' He looked at Lucy. 'For that reason we'd be pleased to take you up on your kind offer.'

'Sounds intriguing,' Lucy said thoughtfully, looking at them in turn. Teddy was frowning, but Tristan's expression was open and calm. She preferred Teddy's honesty, and had a moment's doubt about the wisdom of her invitation, then shrugged; what did it matter what someone had written in some old book two hundred and odd years ago?

'Come to Pencarrack whenever you like. Harry? Come along. It's going to rain again soon and your mother will give us what-for if we return you home soaked through.'

'No she won't,' Hugh said, speaking for the first time since their introduction. 'You're such a marvel with him, Lucy. She is, really,' he added to Tristan. 'You'd think she was his mother, the way she cares for the lad. Patience of a saint. Truly.'

'Hush, Hugh,' Lucy said quietly. She'd have been mortified by the heavy-handed exaggeration of her virtues if she hadn't suddenly felt desperately sorry for him. If Miss Penhaligon and Tristan were spending much time together, which his casual presence in the shop would indicate, then the difference in class was irrelevant. It was

272

already too late.

She made her goodbyes, and her gaze lingered on Teddy only slightly longer than necessary. 'I look forward to facilitating your work,' she said politely. Then, as she stepped onto the street, she flashed him a little grin. 'I'll make sure we have plenty of bandages.'

Freya's thoughts were still muddled when she left work. Without thinking, she walked to the corner of the stables as usual, and had been standing there for more than five minutes before she remembered Juliet would not be coming to meet her. A fresh wave of sadness washed over her, and she remembered Tristan's words of that morning; this was certainly one of the more unexpected things to be hit by. No doubt there would be many more.

As if thinking of him had conjured him up, she saw Tristan crossing the courtyard towards her, drawing one or two speculative looks, and several admiring ones. He did look extremely handsome with his dark curly hair blowing in the breeze, his shirt open at the neck and his well-made frame accentuated by a neatly fitting waistcoat. He held out his arm to Freya, who slipped her hand beneath it, then straightened her summer shawl with her free hand, and looked at him.

'Where shall we go?'

'How about out towards the fort?'

'All right.'

Once past the miners' cottages on Furzy Row, conversation began to flow more freely. Freya found it easier to tell him about the night she'd been swept out to sea, wearing Granny Grace's heavy coat, and had somehow fought her way back to shore, only to fall desperately ill. He put an arm around her shoulder as she talked, and didn't release her even when she told him about Papá's troubles and his reliance on alcohol.

'You're not shocked?' she asked, stopping to look at him, to gauge his honesty when he replied. 'I don't mean he enjoys a pint with his work-mates, I mean if he begins to drink again it's unlikely he'll stop.'

'I understand what you're saying.'

'And it doesn't disappoint you?'

'Of course it does, but not in the way you think. It's sad when anyone has any kind of struggle. But I think no less of him, he seems a good man. He's not fighting it alone now, either, he has Anna, as well as you.'

Freya's insides tightened at that, but she wasn't ready to talk about her suspicions yet. 'He slipped back, the night her husband came and he thought she would leave him, and I'm just worried about what he'll do if it turns out he can't work again.'

'Is that likely?'

'I don't know. It's only been just under two weeks, but I can't imagine he'll ever be too strong in that shoulder and arm again.'

'He seems to be working through it well.'

'*Seems* is just the right word. I'm worried he's keeping something from Anna and from me. He's always tired, and I've seen him go green once or twice when he tries to move too quickly.'

'Has he seen the doctor?'

'Not Bartholomew, but the mine doctor told

274

him to expect it to take a while. The longer it goes on, the more frustrated he'll become, and the less money we'll have. And I know that before, when he and Mama were in trouble, he would–'

'Darling,' Tristan stopped and turned her to face him. His eyes travelled over her face, and she knew he was reading every worried line, every bit of tension she could feel in her own jaw, and the fear that lived permanently in her now. She just hoped he wasn't reading what truly lay behind it all. 'I don't know your father very well,' he said, 'but anyone can see he would do anything for you. Absolutely anything. Including staying sober.'

'He didn't last time.' Avoiding his searching look, she turned her face away, and saw, just ahead of them, the place where the path forked. One way to the fort, one way to Polworra Pool; one way to protection and safety, one way to despair and grief.

Tristan's hands tightened on her arms as he followed her gaze. 'God, I'm sorry. I didn't think...'

'It's all right,' she said in a low, broken voice. 'It's as bad for you. We'll take the lower path.'

'It's such a pretty place, when you get past the noisy part,' Tristan said, as they resumed walking. 'Anna was right to suggest Teddy and I leave it until a quieter time.'

'How do you mean?' Freya squinted at him through the early evening sunlight.

'We wanted to visit the fort – which I still haven't done, by the way – and I wanted to get the lie of the land from above, by the pool. But we met Anna and she said we'd be better off visiting after work here was finished for the day, so we went to Pencarrack instead.'

Freya stopped again, frowning. 'You went to Pencarrack on the day of the explosion, you said. You told the Battens about it.'

'That's right, and the young Miss, Lucy, has now offered us full access to those Batten journals I told you about.'

But Freya waved that away. 'What was Anna doing out here then?'

'She was waiting outside Wheal Furzy to take your father home.'

Freya's mind buzzed, and she shook her head as if she could stop the thoughts from forming, but she couldn't. 'So she was near Polworra on Tuesday?'

Tristan looked at her, clearly puzzled by the slightly strangled tone she could hear in her own voice. 'Not really *that* near. But up at this end of town. Why, what's wrong?'

'How did she seem to you?'

'Well, obviously she was shaken by what had happened. Very distracted.'

'I can't ... I'm sorry. I ought to go home.'

She turned, but Tristan seized her arm and stopped her. 'Oh no you don't! Talk to me! I knew something was bothering you, and you seem to be trying to shoulder it alone.'

'I can't!' she said again, and pulled herself free. 'It's too awful!'

'Freya!'

'I think she killed Juliet!' Freya heard the words burst from her in a sobbing, stumbling voice, but it was too late to bite them back. Tristan's face was a mask of shock, and his hand, which had been reaching for hers again, fell to his side.

'What?' he whispered. *'Anna?'*

'I don't want to think it, but I can't help it.'

'That can't be right. Tell me.' He sounded calm now. She wanted to listen to him talking to her in that steady voice, she would have taken strength from it, no matter what he said. But he fell silent again and eventually she found the words to begin.

'I found some money. Hidden away in Mairead's room.'

Once she began to speak, it all tumbled out: the blackmail money and Anna's reaction to her having found it; the way Mairead had been hastily shipped off to Ireland; Anna's determination not to involve Papá; the fact that no one had seen Juliet since work on Monday night ... and now this double-damning addition of Tristan's.

'She wanted to stop you from coming out here! And you yourself told me about the way this kind of thing can get passed down through generations.'

'But you said it was self-defence, what happened in Ireland.'

'It was.' Freya struggled with the decision for a moment, then sighed; she'd trusted him this far after all. 'It wasn't Anna who killed that boy, it was Mairead.'

As the words had passed from the confines of her thoughts to his she felt the burden lift, just enough to loosen all the rest of her worries. She told him everything she knew, and he said nothing in response, just looked at her with an odd expression of acceptance and finality when she'd finished.

'I love them both,' she said, when the silence stretched too long. 'Mairead is truly like a sister to me now, and I wouldn't wish any harm on either of them. I'd never tell anyone else but you. Not even Constable Couch.'

'But the police investigated. They never questioned Anna or Mairead, did they?'

Freya shook her head. 'I used to think it was a good thing that they're both able to put what happened aside, to carry on as if it hadn't happened. But now I don't know. Even after Anna promised to tell the truth, she lied about the money and what it was for.'

'But that was to protect both Mairead and the memories you have of Juliet.'

'She's still lying to everyone else.'

'So are you,' he pointed out, gently enough but the truth stung. Then she looked at him closely.

'You're hiding something too! What is it?'

Tristan hesitated. 'I don't know if it's important, hadn't thought much of it since, to be honest, but the night I fell foul of Thomas Carne, I caught Anna looking ... I suppose you'd say troubled. She'd been so bright and breezy all evening up until we left, and I remember thinking then how adept she must be at hiding it.'

'She is. Very. That was Monday, wasn't it? The last time anyone saw Juliet was after work on that day.'

He nodded. 'Late Monday evening. And there's something else I have to tell you.' He seemed to want to look anywhere but at her, so she took a half step closer, and put her hand on his face, keeping his eyes on hers. They flickered away

278

briefly, but then came back, looking darker than usual. 'Malcolm Penworthy killed someone,' he said quietly. 'A young girl. And he saw her brother hanged for the murder.'

It all fell horribly into place. 'He fooled everyone too, didn't he?' Freya said in a dull voice. 'And so did she. Both of them so charming, and generous, but he was a murderer.'

'It doesn't mean she's one too. The police are quite sure that Juliet's death was a suicide, you *know* that.'

Freya shook her head. 'She wouldn't have killed herself.'

'I know she was your friend, but–'

'Yes! She *was* my friend! She might not have gone to chapel every week, nor even lived as a good Christian, but she *told* me...' She broke off and hitched a painful breath as she remembered. 'I had to lie to the police, and to go against what I knew she'd have wanted.' Her voice softened in disbelief. 'All to protect the woman who probably killed her.'

'Darling, don't. Please.' Tristan drew her closer, and she wrapped her arms around him so tightly she thought she would crush him. But he held on without complaint.

Eventually she drew back, and her eyes were hot and burning, but dry. 'What do I do about Papá?'

'What do you mean?'

'This will destroy him.'

'He's a grown man, Freya. He should be the one protecting you, not the other way about. And he'd want it that way too, I'm sure of it. I should think he'd be mortified if he knew you were struggling with all this, just to protect him.'

'If it wasn't for the accident I'd tell him everything.'

'I know.' He took her hand. 'But this can't remain hidden forever, and once he finds out you kept it from him, how do you think he'll feel then?'

'Do you promise me you won't say anything about what you've found in the journals?'

His face had a suddenly trapped look, and he let go of her. 'It's my work. I'm sorry, but I can't ignore it.'

'Even now? When you know how it could affect everyone?'

His eyes narrowed, and for a moment he seemed unable to find any words. Then he shook his head. 'I'm staggered to think you'd expect me to protect a murderer. *Three* murderers.' He moved away, his face tight. 'Don't worry, I'm not going to give away your secret about Anna and her daughter, but you can't ask me to cover up the truth about Malcolm Penworthy.'

Freya stared, aghast. She had not even considered he would be so immovable. 'It's past and gone! Why does it matter now?'

'Why?' Tristan looked equally stunned. 'It's *history!* Enough has been rewritten already, without me adding to the lies.'

'Then why not just ... not mention it? You were writing that book before you found out about the journals, so why not disregard them altogether?'

'Those journals are *saving* this book! And my career. Before I saw them I had nothing more than a list of facts.' He ticked off on his fingers. 'Dry accounts with names, dates, numbers.' He threw his hands up, and then ran them through his hair, sending it into even more disarray than usual. 'John Bartholomew has brought this conflict to life. He speaks of things that concerned the ordinary man, sent to fight and leaving his children. The comradeship, including with your own ancestor Stephen Penhaligon! What happened when he was wounded, and Stephen died... Freya, I *can't* ignore his account of what came afterwards just because it doesn't suit this town's image of its founder!'

This speech was delivered with rising intensity, and the same passion and fervour that had drawn Freya to Tristan from the start, but all she could think now was that he would betray everything for it.

'*This* isn't history,' she said, barely able to recognise her own voice for the anger in it. 'This is my family. If you tell everyone you'll upend everything this town is built on, you'll turn everyone against Anna, *and* you'll be putting a bottle back in my father's hand. All for the sake of a book.'

'Freya–'

'No! I'm grateful for your promise not to go to the police with what I stupidly told you, but I don't have to listen to your reasons for destroying everything I've ever had.'

She went to walk past him but he caught her arm. 'Telling me wasn't stupid,' he said, with desperation. 'I'm ... touched, and glad that you felt you could trust me. But I can't lie about this man!' He subsided. 'I won't put it about town though, I promise. And it'll be a long while before the book is published.'

Freya tugged her arm away. 'But it will happen eventually.'

'I can't believe you'd want me to publish a lie.'

'I don't. I just want you to find something different to write about.'

'But this is one of the most important–'

'Hang your importance!' Freya started walking again, throwing her words back over her shoulder. 'Go on and write your truth, Tristan, see how many lives you can break while you're at it!'

'Freya, wait! Oh, for goodness' sake!' Now he sounded as angry as she did. 'You're being ridiculous! Caroline would never have...' His voice trailed away, and she looked back, her heart hurting.

'I thought I'd ask you about her one day,' she said sadly. 'But I don't think that'll happen now, will it?'

'Won't it?' He took a single step after her, but stopped when she shook her head.

'I'd wish you good luck,' she said, and her voice cracked as she realised what she was saying. 'And in all else, I do. I swear. But ... I hope your book fails, Tristan. I do, truly.'

And with the horrible, sinking sense that she had just thrown away the most precious of all the treasures she had ever found, she left him standing on the moor, and went home.

Chapter Sixteen

'You've had a face like thunder all morning,' Teddy observed, as he and Tristan walked towards Pencarrack House.

'It's only ten o'clock,' Tristan reminded him curtly. He caught Teddy's look and sighed. 'All right, no. I'm not happy. The sooner we get these notes taken, the sooner we can get back to Plymouth and some kind of normal life.'

'What?' Teddy stopped dead. 'I thought you—'

'You thought wrong. Well, come on!' Tristan gestured with an impatience he didn't feel; the continual low buzz of excitement and discovery that had thrummed in his blood for the past two weeks had fizzled out, and instead Freya's betrayed face had haunted him through a long, sleepless night, and still did.

'What happened?' Teddy asked, breaking into his thoughts.

'Nothing.'

'But Freya seemed awfully keen the last time I saw her.'

'Freya has other concerns. As do we. We're here to work, so let's get on with it.'

They were let in by Mrs Andrews, who showed them into the library where, despite Tristan's protests, the implacable housekeeper insisted they wait while she fetched the master. Charles Batten kept them waiting almost twenty minutes, and when he arrived he was accompanied by Lucy's elder sister, Dorothy.

Freya had told him about the woman who was known to be a reformed gadabout, and while apparently not a cruel or neglectful mother, neither was she a loving or even particularly interested one. She looked the way Tristan had imagined her; tall and straight, and she introduced herself with a cool kind of politeness, and a speculative appraisal. She clearly had her doubts about the wisdom of letting them loose in the house, unlike her younger sister, but said nothing beyond a polite greeting.

Batten offered them each a drink, but while a distracted Teddy took one, looking anxiously around for sight of Lucy, Tristan refused.

'If you don't mind, sir, my time is limited and I should like to get started straight away.'

'The reason I had you shown in here first, young man,' Batten said, in a surprisingly soft, but carefully modulated voice, 'is because I am about to grant you unfettered access to my entire family history. I'm sure you understand there must be certain restrictions on what you may reproduce.'

Tristan bit his tongue against the same kind of replies he'd given Freya, but couldn't help comparing her passionate fury to this rather cool warning. He'd make up his own mind when the time came, but for now he just needed to see these books.

'Have you read the journals, then? Do you have any particular book in mind that might be a good place to begin?'

Batten looked at him for a moment, then

replaced his glass on the table. 'I haven't,' he said. 'The books were uncovered some time ago after some storm damage, and my late wife suggested we place them under glass in order to protect them further, while still allowing access. It was she who had the interest in our history. I have more pressing concerns.'

'Of course, the mines,' Tristan said. 'I was the one who brought news of the–'

'Mishap. Yes.'

Mishap. Tristan pictured Matthew as he'd been shortly after that 'mishap'; his face pale, the back of his shirt a mass of lumps from the heavy bandaging, and his useless arm strapped tightly across his chest. The man could barely move without feeling faint then, and he wasn't much better now, according to Freya. He felt his own jaw tightening as he looked at Charles Batten – how could he dismiss it so lightly?

But, with an effort, he suppressed that thought since it was not his concern. There were only the books to think about, and then there was escape from Caernoweth ... and from the memory of Freya's dark eyes, looking at him with a pain that came from somewhere far deeper than her confusion over Anna. But surely she must understand? It *would* be like lying, to publish all Bartholomew's gushing praises of the gallant Penworthy in his earlier entries, and not temper them with the truth when it became apparent.

He realised his thoughts were taking him off somewhere else, and brought his attention back to the Pencarrack library. 'I'll be sure to pass all my notes to you for your approval before I leave.'

Even as he spoke he wondered if he would be forced to either compromise his integrity yet again, or completely abandon the biggest find of his career. 'And now, if we might be permitted...?' He gestured vaguely towards the door.

Batten nodded. 'Ensure you pass the notes directly to myself or my daughter. My elder daughter, that is.' He indicated Dorothy. 'And instruct your publisher to send a proof copy to me well before publication. I'll have a document of agreement drawn up for this purpose, which you can sign this afternoon.'

'Of course. And thank you.' Tristan removed the untouched whisky glass from Teddy's hand, and replaced it on the table. 'We're deeply obliged to your family.'

Batten nodded, and before Tristan and Teddy had left the library he was already opening a ledger on the desk, and drawing Dorothy's attention to it. Dorothy flipped a page, and as Tristan closed the door behind him he heard her say, not quite as quietly as she no doubt believed, 'I'd better get Andrews to check the silverware before they leave.'

He relayed this to Teddy when they were alone again in the gallery. 'I don't know whether to be amused or insulted,' he confessed. 'I could understand it when I was walking about looking like a prizefighter on his day off, but I thought I looked quite respectable now.'

'It is a bit thick,' Teddy agreed, looking out of the window. 'Where do you suppose Lucy ... Miss Batten, is?'

Tristan felt an unexpected, and unwelcome,

flicker of irritation. 'We're here for the books,' he said, and fitted the small key into the closest of the three glass cabinets. 'Do concentrate.'

Teddy turned back, eyebrows raised. 'That's not what you've been saying these past few days,' he pointed out mildly. 'What did happen between you and Freya?'

'It doesn't matter.' Tristan lifted the glass lid. 'Here, hold this while I get the book.'

Teddy obediently took the weight of the lid. 'It's a dashed shame, whatever it is.'

'I don't want to discuss it.' The weight of the book in Tristan's hand sent a thrill through him, just as Bartholomew's had, and even banished, for a moment, the uncomfortable knowledge that Freya was right. 'Look at this! It's not the first, though. Where's that one again?'

While Teddy went to search for the earliest dated journal, Tristan began to read the one in his hand. The date was 1669, and in the first few pages it became clear that the writer had been thwarted in the love of a local woman, identified only as 'Jane'. This woman had married a former soldier, and left the country for her new husband's homeland. The Batten who had written this had made no secret of his anger and disappointment, and in the few pages Tristan skimmed he ascertained this Jane was the daughter of a local squire. His heart picking up a faster beat, he found the confirmation he sought on the next page: Jane Penworthy had moved to Ireland with a Michael Garvey. This connection was what made accounts like this spring to life, and even as the thought crossed his mind that he must at least see Anna before he left, Teddy called him over.

'Here's the one you were looking at the other week. The first of them.'

Tristan peered through the glass, and almost dropped the book he still held. 'Look at this! Look closely.'

'D. Batten, esquire,' Teddy read aloud, squinting at the densely packed script, 'dated this fourteenth day of–'

'Not the words, the handwriting!'

Teddy frowned, then his brow cleared. 'I'll be damned,' he breathed. 'It's not exactly the same, but it's close enough.'

'It's more than close. It's the same hand, I'd swear it.'

'So D. Batten is Daniel. The younger Bartholomew son.' He stood straighter. 'I'm not absolutely sure, I'd have to check, but I have a feeling the name Batten derives from Bartholomew, if you go back far enough.'

'I must read it! Here.' He thrust the 1669 book into Teddy's hand and took the very first Batten journal over to the window, where he sat in the shallow, uncomfortable wooden window seat and became lost.

'Look lively!' Fiona Tremar, the head chambermaid, flapped a towel at Freya, who blinked and returned to work with deep reluctance. 'We've only got until half past before the guests come back.' She softened her voice a little. 'Are you sure you should be back at work? I see you staring into space more than I see you changing the sheets.'

'I'm all right,' Freya said. 'I'm sorry.'

'I understand.'

'Do you?' Freya looked at her, startled. Surely news hadn't already spread around town; it was only yesterday evening that she had walked away from Tristan out on the moor.

'Of course. It's a difficult time. Your pa will need looking after for some good while yet. And your ... Mrs Penhaligon has her own place to run. And it's not that long since your grandpa had his stroke.'

'I can't afford to take any more time off,' Freya said. She felt a stab of guilt that her thoughts had not, for once, been on her family and their difficulties. 'I'll do better, I promise.'

'See that you do,' Miss Tremar said, reverting to her former brisk manner. 'I might well understand, but that won't get the rooms done any faster, and it won't cut any ice with Mrs Bone neither, once *her* manager's on the warpath.'

For the remainder of her shift Freya worked harder than ever, less in an effort to appease Miss Tremar than to take her mind off Tristan. But walking home later she found herself looking up and down the busy street, hoping for a glimpse of him. She didn't even know what she would do if she saw him, but in the end that question remained unanswered. She went into the shop, and smiled at Papá, who was leaning over the vice behind the counter.

'Are you back to mending already?'

There was a kind of pleased secrecy about Papá's smile, and when he stood and moved aside she saw, clamped in the widened jaws of the vice and protected by a thick cloth, the *Lady Penhali-*

gon. With an exclamation of delight, Freya peeled off her coat and hat and went to look more closely.

'What do you think?' Papá asked. 'There's a lot to do yet, but will she be seaworthy again?'

The boat had been carefully glued along the split and, while there were still several pieces that were broken and twisted, Freya could see how much work had already gone into repairing it. 'She will,' she said, and gave him a careful, but heartfelt hug. 'Thank you!'

'Thank your grandpa too,' he said. 'I couldn't have done it without his help. And Anna said she could fix the sails, make them just like Granny Grace did.'

Freya stilled, then withdrew, and found a smile. 'That's kind, but I couldn't ask it of her. She has such a lot to do already, with poor Joe gone, and Mairead away.'

'Well, she's a kind person.'

'She is.'

Papá frowned. 'Have the two of you had a falling out?'

'No, of course not.' Freya turned the conversation back to the boat, and asked as many questions as she could about how it would be mended, and whether she could help. As Papá talked, Freya watched him carefully. There were tiny beads of sweat at his hairline, darkening the blond, and puffy purple shadows beneath his eyes. He swallowed frequently, and took the occasional shallow breath, almost a gasp but not quite. He was clearly floundering in his fight against pain.

'Papá, you ought to see Doctor Bartholomew,'

she said quietly, cutting through this explanations.

He looked at her, his eyes duller than usual. 'I'm fine. Doctor Manley says to be patient. And I don't have the money to throw away, just to be told the same thing by someone else.'

She wished she could tell him about the extra money Teddy had promised, but it hadn't arrived yet and until it did she couldn't rely on it. 'Well then, maybe you're trying to do too much.'

'I'm well enough,' he repeated sharply, then softened. 'But thank you. Maybe you're right, I'll take things easier for a bit.'

'Good.' Freya went upstairs to change, and to think. She sat on her bed and let her mind roam over everything; from Papá's accident, through the shock and pain of Juliet's death, the breathtaking suddenness of realising she loved Tristan, and the dismay at her discovery of the money. It was no wonder she could barely scrape through a shift at work without getting into trouble, or arousing misplaced sympathy. One problem at a time, that was the way through this maze of confused emotions.

She knew Anna should be her main concern just now, but even as she tried to force her thoughts to follow through the possible outcome of every action she might take she found them twisting away from her, and finding Tristan instead. Over and over again she saw his bruised, swollen face lose its irritation, and his hand inch towards the books on the counter; she heard his thickened, nasal voice remonstrating with her even as his eyes roved over the journals with a hunger she understood perfectly; she remembered the jolt she'd felt when she'd seen those eyes properly for the first time, and heard the more natural, low-pitched voice breathing her name.

She closed her own eyes now, and let her memory lead her along the tricky, winding path of wanting him, and of being frightened by how much. His enthusiasm, intelligence, and humour, and the feel of his lips on hers ... it all mingled until she was unable to distinguish the physical need for him from the way he had burrowed into her heart and stolen it for himself.

Oh, but he was a stubborn idiot! A surge of frustrated energy drove Freya to her feet, and she began to pace. That same honesty and integrity that had won her over would be the ruin of everything! Why couldn't he understand how dangerous it would be to go blurting the truth? It wasn't even as if it was relevant to his book; he was writing about the Civil War, he'd said so! This new story, this ... *unproven* new story, had nothing to do with the war. Whatever Penworthy might or might not have done after he left the field of battle had no relevance. And if Tristan MacKenzie thought he was just going to slope back to Plymouth and write it all down for the world to see, without hearing further from her on the subject, he was very much mistaken.

Freya took a deep breath then went back downstairs, shouting along the hallway to the kitchen. 'I won't be long!'

A minute later she was striding towards Doctor Bartholomew's house, her face fixed ahead, her mind full. Part of her was concerned the anger

292

wouldn't have dissipated by the time she came face to face with Tristan, but a larger part of her was worried it would have; she would need every bit of it to persuade him he was wrong in this.

She had only just reached Doctor Bartholomew's front door, and not yet even raised her hand to knock, when she heard a window creak open above her. She looked up to see Tristan's head poking out of the small attic window, and she stood back, arms folded. The sight of his face, familiar and already so beloved, nearly toppled her resolve; his dark hair, as tousled as ever, flopped forward over his brow, but she could see anxiety there anyway.

'Freya–'

'Will you come down?'

'Of course, I ... yes. Please. Wait.'

'As if I'd bother to come here at tea time, and then leave,' Freya muttered crossly. She walked the length of the path and back, and then did it again. Her heart was pounding, and her breathing was tight and nervous, but she had to make him understand. Or at least she must try just once more. A door slammed from somewhere inside the house, and a minute later Tristan was closing the front door behind him.

'I'm sorry, you're right.'

'You can't just ... pardon?' She stared at him and he nodded.

'Come with me.' He took her hand and led her away from the house. She saw him fling a look of distaste at the memorial as they passed it, but the cautious hope he'd given her was more important.

Once they were alone, safe from the eyes of the town, Tristan pulled her into a gateway and took her face in his hands. His touch was gentle, but his restless thumbs continually brushed her cheeks, as if he was unaware of what he was doing.

'You were right,' he said again. 'I've been letting my enthusiasm get the better of me, and it's not worth the heartache it'd cause. I'll write about something else. I'll cut Penworthy out of the story altogether, after Stratton Hill.'

'But...' Freya tried to make herself stop talking and just breathe a sigh of relief, but that idiotic part of her that wanted to make him happy, was rising inside her again. 'It'll go against everything you believe in.'

'Not quite everything. Not the most important thing, which is that I love you. I believe in that, more than anything.' He searched her eyes. 'It's all right, even if you no longer love me in return I'll stand by my word.'

'If I *what?*'

'I've been pig-headed and stubborn.'

'I won't argue with that. But do you think that would make me stop loving you?'

'Well, I couldn't blame you.' But there was a light of relief in his eyes, and he no longer sounded breathless and anxious. He dipped his head, and his teeth lightly captured her lower lip. A shock of longing raced through her, and she lifted her hands, linking them at the back of his neck. He pulled her closer, and she felt the racing of his heart through his thin shirt and hers, his hands on her waist, gripping her as if he thought she might try to pull away.

The sun sent its arrows of light deep into his extraordinary eyes, the same light touching his skin and warming it, softening the bold lines of his features. When he smiled it was wide and open, in contrast to the faint shadows that painted his jaw; she wanted to know how that smile tasted, and how it felt, so she stretched up again and her tongue danced across his lips, and she learned that it tasted like evening sunshine, and that the hardness of his teeth pressing against her mouth felt as if he could devour her in a moment if he wanted to. Her fingers traced the groove of his spine, and she could feel the shift and flex of muscle as his hands moved restlessly over her own back, returning caress for caress.

Finally they parted, although neither could bring themselves to break away entirely. Tristan's hand grasped hers and he drew her back out onto the road. It felt as if she was stepping from one version of her life into another, and to talk here about what had passed between them would somehow taint it. It was enough to know that it would happen again, and soon.

'What changed your mind?' she asked instead, as they walked slowly back to the doctor's house.

'I've been thinking about everything you said, and I know we see things differently, but I had to admit you were right. Your reasons for not wanting the story told are more important than mine for wanting to tell it.'

'Your reasons are honest ones too,' she said. 'I wish things were different.'

'So do I. But,' he brightened, 'I found something else very exciting today, at Pencarrack.'

'Oh? What sort of exciting?'

'I'd invite you to my room to see, but that would only set tongues wagging.'

'Fetch your notebook then, and come up to my house,' Freya said, glad of the excuse to stretch the evening further. 'Papá and Grandpa are both there.'

She waited at the end of the path while Tristan went to his room, and when he emerged again he was holding some papers.

'Teddy dropped these in while I was out,' he said. 'Another letter from my stepmother, by the looks. And this.' He handed an envelope to Freya, and with a sudden surge of excitement she tore it open to find the promised advance from Tristan's publisher. He smiled at the look of delight on her face, and dropped a kiss on her forehead. 'Let me tell you what I've found.'

By the time they had reached the shop Freya had learned of the connection between the two sets of journals and her feelings were mixed; Malcolm Penworthy's gift of a small plot of land to Daniel Bartholomew, upon the death of his father, had led to the building of the entire Pencarrack estate. It reinforced Penworthy's reputation for generosity, and would strengthen Anna's standing instead of threatening it. On the other hand, was Freya being a hypocrite to ask him to publish this, and not the rest?

Tristan was tearing open the letter from his stepmother now, and Freya wondered what the woman was like, and how soon they would meet. She looked forward to getting to know his two sisters, too; she already missed Mairead even more than she'd expected to.

Tristan looked up from the letter, his face pale and tight-looking. He laid the paper on the counter and took both her hands in his.

'What is it?' she asked, worried by the combination of frustration and concern on his face. 'Is it your father?'

'Yes.' He took a deep breath, and let it out in a short, heavy sigh. 'I'm so sorry. I have to leave.'

Freya went cold. 'Leave?'

'I hoped it would blow over, but...' He nodded at the letter. 'Catherine – my stepmother – wrote this just after she sent the last letter. My father needs me. Or rather, she needs me to go to him.'

'Is he all right?'

'She says not. She's given to panicking, but this time I'm not sure she's wrong to do so, and I can't ignore it.'

Freya swallowed hard. He couldn't leave, not now! He was the only person she could talk to. She tried not let selfishness win but it was difficult. 'What does she say?'

'Here.' He passed her the letter, and she held it up to the window to catch the late evening sunlight.

My dear Tristan

You will have received my previous letter, setting out dear William's troubles. I write now with urgency, to say that the situation has escalated – the unions are making more trouble than mere demands, and I have fears that violence is coming. William would not tell me this, of course, I have had word from Alexander who is, even now, on his way from New York to Vermont to lend assistance. I must insist you join, them with all possible haste, you know how hot-headed your brother can be, and how stubborn your father. They are in need of your calming influence, and your presence will strengthen them should my fears be realised.

'Violence?' she gave the letter back to Tristan, who scanned it again before folding it and tucking it into his pocket. 'Surely it wouldn't come to that?'

'It might. Especially with Alex on his way. Catherine's right, he's just as likely to stir things up as better them. My other brother Declan would be a better choice, but he's enlisted in the US Army now.'

'Then you have to go.' Freya tried to sound matter of fact, but her voice came out small, and already lonely-sounding. Everyone was leaving...

'Come with me,' Tristan said suddenly. She looked up, to see if he'd blurted it without thinking, but his eyes met hers and there was no regret in them. 'You'd love New England, it's beautiful. Forests as far as the eye can see—'

'Which your father's busy cutting down to make paper,' Freya pointed out, but her heart was starting to beat fast.

'We're replanting as fast as we're cutting,' he protested. 'Well, nearly. Come on, what do you say? The adventure of a lifetime, with me!' He took her hands again and raised them to his lips. 'It needn't be forever, just until my father sees sense, or better still, comes home.'

Freya couldn't help laughing at his excitement, and it was fuelled by her own. Could she really do it? Go all the way to America? The thought of saying goodbye to this man now ... it was as if someone had scooped out her heart and held it ready to throw on the fire. His eyes shone into hers, and that smile was back on his face, their hands clasped between them.

She opened her mouth, certain she was going to say yes, and instead condemned her heart to the flames. 'I can't.'

His expression froze, just for a second, and then the light went out of his eyes. 'I know,' he said, his voice barely above a whisper. 'I know.' He let go of her hands and instead drew her head onto his chest. She felt hot tears in the back of her throat, and stinging her nose and eyes, and when she put her arms around his waist she came within a broken heartbeat of changing her mind. How could she let him go?

But she had to. She pushed herself gently away. 'I'm sorry,' she managed. 'It's only that Papá needs me.' She threw a quick look towards the kitchen door, behind which she could hear her father talking to Grandpa, and lowered her voice. 'If I'm right about Anna, and–'

'I know,' he repeated. 'I can't believe I have to leave you.' A tiny smile touched his lips. 'And I know you think you're going to be lonely, but even if you are it'll not be for long.' He slid a hand beneath her hair to caress the back of her neck, and she shivered, and wished he would stop; he was making it too hard to let go. 'There will be men who want you,' he went on, more quietly. 'They'll flatter you, and court you, and eventually they'll learn to appreciate, and even love you, because who could fail to do that, once they know you?'

He tilted her face so she was looking directly into his eyes. 'But remember, you have *my* heart, and you have my life. I'm asking you to take care of them until I come back.'

'When will that be?'

He looked as if he would reply, but no words came out, and instead he shook his head. Her spirits sank once more; no matter how much both of them wanted to be sure of his return, the future was too uncertain. He gathered her close again, and they remained locked together, restless hands searching for a hold on each other that would last forever. Knowing it never could.

Chapter Seventeen

Porthstennack harbour

Matthew watched while John Rodda tacked up the trap pony. His father's wish to drive into Bodmin today couldn't have come at a worse time, but it would do him good, and maybe the clear air out on the moors would help drive away this fog that was drifting over Matthew's mind, too. He felt woolly and distant, hot and achy, and his back was throbbing more than ever. Freya was right, he was trying to do too much. Perhaps prove too much. After this trip he would take things easy, as promised.

For now, he sought distraction in conversation as he held the pony's bridle to keep her steady. 'You alongshore, or out on the *Pride* today?'

He was surprised by how much the question stung to ask. Time was he and John would have been working side by side, hauling nets, gutting, cleaning ... the boat tipping beneath their feet on the deep coastal swell, hands constantly busy, but one eye on the horizon for any shadow on the water's surface that might herald a squall.

'Out,' John said shortly. 'Always am, these days.'

'Is Ern still acting skipper?'

'Ar. Young Fry don't ever come out no more.'

'What does he do, then?'

John shrugged. 'Bit of lobsterin', bit of paintin'. Not much of anythin'. Got no interest. Either that or he's afeared.'

'He's been out before, used to all the time, under his pa,' Matthew pointed out, climbing onto the seat with difficulty.

'Ar, but bein' in charge is different, we both know that. 'Tween you an' me, I don't b'lieve he's cut out for 'un.' He stepped back and lifted his hand in farewell. 'Go to, lad, get your pa off to Bodmin so you can be back before the weather sets in. You'm lookin' a bit peaky yourself. You all right?'

'Soon will be.'

Matthew drove the trap slowly back along Smugglers' Way to the narrow main street of Porthstennack. As he passed Paddle Lane he looked down through the double row of tiny cottages, and thought back to when James had offered to swap the boat and his house for Penhaligon's Attic. Did the fool really believe it would have been enough, for all three Penhaligons to squeeze into the little two-bedroomed house? Or did he think Freya would have just upped sticks and left town soon enough anyway?

Matthew knew better; her heart was here; she'd proved that by not leaving with MacKenzie when he'd been called away. He could have wrung that young idiot's neck for the pain he'd caused, but Freya had insisted he would be back although Matthew had seen the looks pass between them, and they were not the faces of people who truly believed they would see each other again. They were the faces of young people in love, and hurting because of it. Trying to ease their own pain by pretending to themselves and everyone else.

The trap passed Hawthorn Cottage, and Matthew resisted the urge to lay on the whip and get past it as quickly as possible, but the pony had a long trip to make, and only a short rest before they set off. He'd intended to set his face ahead and not to look into the yard as he passed, but the sudden shout of childish delight struck a chord of memory in him, and he glanced instinctively towards it.

A girl of around the same age Freya had been when she last lived here was running towards the gate. 'Please, Mister! Let me have a ride?'

Matthew shook his head regretfully, although he did rein in to slow the pony. 'Sorry, Tory, your ma would have my hide. Besides, I've got a trip to make. Go and see John Rodda at Porthstennack tomorrow, she'll be back by then.'

302

The little girl climbed the gate and hung over to top of it, her hand outstretched. Matthew obligingly manoeuvred the pony closer, but his attention travelled past the girl to the sitting-room window, where a lumpish silhouette was separating into two distinct figures; evidently Nancy had found someone to help her with the rattling attic latch, after all. His eyes narrowed as he recognised the figure's neat, economical movements and slightly built outline ... then he shook his head and moved on; distasteful as the thought might be, who was he to question? And the rent had to be paid somehow.

Halfway through securing the pony outside Penhaligon's Attic he was overcome by a wave of dizziness, and stood still a moment, his head hanging low and his eyes closed tightly.

'You all right, boy?' A rough hand on his good shoulder brought him back, and he lifted his head. He smiled, but from the look of alarm on his father's face it was not a successful one.

'Just need a minute,' he muttered, and took a deep breath. His back flared with a fresh, white-hot pain, and he turned and spat into the road as nausea rushed up into the back of his throat. 'Get yourself sorted and we'll make a start.'

'We bleddy won't!' Robert gripped his arm, and tugged him away from the trap. 'You'll get inside there, and I'll finish here and fetch Bartholomew. Go and sit in the kitchen.'

Matthew hadn't the strength to argue. He left the pony to his father, and went unsteadily into the kitchen where he wiped his sweating brow with the sleeve of his shirt, and drew a glass of water from the tap. But he couldn't bring himself to drink it and instead he rested his head on his good arm and closed his eyes, breathing deeply and wishing the world away.

He jerked awake some time later, surprised to find he'd been dozing. Pa had returned, and brought Doctor Bartholomew with him, and the two of them were looking at him with deep concern.

'I'll take the trap back to John,' Robert began, but the doctor stopped him with a raised hand.

'Wait. If I'm right, you'll have need of it.'

He ignored Matthew's and Robert's questioning looks, and indicated Matthew should remove his shirt. He did so, with difficulty, and a helping hand from his father, and Bartholomew moved behind him and bent for a closer look in the dim light.

'Put the light on,' he said, and at the same time placed his fingers gently on Matthew's back. The chill of his touch made Matthew flinch, but the pain made him shudder, and the doctor withdrew his hand. 'I'm as certain as I can be that there's an infection in there,' he murmured. 'Probably a stone was missed.' In the flare of bright light he peered closely and pressed again, a little higher, and Matthew hissed.

Bartholomew's hand explored Matthew's upper back for a few minutes that seemed to stretch into hours, then he stood straight. 'There's a muscle back here called the rhomboid major, it seems that's where the problem lies.'

'Doctor Manley said there was muscle damage,' Matthew managed. 'He got the stone out, though.'

'He might have missed a bit.' Bartholomew handed Matthew his shirt. 'Either way, you have a fever, and need to go to hospital. Your father can take you to the Royal Cornwall Infirmary in Truro.'

'What about the shop?'

'Where's your daughter?'

'She'm working extra hours up to the 'otel,' Robert said. 'We'll just close the shop.'

'Your fever's not at a dangerous level yet,' Bartholomew warned, 'but you can't afford to delay too long. I'll leave it to you, but I'm sure you'd prefer to be operated on in hospital, rather than in my back room.'

'Operated on?' Matthew felt a little sick.

'If there's a stone left behind it's got to come out before the infection can be treated. I have instruments, and morphine, but if it's too deep I can't say much for the chances of getting at it before you become really ill.' He picked up his hat. 'You didn't ought to wait until the nine o'clock coach tonight, my advice is to take the trap while you've got it, and get to Truro before the weather turns and you're stuck here. I'll write you an introductory note.'

When he'd gone Matthew looked blearily at his father. 'Someone ought to tell Anna.'

'You heard the doc. No time to lose. We'll leave a note for Freya, and she can tell her.'

Matthew nodded, too tired and sore to argue. Now he knew it was not simply a slow recovery and exertion that was causing the pain, he couldn't so easily put it from his mind. The dizziness out in the street had been frightening, too, and had shaken his natural sense of invincibility as much as the explosion itself had done.

He climbed onto the trap a few minutes later, with his good arm shaking and his legs feeling ridiculously weak, and when they set off he gritted his teeth against the jolting of the cart, and held himself as stiffly as he could to counteract each bump in the road. Truro suddenly seemed a very long way away.

When Freya had left for work that morning the air had already felt heavy and damp. When she returned, at the end of her longer than usual shift, she was startled to see lightning dancing in the distance. No rain, no wind ... not even a rumble of thunder. Just the occasional bloom of light against the ominously dark horizon. Despite her aversion to storms it matched her mood perfectly; all through her shift she had gone over and over everything she had discovered, searching for the faintest glimmer of doubt, something to convince her that Anna was innocent of Juliet's murder, but all she could find in favour of that innocence was Anna herself ... and the bright flare of her character could not quite banish the overwhelming darkness of the circumstances. In the struggle to balance fact against hope, the facts were winning.

It was past closing time, but the sign declared Penhaligon's Attic still open, so Freya pushed at the door, surprised to find it resisting. She felt in her pocket for the front door key instead and went in that way. Papá was likely at the Tinner's, but even though it was still daylight out, it was dim indoors, and none of the lights were on. She felt a tremor of apprehension ... was Grandpa ill again? He shouldn't have been left alone...

'Grandpa?'

There was no reply, and her heart picked up an uncomfortable pace as she went into the kitchen and turned on the light. Her gaze fell on the note.

Freya. your pa is unwell and i have took him to truro. doctor will explain. do not worry. tell Anna too. Love grandpa.

Part of her was relieved Papá had sought help at last, but that he should have been sent to Truro gave her a queasy, squirming feeling in the pit of her stomach; that could only mean the infirmary, her father must have been sicker than they'd realised. She hurried back down the hallway to the front door, noting both her father's and her grandfather's coats still hung on their hooks; they must have left in a hurry then, they both knew the weather was turning. Hopefully they were already either on the train, or at the hospital itself, and would avoid a drenching when the storm finally hit. The last thing either of them needed was to catch a chill on top of everything else.

A bright flash made her flinch as she locked the door behind her, and she looked at the sky. This time the lightning was followed by a low rumble that rattled around the hills, leaving the air feeling stiller and quieter than ever when it faded away. Freya shivered and hurried to the doctor's house. The sharp memory of the last time she had knocked at this door didn't banish the fear, only

307

added to it: Tristan was gone, Mairead was gone, Juliet was gone, and now Papá and Grandpa...

She knocked again, louder, and Mrs Gale pulled the door open. She looked to be expecting Freya, and gestured her in. 'Doctor'll be out d'rectly.'

By the time the doctor had emerged from his office at the back of the house, Freya's imagination had given her a dozen scenarios, each of them worse than the one before, but Bartholomew's smile was reassuring.

'The hospital is far better equipped to help him, that's all. I've just recommended he goes now, on account of the storm. He has a fever, which I believe is being caused by a piece of grit, or a stone, that wasn't removed after the accident. That would also account for the additional pain he's been in. He'll be back home before you know it and fighting fit again.'

'I'd noticed he didn't seem well,' Freya said, relaxing a little. 'Are you sure he'll be all right travelling?'

'If I thought the journey would have shaken him too badly I'd never have suggested they take the trap.'

'The trap?' Freya looked at him in dismay. She pictured the envelope she had left on her dressing table; the extra money for the journals, which would have allowed him to travel in relative comfort, and at much greater speed, and swallowed a surge of frustration and anger at herself. At least that omission had been accidental, unlike the money Anna had deliberately hidden from him.

She thanked the doctor, and quickly walked the

308

short distance to the Tinner's Arms, glancing repeatedly at the ominously lowering sky and arriving at the back gate just as the first heavy drops of rain splashed onto the path. Arric stepped grandly out from behind the hen house then stopped in front of her, making her stumble. Heedless of her frustration he arched his back and opened his mouth in a wide, luxurious yawn that displayed his admirably sharp mouser's teeth, then he spared Freya a cool look and stretched out his front paws, shoving his rear-end into the air and taking his time, until a raindrop landed between his ears and made him flick his head irritably.

The door opened at the other end of the yard, and Anna appeared with her washing basket. Her sudden, unguarded laughter at the sight of Freya trying to step around the infuriating cat only made things more confusing, but it was followed by a more hesitant welcome as their currently uncertain relationship reasserted itself.

'Come away in, you'll catch your death out here in the rain.' She moved to pull the sheets off the washing line, then peered closer at Freya, frowning. 'Whatever's the matter?'

Freya told her about Papá, and watched carefully as Anna's face went through a telling series of emotions: shock, panic at mention of the infirmary, then tentative relief when Freya relayed Doctor Bartholomew's assurances.

She belatedly resumed tugging at the sheets. 'Help me get these in.' Her voice trembled as she added, 'And don't you worry, your da will be well cared for. Robert will see to it.'

Freya helped with the bedding, while her mind

worked just as hard to untangle what she knew from what she suspected. Anna's love for Papá was as deep as it had ever been, there was no doubt about it. But there was just as little doubt about what she was capable of. What would she do if Freya spoke her heart, but promised to keep any more dark secrets that came to light, if only Anna would stay? For a moment she even considered doing just that – what was there to be gained by doing anything else? It wouldn't change what had happened, and it certainly wouldn't make anyone happy.

But ... it wasn't just some distant, unknown person who had died, like that boy back in Ireland, it was *Juliet*. Juliet, whose laugh had been the biggest and loudest; whose wide, guileless smile had helped her out of the trouble her mischief had caused; whose mixed-up heart had confused physical satisfaction with happiness. Juliet, who had fallen foul of her own deep need for affection. Juliet, who lay cold and still, in unconsecrated ground, with her unborn child. Whether it was in cold blood or in a moment of anger, her friend was just as dead. And everything pointed to Anna.

She went into the kitchen, her arms full of damp sheets. Forgiveness pushed at her heart as she watched Anna constantly swallowing her fear, and remembered it was fear that had driven her to do what she had, but she wasn't yet ready to let it in. She worked in silence to spread the bedding to dry, ignoring the little looks Anna sent her way, and the chasm between them widened with each passing minute.

Lightning brightened the window, and she

counted under her breath until she heard the low growl that told her the storm was still some distance away. She could feel her skin shrink on her bones as she pictured it creeping closer, growing in intensity as it fed off itself. Even knowing Papá was nowhere near it didn't help with the suffocating sense of foreboding ... he wasn't fighting giant waves, but he was locked in a deeper, more personal struggle. The as-yet distant storm seemed poised to deliver devastation in one form or another. Perhaps it already had.

She moved into the pub to unlock the front door, but Anna caught her arm as she passed. 'Wait, love. Before we open, I think we ought to have a little talk, don't you?'

'Now?' This was no time for lengthy explanations, but that time would come.

'Look,' Anna said, and sighed as she cast about for the right words. 'I thought you understood why I couldn't tell Matthew about the blackmail, and the money.'

Freya realised then, that Anna had no idea what she suspected. It was probably best to keep it that way, rather than frighten Anna into bolting. 'I do understand it,' she said, 'I just don't like it.'

'Nor more do I.'

'But you're so good at it,' Freya said. 'It seems to be second nature to you.'

'I'm... I've...' Anna shrugged helplessly. 'I hated giving in to Juliet, and then having to lie about it. But you must see I'll do whatever I have to, to protect my family.'

There it was again. 'And how far do you take that?'

'What do you mean?'

Freya just stopped herself from blurting out what she knew. 'I mean will you ever tell him?'

'Of course I will. When ... all this is settled.'

'When everyone's forgotten Juliet, you mean. Stop talking about her as if she's an obstacle to be stepped over!' She went to the door and pulled back the bolt, with a burst of savagery that surprised even her. 'And if you'd been honest, you could have given Papá enough money to travel by train to hospital, instead of taking the trap.'

'Do you think that hasn't been a weight on my mind since you told me?' Anna shook her head, and Freya saw the gleam of a tear, quickly blinked away. 'And about the way I spoke of Juliet ... I'm sorry. I know you and she were close, and you think you knew her, but you weren't here that night.' She lowered her voice, looking at the door nervously. 'You didn't hear how she threatened Mairead. I'd have been delivering my daughter to the hangman myself if I hadn't stopped this!'

Freya blinked. Anna *did* know what she was thinking! And she wasn't denying it. Outside, the rain hissed on the road, and blatted against the window, and thunder rolled across the moor, punctuating the silence in the pub. Anna looked at Freya steadily, and Freya could see her mind working, searching for the words that would explain how things had become so dark and desperate. But what words could? The only question that remained was whether Freya could live with what she had learned, even for the sake of her father and her new sister.

The air between them seemed to tighten as the

seconds ticked away, and they both jumped when the door opened and Ern Bolitho came in.

'Evenin', Missus Penhaligon. Miss Penhaligon!' He rubbed his hands together. 'Weather steals away my work, but gives it to you, I reckon.'

'Your loss is certainly our gain, Mr Bolitho!' Anna smiled. Too easily. 'We'll talk later,' she added to Freya in a low voice.

Over and among the noisy greetings of Ern and the rest of James Fry's crew, Freya heard Anna's voice, bright and friendly, greeting her customers and welcoming them into the warmth. Feeling sick, she painted a smile onto her own face and did the same, wondering if she would ever become as adept at lying as Anna Penhaligon.

Before much more than an hour had passed, she realised she already had. She answered sympathetic questions about Tristan's sudden departure, and commiserated with crewmen about the loss of a night's fishing, and the likelihood of more bad weather to come, she smiled, poured drinks, wiped spills, explained Papá's visit to hospital, and gave every impression she was not feeling the bite of fear and loneliness deeper with every minute that passed. But in the midst of the busiest night she had ever known, she *was* utterly alone. There was no one she could unburden her heart to.

The door slammed open, ripped by the strengthening wind from the hand of the man holding it, and smashed back against the wall. Conversation stopped just for a moment, and when it resumed Freya heard several comments of, 'blowin' up a bit

313

from the east, innut?' and 'long tide, too.' She knew from Papá's stories that an easterly wind, blowing against the tide, would raise a bigger swell, and each of these men would have spent the preceding hours dragging their boats higher up the beach and securing them as best they could. Their quiet appraisal of the weather in no way betrayed the effort, and the worry they lived with.

Even over the noise of a very small pub, filled with chatter, she could hear how the storm was worsening. The tell-tale rattle and scrape of a bucket blowing across the yard; a shutter banging on the house next door; the hollow-sounding echo of the wind itself; and the rain, swept hard against the glass with each fresh gust like tiny stone pellets. The thunder had died, but these sounds were more ominous, and the fishermen were glancing at each other with troubled expressions, particularly those who would have to make their way back down to Porthstennack once the evening of keeping good company was over.

A loud crash from somewhere out the back sent Anna out to make sure no glass had been broken, and Freya went behind the bar to help. The door opened again, bringing Tom Carne and the rattle of wet leaves, blown prematurely from the trees just outside. Grumbles arose as the wind snatched at coats and hats, and Tom slammed the door with difficulty, his gaze falling on James Fry. Freya tensed, remembering Tristan's story of the last time these two had met in here, but this time James was sober and he sat straight. He saw Freya's face, and gave her a wry look.

'Don't worry, I'm not looking for a fight.'

'Maybe not, but I think Tom is.'

'He's not going to get one with me,' James assured her. 'He'd be better off looking elsewhere.' His gaze flicked over to where David Donithorn sat, deep in his cups yet again. An unhealthy portion of Donithorn's wages had gone into the Tinner's coffers lately, from what Anna had said.

'Remember what we said, on the beach,' she said quietly to James. 'It's over and done. Accusing anyone won't bring Juliet back.'

She couldn't help feeling like a hypocrite; she herself was still pulled first one way and then the other, the conflict making her feel nauseous and outside the control of her own thoughts. She had no idea how to resolve it, but somehow, and while Papá was away, she must.

Anna came back into the room, drying her hands in her apron. 'The gutter's down at the back,' she told Freya. 'It'll be all right for tonight, but tomorrow we'll have to get the ladders and see what can be done.'

'I'll help,' James said. 'We won't be putting to sea for a day or two, this storm's likely to blow awhile yet.'

'You never put to sea anyhow,' Donithorn put in, raising his head at last. His half-closed eyes drifted while he found his focus, then he gave a soft snort. 'You're a bloody coward, Fry.'

James replaced his glass carefully on the bar, and turned to Donithorn. 'I have different priorities,' he said, in measured tones. 'And you're drunk.'

'Should've kept Penhaligon on,' Donithorn muttered. 'He's not scared to work out there.'

Freya exchanged a wide-eyed look with Anna; the last person either of them would have expected to speak up on Papá's behalf was David Donithorn. Even after the tentative truce following the explosion.

'Matt and I couldn't work together,' James said, and his voice was tight now. 'Leave it, Donithorn, eh? Go home to your wife.' He stressed the word only slightly, but Donithorn rose unsteadily to his feet and planted his fists on the table in front of him.

'You don't deserve what your pa left you.'

Anna placed a warning hand on James's forearm and shook her head, but James didn't appear to notice.

'I don't think you're the right person to be talking about my father,' he said, 'given you're the reason he lost half the business, and damned near his life.'

Donithorn frowned. 'That was down to Penhaligon.'

'And yet you're the one defending him?'

'Enough!' Anna banged the glass she was holding on the bar, making the two men flinch. 'I'll not have the two of you arguing about what can't be changed! And especially not about my husband, who's sick and in hospital!' She turned to James. 'I'd be glad of your help tomorrow, thank you.'

Tom Carne spoke up. 'Oh, don't make them stop, Miz Penhaligon. It'd cheer a soul to watch the two of them rip chunks out of each other.'

'Don't you start in,' Anna snapped. 'Any more, and I'll throw the lot of you out into the rain. You

316

can do what you want out there.'

'You can try,' Tom said, and Freya realised he'd been drinking before he'd arrived at the pub, and his eyes were glittering dangerously. She moved closer to Anna, suddenly fearful, but Tom had turned to Donithorn.

'You destroyed my sister, just as sure as he did.' He jerked his thumb at James. There was an unexpected note of despair in his voice, and when Freya saw it reflected in James's expression she dared to hope their shared emotion might help dampen the fire a little.

But Donithorn was too far gone to take heed of the rising emotions. 'Your sister was a whore, Carne.' He spoke clearly and slowly, and not quite slurred enough to make the word any less shocking. 'She's the one who ruined everything.' He pushed himself upright, his voice rising suddenly to a hoarse shout. 'She ruined *everything!*'

The next moment Tom Carne had grasped him by the shirt, and pushed, sending both of them crashing sideways into the bar. Freya cried out as the bar top rattled, setting glasses and tankards rolling, and beer splashing the shirts of the men who'd spent their last pennies on it. Donithorn and Carne remained oblivious to the shouts of outrage, and demands for recompense, and as each struggled for a favourable position chairs were knocked over and customers retreated hurriedly from tables before they were drawn into the fight.

Freya turned to ask Anna what she ought to do, but was just in time to see the door swing shut as Anna vanished into the passage. Furious to have been left to manage things, she looked for James instead, but he had already weighed in and was trying to pull the men apart. Thank goodness she could rely on *someone*... She tried to raise her own voice above the shouts of encouragement from the small crowd, and the grunts and gasps of the battling men, but it was easily drowned.

David Donithorn swung his fists several times at Carne's head, but the drink was working against him and he couldn't connect. Which was just as well; Freya had no desire to spend the night mending broken faces. A spike of pain went through her as she remembered Tristan and his foolhardy act, stepping into Donithorn's way, and she felt his loss more acutely than ever.

But she had no time to spare in wishing he was here now. She could see James was having no success, and had taken an elbow to the chest that knocked him backwards. Ern grabbed his arm and prevented him from returning to the fray – Freya couldn't hear what the acting skipper was saying to his boss, but James nodded and rubbed at his chest, and remained where he was.

The noise was rising, and now the shouts were accompanied by the splintering and crashing of wooden chairs as, with what looked to be the last bit of his strength, Donithorn shoved Carne away. Carne landed badly among the broken furniture, and Donithorn lashed out with his boot. Freya's heart thumped hard with rising fear. She'd heard fond reminiscences of bar fights, mostly among men who'd be just as likely to risk life and limb for one another as to land a ringing blow about the head, but this was not like that. Those were momentary eruptions of frustration, easily quelled, and put aside as conversation pieces for calmer times. These two men would do serious damage to one another if they were left to themselves.. Didn't the cheering fools realise that?

Freya could only think of one thing to do, and that was to fetch the constable. She tried to yell across to James, to ask him to go, but there were four men blocking her, all shouting, egging on both fighters equally, content to watch the carnage no matter who won.

The door to the passage bounced open again, and Anna came in carrying a large jug. She took one look at the crowd pressing against the bar, and handed the jug to Freya. It was extremely heavy and icy-cold, and when Freya looked into it she saw bits of leaf and twig floating there; this was from the rain barrel in the yard. When she looked up to ask what Anna wanted her to do with it, her mouth dropped open in surprise; Anna had boosted herself onto the bar, and was actually standing on it. Ignoring the nudges and looks of disbelief from her customers, she leaned down to take the jug off Freya, then rose again and flung the contents over the two fighters, and whoever else was in the way.

For a moment only the rising howl of the wind could be heard, and the slow drip of water from sodden clothing onto the floor. Then someone chuckled, and others joined in, but neither Carne nor Donithorn were among them. As the group cleared away from the bar Freya saw Donithorn's face, dark and tight with fury. He shoved his way towards the door, and, without looking back, he left. The gust of wind that came in, with a fresh scattering of leaves, silenced the last of the nervous laughter, and people turned their attention to straightening the room, politely ignoring Anna as she climbed inelegantly off the bar.

Freya steadied her arm as she slid down, torn between admiration and distrust yet again. Anna was breathing hard, but there was a light of triumph in her eyes, and a flush on her cheeks.

'Well, I never thought I'd see the day I'd have to do that,' she said, brushing at her skirts. 'Uncle Colm would have a fit.'

'Well, you were brought up to be a lady, after all,' Freya said, and Anna had clearly heard the edge in her voice, because the light in her eyes flickered out and she made a pretence of straightening her apron.

'Come on then, there's work to be done.'

Freya was collecting the glasses left behind by the last customer, her stomach in knots as she prepared herself for the confrontation, when she heard Anna cry out from the passage. 'Freya! Come quick!'

She ran into the passage, to see Anna's shadowy, crouching figure at the far end. The garden door was open and banging in the wind, and in the wildly flickering light from the candles Anna had set along the passage Freya could see there was another figure, slumped, just outside the door.

She hurried towards them, her heart pounding, and recognised the figure as David Donithorn. He half-sat, with his back to the hen house, the rain lashing at him, his head drooped, conscious but unable to move out of the weather.

'Is he hurt, or still drunk?'

'I don't know...' Anna tilted the man's head to catch the struggling light. 'I'd say both. It would appear Tom caught up with him after all. He's going to have quite a bruise on that eye tomorrow.'

'Might not have been Tom,' Freya pointed out. 'Might have been James. He called James a coward, remember?'

'Well, whoever it was, it looks from the state of the garden as though they fought right here. Help me get him indoors.'

Together they roused Donithorn and supported his drooping frame between them to the kitchen. Blood dripped from his nose as they went, leaving splashes of deeper red on the earthenware floor.

'This is becoming a habit,' Anna observed as she and Freya hefted Donithorn into the easy chair by the cooking range. She took a towel from the rail and handed it to Freya. 'Dry his hair as best you can, but be careful in case he's got another injury we don't know about.'

She set about preparing a bowl of water to clean the blood from Donithorn's nose, and Freya draped the towel around their patient's shoulders, patting it over his hair to mop up the worst of the wet. Her own hair hung draggled around her shoulders, as did Anna's, and they had both muddied their skirts and boots, leaving dark footprints across the floor. More mess to clean, but Anna didn't seem to pay any heed to that. She looked worried as she wiped away the smears of blood, but her expression gradually cleared, and her manner calmed.

'I think he's all right, just a bit taken by the drink.'

Donithorn jerked and mumbled, and Freya found herself shushing him as if he were a fractious child. He mumbled something else, and she caught the word 'police'. Her eyes met Anna's over his head, and Anna gave a tiny shrug.

'We'll not be calling the constable over a fight, David. Don't worry.'

'Lost her,' he muttered. 'What to do? What'll I *do?*' Then, to both Freya's and Anna's astonishment and dismay, he burst into tears.

Startled, Freya put an arm around his shoulder and drew his head to her, soothing him as best she could. 'Is he talking about Juliet?'

'He must be. I didn't think he cared for her so much.'

Beneath Freya's hand, Donithorn's shoulders heaved and shuddered, and his sobs sounded as though they were being pulled from him. She felt her own eyes prickling with tears of sympathy and with her own renewed grief.

'She in't bad,' Donithorn gulped. It sounded painful, as if he didn't have enough breath to spare, but he had to speak anyway. 'She did a stupid, bad thing, but she in't ... she in't *bad.*'

He looked up through tear-filled eyes, and the waft of stale alcohol washed over Freya's face.

She tried not to flinch away. 'No, she wasn't,' she said softly. 'I told her to say ... to say nothing to no one.'

'Hush, David,' Anna said. 'It's all right.'

'No, it's *not* all right,' Freya snapped, her own

emotions hopelessly entangled with Donithorn's now. 'She's dead!'

Donithorn slumped again. 'She'll hang.'

Anna frowned. 'Hang?' She shook his shoulder. 'Who will hang, David?'

'Ginny.' His voice faded to little more than a mumble, and Freya felt his hot breath through her blouse as he sighed the words, 'Ginny killed her.'

Chapter Eighteen

If astonishment left Anna momentarily speechless, a glance at Freya's face told her the girl was in a real state of shock; discovering Juliet had died by violence, not suicide, must had shaken her to the core.

They both waited as Donithorn tried to pull himself together, and gradually the quiet of the kitchen and the cool of the damp cloth on his cheek began to work. While he gathered his wits Anna thought of every possible scenario in which Ginny Donithorn might have encountered Juliet with such a tragic outcome. Freya's face was completely unmoving, her eyes staring straight ahead, and Anna began to grow concerned.

'What happened, David?' she asked at last. 'Was it an accident?' She understood too well how that might have occurred, and the similarity with Liam Cassidy's death at Mairead's hands even raised a flicker of sympathy towards Ginny

Donithorn. 'Did they fight over you?'

David sat back away from Freya. 'Weren't no accident. Ginny's always had a hot temper. It's what I first liked about her.' His voice was calming as he spoke, and his hitching breaths subsided, making it all too easy to understand him.

'I don't know how she found out about the kid, but...' His fist clenched on his knee. 'Anyway, she did, and she followed Juliet out to the pond Monday night after shift. She knew what she was doing. They fought, Ginny pushed, and when Juliet din't come up again she waited.'

'To see if she could help?' Anna heard the hope in her own voice and knew it was misplaced even before he replied.

'You don't know my Ginny, Miz Penhaligon, if you're askin' that. She said she was makin' sure.'

'And you told no one?' Anna tried hard to keep the anger out of her voice, but David wouldn't have noticed anyway.

'What would be the use? Ginny came to me b'tween my double shifts at Wheal Furzy. Everyone said how nice it was she brought me a bit of dinner.' He gave a short, bitter laugh. 'But she only came to tell me what she done. Then she went home again, and slept like a lamb while I spent the whole night in the dark, picturin' it. My *baby.*'

He sniffed and wiped his nose on the back of his hand, then looked at Anna with brimming eyes. 'I reckon you'll be tellin' the constable now then?'

'That's your job,' Anna said curtly. 'Where is Ginny now?'

He shrugged. 'Gone. She left the day after the explosion, she prob'ly thought I'd tell the Cap'n the real reason why I wasn't in my right mind.' He caught her questioning frown, and shrugged. 'Her brother moved to Camborne, back along, she most likely went there to start with.'

'That's probably not far enough.' Anna rose unsteadily to her feet. 'She won't stay at large for long, and rightly so. The police will know to look for her where her family are. And you *are* going to tell them, aren't you.' It wasn't a question, but David nodded miserably. Now he'd confessed to them, there was no reason to think he'd protect the murderer of his child, but he must be torn in half, and Anna couldn't help feeling sorry for him, despite everything.

She turned to see Freya, also rising, and was startled at the look of guilty dismay on the girl's face. 'What is it, love?'

Freya looked as though she had a hundred things to say, but nothing came out. Her cheeks were stained crimson, and her eyes were open wide, as if a dozen small truths were falling into place. She shook her head and came over to Anna, and put her arms around her. Relieved, Anna returned her embrace, feeling the slender shoulders shaking under her hands, although she was sure Freya wasn't weeping. Perhaps she was the one who'd told Ginny? If so then no wonder she was so shocked; she would feel completely responsible for the death of her best friend, not to mention terrified of any retribution Donithorn felt inclined to administer.

Anna held Freya close, her narrowed eyes still

on David. His head was drooping, and his hands working before him as if he could wash them of the knowledge he had never wanted in the first place... She herself was tensed to do everything necessary to protect Freya, but David would have much worse than Anna to answer to if he hurt the girl – broken arm or not, Matthew would lay the younger man to waste.

But David was fighting a more immediate battle. As Anna watched over Freya's bent head, he half-straightened and began to take deeper breaths, and her heart sank as she saw him swallow hard once, twice, then surrender. He lurched forward off the chair and onto his knees, and vomited, pure liquid that spread in a wide pool across the kitchen floor. She turned up her nose at the smell, and Freya lifted her head.

'I'm sorry,' she said in a hoarse voice.'

'What for?' Suddenly worried Freya was going to confess to having told Ginny, Anna went on quickly, 'Never mind, we'll talk in a while.'

'But I should have known,' Freya insisted. 'You could never have done something so awful.'

Anna stilled, and looked more closely at the girl in front of her. Freya's eyes were still dry, but her face had gone from flushed to pale. What did she mean? *Done something so...*

It hit her, then. Like the hardest slap, jerking her out of her tumbling thoughts, her worries over who had told Ginny, and her longing for Matthew's return. 'You thought I killed her,' she muttered. Of course. It was blindingly obvious. But *why?*

She was prevented from asking the most

important question of all by David barking a last, retching belch, and sitting back, his eyes streaming. 'I'm that sorry, Miz Penhaligon.'

'Go home, David,' Anna said, her eyes back on Freya. 'We'll clean this.'

'What do I do?' he asked again. 'Will the constable arrest me too?'

Anna's patience snapped. 'I don't bloody know! Get out, go on!'

The kitchen door swung shut behind him, and they listened to the scrape of chairs and tables that marked his unsteady progress through the pub to the front door. When it had fallen silent again Anna turned to Freya, aching with the effort of reining in her anger.

'How long have you thought this evil thing of me?'

Freya winced. 'I didn't want to think it.'

'Then why did you?' Anna was aware she sounded harsh and unforgiving, and she tried to soften her voice but she felt too raw. 'What could possibly have made you think I could kill anyone, let alone a pregnant young girl?'

Freya sat at the table and began to talk, and by the time she had reached the part where Tristan said he'd seen her outside Wheal Furzy on the day Juliet had died, and had talked him out of going to the pool, Anna's mind was too full to do more than ask, 'Why, for the love of all that's holy, didn't you come to me? To ask?'

'I thought you already knew what I was thinking. You kept talking about how you'd have done anything to protect Mairead.'

'And so I would. But ... *murder?*'

'I supposed at first that it was an accident. That you'd fought, or she'd fallen.'

'Like Liam Cassidy.'

'Yes. But then with the blackmail, and what with everything that's come out about Malcolm Penworthy, and Tristan talking about how character traits can follow down through families–'

'What?' Anna held up her hand. 'What's that about Penworthy?' Freya fell silent, but Anna's insides churned at the look on her face. 'Freya?'

'He's a murderer. It's in the books.'

'The books? The journals?' Anna shook her head. 'I can't take this in, not today.' She felt unutterably weary, and heart-sore, and Matthew occupied the forefront of her mind even now.

'This is the only thing that's stopped you telling your da about the money, isn't it?'

Freya hesitated, then nodded. 'I thought you might use it to run away if you thought anyone knew what ... what I thought you'd done.'

'And now?'

'Will I tell him, you mean?' Freya looked at her steadily. She still looked guilty and sorrowful, but there was a firm set to her jaw, and her eyes were calm. 'No. But I still think you ought to.'

'I will.' But even the relief of unburdening herself to Matthew wouldn't remove the sour taste of Freya's doubts. 'This must have been difficult for you,' she said, her voice quiet. 'I'm sorry I haven't given you a good reason to believe anything I say, but please, believe this. I love your da, and I love you. What I've done for Mairead, I would do for any one of you. That's how deeply you're in here.' She lay a hand over her heart, and

328

struggled to control the rising emotion in her voice. 'I know Juliet was your friend, but she was my enemy. That sounds harsh, but it's the truth. I'm sorry she's gone, but that night I hated her, Freya. I truly did. What she was prepared to put my daughter through... And she'd have punished you too, by taking Mairead from you.'

'She was desperate.' It was an old argument, and Freya sounded as tired of it as Anna was.

'She was at fault. You know that.'

'She didn't deserve to die.'

'No, she didn't.' Anna hesitated, but if she couldn't ask now, she never would. 'Was it you who told Ginny Donithorn about the baby?'

'No! I hardly know Ginny, and I did everything I could to make sure no one knew.'

Anna nodded. 'I had to ask. You were the only other person who knew.'

'Apart from Brian Cornish, and whoever else was within earshot in the pub the night *you* told him,' Freya pointed out.

'There wasn't anyone else in the pub,' Anna said, trying to ignore the accusatory tone. 'It was early. Brian wouldn't have told anyone else, it took him two days to tell James. You know he did right, you yourself tried to persuade Juliet to tell him.'

Freya sighed. 'I know. And Ginny had as much right to know as James did, but I wouldn't want to be in the shoes of the person who told her.'

'I had no idea she was of that mentality,' Anna said. 'Ellen just said she was sad she'd not been able to give David a child, never hinted that she was the fierce type.'

'She kept mostly to herself,' Freya said. 'I don't think anyone but her family really knew her, and half of them don't live here any more.'

'And now she's gone.' Anna caught a strong waft of David Donithorn's vomit, and her throat clenched. 'Go home now. Get some sleep, it's been a long day. I'll be up to the shop in the morning, before you go to work.'

'I'll help you clean here.'

It was something of an olive branch, but offered very tentatively, and Anna shook her head. 'No, you go on. I won't sleep yet awhile.' She tried to smile. 'I hope one day you'll come to trust me as much as you trust your da.'

'Of course I trust you.'

Anna compared Freya's cautious acceptance with Mairead's wholehearted, unquestioning love, and her heart ached with the longing to see that sweet, earnest face again. Freya had shown her true feelings tonight; and even Matthew had doubted her – once he learned she had continued to lie to him she would be lucky if he ever trusted her again. It felt as if, despite her desperate struggle for this new life, and the people in it, she would still lose everything, and after tonight she didn't know how much fight she had left in her.

She woke into utter blackness, her heart racing for no apparent reason. The wind had risen even further since she'd come to bed hot, sweaty and exhausted, and stinking of carbolic after scrubbing the kitchen floor, but she was so tired that the noise of it hadn't prevented her from falling into a heavy slumber almost immediately. It howled around the corners of the pub, and the back gate, usually wedged into the clumps of grass by the wall, now banged rhythmically against the stone post. Maybe that broken guttering had collapsed even more and that was what had wakened her?

She fumbled for a match, and, still listening hard, she lit the paraffin lamp that stood on her bedside cabinet, and turned the flame high. There was a rattle of loose slates above her, and she shivered as the rain lashed at the window pane, each gust sending a fresh burst until it sounded as if it were only a matter of time before the glass broke beneath the onslaught. Her thoughts went to Ellen and little Eddie in Porthstennack, and she drew her knees up and hugged them, trying to quell the nasty suspicion that things at the fishing hamlet might actually be dangerous now, as this seemingly endless night went on.

At last she rose and dressed, wondering what time it was. It was still dark, and in August too, but it might be any time from two o'clock to five o'clock given this weather. She pulled on her boots, and took her heavy coat down from the top of the wardrobe. Emerging from the back yard onto the road, she saw she was not the only one to have concerns, although it looked as though the people of Caernoweth were well used to lending a hand, and knew exactly what was needed; people hurried past with blankets and boxes, extra clothing and tools, and Anna followed.

The gas lights trembled, and Anna staggered forward as the ferocious easterly wind pushed her towards her destination, as if urging her on. She heard a voice call her name, and Freya caught up with her.

'What woke you?' Anna asked, grasping her hand. 'It's not thundering any more.'

'It's the sea,' Freya told her. 'Can't you hear it?'

With a jolt, Anna realised she could. It was such a familiar sound it hadn't occurred to her that she shouldn't be able to hear it so clearly all the way up here, but now Freya had drawn her attention to it she shuddered at the distant, furious roar.

'Are you going to be all right, love?' She tugged at Freya's hand to stop her. 'I know how storms take you, and to go down to the beach...'

'We're all needed,' Freya said. She nodded at the basket she carried. 'They're saying there hasn't been a storm like this since the one that broke the pump at Wheat Furzy back along, and flooded it out.'

'Wait, let me fetch something and come with you.' Anna hurried back inside and returned with an armful of blankets, and the two joined the steady flow of people making their way to Porthstennack, to lend strength where they could. Behind them the sky was lightening, but ahead all was still in darkness, and those who knew the road best hurried past the others, pushing them aside in their haste. Anna found herself shoved into the hedge more than once, and brambles tore her skin, but the lashing rain soon washed away any blood. They passed the big stone barn that belonged to Priddy Farm, and as the first rays of the day's light touched the roof Anna saw a gaping hole and crossed her fingers for the hay harvest.

Porthstennack was alive with people, hurrying from house to house, checking on neighbours. Parents called to their children with an anger born of panic, their shouts punctuated by the sounds of splintering wood and pounding surf. The boiling sea rose, its waves dwarfing the harbour wall, and as the inky black of the sky faded it was possible to see tiny black outlines of boats, ripped from their moorings and dancing on the surface with eerie grace before vanishing into the troughs.

Paddle Lane bore the brunt of the storm's fury. Running along the length of the shingle shelf, the houses that backed onto the beach were battered time and again as rocks both big and small were picked up by the tide and flung like bullets against crumbling, salt-eroded walls.

Anna had never witnessed anything like this before, even when she'd lived on the cliffs in Ireland. Her former home had never come under attack from the sea; on stormy nights she, Finn and Mairead had simply closed the curtains, brightened the lamps, and read quietly, lulled by the crackling fires and the distant sound of the wind. Cosy. Warm. Safe. Now she realised that, all that time, there had been scenes like this just below the Caseys' fortress; people forced from their homes to save their belongings, and each other. Fishermen fighting the monstrous tide to rescue their boats – their livelihoods. Broken glass flung into bedrooms and kitchens, and slates sent spinning from roofs to land in the road, exploding deadly shards in all directions.

Freya must have been fighting the memories of

that other horrific storm; Anna could hear her breath coming short and shallow, and her hand was tight on Anna's arm. Someone pushed past in the darkness, and they both stumbled but held each other upright. Anna realised she had no idea what to do next; she'd been driven here by instinct, and then swept along by the tide of townspeople hurrying to help, but what should she be doing?

Another shadowy figure barrelled into them, and Anna heard a familiar voice. 'Keep a hold of me!'

'Brian?'

'Miz Penhaligon?' Brian and his wife stopped, their boots scraping on the wet road, and Anna flung her arm up to block the buffeting wind.

'Are you all right? What can I do to help?'

'Go to Esther!' It was the first time Anna had heard Mrs Cornish speak, and her voice was surprisingly low and melodious, even in her agitation. 'She'm refusin' to leave! We can't make her—'

'What!' Freya was already starting in the direction of Paddle Lane, but Anna pulled her back.

'Wait! It's dangerous down there!'

'Exactly!' Freya jerked away and grabbed at her skirt, lifting it free of her boots. 'Come on.'

Anna's hair whipped across her face, stinging-wet and momentarily blinding her. When she had pushed it aside she saw Freya had already begun running, and it was only then that she realised the night had finally retreated, letting the grey daylight wash over the hamlet and showing the extent of the devastation of Paddle Lane.

She fumbled her key from her pocket and

spoke quickly to Brian's wife. 'Go to the Tinner's. Tell everyone else the same. Make hot drinks until you can't make any more. Take any clothes or blankets you can find, and share them out. Here, take the key.'

The wind tried to whip her words away, but she made sure the Cornishes had understood, then turned and followed Freya along the narrow lane, her boots crunching on pebbles, and knocking aside bigger stones and bits of broken fencing. Her heart leaped in horror as she saw the girl dodge a flying slate, barely breaking her pace as she ran up the short path to the front door of Esther Trevellick's little house.

A loud cracking sound further along the lane snatched her attention away from Freya. James Fry erupted from his own front door, his face ghost-white in the dawn's light. He looked behind him, and Anna saw him flinch at whatever he was seeing.

'James!'

He jumped, and turned. 'Go back, it's dangerous! My back rooms–'

'Esther won't leave! Will you help us?'

He looked back at his own house again, then at Esther's, and a moment later he was running towards the Trevellick house. 'Christ, we have to get her out...'

Anna cried out as seawater foamed up through the narrow gap between two nearby houses as she passed them, soaking her skirt to the knee. The iciness of it was bad enough, but the strength that the wave still carried, even after being spent on the road, nearly tugged her off her feet. The surf thundered and roared on the other side of the houses, and she could hear raised voices at the end of the lane, in the middle of the little hamlet. But there was no time to turn and see what fresh damage had been done by this latest surge; Freya was rattling at Esther's front door, and James pulled her, none too gently, out of the way.

He put his shoulder to the old wood and pushed, then stood back and raised his foot to deliver a powerful kick, directly beneath the handle. The door smashed inward and James staggered back into Anna and almost knocked her over. There was no sign of the old woman, but the kitchen door was closed, and from beyond it they could hear the sound of the sea ... too loud. Too close.

She pushed open the door. The window was smashed, and the kitchen awash with floodwater, wet sand, and stones. But there was no one there. She turned to tell the others to try upstairs, and a hollow boom from just outside the window stole her words, and her breath. The next moment it was as if someone had emptied a bucket of chilled water down her already soaked back, and the force behind it sent her staggering.

'If Esther stays here, she could die,' James said grimly. 'My own house is all but destroyed at the back.'

Freya led the way upstairs, calling to Esther but receiving no reply. Anna followed, her insides tight with dread, and James was close on her heels, pushing her on.

'It's that room there,' he said, pointing straight ahead.

Freya went in. The window beside her was in the same jagged, smashed state as the one in the kitchen, and the curtain rail had been pulled down and lay askew across the floor. Esther herself sat huddled in the corner, and in the dim light Anna could see there was blood on her face and her hands.

'Come with us, Esther, please! You're hurt, we can help you.'

Esther shook her head, and Anna was about to sharpen her voice, just to break through the old woman's mantle of shock, when James moved past to crouch in front of her.

He spoke gently, but with an edge of urgency. 'He wouldn't want you to stay, not when it's so dangerous.'

Esther looked towards the bed. 'I can't go away an' leave 'im.' Her voice was low, shaking, and James put his hand over hers.

'He's not here. And if he was, he'd tell you to go with Mrs Penhaligon, somewhere safe, so you could keep remembering him.'

Esther raised flooded eyes to him, and Anna turned away to find a dry blanket in the wardrobe. There was a pile of neatly folded clothing there too – she'd come back for those later; it didn't seem right to salvage such things now, in the face of Esther's grief.

'Come on,' James said, and Anna tried not to shrink away as a wave thundered against the side of the house, sending spray and more broken glass all over the bed. Esther finally allowed herself to be raised to her feet, and Anna draped the blanket around her shoulders.

'We'll take you back to the Tinner's,' she said, 'get those cuts looked at.'

Stepping carefully over broken glass, they led Esther back out into the lane, where the daylight made them squint with its contrast to the dim sitting room they had left behind. As they reached the end of Paddle Lane they delivered the trembling Esther into the hands of Alice Packem and Martha Rodda, who promised to see her to the Tinner's, and give her a hot drink.

The wind still raged, and pushed against the incoming tide, raising a swell that drew even the most reluctant eye in mute fascination. Anna found her gaze pulled time and time again to the heaving grey water, hypnotised by it, and had to be dragged farther up the road to avoid a second head-to-toe soaking. Once he was satisfied they were safe, James left them and went, with obvious reluctance, to discover the fate of the *Pride of Porthstennack.*

Anna pulled her wet coat tighter around her, taking meagre comfort from the act itself although she was no warmer for it. 'We have to help them save their belongings if we can,' she said to a shivering Freya. 'But I don't know how.'

'What about the barn at the bottom of Priddy Farm? We might be able to dry some of the clothes and blankets in there.'

'Perfect. Come on.'

Together they went back along Paddle Lane, heads bowed against a fresh onslaught of stinging rain. The worst-hit houses were Esther's and the two next to it. James's shouldn't have been as bad as he said, and, curious, Anna went in to see if she

338

could salvage some clothing for him. He was right; the rooms at the back were uninhabitable; the kitchen and main bedroom windows smashed, just as Esther's was, but the frames were hanging loose in all of them. She remembered him saying he'd be making fresh plaster at the weekend, but he had not yet done it, and the walls were bare around the window where he had knocked the old stuff away.

In the other bedroom, the occupied one, the story was a similar one, but Anna wasted no time trying to work out the extent of the damage. She opened the wardrobe and found dry clothing, and took as much as she could carry back out into the rain. Hunched over it to keep it as dry as possible, she ran to the bottom of the hill and cut across the field to the Priddy Farm barn. The hole in the roof had let in a considerable amount of rain, but Farmer Pawley had known as well as anyone that the storm was coming, and so the hay was covered, and safe. She left what she'd brought in a corner and went back for more.

Gradually more of the stricken people began to do the same instead of hurrying back to the safety of Caernoweth and the Tinner's Arms. Wet blankets were spread to dry, wearable clothes were shared out among those who most needed them. Boxes were brought from flooded homes, containing treasured personal items, letters, photos ... anything that could be rescued was brought to the Priddy Farm barn.

Farmer Pawley and his right-hand man, Alfie Nancarrow, set a ladder against the side of the barn, and Pawley and another labourer held it while Alfie, as the youngest of them, climbed up to cover the hole as best he could. It was a terrifying thing to watch, and Nancarrow's progress was slow and wary as the wind tugged and pulled at his clothing and at the huge sheet of canvas he dragged behind him. The ladder slid and wobbled despite the men's best efforts to hold it steady, and Nancarrow stopped often, his head down, his knuckles white as he gripped the side of the ladder with his only free hand as he waited for the gusts to subside. Eventually the tarpaulin was stretched across the ragged hole and nailed tight, and Nancarrow returned to the safety of solid ground and accepted a hot cup of tea, pressed on him by a grateful farmer's wife.

Anna paused to catch her breath during one trip from Porthstennack, her arms straining beneath the weight of sodden pillows and sheets, and she looked out to sea. The rain splattered against the back of her head, and the still-fierce wind pressed her soaked skirts against the backs of her legs, but she hardly noticed it any more. Daylight showed a seascape that was at once terrifying and glorious. The rolling swell, the spume flying as the waves dashed themselves against the rocks and the harbour wall, the unceasing roar... The beach was covered with the wood of a dozen smashed boats, but the larger vessels appeared to have ridden out the worst of it without too much damage.

She tried to picture how it must be to be caught out there in the middle of the sea, and couldn't. Matthew had told her stories that had made her stomach shrink and twist with fear on his behalf, and she knew that, seeing the water behaving exactly as he'd described, she ought to be able to put herself in his place, but it was impossible. She'd never know the fear and exhilaration of fighting, and besting, such a beast. Matthew did, and it was where he belonged. She longed to be able to turn to him and ask him what it was like; to while away this exhausting and frightening time listening to his low voice and being able to reach out and touch him ... to take strength from his presence. Please, God, let him be all right...

'Anna!' She turned to see James coming towards her. 'Let me take some of those.'

'Fair enough, it's yours anyway.' She surrendered half her burden to him, and he looked at it in surprise.

'So it is.' He hefted his share, and gave her an odd look. 'You never cease to surprise me.'

'Oh?'

'You're as close to royalty as this town gets, and yet here you are, soaked to the skin and working like a carthorse.'

Anna shrugged, trying not to think too hard about her connection to Penworthy, after what Freya had said. 'Aren't we all?'

'I've heard you've given up the Tinner's to those who've been put out of their homes.'

Anna gave him a wry smile. 'Well, they'd all better like each other a lot, because they'll be bunking down in the bar. It's not a coaching inn, just a house.'

'Nevertheless people won't forget that kind of generosity. You're obviously a true Penworthy.' He smiled and walked away, and Anna was left staring after him, her spirits sinking. *He's a murderer, it's in the books...*

When whatever was in those books came out, she would be tarred by the very same brush she had been so happy to make use of when she'd first come here. If only she'd made less of her relationship, her actions might have spoken for themselves. As it was, she was merely seen to be living up to the expectations of her family roots.

And they were rotten right through.

Chapter Nineteen

Pencarrack House

The song of the wind rose and fell, and Lucy's body moved with it. She had opened her bedroom window a crack, and it made the song high and discordant; sinister and eerily beautiful. The dance that it wrung from her was equally wild, and her hair spun outward, kept there by her spinning form and the whipping motion of her head. The storm had awakened something so deep in her that she had been dancing since the very first light had crept across her ceiling – it was past breakfast time now, and she was exhausted, but the wind still shrieked in through the tiny gap in the window, and set the wooden frame rattling, and it became rhythm and song together in her mind.

At last she fell still, but did not collapse across

her bed as she usually did, panting and smiling. Instead she stood in the middle of the floor, her head down, her hair now sticking to her face, her blood still thrumming with the ferocious howl just beyond her bedroom walls. It was not enough to listen to it. She needed to feel it. She went to the window and pushed it wider, leaning out as far as she could before her balance began to waver.

The rain had stopped, but the trees in the garden had been stripped practically bare overnight, despite it being only August, and their branches were dark spikes against a grey sky. The hedge that ran the length of the garden to the gate swayed and bent, twisting away from the wall until it seemed it must soon be laid flat. Lucy watched, breathless and fascinated, her hair tugged forward and her skin grateful for the cool air.

The moment she pulled her head back in she felt the heat of her room again, and her damp, sweaty clothing stuck to her body. She pulled a face and tore her nightdress off, listening to the wind, and resisting the temptation to go to the window, unclothed, and let the weather at her skin. After a very quick wash, she dressed and went downstairs, already thinking ahead to how it would feel to walk in that gale, and feel the delicious, cool pressure of it.

'Where do you suppose you're going?' Charles Batten's voice was as soft as ever, and every bit as impossible to ignore.

'Just for a walk.'

'Don't be silly, child. The wind will knock you over.'

Lucy laughed. 'It's not that bad.'

'You can go out if you take your lazy brother with you.'

'Hugh's not lazy,' Lucy protested. 'He's just ... well, he has things to attend to at home.'

'Indeed.' Her father raised an eyebrow. 'He's currently attending to them from a prone position in the big sitting room, I believe.'

Hugh was, indeed, asleep on the chaise, his hand tucked beneath his head like a child, snoring softly, still wearing his dressing gown and pyjamas. Lucy leaned down and gently pinched his nostrils shut, and he spluttered awake, batting her hand away.

'What the blazes? Lucy!'

'Come for a walk with me?'

Hugh struggled to a sitting position and scowled. 'Absolutely not. I spent all last night here thanks to the loose slates banging above my room. It's not nearly as comfortable as it looks. Besides,' he cocked his head, listening, 'it's still blowing a gale out there.'

'Exactly!' Lucy spun away, eager to be out. 'Just think how alive we'll feel!'

'I'd rather not.'

'Oh, come on, Hugh!' She tugged at his hand, to no avail. 'It'll be glorious, so exciting. We could go out past the fort, and look down at the sea! Imagine how majestic and wild it will look.'

Hugh groaned and dropped his head into his hands. 'What rot,' he said. 'You go. Just don't fall off the cliff, or Father will have my hide.'

'We might see Freya,' Lucy said, playing her trump card. 'I'll bet she'd be pleased to see you,

344

too.' That part she was less sure about. But Tristan MacKenzie had left now and, from what Teddy had told her, he would not be back. 'You could buy Harry some books to take away to school with him next month. He'd love that.'

'Where is he, anyway?' Hugh's voice had lost the gruff, out-of-the-question tone, but he still remained sitting. 'He's usually running about like a firework this time of the morning.'

'He and Maddern left for Plymouth last night. Today's when they're visiting St Boniface's school.'

'Oh, yes. Rather typical that he should be taken by his tutor, rather than his mother.'

'Never mind that! Are you coming out?'

Hugh sighed. 'Yes! All right. But only to stop you from wittering and whining all day. No other reason.'

'Of course not,' Lucy said demurely. 'I'll wait by the front door. Hurry now, before the wind drops and all the fun goes out of the day.'

Pencarrack House had nothing to break the easterly gales but a few trees along the top of the garden, and although Lucy's hat was tied tightly she still had to hold it in place with one hand. The wind snatched her breath away, and felt absolutely delicious as she started towards town on her reluctant brother's arm. It was pointless trying to talk, so they just held onto each other until they had dropped down a little, out of the most exposed part of the garden.

Lucy let go of Hugh when they reached the gate, and enjoyed the feeling of her coat and skirts pulled first one way and then the next as she changed direction. One minute she could lean into the wind completely, relying on it to hold her up, the next she was being pushed from behind, and having to run a couple of steps to prevent herself falling flat on her face.

Out here the music was less, the roar was everything. She had to turn her head sideways to hear anything Hugh was saying, but it was mostly complaining about Dorothy so she soon ceased to bother. The road into town was predictably empty, but when they approached the top of the hill, where they could look down its length at the shops and houses that lined the sides, they noted a surprising lack of activity there, too. Surely people still had to work? It was only a normal Thursday after all, and the Penworthy Festival wasn't due to take place until next Monday.

But no shop doorways opened or closed, no delivery carts stood in the road, no children hurried with their parents to Priddy Lane school. Planted nets swung wildly in front porches, spilling soil and flowers, and now and again something not sufficiently secured would blow across the road. But apart from that, and the noise of the wind and the sea, there was no sound. It was quite eerie, and – Lucy shivered – as if the town had been deserted overnight.

She staggered in a sharp gust and Hugh caught her arm. Then as they moved down the hill she peered ahead, to where a small group of people was straggling up the road past the memorial. 'Look there! She looks the right age, is it Freya?'

Hugh followed her pointing finger. 'I suppose it

could be.'

Lucy threw him a sideways look, amused at his attempt to sound casual. 'I wonder where she's been so early in the day?' She stared harder. 'Gracious! She looks a fright!'

'She doesn't, she just looks as if she's been caught in the rain.' Hugh moved on, clearly with the intention of meeting Freya at the shop.

When they drew level, Lucy saw just how bedraggled and dirty the Penhaligon girl was. It reinforced her original opinion, although all the messy hair and clothes in the world couldn't disguise the purity of the girl's skin, or the clear, dark beauty of her eyes. She looked ready to collapse, and her hands were bleeding in places – she had clearly wiped them on her wet skirts several times, too; there were dark brown smudges and smears on the plain grey material.

'Mr Batten, Miss Batten.' She gave a tired half-bob as she took a key from her pocket, then turned away to fit it into the lock.

'What's happened to you?' Hugh joined her at the door as it swung inwards, and Freya turned to her four companions and gestured them all indoors. They all looked almost as beaten and shattered as she did, and Lucy frowned as she watched them troop wordlessly past, into the shelter of the dark shop.

'Take what you need,' Freya called after them, then looked back at Hugh and Lucy. 'Porthstennack was badly hit by the storm early this morning.'

'But that's Porthstennack,' Lucy said. 'Why is no one working here in Caernoweth?'

There was a faint look of distaste and frustration in Freya's expression, as if she couldn't quite believe she had to explain. 'All of the townspeople, or most of them at least, have gone to help.'

'I understand how extra hands might be useful if the houses there are flooded,' Lucy said, stung by the girl's attitude. 'But people must still work, or they'll all be out of pocket.'

'When I say badly hit,' Freya said, with a touch of irritation, 'I don't mean a bit of a leaky roof, or some spoiled food. I mean there are houses that will never be usable again. *That* bad.' She seemed on the verge of saying something else, and stopped herself. But she didn't need to say what was clear on her face; that she couldn't expect people like the Battens to understand real hardship, much less real community spirit. Perhaps she had just remembered that, while the Battens did not own Penhaligon's Attic, her father still relied on them for a job. Lucy remembered it was Freya's father who'd been hurt in the explosion, and the little flare of annoyance subsided. The girl couldn't really be blamed for being less than polite at a time like this.

Freya went in and put the light on, and Lucy and Hugh waited outside, not sure if it was polite to simply walk on now the conversation was over. They exchanged a questioning look, but just as Lucy was about to urge Hugh away Freya returned. Lucy waited for her to invite them in, after all they were potential customers, but instead she moved to shut the door.

'Excuse me,' Lucy said, putting her hand out to

stop her. 'My brother would like to purchase a gift for our nephew.'

'I'm sorry, the shop's not open,' Freya said, with ill-concealed impatience. 'I'm just changing into something dry, then I'm going back out.'

'To Porthstennack?' Hugh was looking at her with an expression Lucy found it all too easy to read. 'I'll come with you.'

'And do what? Dispense your valuable wit and wisdom? What they need is someone who can shift rocks and sand, and hammer boards across empty windows. Can you do that?'

'About as well as you can,' Hugh said, his eyes narrowing. 'Go and get changed.'

Lucy was watching the people who'd arrived with Freya: three women and a young girl of around Harry's age. They looked as though they didn't have a coherent thought to share between them – blank-eyed and numb, drenched and exhausted.

The truth hit her hard at last: all her romanticising about the wild beauty of a storm, the music it made, the power of nature's fury, unleashed on the great open sea ... to these people it meant something very different. She swallowed hard, hardly aware of the door closing gently in her and Hugh's faces, and tried to banish the images that had suddenly risen in her mind as she looked at those nameless strangers: chaos, terror, violence and maybe even death ... and all the while she, Lucy, had danced. She felt sick, and turned away.

'Where are you going?' Hugh asked.

'Home. To get...' she shrugged helplessly, 'I don't know. Food. Cocoa, tea. Blankets. What-

'ever I can find.'

'And do what?'

'Bring it back here. For them, and whoever comes after them.' She hesitated. 'Are you really going down to Porthstennack with that girl?'

'Yes.' Hugh winked. 'I think I can prove a thing or two, don't you?'

'Is that why you're doing it?'

'No.' He sobered. 'I think I've just learned the same thing as you have.'

She nodded, then stretched up and kissed his cheek. 'Take care, darling.'

'You too. And don't let Father or Dorothy catch you.'

Lucy gave him a wry little smile. 'I think I can prove a thing or two, don't you?'

The tide turned at last, giving the people of Porthstennack some much-needed breathing space. They took the opportunity to secure the boats that remained undamaged, and to drag the others higher up the beach ready for repairing once the weather allowed. It was unthinkable that anyone should put to sea, no matter how sturdy their craft, and so the fishermen worked instead at clearing rubble and making the lesser-stricken houses habitable at least. The worst-hit would require days of work, if they could be saved at all, and the women and children of those houses were being cared for in town, while the men worked alongside their crewmates and friends.

Anna concentrated on staying upright against the wind as she made her way towards the barn with yet another armful of wet towels. Her hopes for Matthew were hopelessly conflicted; she desperately wanted him well enough to come home, but the thought of that little pony and trap battling their way back towards Caernoweth in these high winds gave her horrors. She imagined the worst every time she swayed under a new gust; the trap sliding across the road, tipping Matthew and his father out, the pony stumbling, perhaps breaking a leg. Matthew and Robert lying bleeding in the rain, and no one finding them because no one would be foolish enough to come out in such dangerous weather.

Ahead of her on the road, she saw the slight form of a young boy, pushing through the gateway of the field where the barn stood, and she called out, grateful for the distraction.

'Eddie?' She peered over the top of her burden. 'Where's your ma?'

'She's down Paddle Lane, with Granny Alice.'

'And what are you up to?'

'Ma told me to go to the barn and help sort out clothes for the babies.'

'Good lad. I'll walk with you. Here, take the top towels for me?'

Eddie obediently took an armful of towels, and hurried ahead of Anna towards the barn. Anna ensured he was put to work alongside Susan Gale and the others, spreading wet clothing and blankets along the drystone wall, now that the rain had stopped. Then she made her way back to Paddle Lane. Eddie had unknowingly reminded her that she hadn't yet picked up Joe Trevellick's old clothes from Esther's house – even if they weren't needed for someone else, the room was in such a dreadful state she ought to try and rescue as much from it as she could; Esther would have need of it, even if it went to the rag and bone man for a few pennies.

The tide was no longer hammering at the back walls of the houses on this row, but the wind was getting under the loosened tiles and slates, and she could hear them slide and smash with worrying frequency; it was time this road was left alone, to either survive the last of the storm or to fall beneath the onslaught. Esther's front door was banging rhythmically, its broken latch and splintered wood crunching with each impact. Inside, Anna could smell the salt from the sea, and from the sand deposited throughout the lower floor, and her feet squelched on sodden rugs as she crossed towards the stairs.

'Anna?'

She turned to see Ellen stepping over the threshold, a scarf clasped over her head and beneath her chin. 'Have you seen Eddie? He–'

'He's well, and safe,' Anna said quickly. 'He's at the barn with Mrs Gale.'

'Oh, thank God.' Ellen visibly sagged in relief. She pushed the scarf off her head so it fell around her shoulders instead. 'Never thought I'd need this at this time of year.'

'It's very pretty,' Anna murmured absently, her mind on anything but scarves.

'It was the last thing my Ned gave me, the Christmas before he died.'

It was only then that Anna saw the fear and the sorrow in her friend's face, and she pressed her arm. 'It must be a great comfort to you, then.'

She wished she had something of Matthew's she could wrap around her and pull close.

Ellen nodded. 'What are you fetchin'?'

'Just some things for Esther. You go on and find Eddie, I'll catch you up.'

'No, now I know he's all right, I'll help you.' Ellen's ill-fitting boots clunked on the stairs behind Anna, and they went into the Trevellicks' bedroom. Ellen caught her breath. 'Oh, my word ... look at that.'

'At least the tide's turned.' Anna went to the wardrobe. 'If the wind drops before it turns again the house might be saved. Otherwise...' She sighed. There was no need to continue, Ellen had lived here much longer than she had and knew the dangers infinitely better. 'Actually, I'm glad you're here,' she went on. 'There's something I need to tell you.' She wondered if it was wise to go on, but the weight of secrets was always an ugly one, and Ellen had every right to know. 'It's about your sister-in-law.'

She kept working as she talked, pulling out Joe's few and familiar sweaters and jackets, and dropping them to the floor beside her. She told Ellen everything David had said, ending with the news that Ginny had fled Caernoweth. 'She must know she'll hang if they come after her. And they will, I'm sure of that. I'm so sorry.'

Ellen was staring at her, her face slack with shock. Her eyes skipped left and right as she struggled for words. In the end she went to the broken window and stared down at the shingle slope, her arms folded, and said nothing.

Anna went over to her. 'Come away, Ellen. It's

353

not safe.'

'I don't deserve to be safe,' Ellen whispered. She twisted her fingers in her scarf and looked at Anna, her face white. 'It was me. I told Davey about the baby. It's my fault Juliet's dead, and my fault my brother's lost his baby and is goin' to lose his wife too.'

For a moment Anna didn't know what to say, because if it was Ellen's fault that these three lives had become tragedies, then it was equally hers for blurting out what she had to Brian. 'How did you find out?' she asked at length, fighting rising nausea.

'I 'eard the two of them talkin' on their way from work.'

'David and Juliet?'

Ellen shook her head. 'Juliet and Freya. Freya was lookin' around, like as if to make sure Ginny weren't around, and she weren't. But I was.' The wind blew sharply, and above them something creaked.

'Come away,' Anna said again, with real urgency now.

'He's my brother! If he had a right to know, then so did his wife!'

'I know,' Anna soothed. She looked nervously at the ceiling, and reached for her friend's hand. 'You weren't to know what would happen, don't blame yourself.' She wished she could take comfort from her own words.

'I didn't mean for–'

But Ellen didn't finish her sentence. An almost human-sounding groan came from above them, followed by a deafening splintering sound, and the window frame collapsed, bringing down the entire top half of the wall, and the roof. Anna snatched a sharp, panicked breath, and both women lurched away towards the doorway as the air was suddenly filled with noise and flying debris. Ellen moved the quickest of the two, pulling at Anna's hand as she went.

Anna's boot came down awkwardly and she staggered to the side, a mis-step that saved her life even as it pitched her to the floor. As she fell sideways, an enormous chunk of ceiling plaster smashed into the floor where she should have been standing, and shattered, sending a cloud of choking dust into the air that completely hid Ellen from view.

'Are you all right?' Ellen cried, her voice shaking. 'Anna!'

'Yes!' Anna coughed and shook her head. 'Mother of God ... I actually am!' Her voice was hoarse and trembling with shock, but she managed a short, incredulous laugh. She put her hands down to the debris-strewn floor, and had just raised herself onto her knees when her world burst into flame, then went black.

Chapter Twenty

Freya's coat was still wet, but at least her shirt and skirt were dry next to her skin. Going back downstairs, she listened to the wind shrieking around the corner of the building, and thought of the many days she had lain in bed in the early hours, listening to Papá stumbling around in the dark, preparing himself for a day's work despite the weather.

She went into the shop to make sure her charges were settled, and noted that neither Hugh nor his sister had come in. Although not deeply surprised, she couldn't deny a certain disappointment; she'd thought better of Hugh, at least, since he had voiced his wish to help.

Little Sally Gale's wet clothes had already been removed by her mother, and spread to dry on the shop's counter, and Miss Pawley was taking a dry dress for her from her basket. Miss Trethewey, who taught the younger class at Priddy Lane, had gone into the kitchen to make them a hot drink while Sally's mother, Jenny, was already preparing to return to Porthstennack with Freya.

Freya waited for Jenny, then opened the door to the street. She blinked in surprise to see Hugh Batten still standing there, his hat in his hand, and his hair standing up on one side of his head with the pressure of the wind.

'Well, come on,' he said, in the same impatient tone she herself had just used with his sister. 'We've got work to do, haven't we?'

Freya didn't quite know what to say, so she just nodded, and Hugh walked at her side, making nothing of the silence between them. It wasn't until they reached the hamlet itself, that she looked at him properly.

'It's really not a day out,' she said, and his frown deepened.

'I know. Just because we live in a big house

doesn't mean we're not sensible to the hardships.'

'Miss Batten didn't seem quite as touched by it.'

'Lucy is a romantic. But she might surprise you yet.' He went on to explain how Lucy had run back to Pencarrack, and what for, and Freya regretted her snippy tone.

'That's good of her,' she said. 'I didn't realise.'

He gave her a quick smile. 'No reason you should. Right,' he looked around them. 'Which houses need most work?'

'You're not exactly dressed for it,' Freya pointed out.

Hugh considered her for a moment, then looked at the hat in his hand. 'Hie, you boy!'

The boy hurrying past, clutching his little sister's hand, stopped and looked at him in surprise, then embarrassment. 'Yes sir?'

Hugh planted his hat on the boy's head, and pushed it firmly down. 'Looks far better on you anyway. Hold onto it, you'll soon lose it in this wind. Come on,' he added to Freya, and set off through the narrow, winding streets towards the sound of the pounding surf.

On the wrong side of the sea wall, on Paddle Lane, the unbroken waves had first weakened the old walls, then lifted the plaster and cement render, and in places exposed the cob beneath to the wind and the tide. Even from the end of the road, Freya could see the way the roofs of the middle few houses had sagged, giving the whole shore-side row the look of a long-derelict ruin rather than a place where, only hours before, people had been sleeping, talking, fretting ... just living.

Ern Bolitho and his crewmate, John Rodda, were urging people to stay back now, and to concentrate on the houses on the other side.

'T'idn't no use, maid,' Ern shouted against the once-again rising wind. 'Nothin' to be saved from those 'ouses now. Trevellick's has just collapsed at the back, and Mr Fry's in't a lot better. Others are likely to go anytime. Better off helpin' over to Gales' place, and along Smugglers' Way.'

'All right!' Freya started to leave, then turned back. 'Have you seen Anna Penhaligon?'

'Last I seen she was up to Priddy's barn with young Eddie Scoble.'

Hugh was looking worriedly out to sea. 'How long before the tide comes in?'

'Should begin to turn around lunchtime,' Freya said. 'High tide'll be around six tonight.'

'And if the wind keeps up?'

Freya set off, calling back over her shoulder, 'Then most of Paddle Lane's probably going to be washed out to sea.' She turned, still walking. 'But we can make sure the people who live in Smugglers' Way don't lose everything too.'

They worked all morning, going into each of the fishermen's cottages and retrieving armfuls of belongings to carry further back into the village. Most of the Caernoweth residents had returned to town to attend to their own jobs and houses, but several Porthstennack houses, more happily situated than Paddle Lane and Smugglers' Way, had been opened by their tenants and owners, and room given over to storage, clothes-drying, and the feeding and entertaining of the temporarily homeless children. Several of the women were engaged in bandaging torn hands and broken blisters, and removing splinters, and the older girls were kept busy washing cloths at the well, and spreading them to dry so they might be used as clean bindings.

Mrs Kessell, the baker's wife, had brought an entire morning's bake and delivered it to the barn, before hurrying back to use the last of her supplies so as not to put herself out of business. Mrs Watts, the grocer's wife, had brought various tinned goods, and Susan Gale doled it all out with a sharp eye, and a warning look at those who she felt had already taken their fair share of the generous, but ill-afforded offerings.

The weak sun was high overhead by the time Freya stopped to rest. The wind hadn't dropped much, and the sky was an ominous grey and still spat the occasional heavy shower. There was a good deal more to come, and the tide would have turned by now and be making its way back into shore. Another bad night was in the offing, and there was much more work to be done to secure loosened tiles and damaged property, to avoid further injury.

The air was still very cool for August, but Freya was hot and sweating, and she rolled her shoulders, to ease the ache from carrying heavy boxes and seawater-sodden bedding, before accepting a cup of tea from Mrs Gale.

Hugh had worked tirelessly at her side all the while, keeping her flagging spirits up with tales of his more outrageous friends, and how his older sister had been such a tearaway in her youth.

Freya was aware she was probably being less than gracious, but she was also acutely aware of the looks the two of them were getting as they worked together. 'Stennack folk were polite, but proud, and did no more to acknowledge the presence of a Pencarrack Batten than a nod or a murmured greeting. But Hugh didn't seem to take it amiss, which did much to endear him to Freya.

'You're almost like a real person,' she teased, as she led the way out to the drystone wall behind the barn. She eased aside a piece of nearly-dried sheeting, and sat down. The rocks were uneven and jagged, and bit into her flesh, but it was such a relief to take the weight from her feet that it didn't matter. Even the wind, buffeting them as it came right off the sea over the tops of the hamlet houses, was more of a relief than a discomfort.

Hugh looked absurdly happy for someone who had spent the morning dragging broken boats around, and pulling loose slates from roofs. His clothes were torn and wet, and his hair plastered to his head from where he'd been standing beneath Mrs Gale's broken guttering and received a drenching when it had given up its moorings entirely, but his smile, though tired, was easy and unforced.

'I'll accept your words as the compliment they were no doubt meant to be,' he said with a wry look, and saluted her with his teacup. He sat beside her, and they remained quiet for a minute or two, enjoying the chance to rest their aching muscles. A drop of rain landed in Freya's tea, and she began to drink faster, keen to enjoy it before the downpour began in earnest.

Eventually Hugh cleared his throat and said what had clearly been on his mind for some time. 'I gather your chap has left town?'

'My chap?' Freya's voice held an amused note, and she wished she felt that amusement, or at least something other than the thin slice of pain in her heart. 'Yes, he's been called away on family business.'

'Will he be away long?'

Freya gave him a quick, sidelong look, wondering if she was imagining the suddenly tight-throated sound in his voice, but he appeared engrossed in chasing a stray tea leaf around his cup. 'I imagine so,' she said. 'He's going to America.'

Hugh looked up, and she knew she wasn't imagining the faint flush on his cheeks. 'That's ... too bad.'

'Is it?'

'Isn't it?'

'It is for me.' There followed an awkward pause, the first they'd encountered that long, long morning, and Freya wished she hadn't spoken. But the words had just popped out, and since they had sounded so blunt she sought to soften them. 'Hugh, you must understand–'

'I do. It's quite all right.' Hugh threw his tea away onto the grass, and Freya fought a surge of annoyance; someone else might have benefited from that hot drink. A disappointing display of thoughtlessness, from someone who'd never had to save anything.

She held out her hand. 'Shall I take your cup, since you've clearly had enough?'

Perhaps she hadn't made as good a job as she'd hoped of suppressing her feelings, because Hugh looked from the empty cup to the splash of tea on the grass, and his flush deepened. 'Not yet. Let's sit a while, we've earned a rest.' He waited a moment, then shifted so he was looking more fully at her.

'Freya, you know I'm quite keen on you, don't you?' He held up his hand to stop her, before she could reiterate her attachment to Tristan. 'I know your heart lies elsewhere, but I didn't want there to be any more awkwardness between us. Better I just say it, and then we can stop pretending ignorance.' His hazel eyes rested on hers, and the noon sun lit the clean lines and strong, firm chin... He was a very good-looking young man. But he wasn't Tristan.

'I like you very much too,' Freya began. She hesitated, not wanting to hurt him. 'You're proving to be a good friend, and I'm glad we can talk honestly.'

'Always, with you,' Hugh told her. 'There will never be anything but honesty whenever I talk to you, you can rely on me for that, at least.'

Freya was reminded of the pledge between Anna and Papá, of that very same thing, and her heart tightened. Why did people make such promises when they could not hope to keep them?

'The thing is,' Hugh went on, 'it's hard for me to separate what I'm feeling from what's appropriate. What I do know is that, if not for you, I would never have come here today. I wouldn't have seen the devastation for myself, nor swapped words with half these people. And they're good people.'

'They are. Mostly.'

'You'll always find a few rotten apples,' Hugh agreed, with a little smile. 'Anyway, I'm a nosy parker, Lucy always says, so tell me about Mr MacKenzie and why he's in America.'

Freya explained about Tristan's father, and his troubles with the union at the paper mill. 'He's in Liverpool just now, Teddy wired to say he'd seen him onto the train in Plymouth. He's going to pick up a ship called the Moira-something, and according to Teddy he should be in New York within five days.'

'Ah, that would be the RMS *Mauretania*. That little beauty will fly.'

'Well, it'll be another two or three days after that before he gets to New England, and he'll write when he knows what's happening.'

'Do you think he'll be back?'

The question was direct, and unexpected, and Freya was momentarily unable to find a reply. America was a terribly long way away, and she and Tristan had known each other such a short time... Her heart screamed, 'Yes!' but she finally accepted that her mind knew better. The response was hardly more than a whisper, but it was no less certain, for all that.

'No, I don't.'

Silence fell once more between them. Freya tried to tell herself she was wrong, that Tristan would not allow himself to become embroiled in his family's business, but the fact that he had asked her to go with him told her he'd known he would be away for a long while. Perhaps forever.

363

And even if he returned, the distance and the time between them would be sure to have a cooling effect on the warmth of their memories.

'If he doesn't come back,' Hugh ventured, dragging her back to the moment, 'might you one day consider allowing me to call on you?'

Freya finished her tea before answering, then chose her words carefully. 'What would your father say to that?'

'What does it matter what he thinks?'

'Quite a lot, I should have thought. What with you being the heir to Pencarrack and all.'

'Just pretending, for a moment, that I wasn't. What would you say?'

Freya looked at him again, properly this time. Contrary to what he probably thought, she was not assessing his physical attractiveness, she was noting the smudges of dirt on his face, the wet hair, the dirty clothes and the grazed knuckles; she felt a sharp sense of shame at the way she had tightened up, just because he had thrown a splash of tea onto the grass.

'Supposing,' he tried again, 'I asked your father first, and he was happy for me to take you for a drive?'

'We're supposing an awful lot,' she ventured. 'In the spirit of that, I *suppose* I might find it quite nice.'

Hugh grinned, but before he could respond they were interrupted by Eddie Scoble, who'd come out of the barn and seen them.

He hurried over, recognising a friendly face. 'Miss Penhaligon! Why hasn't Ma come back yet?'

'From where?'

Eddie's face was pale and pinched-looking. He'd clearly been troubled for some time. 'She was in Paddle Lane. I told Mrs Penhaligon so, an' I thought she were goin' to fetch her back.'

'When was this?' Freya stood, her heart starting to beat fast.

'Just after you took Sally Gale an' that, up to town.'

'That was hours ago. Has no one seen her since?'

Eddie shook his head, and large tears spilled over onto his thin, grubby cheeks. 'Can you find her?'

'I'll try. You stay here. Promise me, now? I'll go and ask in the village.' She smoothed his salt-caked hair, and made sure she sounded much calmer than she felt. 'Don't worry, they've probably stopped for a bite of lunch.'

As she and Hugh arrived at the junction of Paddle Lane and Smugglers' Way, with the slope down to the beach directly ahead of them, it was clear that tide and storm were returning together. The rain became more than the occasional splash, and Freya pulled her coat tighter. Hugh expressed mild disappointment that he'd given his hat away, but he'd have been hard pressed to keep it on his head in any case; the wind gusted much more fiercely here than it had even just up the lane at the barn.

Freya hailed Brian Cornish, who was helping Arthur Gale drag a battered rowing boat across the narrow entrance to Paddle Lane. She had to raise her voice to be heard above the crashing waves, and the roar of the wind. 'Mr Cornish, have you seen Ellen Scoble, or Anna?'

'Not for a good while,' he shouted back, dropping his end of the boat and arching his back. 'Probably gone up to town.'

'Eddie Scoble says they were down here.'

'Eh? Nah. Too dangerous, that's why we're puttin' this here.' He picked up a pot of whitewash, and scrawled KEEP OUT across the hull, while Arthur tipped a waiting barrow-load of rocks into the boat and stepped in to spread them evenly, weighing it down.

'That should do it,' Brian said, stepping back. In the relative shelter created by the two end houses, the barrier should withstand the worst of the weather. He looked back along the road sadly, towards his own home. 'Be a brave lot of work to put these places to rights.'

'My Bobby was turnin' people away, on account of the flyin' slates and such,' Arthur put in, 'but he've gone to your place now, to find 'is sister.' He raised his voice again as Freya walked forward. 'Best you go on there too, now, Miss. Not much more we can do here.'

'Not yet.' She stepped around the boat and started up the lane, ignoring Brian's shout and drawing a deep breath to deliver one of her own. 'Anna! Ellen!'

She heard Hugh following, and turned to see an admiring grin on his face. But before she could send him back, with a repeated admonition that this wasn't a game, he stopped and tilted his head. 'What's that?'

'What?'

He frowned and turned further aside. 'That. A voice.'

Freya knew all too well how the strange calls of the gulls could sound like voices sometimes, and she was about to caution him against hope when she heard it herself. He was right. Two houses up, where Esther Trevellick lived, and where the roofs had sunk in the middle on the seaward side, the front door swung open and banged against the jamb. She remembered James kicking it in, but it was as if it had happened a week ago – it hardly seemed possible that it had only been this morning.

From beyond the splintered wood she heard a hoarse, sobbing cry. 'Help us...!' It sounded like Ellen Scoble, and Anna must be with her. Her heart lurched, and she began to run. The pathway was strewn with broken pieces of tile, and she kicked them aside as she hurried along the path and through the front door.

Immediately she stopped, and stared in dismay at the staircase along the back wall. The next floor was not very high – the ceilings were low in all these cottages – but it might as well have been twice as far for all the chance Freya had of getting there. The upper part of the back of the house was utterly destroyed; the staircase a mass of smashed plaster, crumbled cob and jagged glass. On the other side of it, from around halfway up, she could see the grey swell of the sea, still out a long way, but already making its way back. The rain blew in, drenching everything, and sending tiny waterfalls over the debris.

From the room beyond the top stair she heard sobbing again, and she turned as Hugh came in. 'They're upstairs.' She scrambled over chunks of plaster and splintered wood, and peered up. 'Ellen? It's Freya. Is Anna with you?'

'Oh, thank God. Yes! But she's hurt. I think it's bad ... I can't wake her!'

There came the sound of slipping, sliding foot-steps from the floor above, and Ellen's voice came again, a little closer. 'The roof came in, she was hit by one of the beams. There's a lot of blood...' She dissolved into gulping tears again, and Hugh gently eased Freya aside.

'Ellen? My name is Hugh. I'm going to try and climb up, is there anything I ought to know? How strong is the floor at the top of the stairs?'

'I don't know. I can't get to the doorway.'

'All right. Don't try, just sit tight!'

'I'll get the others,' Freya said, and turned to go for help, but a gust of wind shook the cottage, and a fresh burst of rain blew in. She froze as a loud crack came from upstairs, and Ellen screamed out, 'Hurry! Please...'

'There's no time to wait,' Hugh said. 'You go on, I'm going to start climbing.'

'I'm lighter, let me.'

'No!' He put a hand on her shoulder to keep her from pushing back past him, then turned to face the shattered staircase again. 'Go for help, I'll need it.'

Freya hesitated, but Ellen had said Anna was already badly hurt, there was a lot of blood... Hugh shoved aside some of the bigger obstacles and began to climb, and Freya scrambled back outside into the street where Brian and Arthur were standing halfway along the lane, staring towards the house.

'Hie! We need help!' Freya yelled, her voice torn away by the wind. 'Please!'

As soon as they began moving towards her she went back into the house, and her heart leaped into her throat as she saw Hugh balanced precariously halfway up the stairs. He had reached the point where nothing now lay between him and the tiny garden and the shingle shelf outside, and the wind pushed at him, as if deliberately trying to topple him before he reached the top.

Freya dared not speak, and distract him, but her worry for Anna was consuming her now. How long had she been unconscious? She silently urged Hugh to greater speed, her fingers twisting together as her agitation grew. She heard a low, horrified curse from either Brian or Arthur, but she didn't know which; her eyes were fixed on Hugh.

'Anna's hurt,' she said, still without looking. 'Ellen's with her.'

'What was they bleddy doin' down 'ere in the first place?' Arthur wanted to know. 'Everyone knew 'twas dangerous.'

'Trying to help! Like we all are.'

Hugh grunted as his foot slipped, and he reached out to grab the jagged edge of the broken stair rail. Freya's breath halted, and only resumed when he pulled himself straight again.

'We need to be ready,' she said, moving to stand at the foot of the stairs. This close, and sheltered by the lower wall which was still more or less intact, she could hear the sounds from upstairs a little better.

Ellen was talking in a low voice. 'Your girl's

goin' to help us, Anna. We'll be all right. We'll get you to the doctor, you'll see. It'll be difficult gettin' down them stairs, with no wall an' that, but we'll help you.'

For a second Freya's hopes flared, but there was no reply, and she realised Ellen was simply doing what she'd no doubt been doing since the roof had collapsed: keeping herself calm.

Hugh reached the top of the stairs, pulling himself up the last bit by the part of the broken rail that was still secured to the wall outside the bedroom. From where she stood Freya could see the door was hanging by one hinge, but that beyond it lay a massive roof beam, which had fallen and smashed through the floor, blocking the doorway.

'Ellen?' Hugh said, and his voice was steady although Freya could see him breathing hard. 'I can see you both now. I'm going to try and climb over this. We ... we have to get Mrs Penhaligon out first, do you understand?' He glanced back at Freya, and his expression sent a chill through her. He looked both scared and regretful.

All the past days' angst and anger were banished in that instant; Anna's life meant more than any of it, and not just for Papá's sake. Freya's vision blurred and she blinked, feeling Brian's hand on her arm.

'We'll get her out, maid.'

'What if it's too late?' she managed. She watched as Hugh began to climb over the huge beam, and couldn't help the icy thought that if it was one of those that had hit Anna then she must surely be dead.

Hugh disappeared from sight, and she heard him crossing the floor, crunching plaster and glass underfoot. She looked at the stairs, and then back at the two men behind her. 'Help me.'

She began to clear as much of the stairway as she could, throwing debris down into the sitting room, exposing the broken stairs beneath, but at least they could see where the worst places were now. As she moved higher, to where the wall had vanished, her hair was tugged over her eyes by the wind, and she felt the strength of it as Hugh had done, trying to throw her off. Her skirt blew flat against her legs, and she had to lean slightly into the wind to stop herself tumbling off the staircase... She could only pray it didn't suddenly drop, or she'd be falling in the other direction, onto the waiting ground below.

Hugh appeared in the doorway above her, and she stopped, her heart plummeting. In his arms he held the limp form of Anna, her face covered in blood. Ellen had clearly tried to bind the head wound with a scarf, but more blood soaked this makeshift bandage, and Anna's slack face was doughy white.

Freya was startled to find a pair of hands gripping her waist, and she turned to see Arthur Gale, who lifted her from her unsteady perch. Then Brian was in her place, reaching out his hands for Hugh's burden.

'Give her to me, lad. You help Mrs Scoble.'

Hugh passed Anna over the top of the crooked roof beam, into Brian's waiting arms, and Arthur steadied his friend as best he could, as he negotiated the difficult path back down. Freya watched, with her heart in her mouth, and the moment Brian reached the floor, she was at his side.

Somewhere above her she was vaguely aware of Hugh and Ellen beginning their descent, but all her attention was on Anna. With trembling fingers she brushed rain-wet, bloodied hair from Anna's face and saw that more blood coated her eyelashes and pooled in the corner of her eye, but that there was a pulse fluttering in the pale throat.

Hugh appeared at Brian's side, with Ellen behind him. 'I'll take her up to the doctor's. Is there a cart or a trap we can use?'

'All the ponies been took to shelter.' Brian passed Anna back to him. 'You'm gunna have to carry her.'

A shadow crossed Hugh's already exhausted face, but he shifted his grip on the unconscious woman, and moved towards the door. Freya followed, her estimation of him rising with every step and with every encouraging word he threw her way as they climbed the hill to Caernoweth.

Bartholomew had been tending a string of minor, storm-related injuries, presumably free of charge, but he took one look at Hugh's burden, and his face paled. Freya knew he had a great respect for Anna, and to see his dismay at the sight of her brought her fear rushing to the surface again; he looked as if he already expected her to be dead.

'I'm sorry, everyone,' he called to the waiting patients. 'You'll have to wait, or come back later.' He led Hugh and Freya down the corridor and into a room with a high, narrow bed in it. 'Leave her here, I'll see if there's anything I can do.'

Hugh surrendered his charge to the doctor's care, and guided a reluctant Freya back outside. She could feel his arm shaking with fatigue. 'There's nothing more we can do,' he said, after a minute or two of silence between them. 'Go back to your shop, tell whoever needs to know that they can't go back to Porthstennack today.'

'No, I'll stay here and help out with these people. I'm sure I can clean a few cuts, and put the odd bandage on.'

He gave her a small smile. 'I'm sure you can.'

'And what will you do?'

He looked at her steadily for a moment. 'What do you want me to do?'

'What do you mean?'

Hugh took her hands in his, and raised the bloodstained knuckles to his lips. 'I know today wasn't typical of how our lives are, and this sounds suspiciously like madness, but I have enjoyed getting to know the real you today.'

'And I you,' Freya said. It was true enough; he'd proven himself to be hard-working and courageous, she'd always found him attractive, and she knew him to be amusing and intelligent. So why, then, did her heart sink as his flawlessly handsome face moved closer to hers, and his hands tightened on her fingers?

The touch of his lips was light, and flatteringly hesitant, and she willed herself to respond the way she had to Tristan. She returned the slight pressure, but her heart lay dead in her chest. Perhaps it was exhaustion, worry, the discomfort of wet clothing and aching muscles ... but she

373

didn't think so. If this had been Tristan in front of her she knew her response would be immediate and fierce, and that his touch would banish most of those other considerations for as long as it lasted.

Hugh put his hands on her shoulders, and as he lifted his mouth from hers, and whispered her name, she felt his breath warm on her cheek. But she felt nothing else; she stood as if wooden, wondering at her own coldness. At last he sensed her reluctance, and drew back.

She looked at him, and could only shake her head. 'I'm sorry...'

He nodded. 'So am I.'

'I know he's not coming back.'

'No, he's not.' He stepped away. 'I'll be waiting when you realise that you're wasting your life on a memory.'

'It doesn't make any difference though. You're still a Batten, and I'm a Penhaligon.'

He gave a short laugh. 'Hardly Romeo and Juliet though, are we?'

'Even if I felt–'

'You can stop now.' He sighed. 'I know what you're going to say. I'm the heir to Pencarrack. Except I'm not.'

'What?'

'It doesn't matter. Perhaps I'll explain one day.' He found a smile, and she could see it hurt. 'Thank you for teaching me how to be a real person, Miss Penhaligon, I'll try and put it to good use. Do please tell my sister she'll be needed at home at *some* point. I have a feeling she'll have enjoyed playing Florence Nightingale too.'

Before Freya could respond he turned and walked away down the path, and was gone. Saddened at the way he'd left, Freya went back into the doctor's house; Mrs Gale was presumably still at the barn, and there was no one to stop her walking past the queue of waiting patients and into the doctor's treatment room.

Doctor Bartholomew had unwound the blood-soaked scarf Ellen had used to bind Anna's head, and his face was still drawn and worried.

'I'll do what I can, but I don't know if it'll be enough.'

'I want to help some of those people out there. Is that all right?'

He nodded. 'Thank you. You'll find what you need in the office, across the hall.'

Freya looked down at the deathly still form, the waxy skin and the blood that was trickling again down the motionless face, and bent and kissed Anna's brow. 'I'm sorry,' she whispered.

'What are you sorry for?' Bartholomew asked, as he moved to begin his work. 'What happened?'

Freya told him about the roof-fall, but did not offer an explanation for her regrets. Nothing mattered now, after all, but that Anna should be saved.

Chapter Twenty-one

Matthew returned to Caernoweth three days later. His right shoulder was freshly padded, and he sported a plaster of Paris cast on his arm, keeping it immobile. Freya needn't know how dangerously high his fever had been by the time he'd reached Truro; there was no sense in worrying her now. Robert had sent a wire to tell her all was well, and that she was to expect them home within the week, and then they had both waited to see if that was the truth.

The two days following the operation had passed in a cloud of pain and confusion, and a sudden onset of vivid dreams that took Matthew back to his youth. He'd seen his little sister Julia, and spoken to her; he'd laughed with James Fry over some trick they'd played on Joe Trevellick; he'd watched Dorothy Batten from a distance, admiring her cool beauty and her don't-care attitude. During that time Matthew had been only vaguely aware of his father's presence, and Robert's voice seemed to come from a long way away, but it had been a constant comfort. It seemed that the last of the broken feelings between them had mended at last.

Outside Penhaligon's Attic Matthew climbed down from the trap with Robert's help. He accepted his father's arm as they walked stiffly to the house, his mind already reaching for the moment when he would see Anna again, and his homecoming would be complete.

The shop was closed, but the momentary surprise faded when he remembered it was Sunday. He glanced absently at the coats hanging on the hooks, remembering Pa's dismay when they'd realised they'd left them behind. Then he looked more closely; Freya's coat – his mother's old one, that she insisted on wearing – was missing, but in its place hung one he'd never seen before. Not a new one though, in fact as ratty-looking as any he'd seen.

The kitchen was alive with unfamiliar voices. He frowned; no, not quite unfamiliar, just unexpected. Brian Cornish was one of them, Ern Bolitho was another. He exchanged a puzzled glance with his father, and pushed open the door.

'Mercy!' Brian's wife exclaimed, almost dropping the casserole dish she'd been carrying from cooking range to table. The three men at the table looked up at the same time, and Ern and Brian looked quickly from him to James Fry and back again. They had clearly not expected him today.

'What the bleddy Norah are you party doin' in our 'ouse?' Robert demanded, pushing past Matthew, who couldn't speak, much less make demands.

'Freya ... Miss Penhaligon, did give her permission,' Ern began. 'Matthew, it's good to see you, lad.'

'Where *is* Freya?' Matthew managed at last. 'And what...' He gave up again and shook his head, bewildered.

'She'm stayin' at the Tinner's with Esther Trevellick.'

'What?' Robert stared.

'Well she can't be stayin' here in a 'ouse with strange men.'

'I think you'll have to give us a bit more than that,' Matthew said after a moment. He pulled out the last unoccupied chair and sat down. He probably should have left it for Brian's wife, or his own father, but he was feeling dizzy and a little bit sick. Not to mention baffled.

Ern, Brian and James all looked at each other, then James began to talk. As the news of the storm's devastation unfolded in his precise, well-educated tones, Matthew felt his insides alternately tighten and loosen and, as James explained how temporary homes had been given to those most in need, following the disaster on Paddle Lane, he found the only other question that mattered.

'Where's Anna?'

'Matt, listen–'

'Where is she?' Somehow he stood, and his voice came out flat. 'Is she ... alive?'

'Yes.'

He closed his eyes. 'Where?'

'She's proper sick, lad,' Ern put in. 'Sit a minute, and we'll tell you what happened. Brian was there, wun't you, Bri?'

Brian took up the narrative, and explained what had happened in Esther's home. 'The young Batten sir took her to Doc Bartholomew.' His voice gentled. 'She ain't woke yet.'

Matthew knew he ought to sit down again, but he couldn't. Nor could he move in the direction he wanted to go in – the door. His throat was dry, and his gaze moved to the cup of beer that stood at James's elbow.

James saw him looking, and he draped a napkin over it and rose to his feet. 'Come on, I'll take you.'

Out in the fresh air, Matthew was relieved to find himself coming to life again. James walked with him as far as the gate at the bottom of Doctor Bartholomew's path.

'I hope she's all right,' he said, unnecessarily. Then he cleared his throat. 'For what it's worth, I'm glad you're all right. I truly am.'

Matthew looked at him, and saw the sincerity in the familiar blue eyes. 'Thanks. Look, tell everyone they can stay. We'll work out how later. For now...' He gestured at the doctor's front door, and James nodded.

'Of course.'

Matthew knocked, and waited, and eventually the doctor himself opened the door. He was looking flustered and hot, and when he saw Matthew his face split in a wide grin. 'She must have known you were back!'

Matthew's heart stuttered. 'She's awake?'

'Just in the past half an hour. I've spent the time checking her over... But come in, come in! How are you?'

Matthew blinked. He'd forgotten in that instant that the last time he'd seen the doctor he'd been on the verge of fainting with pain. 'Much recovered. Where is she?'

'Upstairs. The attic room.'

Matthew ducked his head to go through the low doorway at the top of the house. Anna lay in a large bed, with her eyes closed. A white bandage was wrapped around her head, and her face was nearly the same colour.

'Anna,' he whispered. Her eyelids flickered open, and she stared through him for a moment before she focused, and gasped.

'Matthew!'

'Don't try and sit up!' Doctor Bartholomew hurried forward to stop her. 'Just stay very still. I'll explain all I can.'

Matthew held tightly to Anna's hand while the doctor described the past few days, how he'd initially been certain they were going to lose her, that he couldn't find evidence of any deeper injury but she'd remained deeply asleep. Mrs Gale had tended to her baser needs, and had offered to stay today, but she had a large family who needed her, and the doctor had told her to take her Sunday.

'I was sitting by her side, just wondering whether we ought to transfer her to hospital, when she woke.'

'Why didn't you do that sooner?' Matthew said, unable to take his eyes off her.

'Well,' the doctor looked embarrassed. 'It's a difficult situation, isn't it? How to explain to the hospital who she is? And besides, I was keeping a close watch; her blood pressure was good, her pupils reacted as I'd expect, her heart rate was steady. You can rest assured that if any of those things had given me concern, I'd have driven her to Truro myself.'

Matthew subsided, nodded. 'Of course. I'm sorry.'

'I think now that her mind was in full control and was giving her time to heal naturally. We're little miracle-workers really. Anyway, I'll leave you two alone. Don't tire her out.' The doctor squeezed Anna's hand, patted Matthew's shoulder, and left.

Anna caressed the fingers of the hand in the cast. 'This looks very dashing.'

'That's the only reason I'm wearing it,' he said, with a smile that faded as quickly as hers. 'What's wrong, are you in pain?'

'I have things to tell you,' Anna said faintly, closing her eyes again. 'Horrible things, they seemed at the time, but I think... I think it will be all right.'

Matthew drew back, growing wary. 'Horrible things?'

She shifted on the bed, and winced. 'I've not been honest with you. I'm sorry.'

'You'd better tell me.' Matthew tried to quell the disquiet that stirred in him as she hesitated, and despite the anxiety he was determined not to rush her into it. But as the story tumbled out, and the burden of her secrets lifted, he noticed she seemed to get stronger.

The story itself left him reeling. Murder, blackmail, a mess of misunderstandings and suspicions... It was no wonder she'd seemed so strained these past weeks, and on top of that she'd kept it all to herself. So this was what lay behind

Freya's reservations about asking her to fix the *Lady Penhaligon's* sails.

'Didn't you trust me?' he said, when she'd finished. 'Did you think I'd fall apart under all this?' He rose and went to the window, looking down onto the garden below, where a strong wind still battered the hedges.

'It's not a matter of trust,' she said. 'You know how it would have looked if word got out about that money. I was terrified I'd have to leave.'

'And that I'd pick up the bottle again.'

'Yes! All right? Yes.' Anna sighed, and her hand rose to her bandaged head, wincing at her own shout. 'Can you blame me, after the last time?'

'I'm stronger now.'

'I know you're getting better, but–'

'No.' He came back to the bed and took her hand. 'I mean I'm stronger because of you. When I thought you were going to leave with Finn, I believed it was because I wasn't enough for you, and if I wasn't enough, then I wasn't worth saving. But now I actually believe in what you've made me.'

Even as he spoke he wasn't sure if he meant it, or if he was simply buying time with meaningless words, hoping he would be right one day. But it didn't matter, he would do whatever he had to, and say whatever it took, to keep Anna here.

'I'm glad,' she said, relaxing against her pillow. 'Now tell me what happened in hospital.'

So he told her, and then they spoke of Freya, sharing their disappointment that Tristan had not been the one to make her happy after all, and of Mairead, from whom they decided to keep the news of the storm, at least until things returned to normal. When Anna showed signs of growing tired again, Matthew leaned over to turn down the paraffin lamp that stood on the bedside cabinet, and Anna touched the bump at the back of his shoulder, where the fresh padding lay beneath his shirt.

'*Are* you all right, really?'

He looked at her, at the worry on her face, and he read past the concern for his physical health and into what lay deeper. 'I am,' he said seriously. 'But we have a bit of a problem.'

Her expression clouded again. 'What's that?'

'My house is full of people who don't live there, and so is yours.'

A light flashed deep in Anna's green eyes, but her voice was sympathetic. 'So ... you've nowhere to sleep tonight?'

'Nowhere,' he sighed.

'Well, we're married. In a manner of speaking.'

'So we are. In a manner of speaking.'

Anna patted the bed beside her. 'The doctor's a grand host. He'd not see you turned out.'

'You do need someone to keep an eye on you,' he pointed out. 'And neither of us is likely to be doing anything untoward for a while yet, in any case.'

She stroked his cheek, her eyes burning into his for a moment, then she pulled him closer and, with her mouth almost touching his, she whispered, 'You *are* worth saving, you do know that?'

'I do.' He kissed her, and as he felt her mouth widen in her beautiful, familiar smile he realised he was telling the truth.

383

Epilogue

December 24th, 1910

Freya stretched up to fix the holly more firmly above the window. The kitchen was warm, and filled with wonderful smells, and a variety of noises – so much so that it was hard to think straight. So many things to remember; there were the almonds still to blanch, and the candied peel to chop, and the puddings hadn't even had their final stir yet.

Anna and Mairead were arguing over whose turn it was to use the good knife, and who must make do with the blunt one, and Grandpa was knocking his pipe out on the table and ignoring Freya's exasperated sighs and repeated requests for him to take it elsewhere. Instead he was regaling them with tales of when Papá and Julia had written Christmas poems to read out at dinner. 'Fair talent,' he conceded, 'but usually about nonsense.'

'I read one of Matthew's poems once,' Anna said, and rose to fetch Granny Grace's cookery book. 'Here. I think this is actually what made me fall in love with him.'

Freya grinned as she read it; it had to do with Papá's dislike of green vegetables, which was something that hadn't much altered since he'd written it, at the age of ten. 'Give him extra cabbage tomorrow,' she advised, glancing at the door to make sure he wasn't listening. But he was in the shop, having taken himself safely out of the way of cross-cutting sprouts or peeling potatoes.

The shop was closed, and had reverted once more to the sitting room it had been before – the bookcases pushed to the back wall, leaving enough space for chairs, and for charades tomorrow, and Papá was putting the finishing touches to the Christmas tree he and Grandpa had brought in this morning. It was almost supper time, and Freya counted out six plates, enjoying the excitement that accompanied this particular Christmas – Penhaligon's Attic would see a houseful, for the first time she could remember since before she and Mama had left, and it was already a glorious, noisy mess.

The holly slipped again, and she sighed. 'Where's James? He's the tallest, apart from Papá.'

'Finishing in your grandad's room,' Mairead said. 'He's putting up the campaign bed in there.'

'Could you ever believe he's spending Christmas under the same roof as your da?' Anna said to Freya with a smile. 'Never thought I'd see the day.'

'Well let's hope they don't start tearing into each other over who gets the silver sixpence.'

'It was very good of him to help with the attic conversion,' Mairead put in, a little archly. *'I'm glad they're friends again, anyway.'*

'So am I,' Freya assured her. 'It's just … surprising. I keep waiting for them to fall out again, but it's been four months now so it seems safe enough.'

Four months. Freya swallowed a little flutter of sadness; it was lessening with each week, but it was still there. The letter from Tristan still sat on her dresser where she read it again every single night. She knew it by heart now.

Dearest Freya

Things here in New England are much worse than I'd imagined, but my father is sticking firm. I'm taking over much of the business with the unions but it is not going well, and Alex isn't helping at all – he's too volatile to be of any calming influence. I am keeping things as steady as I can.

I'm lost without you. I would beg you once again to come to America, and if you chose to do so I would keep you as safe as I could, but this situation is dangerous, and your disposition too trusting. If I failed you I would never forgive myself.

Darling Freya, I love you. You know I do (I hope). But I can't see a way back to you soon, and it's not fair to ask you to wait for me, when it might never happen at all. I want you to find a different path to happiness, and am more sorry than you will ever know that I can't be the one who waits at the end of it.

Yours always,
Tristan.

Hugh had called on her just once, since she had received that letter, and even as Tristan's words paraded through her mind, and she knew Hugh would do everything in his power to make her happy, her heart was locked. But at least that way it was safe.

The past four months had been a strange and hopeful time. James and Papá's friendship had found a new footing, albeit a shaky and slightly uncertain one. James had offered to help Papá clear the attic and build the bedroom for Mairead, which meant that she and Anna could move in properly. The now-homeless Esther Trevellick had been persuaded to give up her ruined cottage and instead live at the Tinner's, and Papá had cautiously suggested that she might need live-in help. She had bristled at first, and denied it, until he had named her elder grandson Alan as the best person for the job.

'He's too sick to be working down that mine, you know it.'

Esther nodded. 'True enough. An' he's a good lad.'

'Mrs Penhaligon will pay him a wage, but it won't be anything close to what he's earning at Wheal Furzy. He'll have a roof over his head, though, and the room's just about big enough for him and Tommy to share. Closer for Tommy to get to work, too.'

'It'll do, I reckon,' Esther said. And Papá had suppressed a smile as he shook her hand.

Such a change in James too, these past few months. His own home still uninhabitable, he had moved into the spare room at Dr Bartholomew's as soon as Anna had been allowed home, and as he worked with Papá every day on the attic Freya had come to recognise something in him; the longing, just like hers, for a big family. The attic had long since been completed, but he remained a constant visitor – when Freya had invited him to stay at Christmas she'd thought he might just melt with gratitude and excitement.

Mairead had noticed it as well, and Freya couldn't help wondering about the odd and un-usual closeness she and James shared. Mairead had always said she couldn't imagine being happy with a lot of brothers and sisters, but perhaps an older brother was what she needed. Although he was a *lot* older...

'Freya!'

Papá was calling from the shop, and Freya put down the toffee hammer she'd been using to try and fix the holly bough. 'What does he want now?'

Anna looked up and smiled a little distractedly and, just as Freya turned away to answer her father's summons, she caught a gesture from the corner of her eye. Just a *tiny* gesture ... but it was enough: Anna smoothed her hand over her apron. She caught Freya looking, and snatched her hand away, but it was too late. The belly beneath was still flat, but there was something in the protectiveness of the gesture that brought with it a strong, bittersweet reminder of Juliet.

Freya nodded towards the shop, her eyebrows raised, and Anna shook her head, but her smile lit the room, and when Freya went through to the shop she was able to use her own smile to express her pleasure at the work Papá had done in there. The tree was not a big one, but it was laden with pine cones, home-made streamers, and all kinds of nuts hung on string.

'It's beautiful,' she said, with real delight. 'You've worked so hard.'

'I wanted you to be the first to see it,' Papá said. He had his own secretive little smile flickering around his eyes. 'And I wanted to give you this, while it's quiet, and while it's just you and me.'

He bent and picked up a box, a little awkwardly, but with two hands, and passed it to her. She already knew what would be inside, and her breath caught. 'You've finished it?' She lifted the lid. 'It's as good as new!'

'The *Lady Penhaligon* lives again.'

'Thank you!' Freya put the box on the counter top, and hugged him.

'Exchanging gifts already, are we?' James's voice came from the doorway.

'Just one very special thing,' Freya said. 'Everything else will be tomorrow.' She changed the subject, keeping in mind her father's wish to keep it between them for now. 'Do you think you'll sleep all right on that camp bed?'

'I'm sure I shall.' James looked nervous as he turned to Papá, and Freya frowned. She hoped he wasn't going to spoil things somehow.

'Matt, can I talk to you a minute?'

'If you can make it quick, I have a pudding to stir, apparently. What is it?'

'It's a ... a proposition.'

'Oh?'

'I want you to buy the *Pride of Porthstennack*.'

Papá went very still. 'Buy it?'

'For a good price, one that suits us both.'

'You don't still want to swap it for this place?'

James shook his head. 'That was stupid, and thoughtless.'

'And sly,' Papá said. 'I always knew you were

better than you were that day.'

'Then let me prove it. I want the *Pride* to be yours, Matt. Pa would too, I know that.'

'Even though he left it to you?'

'He wanted me to have the chance to find out. I'll never be a sailor, nor a fisherman, it's not in me. It's in you. It's in your bones, just like stone work's in mine.' He cleared his throat and flushed faintly. 'It took a very wise woman to remind me of that.'

Papá raised an eyebrow, but James didn't elaborate and instead of pressing the point he looked at his slowly mending arm. 'It'd be a while before I could work.'

'Ern's a good skipper. He'd work hard for you as long as you needed him.'

'How much?'

'Make me an offer. I'll accept it.'

Papá gave him a crooked little smile. 'You don't know what it is yet.'

'I trust you to know a good business when you see it, and understand what it's worth.' James shrugged. 'And I also trust you to know when a friend is trying to make amends.'

Papá eyed him steadily. 'I was as much of a bastard to you as you were to me.'

'Which is why I know your offer will be a fair one. Think it over. Talk to Anna. Offer what you can afford, and if we have to haggle we will.'

Freya exchanged a glance with Papá, and knew from the gleam in his eyes that Anna had told him about the money she still had hidden away. What better use for it? It seemed that everyone was getting what they most wanted for Christmas

– or nearly everyone. But this was no time to dwell on what was missing, and Freya watched with relief as Papá held his hand out to James, his smile spreading from his eyes to the rest of his face at last.

'We'll talk after all this is finished.' He fixed his old friend with a steady look. 'New beginnings for all then, is it?'

'New beginnings,' James agreed. 'Good ones.'

A knock at the shop door broke the moment, and, still smiling, Freya went to open it. If someone was looking for a last-minute gift they were destined to be disappointed, but instead of a hopeful shopper, quite rightly expecting the shop to be open on a Saturday, she found the telegram boy.

'Miss Penhaligon!' He thrust the envelope into her hand and pedalled off, yelling, 'Merry Christmas!' as he went. Freya shut out the icy December chill, and pulled out the telegram with shaking hands that owed nothing to the weather.

Coming home for new year save some mistletoe. Tristan.

Acknowledgements

My sincere thanks and admiration to the staff at the incredible Geevor Tin Mine Museum, near Penzance. So helpful, friendly and informative, your tireless work to keep alive the spirit of Cornish mining is something to be valued.

My thanks also to my agent Kate Nash, and to my editor at Little, Brown, and, as always, a special shout out to my SCWG – keep ranting and writing, my lovelies!

To ALL my family and friends, for your support, and your energetic cheerleading; for buying my books; for spreading my words; and for gently prodding me when I spend too much time on social media.

And a massive 'thank you' to everyone who read *Penhaligon's Attic,* and who let me know you cared enough about the characters to ask for a sequel!

The publishers hope that this book has given you enjoyable reading. Large Print Books are especially designed to be as easy to see and hold as possible. If you wish a complete list of our books please ask at your local library or write directly to:

Magna Large Print Books
Magna House, Long Preston,
Skipton, North Yorkshire.
BD23 4ND

This Large Print Book for the partially sighted, who cannot read normal print, is published under the auspices of

THE ULVERSCROFT FOUNDATION